LIQUID
FIRE

A Novel

by

Melanie Kallas

Liquid Fire

Copyright © 2022 by Melanie Kallas

ISBN: 978-1-943515-45-5

AcuteByDesign, Publisher
Book Interior and E-book Design by Amit Dey | amitdey2528@gmail.com

Printed in the United States of America

ACUTE BY DESIGN
the little book company that could
A Michael Marion Sharpe Company

Michele Thomas
Executive Publisher

The Janissary

1.   Psychic Schools

The Janissary has six schools known as the "big six." At the Janissary Academy, teachers test their students' psychic abilities, placing them into ascending levels as the students master their powers. Each school has five levels with the most advanced being level five.

A.   Telekinetics
Level 1: Push or pull small objects
Level 2: Airwalk and frictionless surface
Level 3: Binding
Level 4: Levitation
Level 5: Repulsion field

B.   Mind Control
Level 1: Empathy
Level 2: Emotion control
Level 3: Mind reading
Level 4: Telepathy
Level 5: Mind domination

C.   Awareness
Level 1: Short-range clairvoyance
Level 2: Clairsentience

Level 3: Clairtangency
Level 4: Clairaudience
Level 5: Astral projection

D. Level 1: Leaping
Level 2: Quick reflexes
Level 3: Overclocking
Level 4: Physical modulation
Level 5: Body supremacy

E. Energetics
Level 1: Manipulate small amounts of quick
metal in close contact
Level 2: Heat quick metal
Level 3: Manipulate large amounts of quick
metal at distance
Level 4: Quick metal intuition
Level 5: Quick metal solidification

F. Precognition
Level 1: Premonition
Level 2: Postcognition
Level 3: Presentiment of future emotions
Level 4: Omnicompetence
Level 5: Predict the future

2. Branches

    The Janissary is divided into six branches. Upon
    graduation, Academy students intern at their
    designated branch.

    A. Administration
    B. Logistics
    C. Security
    D. Diplomacy
    E. Engineering
    F. Operations

Prologue

Mist danced off frosty coastal waters. A dark figure dropped off the military warehouse's slanted roof, tumbling to the faux wood planks of the wharf. He was dressed in a skintight suit, all black save for the pale janiform insignia, one face looking forward, the other back placed reverently over his heart.

As a janissaire, he had jurisdiction in most places around the world. However, Isle Royale was the Imperium's capital, so he had to tread lightly, especially where the military was concerned.

The janissaire tried the warehouse door, surprisingly unlocked. This part of the city was designated a depressed socioeconomic area, yet the crime rate was nearly zero. Per municipal codes, repository doors were supposed to be locked. He would have to call it in.

"This is Janissaire Eacles. I'm at the military warehouse on 34th Avenue," he whispered into his headset. Only static reverberated over his earpiece. Eacles slid his skean out of its scabbard. The short, bronze-colored double blade gleamed in the city lights. With his free hand, he slowly slid open the door until there was just enough room to squeeze through. Eacles touched his visor to activate his night vision. Nothing happened. He tapped the visor again. Nothing.

"This is Janissaire Eacles. My electronics are on the fritz," he said. The only answer he got was the continued hiss of his communication system. Eacles shook his head and pulled out his pistol. With his thumb, he pressed the smart buttons near the trigger. The pistol did not light up as designed. He holstered his firearm with a long sigh.

Concentrating, Eacles forced the blade of his skean to lengthen. He stared down at his skean, furrowing his brows for a second until the blade started to grow. He smiled at the ease of the transformation. Most janissaires scored a zero in energetics, but Eacles was baseline in this psychic ability, giving him the minimal power to alter quick metal and, therefore, the right to carry a skean.

Now, Eacles gravely wished he had scored higher in the awareness ability so he could avoid having to physically enter the darkened warehouse. With even a little clairvoyance, he could stay near the entrance and still search the interior.

Thumping footsteps alerted him that a heavy bot was approaching. This was a military building, after all, so there ought to be sentries. Eacles slipped inside as though on cat's paws, closing the door behind him. His heel caught a rut in the floor. Steadying himself, he quietly recited his favorite Benevolent Imperator maxim, "Balance comes from strength."

Letting his eyes adjust to the darkness, he surveyed the stacked shipping cubes around him. Overhead, shafts of dim light shone through broken windows as the wind whistled across the broad storage area. Peering up, Eacles found a rectangular light fixture swinging lazily. As his gaze drifted back down, he froze.

Within striking distance, six stationary military bots stood over seven feet tall. Their demon heads sat atop grotesque humanoid frames. Spiked shoulders led to thick arms with retractable auto-guns. Emblazoned across the entirety of their barrel-shaped chests were imperial moth insignias. In the faint light, Eacles could still make out the moths' outstretched yellow wings and purplish markings. While moths did not necessarily look intimidating, most people were scared enough of military bots to run away no matter what was on their armor.

The thumping from outside drew closer. The heavy sentry bot must have stopped within feet of the only exit. Slowly, Eacles inched forward, holding his breath. He steered to the middle of the warehouse where there were no ruts to trip him up again.

A red light blipped on the head of the bot nearest him, as more lights cascaded off its demon face in a pretty rainbow that would have been hypnotically beautiful had the bot itself not represented certain death. Horrified, Eacles heard the startup of hydraulic pistons. Without hesitation, he slashed his skean across the bot's neck. Sparks arced across the otherwise darkened warehouse, fizzling out as they dropped. An ugly head bounced across the dusty floor.

Turning, Eacles's eyes widened as he found himself facing down five more bots that were closing in on him. He leaped with preternatural strength at his nearest attacker, his skean raised above his head. As he descended on his target, the bot lit up with honeycomb force shields protruding from the tiny pores all over its body.

Eacles landed on the bot and stabbed through the creases of its shields, willing his flexible blade to dig deeper. A wallop cracked across his hand. His fingers slipped off the hilt of his skean. The barrel of the bot's auto-gun slammed hard onto his skull. Ears ringing, he fell limp to the ground, kicking up more dust. Nausea gurgled in his stomach and climbed up his throat. The buzzing in his ears faded.

Eacles's world grew suddenly dark. Strange visions floated across his mind's eye. A woman was hailing him, calling for her "brother." *Who am I?* he thought. *Am I late for work? Do I have a job?*

Bit by bit, his brain rebooted. A metronomic orange blob flashed incessantly in his eyes. *That's an annoying alarm clock,* Eacles thought as he groped to turn it off. His hand tapped the dirty floor; pain shot up his finger. As his heart raced, he blinked his eyes open to find the rectangular light fixture swaying above him, spraying rays of orange light across the dingy floor.

The throbbing pain in his ring finger brought him back to reality. He raised a ruined fingertip across his outstretched body. The skin was torn open, and sinew had burst out like a hotdog left too long on the grill. Blood dripped onto his pale janiform insignia, covering one face entirely.

The taste of copper filled his mouth. Probing with his tongue, the inside of one cheek was chewed up. He must have bitten it during the fall. Still dizzy, he lifted his head to get a better view of his surroundings.

"This is unreal," Eacles muttered as he surveyed the storage area, the orange light shifting from side to side like a searchlight, revealing perfectly stacked cubes about a yard in length. With his uninjured hand, he reached to rub his eyes, but his hand knocked into something. Peering through the glass over his eyes, the janissaire examined his hand. *I'm wearing a virtual reality visor?*

When he pulled the visor off, the scene looked the same. The floor was still dusty. The bots were still ugly. With difficulty, he turned his head to see the vague silhouette of a prone sniper atop a cube about sixty feet away. It was an easy shot for anyone with the training. Orange light glinted off silver, metallic arms.

"Do not get up," said a mechanized, feminine voice, echoing from all five speakers of the remaining bots. "How did you find me?"

Eacles spat blood. "It's what I do," he said with some bravado, considering his position.

"Who tipped you off?" asked the haunting voice through the five speakers.

"I just followed your breadcrumbs," Eacles responded brazenly. Taking a moment to gather his courage, he squared up to this lost cause. "You practically drew me a map."

I must be on a quest in some VR game, he thought. The ripping pain in his finger, however, belied such speculation. With his thumb, he gently tapped the injured ring finger, which was strangely numb. *Looks like I tore a tendon as well.*

"You are very calm for a man who is about to die," said the harsh, mechanized voice over the bots' five speakers. *The sound quality is pretty bad in this game.* "I'm not too worried," said Eacles, "I'll just respawn and come right back here."

Chilling laughter resonated across the speakers. Eacles frowned. The dull ache in the back of his head left everything a bit fuzzy. *This can't be real, right?* Before he could answer his own question, though, the five military bots began stomping in lockstep until they formed a pentacle around his fallen body. Eacles cringed as he noticed the pattern. No bot was directly in front of another so as to avoid friendly fire. With terror, Eacles eyed the barrels of the auto-guns. They all opened fire.

Chapter 1

Tightening the belt of her terrycloth bathrobe, Olivette stepped barefoot into the dining room to the aroma of bacon and eggs. She smiled, looking over to her roommate. "You didn't have to cook breakfast again."

"My stipend doesn't even cover half the rent, so I figured I'd help out where I could," responded Piero as he moved from the kitchen. Of course, he was already dressed in his ash-gray, loose-fitting tunic, ready for work. He wore the pale janiform insignia over his heart.

"Why are you staring at me like that?" Piero asked, scrunching his eyebrows slightly as he sat down at the small table.

Olivette slid into the seat across from him. "I'm just jealous that you're the *only* one who can dress casually at the office."

"Ah, those days are over," he began jokingly. "My new protégé is meeting us at work, and she'll dress even more shabbily than me."

"How did you become a mentor so quickly?" asked Olivette while slurping eggs into her mouth. Strands of her reddish-brown hair dangled onto her plate.

"It's just individual attention for the minimally exceptional."

Olivette laughed. Her slight frame shaking under the bathrobe. She covered her mouth to avoid spitting up her meal. "You're not a minimalist!"

"The Janissary Academy would beg to differ. I scored a one on all six psychic schooling tests. That's baseline for the big six."

"You're still a janissaire," Olivette offered. "Don't you have to be at least baseline on all the big six tests to become a master?"

"Not exactly," Piero corrected. "To become a master, you must reach the fifth level in one psychic school and still be at least level one, also called baseline, in the remaining five schools. For example, Master Albus, my boss, reached the fifth level in awareness. That's scary high. He could be using his astral projection to watch us right now!"

Olivette chuckled as Piero looked under the table. She instinctively clapped her knees together. Their relationship was strictly platonic, even though Piero was lean and oddly handsome. He had dark hair and thick eyebrows. To appear older, he grew a beard but shaved off his chin hair.

A strict code of conduct had been instilled upon poor Piero since he was four years old, the age children started the Janissary Academy. Those gloomy kids never saw their real family again and were prohibited from external relationships. The Academy taught that attachments led to depravity. The teachers told their pupils that they were all brothers and sisters. Any physical contact was forbidden. At puberty, the teachers fed their students libido inhibitors which impaired any further yearnings. Moreover, Piero was not dramatizing about barely qualifying to be a janissaire. While he showed early progress in all psychic schools, he bottomed out early. Dregs like him were destined to fill the lowest ranks of the Janissary.

"Isn't Master Albus in the Septenary?" Olivette asked to break the silence.

"Of course," Piero replied. "He's the head of the Awareness School *and* the Logistics Branch of the Janissary."

"So, you report directly to Master Albus?"

"For the time being, he's my supervisor," Piero replied. "The Septenary reports directly to the Office of the Benevolent Imperator."

Olivette winked. "I didn't know you were so connected, Pi."

He winced, forming a little vertical crease between his black eyebrows. It was obvious that he hated his nickname. Grabbing a dirty plate, he said, "If you're done eating, I'll clean up."

Olivette nodded, watching him clear the table. *A janissaire served me breakfast for the last month and cleaned my laundry without complaint,* thought Olivette. *It's his first real home outside of the Academy, and I have to cover his rent. Alas, these are the sacrifices I make for my family.*

"You seem melancholy this morning," Piero said.

"Are you reading my mind?" she accused.

"I'm not nearly that powerful," he responded with a note of shame in his voice. "That's a third-level mind control ability. The only people who have that ability are the Benevolent Imperator and a handful of janissaires, namely Mistress Raven, Hatchette, and, of course, Elvene."

Ah, Elvene, reminisced Olivette. *I hope you have one foot in the grave.* "How's your old mentor doing these days?"

"The doctors had to amputate her legs."

Olivette giggled. *Make that two feet in the grave.*

Piero looked at her crossly. "What's so funny about that?"

Good! He can't read my mind. Olivette casually wiped egg yolk out of her hair. "Oh, I was just recalling a funny scene from Mystic Mike's banned viral video."

Piero shook his head. "Anyway, as a baseline for mind control, I only have the empathy ability. Earlier, I could tell that you were sad about something."

Olivette smiled and stared him deep in the eyes. *Yes, dear boy, you have struck too close to home and overstayed your welcome. You would be sad too if you knew what was coming.* "Don't work too hard; I have a surprise for you tonight."

Chapter 2

The lights in the control room blinked relentlessly when the protégé passed the security door. She looked around, bemused at the oversized room containing only two other people.

"That's our alarm going off," Piero said testily over his shoulder. "You must have some kind of recording device on you."

"It's just my phone," the protégé replied gruffly.

"Who is this mysterious lady?" coyly asked Olivette while lounging in a rolling chair at the far end of the console in her pressed, stark white uniform.

"Ah, introductions *are* in order," announced Piero. "Riley, this is my coworker, Ensign Olivette Demedici. Like everyone else in this building, she works for the military."

"Your uniform gave you away," Riley said snidely. "Are you related to anyone in Demedici Shipping?"

"I'm afraid so," Olivette admitted. "Cosimo Demedici is my father, but I don't—"

"Is this where I'm going to intern?" interrupted Riley with a frown, looking to Piero.

The flickering lights continued unabated. Exasperated, Piero made a shooing gesture." Step back out and put your phone in one of the lockers in the antechamber."

As soon as Riley left the control room, the lights returned to normal. Olivette rolled her chair over to Piero, a teasing glint in her eyes. "You forgot to mention that your protégé was so pretty."

"This is the first time we've talked," Piero shot back. "All I know is she's eighteen and was reassigned to me when her mentor went absent without leave."

Riley strolled back into the control room, shaking her slick black hair that bounced off her shoulders. Piero turned his head to glare. She was shorter than him and wore too much cheap, dark eyeliner. Riley strode up to her new mentor, exclaiming, "So, I'm stuck in Logistics with *you!*"

"What branch were you in before?" asked Olivette nervously as she wheeled her chair back to the far end of the console.

"Operations." Riley eyed her. "I'm a level two for precognition and telekinetics but just baseline for energetics and body control."

"So, in two schools, you rank higher than Pi, your *mentor*," Olivette said jokingly. "How is that going to work?"

"It's not." Riley planted her feet and leaned her head back. "Pi can't teach me a damn thing about precognition or telekinetics."

"What do you get as a level two precog?" Olivette asked worriedly.

"Aside from the danger sense that comes with level one, I also have postcognition," Riley explained matter-of-factly. "I get a flash of memories that will have something to do with my future."

"Pi won't be of any help there." Olivette relaxed in her chair. "He can't even remember to put the toilet seat down."

Piero grimaced before addressing his protégé. "I'm going to instruct you in logistical procedures. It doesn't mean that you'll never go back to the Operations Branch. For instance, I started in the Administration Branch, and I considered going back."

"With your qualifications, I bet they'll let you teach kindergarten," Riley said in a heavily sarcastic tone.

"I wish," replied Piero. "My job was to test toddlers for psychic abilities."

Both Riley and Olivette burst into uncontrollable laughter. Riley wiped mascara-laden tears from her cheeks before they dripped onto her steel-gray tunic. Piero smiled and then joined the jollity. "I know it sounds lame, but I stayed out of trouble and worked my way to this job, which had a vigorous screening process. I now have top secret clearance with both the military and the Janissary."

As an aside to Riley, Olivette teased, "By the way, the first thing you're told when you get a top secret clearance is never to tell anyone you have a top secret clearance."

"Thanks for the tip, but I'll never pass the vetting process," Riley muttered. "I have a checkered past."

Why did the Academy give me this delinquent? Piero asked himself. *The girl will be the death of me. I better smooth things over before Olivette starts to lecture.* "Bet your juvenile record is already sealed, so you—"

"Stop the chitchat and let's get down to business," Olivette ordered as she cracked her knuckles.

Piero slowly closed his mouth. *Too late.*

"From all over the world, janissaires send Piero requisitions. The Janissary is a separate institution from the military, but we still work closely together. When he approves a valid requisition, Piero kicks it over to my terminal. I then have the unenviable task of summarizing whether the military should honor the requisition, paying or reimbursing the *jinn.*"

"The military refers to us by the derogatory term, jinn," added Piero. "Individually, the slur is jinni."

"Jinni has a nice ring to it even though it's girly," Riley commented. "So, Olivette decides who gets paid?"

"I just make the recommendation," Olivette responded. "My boss, Commander Olaf, makes the final decision. He'll call me to his office on the top fl oo r to berate me when I make a bad approval."

"Ergo, Olivette is highly motivated to deny a janissaire's requisition," added Piero. *She takes a little too much pleasure in denying our requisitions. Sometimes I wish I wasn't able to feel her schadenfreude. Empathy is a fickle beast.*

"On the plus side, Commander Olaf rarely comes down here," Olivette said cheerfully.

"Can you pull up any janissaire's requisition?" Riley inquired.

Piero turned back to his monitor. "Just give the computer a verbal command."

Riley cleared her throat. "Computer, pull up all requisitions from Janissaire Eacles."

The screen shimmered and faded out. Then, streams of data rained down from the top of the monitor. Piero pointed to a line. "I remember this requisition. Eacles discovered some graffiti, calling them hex signs. His report said it belonged to a gang known as Hexahedron."

"That was only a few weeks ago," Olivette said from the end of the console. "Olaf denied the requisition because it wasn't a military matter."

That's a half-truth at best, thought Piero. *Olivette recommended the denial, and Olaf just signed off on it. I recall her shameful joy.*

"What did Eacles want?" Riley asked intensely.

"He wanted equipment hardened against electromagnetic attacks," Piero said while pointing to the screen. "That equipment is pro stuff only authorized for military personnel."

Riley gazed at the screen with a solemn face. "Maybe, if he had the equipment, Eacles wouldn't be missing."

"What was Eacles's job?" Olivette inquired.

"He hunted down rogue psychics," Riley said. "We worked together as partners. Eacles was on routine patrol without me the night he went missing."

"Is it common to patrol alone?" Olivette asked.

Riley looked down forlornly. Piero felt ripples of shame from her disconsolate mind. She cleared her throat before muttering, "Only when your protégé fails to show up."

Chapter 3

After escorting Olivette home, Riley followed Piero across the broken, trash-strewn sidewalks towards the Academy. Although it was very cloudy, Piero still wore his red-tinted glasses. Riley caressed the pommel of her skean, eyeing anyone who passed too close. "Why are we walking through this slum?"

"This is an up-and-coming depressed socioeconomic area," Piero replied favorably.

"It's a migrant ghetto," Riley retorted as she pointed to a man hauling a garbage bin. "What do you call that poor guy?"

Piero quickly walked past the worker in dirty coveralls. "Waste disposal personnel."

"He's a damn garbage man," Riley growled. "Where do you think he's going to drop off that trash?"

"He will drop off the waste at the volume reduction center."

"It's called the town dump."

While passing an alley, Riley bumped into a disheveled man who reeked of cheap rum. Immediately, she shoved him into some wilted cardboard boxes. The drunk rolled around listlessly before giving her a vacant gaze. Riley patted herself down to make sure she still had all her possessions. She gave a half-shrug as she inspected the front of her steel-gray tunic. "That bum got some goo on my chest."

Piero stopped to consider the man now snoring on the crushed boxes. "He's a displaced person."

"You're assuming that he came from someplace," Riley snapped. "He has likely been roaming these streets his entire life."

Piero stopped to consider a cinder block wall in the alley. "Ah, here's what I wanted to show you."

The cinder blocks were covered in graffiti. Piero pointed to a tilted blue cube, showing three sides, each displaying a number: six, one, and finally four. Red paint encircled the cube, and various colors filled in the empty spaces.

"It's the hex sign mentioned in Eacles's requisition," Riley said dumbfounded. "How did you know where to find it?"

"I pass by here on my walks to the Academy," Piero responded.

"Why don't you just take an auto-car like everyone else?"

Piero tapped the pommel of his skean. "I've never been mugged. Besides, I enjoy watching the activities at street level. The displaced persons are quite entertaining."

Riley studied the hex sign. "This cube looks like a die, the kind used for gambling, but somehow off."

"I noticed that too. Dice have the numbers, one and six, on opposite sides. Since this isn't an accurate representation of a die, the number 614 seems significant. The colors bordering the cube may have some importance."

"Random number generators screw up our precognitive abilities," Riley asserted. "Criminals will sometimes roll dice to determine which place to burglarize."

Piero touched the side of his glasses, emitting a flash against the alley wall. He took three more pictures of the hex sign at different angles and then just stared at the wall.

"What are you doing now?" Riley asked, tugging on his tunic.

Piero was startled out of his trance. "Just attaching the photos to the message I sent to Master Albus. Maybe he'll pass them along to whoever's investigating Eacles's disappearance. Let's keep moving, or we'll be late for training."

"Let me call an auto-car." Riley reached for her phone.

"If we take an auto-car, we'll get to the Academy way too early. It will screw up my whole itinerary."

Piero stepped out of the alley and walked at a quick pace. Riley trailed behind, saying nothing. They had to march single file most of the way as they weaved around derelicts and toppled trash bins.

A greasy migrant toting a pail collided with Riley at the corner of a busy intersection. Before she could pull out her skean, the man had trotted down the lane. Riley gave the oblivious migrant a rude gesture when she discovered a black smudge across her waist. *This brings back bad memories,* she thought. *I haven't been this dirty since the summer I worked at the aluminum recycling plant.*

Years ago, an academic advisor had thought it prudent to explore Riley's abilities in energetics. While she excelled in telekinetics and body control, her power to manipulate quick metal had not advanced beyond the simple use of a skean. The advisor assigned her to the third shift at a recycling plant in the hopes that she would form an interest in metalworking.

However, Riley resented this placement with her usual hostility. At the plant, the women's locker room looked as though it had been ransacked. Gang graffiti covered the rusty steel lockers. How did gangs get into this facility? *Riley thought to herself.* Oh, that's right; gangbangers must work here.

A cold breeze unsettled her. She looked up to find missing tiles in the ceiling and could see straight up to the rafters. When she opened a locker, the rusted steel door fell off its hinges. Why wouldn't they just use aluminum? *After two more tries, she found a working locker and dumped her backpack inside.*

Riley walked to the main floor, where lengthy columns of aluminum were stacked up like logs at a lumberjack camp. She was shocked to find scores of migrant workers scurrying about. They formed small groups and stared at her. There were no service bots in the entire building.

The frazzled plant manager did not know what to do with her. After quizzing her about her skills and finding that she had none, he finally gave Riley a spray bottle filled with green goo, instructing her to wipe down all the yellow safety railings. Of course, the railings protected loud, fire-belching machines that spurt out grease. Several times that first night, she had vowed to quit. Since no one had given her gloves, sticky oil had blackened her nails. When she went to the restroom to wash her hands, she caught her reflection in the large mirror over the sink, noticing heavy black smudges over her eyes. She must have rubbed them earlier.

Riley decided not to tidy up. The black smears on her eyes and fingers confirmed that she was working hard. Now, she was just as greasy as the other workers who did not give her a second look. For once, she fit in.

Another thump brought Riley out of her nostalgia. *My postcognition is kicking my ass today,* she thought. This time, she collided with a bag lady's cart. Piero looked back and shrugged before maintaining his quick pace. After twenty minutes, the pair approached the large plaza in front of the Academy. From a couple of blocks away, Riley could hear the uproar of protestors. The plaza was crowded again with bums and migrants chanting in unison near the Office of the Benevolent Imperator.

Piero circled a huddle of migrants. A young woman was shouting orders. She sported a white armband with a hand-painted green cross and the word "medic" scribbled underneath. Riley watched dumbfounded as the medic poured milk over the eyes of a fallen elderly man. An older woman in rags cried as she supported the man's head.

"Hurry up!" yelled Piero over the roar of the crowd. Riley did not realize that she had stopped. She called back, "Why is OBI using pepper spray?"

Her mentor just waved her on. Riley pushed through the huddle, catching up to him near the street. They slipped past some more protestors as fire suppression vehicles hovered menacingly about seven yards above. Riley noticed that their nozzles were pointed at the center of the mob.

"Let's hurry before we get wet!" Piero yelled.

They just made it to the crosswalk when the flood began. Riley looked over her shoulders to see waterfalls shoot out of the tubby bellies of the Fire Suppression Vehicles. The few brave demonstrators who had crossed the street to the OBI ended up in the gutter under tons of falling water.

Piero and Riley bounded up the steps of the Academy. The parade doors were on the third-floor landing, which could easily accommodate auto-cars.

As they reached the top, a narrow-skulled sentry bot greeted them. "Welcome Janissaire Piero and Protégé Riley. In five minutes, you have a training session with Janissaire Dirk."

"Acknowledged," responded Riley as she sped up through the open doorway. Piero followed closely behind. They twisted through the intersecting halls and down two flights of stairs. They reached the training room to find a bald man meditating on the practice mat.

Dirk's eyes popped open. "I sensed you running here. I hope you're already warmed up for today's exercise." Laughing as he slowly stood, he presented his bronze skean. Fascinated, Riley watched as Dirk's skean began to glow and then turn bright red. From a yard away, she could feel its heat.

Riley grabbed a dull sparring skean from the weapons rack and twirled the blade in her hand. She waited on the practice mat as her mentor took off his red-tinted glasses and utility belt, placing them in a cubbyhole against the back wall. Piero hurriedly pulled a sparring skean and joined her.

"With baseline energetics, we can manipulate the molecules of quick metal into various shapes." Dirk's skean lengthened into a blazing scimitar. "By quickly moving the molecules, I heat the blade, allowing it to slice through armor. Now, touch my blade with the tip of your skeans."

Riley was the first to comply. She lengthened her skean so that the tip touched the scimitar, marveling as her skean began to turn cherry red. She trusted that the rubber-treated handle and the protective guard would prevent her palm from frying. *The burned hand teaches best. Was that a Benevolent Imperator maxim or just some line from a fantasy novel? Maybe both.* Piero followed suit and likewise heated his blade.

"Also, you can heat your skean manually by just touching the tip to a hot surface," Dirk continued. "The molecules of quick metal are designed for easy motion."

"Dirk, I get that you're high level for energetics, but we're just run-of-the-mill baselines in that school," Riley said dismissively. "I can barely form a long blade."

Dirk seemed to ignore her, continuing, "Another advantage of a hot blade is that it will cast light. An illuminated blade also reveals any defects, called *hot tears*, that form when your blade moves from part liquid to part solid."

Ugh, Dirk is such an amateur, thought Riley. *He's mispronouncing hot tears like ears.*

Dirk pontificated, "These ho*tears* will make your blade vulnerable to failure when—"

"The defect is called hot *tears* as in Goldilocks and the Three Bears!" corrected Riley.

"They're *tears* as in a pack of deers!" Dirk shouted back as sweat trickled down his bald pate.

"First of all, they are just called deer," she argued. "And, deer travel in herds."

"We're talking about metallurgy, not barnyard animals!" Dirk shook his blade menacingly.

Riley rolled her eyes. "The defects are called hot *tears* because they are long cracks where the metal is torn."

"Hot *tears* look like tiny teardrops!" spat Dirk. "Before coming over to the Administration Branch, I spent three years in the Engineering Branch, studying this stuff!"

With her free hand, Riley pulled out her phone. "I actually worked with aluminum and I can show you photos of hot *tears*!"

She felt a hand on her elbow. Her mentor pushed her arm down. Piero smiled. "Pick your battles."

Dirk seemed to gather his composure when Riley pocketed her phone. He took a deep breath and continued the lesson as if nothing had happened. "The quickest way to cool down the blade is to dip it in water or snow."

"What should I do if there's no water or snow around?" Riley asked.

"Improvise!" Dirk snapped.

"Can I put my hot skean in a freezer?" she quipped.

"For today's lesson, we will use water." Dirk crossed the mat and dropped his skean into a metal rain barrel, causing a gush of steam. More water droplets pooled on Dirk's scalp. Piero and Riley imitated him by dumping their sparring skeans into the barrel.

Dirk returned to the center of the mat as he pulled another skean out of his belt's scabbard. "Pi and Riley, you must learn to work as a team. Go fetch new sparring skeans and try to strike me."

Riley snatched a skean off the weapons rack. She considered her opponent who was still lean and athletic despite being in his forties. The recessed lamps glistened off Dirk's shaved head, giving him a faint halo. Meanwhile, Piero slashed his skean as he circled behind Dirk.

"I don't hear any chatter," commented Dirk. "You have to communicate."

"What's the point of sparring against an adversary who is armed with a skean?" Riley asked disapprovingly. "It's not like we're going to fight other janissaires."

"That's the smartest thing I've heard you say all day," Dirk replied as he tossed away his skean, which skidded across the mat and jarred into the rain barrel. While still facing away, he raised one hand to Riley, motioning for her to come at him.

She did. With a lunge, Riley leapt off the ground. Dirk spun and deflected her blade arm at the wrist. Riley rolled past him and into a charging Piero, taking out his legs. Piero landed atop Riley in a tangled mass of limbs.

"Never leave the ground if you don't have to," scolded Dirk. "Once you're airborne, you have little control. Always, run through your opponent."

Riley was still pinned under Piero, who just noticed their compromising position. She felt Piero's breath on her neck and his chest rapidly pulsating against hers. As Piero started to demurely push himself up, Riley grabbed his collar, pulling him closer. She whispered in his ear.

Nodding, Piero stood and stretched his arms over his head. Circling the mat, he elongated his skean into a lean rapier. Piero swiped the air several times, getting a feel for the new blade.

"So, you're going for reach," Dirk taunted. "You'll need every inch."

"I just have to touch you with the tip," Piero retorted.

Dirk turned back to Riley, who was on her feet and tapping her phone. Dirk tilted his head, seemingly astonished that she was making a call during a match. Riley looked up for a moment and then peered at the screen. She winked before putting her phone away.

A guttural shout and the stamping of feet broke the interlude. Dirk turned to find Piero charging again, rapier held high. Dirk leaned under the thin blade, redirecting it up. Using Piero's momentum, Dirk pulled him close and kneed him in the groin.

Behind, Riley used her telekinetic ability to step on air. In quick succession, she silently strode up five feet, kicking Dirk in the back of the head and sending him sprawling to the mat. Riley landed in a crouch. She walked over to Dirk's motionless body and tapped him on the back with her skean. Slowly, Dirk rolled and pushed himself up on his elbows, moaning his disapproval.

Clutching his crotch, Piero rose unsteadily to his knees. "How did you do it?" he asked in a high-pitched voice.

"It was a rigged match," Riley intoned while eyeing her fallen opponent. "Dirk was using his precognitive abilities to predict our moves. In my head, I enumerated ten different attack options and used my phone to pick a random number. The last digit turned out to be a five, so I went with the fifth attack option which you just saw, but Dirk didn't."

Dirk shook his bald head. "That wasn't the point of the exercise."

"Wasn't it?" Riley held out her hand to Piero who grabbed it and hoisted himself to his feet.

"Now, that's what I call teamwork," Piero said while stumbling out of the room hand in hand with his new protégé.

Chapter 4

Olivette stared at her reflection in the mirrored wall. She wore a black lace mask and matching black tasseled gown, showing off her slender figure. Her only accessories were a gold necklace and a black veil, which she attached to her pinned-back hair.

A soft knock broke her self-absorption. The door opened slightly letting in the noise from the party. "Are you decent?" asked a shy voice.

"Please, just come in," Olivette said testily. "It's not the first time you watched me dress."

Piero poked his head inside. "I don't know the decorum for visiting my roommate in her father's house."

Olivette looked him over and shook her head. "I told you the holiday party was a masquerade."

Piero poked his hand through the doorway and dangled a black velvet mask. She grabbed his arm and pulled him inside. Olivette closed the door, shoving him against it. She glanced down at his body, smiling.

"Do you like the clothes I bought you?" she asked playfully.

"It's a nice costume." Piero looked around nervously as she pressed up against him. "This is the second time tonight that a woman has pinned me."

"Did your protégé play too rough with you?"

"Riley is like family to me. We're already experiencing sibling rivalry."

"Tell me about it," Olivette grumbled as she returned to the mirror and straightened her veil. "This was my bedroom until I moved out. My little sister, Daisy, has it now."

Piero gulped. "I thought Daisy was just your half-sister?"

"No, she's my full sister. I do have six half-brothers and four half-sisters though, all of whom are older than me. Father's been married a few times."

Piero turned his head as the music began downstairs. "We should get going."

Instead, Olivette grabbed his arm and directed him in front of the mirror. She took his mask and placed it gently on his face. Olivette then peeked over his shoulder. "I like your disguise."

"Do you think anyone will recognize me?"

"Not if you're lucky," Olivette joked as she sidled up next to him.

"Let's go before someone gets the wrong idea about us."

Olivette began to say something. She stopped and smiled at their reflection. Piero knew exactly what she was feeling. His uncomfortable expression gave him away.

They walked down the main stairs together to find the Demedici holiday party to be a crowded affair. Olivette was permitted to invite a single guest. Piero was surprised that she had chosen him over her many socialite friends, considering the guest list. He felt overwhelmed by the wealth and power packed into this party.

The Demedici family home was a mansion on Isle Royale. The Capital was built on the south shore along Siskiwit Bay. However, in less than a decade, the city sprawled to take over the entire island. The Demedicis lived in the glitzy, entertainment district of North Point, so the property had cost a fortune. However, the family could easily afford it. Cosimo Demedici owned a multinational corporation, holding a special license for shipping to countries outside the Imperium. It was a lucrative market as long as it lasted. Every year, more foreign countries petitioned to become Imperium territories. After a short time, those territories were always absorbed into the Imperium.

To complicate matters, a group of third-world countries formed an alliance called the Free States League, whose sole purpose was to curtail Imperium expansion into the Southern Hemisphere. The "Leaguers" enlisted privateers to capture commercial ships, leading the Imperium to place merchant marines on Demedici freighters. Months ago, rumors abounded that Cosimo had bribed senior officials in the Office of the Benevolent Imperator to procure this favored status. The fine line between government and capitalism had eroded over the years.

"You're not the only janissaire at this party." Olivette nudged Piero who followed her gaze across the congested dance floor. He spotted his former mentor, Elvene, who looked good for being in her late forties. She donned a red bird mask covering her long nose but could not hide her prominent, bold chin. Conspicuously, Elvene was dressed in a floor-length gown, veiling her new robotic legs.

"What's she doing here?" Piero asked. When Olivette did not respond, he touched her elbow. "Is Elvene someone's guest?"

"She comes to all our parties."

"Since when?"

"Elvene is a family friend," Olivette pulled him down and spoke directly into his ear. "That's how I got my job here after graduating from the Military Institute."

Piero's eyes lit up. "I didn't know janissaire had personal relationships like that."

"Why so surprised?" Olivette asked. "You're a friend of the family too."

Goosebumps tingled his forearms as Piero sensed danger approaching. Without looking, he suspected that Elvene had zeroed in on him. He braced himself, smiling as he turned.

"I've been waiting to talk to you all evening," Elvene said as she passed him and hugged Olivette with faux kisses on both cheeks. "How has Commander Olaf been treating you?"

"Like a dog treats a fire hydrant," Olivette joked.

Piero stood to the side as the two ladies laughed. He was used to being left out of the conversation back when they all used to work together. In fact, he was secretly glad when Elvene had retired for medical reasons.

"What have you been doing with yourself?" Olivette asked.

"It's too crowded in here," Elvene complained. "Let's go somewhere more private."

Piero was relieved to see them depart. Elvene limped and had to lean slightly on Olivette's shoulder for support. The last time he worked with Elvene, she was in a hoverchair.

Once the two women had walked away, Piero began to worm his way to the back of the hall, following the scent of hors d'oeuvres. Behind a table containing little plates stood a cute, young Asian server. Piero pointed to the trays of canapés behind her. "May I have something with caviar?"

"At a later time," she said, smiling.

"Well, when can I get some caviar?"

"Let me consider it."

"Are you saying you cannot give me any caviar?" Piero pointed to a tray behind her.

"I will have to get back to you." The server stood stock-still.

A gruff voice drawled, "You'll never get a 'no' out of this migrant. By the looks of her, she's from Nippon province. In the Japanese language, the most straightforward way to say 'no' is rarely used since it often comes out as too blunt. So, those folks use a wide range of expressions to avoid it."

Piero turned to find a mustachioed, older man wearing a white cowboy hat and black mask. The cowboy pointed to a tray of small, dark beads on crackers, "He'll have some of that."

The server bowed slightly and grabbed a small plate, stacking it with canapés. The server bowed again before handing Piero the plate.

"The Demedicis don't eat any animal products," the cowboy said as he pointed to a tray of orange hors d'oeuvres. Piero was about to say that he cooked bacon and eggs for Olivette but stopped himself. "That's interesting."

"I'm guessing this is your first hoedown at the Demedici estate."

"I work with Olivette."

The cowboy shoved something orange in his mouth which dribbled down his chin. "You must be replacing the other jinni."

"Well, I've replaced the last *janissaire* at the Logistics Military Office if that's what you mean. I've been working there for about eleven months now."

The cowboy looked at him as if he was naïve. "The Demedici family has always had a house jinni that I can recollect. With Elvene moving to greener pastures, you're the new stallion in the stable."

"Where's Elvene going?" Piero munched on a cracker with a dark topping. "This tastes exactly like caviar," he said, looking down at the food in confusion.

Things seemed to have reached critical mass with the friendly stranger. The cowboy squinted, tapping his hand against his thigh as if he was getting ready for a showdown.

The cowboy drawled, "Demedici Shipping is having problems in Guyana—"

"That's where Elvene is going?"

"That's where you're going."

"I'm sorry, but you're mistaken. I already have a job, which I mentioned before."

"Did you just train another *jinni* for your job?" The cowboy's bushy eyebrows rose over his mask.

"That's classified information."

"Well then, let me ask you another question. Do you think the Janissary would send a middle-aged woman with robotic legs into the Guyana jungle?"

"I can't talk about Janissary business." Piero turned to order some more hors d'oeuvres.

"When you're in the Guyana Highlands, check out Kaieteur Falls," the cowboy said as he moseyed away.

Piero shook his head and surveyed his hors d'oeuvres options. As an aside to the server, he asked, "Do you think that cowboy was joking?"

"Let me consider it," the server replied with a smile.

"Am I crazy to think that the military will ship me off to a hostile country?"

"I will have to get back to you."

"May I have some of those yellow hors d'oeuvres?"

"Yes."

Piero traded his empty plate for one filled with gooey, yellow treats. He sampled one that tasted like shrimp. With his free hand, he pulled out his red-tinted glasses. When he tried to put them on, they bounced awkwardly off his mask.

"Was that sophisticated?" Piero snorted as he put his glasses away.

"Let me consider it," piped the server.

Piero spied a pretty masked debutant weaving through the crowded dance floor, making wide turns to allow for her short, black, projecting skirt. *Ah, that's clever,* he thought. *She's wearing a modern tutu but a leather mask that was customary for 17th-century ballerinas.*

Although Piero was forced to take libido inhibitors every month, the medication's potency seemed to have waned over the years, doing little to curb his attraction to women. At best, the pills prevented any feeling associated with attraction.

Even so, Piero goggled at the young lady as she danced up to him and gave him a theatrical bow. She snatched one of his shrimp flavored hors d'oeuvres and popped it in her mouth. The ballerina daintily chewed the morsel before asking, "Don't you recognize me?"

Piero considered her attributes: the lilting, soft voice; the slight build; and the pinned-back auburn hair. With a knowing smile, Piero said, "I see through your disguise, Daisy."

"I do believe you're blushing, Pi." Daisy took the last treat off his plate and nibbled, enticingly.

"Your costume is very . . ." Piero struggled to find the right word to describe the tight, low-cut outfit.

"Revealing?"

"Beautiful."

"It doesn't take a mind reader to know where your *head* is at." Daisy giggled. "Olivette cryptically told me that she was bringing a chaperone. I was hoping it would be you."

"I thought I was her date."

"Nope," she said without hesitation as she rubbed her arms. "Is it cold in here?"

Piero tore his gaze away from the twin peaks poking through Daisy's costume and looked at her mask. He found it hard to keep his eyes from drifting downward. "Are you graduating from the Conservatoire soon?"

"Later this year, I'll have my bachelor of fine arts in dance. I've been very busy as the prima ballerina for the Othello ballet at the Isle Royale Opera House that started four weeks ago. Would you come to the show if I got you a couple of free tickets?"

Piero scanned the dance floor. "I wouldn't know who to bring."

Daisy smiled devilishly. "How about I give Olivette two tickets for the Saturday matinee and then she can bring you along?"

"I may have some competition." Piero looked around to see if anyone was listening to their small talk. He desperately wanted to be alone with Daisy to have a real conversation. "Next to you, Olivette is the top bachelorette in the Capital."

"Alas, you're always right," Daisy said dramatically. "Olivette would squander her ticket on some sycophant fool. I suggest that you try to make her jealous. I'll find you a respectable girl to chat with. However, I need you to find someone for me."

"Name him."

"I need a girl," Daisy said coquettishly. "To be precise, I'm choreographing my final ballet recital and I want a girl from your Academy who can walk on air."

Piero sensed waves of enthusiasm radiating off her. "That's oddly specific."

"My recital is about a girl in the Janissary who falls in love with a ballet dancer. At the climax, he throws her into the air, and she hovers over the audience."

I need to get off this subject, Piero surmised. "Why are you the only Demedici who didn't go to the Military Institute?"

"I'm an artist. What kind of art did you study at the Academy?"

"Martial arts."

"That's a combat skill. Surely, you have a passion for art."

"I enjoy writing fiction."

"That's a craft. Writers are lonely wordsmiths. If I had your empathy, I'd be the greatest choreographer in the world. Don't you want to give some young, deserving girl a chance to dance at my recital?"

A cruel thought crept into Piero's head. "Not at this time."

"So, you don't know any girls who can airwalk?"

"Let me consider it."

"Will you help me?" asked Daisy through pouty lips.

"I'll have to get back to you." Piero backed into the table, rattling the plates. When he looked over his shoulder, he noticed that the server now had her arms crossed and glared at him.

As an aside to the server, Piero said, "Don't judge me." He felt a warm hand on his chin. Daisy slowly turned his head, so he was facing her again.

Her eyes looked sincere behind her mask. "Find me this girl and I will get her a room at the Conservatoire's dormitory where she can eat for free at the cafeteria. All she has to do is dance at my recital."

Piero fumbled for his red-tinted glasses. He tried to put them on, but they bounced off his mask again, eliciting laughter from the server. The lenses were flashing, indicating that he missed some urgent texts. "I'll have to contact my boss to get approval."

"Thank you, Pi." Daisy smiled and promptly clapped her hands. She then craned her neck and kissed his cheek.

Piero lingered, watching her dance away gracefully. After a few rapid heartbeats, he followed the back wall until it came to a doorway, leading to a foyer. After finding a quiet nook in the wall, he checked his lenses again to discover four identical texts from Riley, stating: "Call me back now." Piero manually hit the callback icon and waited.

"Why do you have me on audio?" snapped Riley.

Piero sighed. He turned his glasses around, so the camera faced him. One lens showed Riley and the other reflected his own masked image.

"How are you doing?" asked Piero indifferently.

"Not as well as you. Are you at some weird fetish ball?"

"You marked your texts as urgent."

"I need to crash at your place for a few nights."

He sighed. "You're already getting free housing at the Academy graduate dorms until you finish your internship."

"I've got to get out of here for a while. Dirk is whining that I *intentionally* kicked him in the head. I find that odd, considering he kneed you in the balls. Anyway, the higher-ups are going to ask for your statement—"

"I'll write my mentor report tomorrow. I'll just chalk it up as a training accident. That's what it was . . . right?"

"Sure," said Riley unconvincingly. "Still, I need to stay with you until this all blows over."

"I know another place where you can stay for free." Piero smiled slowly. The wheels in his mind started turning. "Have you ever been to Blake Point?"

"That's way too upscale for me. What's the catch?"

"Tomorrow's a holiday, so you'll have the day off. Pack your meager belongings. I'm sending you a link to someone who'll take care of the specifics."

"What have you gotten me into—"

Piero disconnected the call; the lens holding Riley's angry face blipped off. On his red-tinted glasses, he thumbed Riley's contact information into a message to Daisy. Piero stared at the ceiling as he contemplated the best advisor to push this recital through.

"Working at a party?" sang a birdie voice.

Piero looked down to find a woman in a red bird mask. *How did she sneak up on me?* Elvene tilted her bold chin up at him. "Daisy sent me to find you."

"Of course, she did," Piero muttered. "She wants me to find a dancer for her recital."

"Who's the hapless victim?"

"I volunteered Riley."

Elvene twittered to what amounted to her laugh. "I will smooth things over with the Septenary. You will have to manage Riley. *I'm sorry to hear about her training accident.*"

"Ah, you were spying on me. I'll have to be more careful with my calls in the future."

Elvene tugged on her earlobe, which evidently concealed her embedded listening device. "These parties are great for Janissary intelligence. The Capital's movers and shakers all come to this masquerade where deals are made. For instance, we loan an Academy graduate, not even a janissaire, for a dance recital. Now, Demedici Shipping owes us a favor."

"I'm really not comfortable with these backroom deals."

"Get used to it. It's a simple *quid pro quo.* I'll scratch your back if you'll scratch mine. As your mentor, I gave you excellent reviews, so I expect something in return."

"I thought I deserved those reviews."

"Well, you didn't," explained Elvene. "At best, you excelled at mediocrity."

Piero's eyebrows rose as his mouth dropped. He shook his head in disbelief. But Elvene was not finished. "I'm a trusted advisor to the Demedici family, but someone wants me out of the way."

You're more like a house jinni than an advisor, thought Piero. "How can I help?"

"I'll try to pull some strings backstage, but you will have to do the *legwork*." Elvene laughed as she pulled up her floor-length gown, showing off a chrome foot. "I can't even wear shoes with these robot feet."

"Why me?"

"I don't understand your blathering."

"Why send me to Guyana?" Piero asked anxiously.

"I'm not sending you anywhere. I want you here in the Capital."

"There's an elderly man at this party dressed like the Lone Ranger who said you were leaving, and I was going to the jungle," Piero explained. "I've never been out of the Imperium. I don't even have—"

"Just playback the conversation," Elvene snapped.

"I'm not recording anything!" Piero said flabbergasted. "That's illegal. Are you recording me right—"

"Shut up, you moron," Elvene whispered as a couple of partygoers passed behind. She plastered on a fake smile and talked through her teeth.

"If anyone asks, I was just recording for employee quality assurance purposes."

Piero studied Elvene's red feathered gown but could not see any recording device. Instead, he listened intently and thought he heard a buzz coming from between her breasts.

"Stop staring at my boobs, pervert," Elvene whispered without moving her lips. "Whatever happens tonight, just refrain from saying 'no.' You feel as though it is the right thing to do, don't you?"

Piero felt a slight pressure at the front of his skull. He recognized the subtle, emotion control technique common to janissaires with level two mind control. Once exposed, Piero enacted his countermeasures, chasing Elvene's pressure away. "Let me consider it."

Elvene seemed satisfied and limped away. She trailed one hand against the marble foyer wall as she hobbled back to the dance floor. A flash of light pulled Piero's attention away from his old mentor's abnormal gait. His red-tinted glasses were flashing like a strobe light. Piero clicked the callback icon.

"You're trying to put me in dance classes!" Riley yelled.

Piero flipped the lenses around to find her enraged, red face. "Consider that the side benefit."

"The side benefit of what?"

"Oh, you're talking to Riley," said a girlish voice from down the foyer. Piero flinched as the ballerina ran up and hugged him. He now saw himself with a masked Daisy in one lens and a fuming Riley in the other.

"I'm glad you're not a porker," Daisy said melodically to the lens. "I already checked your Buddy profile on the Academy's social network; you have the firm body of a dancer."

"I'm so very flattered," Riley responded sarcastically. "Do I get to wear a burlesque mask like a dominatrix?"

"You're far too pretty to hide behind a mask," Daisy purred as she took off her leather mask.

"Really?" Riley asked tenderly. "You think *I'm* pretty."

"Of course, you're sensual," the ballerina replied. "You're a nine, but I can make you a ten."

"I think you're a ten." Riley tilted her head and smiled. Piero handed Daisy his glasses and stepped out of frame as the two admirers continued trading compliments. He stood a few feet away while they debated who was prettier. Daisy posed in front of the lenses; her profile was striking. She had perfectly symmetric, arched eyebrows that wrapped around pure blue eyes. Daisy's pouty lips looked like matching couch pillows. He resisted the urge to rub her inviting, alabaster shoulders.

Piero walked to the end of the foyer, which led to a patio. The doors were open, and he could see the lights from Thunder Bay. Piero stepped outside to cool off. He breathed in the fresh, lakeside breeze and was grateful that the patio was empty. He closed the glass doors to give himself a moment of peace.

This side of Isle Royale was much less gritty than where he lived. He envied Riley. She would live in the most exclusive neighborhood on the island. *I'm not up to chitchatting with these elites. I can't even socialize properly. There's no point in getting comfortable; they'll just replace me with someone from the Diplomacy Branch.*

A foghorn softly sounded. Piero saw a lighted ship on the horizon. *Did Olivette and Daisy stand here looking at ships in the night?* The patio door opened, letting the noise out. Daisy held out his glasses with one hand and placed the other on her hip, still holding her mask. He concentrated, finding her mood to be amused.

"So, you like her." Piero took his glasses and placed them in his shirt pocket after a few tries.

"I like you better."

"The feeling is mutual."

Daisy hugged him from the side. Her black tutu ruffled against his thigh. "I'm guessing that's the closest to affectionate words that you're willing to give me. When writing my recital, I was thinking of you. I turned the janissaire into a girl to hide the truth that I love you."

"My whole life has been dissuading the truth. I try to concentrate on the things that I can control."

"You cannot control love," she whispered and stared into his eyes. "You have to grab it and ride it out."

"I feel like your father is grooming me for something but not to be his son-in-law."

"Oh, think of the scandal that would make." Daisy hugged him tighter. "You live with one sister but marry the other."

"I think of Olivette as a sister already."

"Then, it will be an easy transition when we're married."

"Janissaire cannot legally marry," he told her.

"Just leave the Janissary," Daisy proposed. "Many students wash out of the Academy."

"There's still the restriction on reproduction."

"Do you want to marry me or not?"

"I do," Piero admitted.

"Then, we *are* secretly engaged," she affirmed. "We'll work out the details soon enough. For starters, I'll find you a new place to live. I think Olivette might have a thing for you."

"I read her emotions every day. I can assure you that she doesn't."

"Let's keep it that way."

"I can't afford the rent anyway," Piero said sincerely. "But I don't want to leave her in that depressed socioeconomic area all by herself."

"Pi, why can't you just admit that you enjoy living with a pretty woman?"

"I want to live with you if it were only possible."

Daisy rested her head on his shoulder. "Everything is impossible unless you try."

"I've spent the better part of the night pretending that I barely know you," he said glumly. "I'm tired of pretending."

Daisy placed her mask in his hand. She stood in front of him facing the lake. "Help me with my disguise."

Chapter 5

Piero cast a languid eye over the rows of amber streetlights swaying in the breeze like cornstalk tassels. When his auto-car taxi lowered over the city, he noticed that every streetlight dotted yellow pools on an otherwise dark landscape. At night, everything was either yellow or black. Even his taxi had yellow and black stripes. The faux-leather seat quickly inflated to hold Piero in place as the auto-car dove. *I feel like I'm in a giant bumblebee that's dipping into a flower petal.* The buzz from the auto-car's four-rotor blades added to his delusion.

In front of him, the screen flashed a red skull icon, followed by the warning: "You are entering a sector susceptible to insurrection. Probability of your violent fatality is imminent." The auto-car quickly landed at the corner of Mulberry Street and 45th Avenue, colloquially known as Murder Mile and Skid Row, respectively.

Piero exited the vehicle, which speedily whisked away. He was going to have a hard time finding another ride home. His mask dangled from his belt as he walked under the arched streetlight. Piero put on his red-tinted glasses and tried to open his text messages but realized his glasses were not working. He tapped the side again to make sure. For the first time in this neighborhood, he was really worried.

While at the Demedici mansion, Riley had sent him a text explaining that she found another hex sign. After finishing his plate of hors d'oeuvres, Piero had immediately left the party and hailed an auto-car taxi. He followed the coordinates here even though it was well past midnight. He circled in place but did not see anyone moving on either street. On closer inspection, Piero did spot two bodies splayed on the blacktop about a block up Murder Mile. They had probably been dumped out of a gangster's auto-car hours ago. Without a communication device, he wouldn't be able to call it in.

"Riley, if you're around here, I'm going to need your help," Piero called out. When there was no response, he set off south on Skid Row towards the wharf. After walking a few yards, he spotted a vandalized streetlight that was spitting out sparks from a cracked fuse box. Piero pulled his skean out of its scabbard and stuck the tip into the box. As hoped, the skean's bronze tip illuminated bright red, which traveled down the length of the blade.

There was a loud bang. Piero spun and slashed the air with his red-hot blade. A dark figure charged out of the trash-strewn alley. Piero sidestepped like a matador, letting his opponent pass him and crash into the streetlight. With an earsplitting thud, the figure cracked its bulbous head and fell back onto the sidewalk.

Piero jumped back, wobbling on the curb. He peered down at his assailant who was now shuddering uncontrollably. The metallic sheen indicated that it was an older model service bot. Piero extended his arm, letting the red glow of his skean wash over the bot that was still in the throes of conniptions.

The bot's speaker crackled to life. A mechanized, feminine voice said, "I don't wish to harm you."

"You can't even get up, so how would you harm . . ." Piero paused as he noticed a green dot on his fancy dress shirt that was not there before. He traced an invisible path to a gleam from an open window on the second story of a corner apartment building. Piero sighed, knowing that he had been in the sniper's crosshairs since he landed. He intently watched the green dot move in slow circles on his chest.

"If you want to leave the Janissary, I have a position for someone with your talents," crackled the speaker. "Just follow the hex signs."

Piero scoffed, "Next time, just send me a text."

"There is a janissaire with precognitive abilities who can sniff out deserters before they know they want to defect. I rolled the die, and this chance meeting was random enough to go undetected. I have some access to the Janissary network, but I need your password for the Logistics Branch."

A soft whooshing noise was creeping up the road. Without turning his head, Piero recognized the sound. The sniper was likely focused on keeping the laser-sighted green dot on his chest and was too far away to hear it.

A slight breeze kicked at Piero's ankles. Suction was pulling trash towards the street sweeper just off to his left. In his peripheral vision, he saw the blocky, yellow vehicle moving towards him, just clearing under the streetlights. And then, it was inches in front of him blocking the sniper's line of sight.

Bang! Something struck the street sweeper. Bang! The sniper was shooting at him. After a loud hiss, the whooshing noise stopped. Piero ducked down the alley; he hugged the left wall to keep out of the sniper's line of fire. Peering d own the dark lane, he could not see an exit on the other side. However, about fifty feet down, the alley seemed to hook right.

The street sweeper whined back to life, going in reverse and taking a sharp turn towards the other side of the street. Piero noticed that the vehicle's camera had pivoted towards him. Like most vehicles, the street sweeper was just a large bot that was programmed for one task. However, Piero couldn't help but think that the street sweeper still appeared to be eyeing him.

The wall across from Piero exploded; chunks of concrete rained on his fancy clothes. He gawked at the foot-sized hole in the wall just five feet away. Momentarily distracted, he failed to notice the blocky street sweeper bearing down on him. The vehicle jumped onto the sidewalk. Piero sprinted down the alleyway. Sparks flew as the street sweeper ground against the walls. Something crashed a few inches away from him. It was long and metallic. Piero cringed, realizing a falling streetlight had nearly crushed him. The cylindrical, metal pole moved alongside him. Without looking back, he knew that the street sweeper was pushing the streetlight, along with everything else, towards him.

The alley did hook right after fifty paces. Piero hopped over the streetlight that was crunching against the wall in front of him. As he turned the corner, the blocky street sweeper smashed into the concrete wall behind him. Piero sucked in a deep breath, knowing he had almost been flattened. Looking over his shoulder, the vehicle filled the alley like a big yellow barricade.

Piero turned back to find that the alley's bend abruptly stopped twenty yards in front of him. The walls were four stories high with no windows and no fire escapes. He desperately looked for a way out, but his only egress would be to climb over the street sweeper and then back out the way he came towards the sniper.

I'm panicking, Piero thought as he trembled. *I need to calm down and think of an exit strategy. Remember the Benevolent Imperator maxim, "Terror is the mind slayer."* He walked to the end of the alley and slumped down next to a hollowed-out dumpster. He leaned back against the wall and gazed up at the purplish sky.

A muffled cough hackled t he h airs on the back o f his neck like a ghost's caress. Within arm's reach, Piero spotted four figures huddled together i n t he d ark. Scrutinizing closer, he determined that two of them were mere children. This part of the town enticed migrants, mostly from Asia, with low-paying jobs and no questions about their residency status. While citizens of the Imperium were allowed to freely travel within its borders, they were only allowed to live and work on Isle Royale with permission from the Office of the Benevolent Imperator. Violators were quickly snatched up and sent to labor camps.

After determining they were harmless, Piero offered, "I'm sorry to bother you folks, but I'll—"

"Be quiet, this is robot country," whispered the man with bleach blond hair.

The boy jerked his head to the side, shouting, "Coquetry, adultery, mockery, sorcery, *hexerei*!"

"What's the kid's problem?" Piero asked in a hushed tone.

"My boy, Wunnut, suffers from rhyming syndrome," the man explained. "It only happens when—"

Wunnut lurched, yelling, "Oxygen, halogen, fountain pen, *hexahedron*!"

Piero pointed at the boy. "I heard it again."

"Glen, yen, ten, regimen, *marksmen*!" shrieked Wunnut.

The little girl in the huddle put her hands over her ears. "Make him stop, Mama."

Wunnut twitched, crying, "Mullah, tarantula, insomnia, Andromeda, *hexahedra*!"

"Stop!" exclaimed Piero. "I heard it again! It was a plural this time, but he said it clearly!"

"Wunnut doesn't know what he's saying," scolded the mother.

Fear gripped Piero as he recognized something directly over the family's head. "I need some light."

"No light," whispered the father. "Light attracts robots."

Piero peered over his right shoulder at the smashed, yellow street sweeper. He felt something warm near his thigh; he was still clutching his red hot skean. In his panic, Piero had maintained a death grip on his only weapon.

He stood and held out the blade. All four refugees pushed back against the wall. Piero held his skean over them, letting the soft, red glow flicker off the wall above them. He recognized the graffiti as the same blue cube with numbers on three sides. Piero read them aloud: "six . . . six . . . six."

The sound of a thousand hummingbirds fluttered down from above. Piero contemplated the purple, hazy night sky as an auto-car drifted into view. "Is there a way out of this alley?"

All four refugees pointed in the direction of the smashed street sweeper. Piero shook his head and scanned the rooftops but did not see any way up. "Where's the sewer?"

The father looked at the hovering auto-car with dread-filled eyes. He crawled to a beaten-down cardboard box and pushed it aside, revealing a large metal grate on the ground. Piero grabbed the meshed cover with one hand, pulling up sharply. Stuck. Not giving up, he stabbed the grate with his skean. The metal grill melted away as Piero traced a rough circle with a three-foot diameter. With a quick stomp, the center of the metal grate fell, clattering against the bottom of the storm sewer.

Immediately, the father jumped down. The mother picked up the girl and lowered her into the hole. She next grabbed the boy and repeated the getaway. After looking into the hole, the mother jumped down with her arms stretched over her head.

A gush of wind was Piero's only warning. With an instinctive reaction, he leapt back towards the street sweeper. An auto-car fell sixty feet, nearly smashing him. Hunks of crushed auto-car shrapnel exploded in every direction. Piero quivered as he patted down his body, feeling for injuries. Thankfully, he was unscathed.

More humming approached. Piero did not wait to see how many auto-cars were en route. He scrambled over the smoking, crushed auto-car. *Blessed be the Benevolent Imperator,* Piero thought as he looked down at the exposed metal grate. He could not believe his good luck. There was just enough room to squeeze past the flattened auto-car and into the hole.

Dropping into the storm sewer was like falling into the blackest abyss. Piero held out his skean and headed in what he thought was a southerly direction towards the lake. He flinched at a deep booming thud that echoed through the sewer, indicating another auto-car had dropped.

Piero moved at a quick pace, resisting the urge to bolt. The refugees were nowhere in sight. *May the Benevolent Imperator protect them,* Piero prayed quietly. After nearly a hundred paces, he felt a vibration coming from his shirt pocket. Joyfully, he pulled out his red-tinted glasses and put them on. The sewer lit up as he activated its night vision mode. Despite the large rats that were bumping his ankles, Piero was ecstatic that he could make phone calls again.

He was about to click the icon for the Janissary hotline when he hesitated. *This whole fiasco started after I sent the Janissary my pictures of the hex sign. The enemy has compromised our communications, and I would be foolish to give away my position.*

Piero decided to stay hidden and followed the sewer on a gradual decline. After half an hour, he reached the end of the line. Lake Superior had receded over the years due to the many cold-water reactors lining its shores. Piero walked out of the sewer to a muddy, polluted beach. Given his recent experience with auto-cars, Piero chose to walk home. By comparison, the gritty streets seemed less daunting.

After a twenty-minute stroll across littered sidewalks, Piero found the street-level entrance to his apartment building. He tore off his shoes and socks, throwing them into the trash bin. After rolling up his sooty pants, he climbed the stairs barefoot, not trusting the elevator.

The apartment was empty; Olivette was still enjoying her big night with her many suitors at the masquerade. Piero dumped his formerly nice clothes into a plastic garbage bag. With any luck, they could be salvaged. After brushing his teeth, he took the longest shower of his life.

Piero had just put on his silk pajama bottoms and settled into his waterbed when he heard Olivette come home. Through his open doorway, he could hear Olivette enter the bathroom. He waited patiently in the near dark, unable to sleep anyway after his long night. After twenty minutes, he heard the patter of soft feet.

The left side of his waterbed sloshed, and a warm body snuggled up next to him.

Olivette laid her head on his shoulder while he slowly wrapped his arm around her. He patted her hip, feeling soft fabric. She must have been wearing her favorite flannel pajamas. He took a deep breath; he liked the scent of her perfume, which barely masked the stench of alcohol and vomit.

"I had quite a stressful night," Olivette slurred.

Piero sighed. "Do you want to talk about it?"

"Only if you promise not to fall asleep again." She tickled his ribs.

He trembled involuntarily. "Stop it before you get me excited."

Olivette giggled as she snapped his waistband. "If only that was possible."

Piero wavered. The Janissary's limits on reproductive rights were severe. The Janissary claimed that it was just a precaution to protect his DNA, but Piero felt there was more to it. "I have to tell you something and I'm afraid that you will hate me."

"You can always be honest with me." Olivette laid her palm on his chest.

"A year ago, I took a bunch of prospective Academy children to the beach," Piero began. "I was still working for the Administration Branch back then. I met a girl; we secretly started dating. We weren't intimate, of course, but fell in love anyway."

"Don't your libido inhibitors keep you from having any real feelings?"

"The feelings persist, but I cannot act on them."

"I *feel* your heart beating through your chest. Do I know this girl?"

"My girlfriend is a college student. At first, I didn't know that her family was wealthy. I respected her privacy. She told me her name was 'Dee-Dee.'"

Olivette giggled. "That's a dumb name. My sister always tried to get the rest of the family to call her Dee-Dee, for short. I tried to tell her that Dee-Dee had two syllables just like her name. However, she claimed 'Dee-Dee' stood for her initials, so it was short for Daisy Demedici . . ."

The pause lasted several heartbeats. Piero felt her soft palm curl into a fist. Olivette lifted her head. "Tell me that you are not dating Daisy."

"She started school again and I got a new job in the Logistics Branch. A few months later, you became my coworker. Tonight was the first time we've been together for several weeks. Still, she asked me not to tell anyone, especially you."

"Stop saying 'she' when you refer to my sister."

"I wanted to tell you right away."

"Why?" Olivette asked.

"I trust you."

Olivette laughed hysterically. She pulled away and rolled out of the waterbed. Riding gentle ripples, Piero sensed her amusement from across the room. *Did I misread her that badly? We have a special bond.*

"You really are a fool." Olivette laughed some more, almost manic.

Okay, that bond has been pulled thin, he admitted to himself.

"You think that you'll marry *my* sister and have baby jinn?" Olivette demanded as she stomped around the bedroom. "Wait until they turn four and the Janissary takes them away! Do you think Daisy will still love you then?"

"I see you have put some thought into this."

"The reason you can't get it up isn't for your protection . . . it's for *our* protection. I can speak for the rest of the citizens who don't want to get mind raped," she snapped, looking angrier than Piero had ever heard her.

Piero felt a deep pain in his gut. It was far worse than getting kneed by his trainer. The agony slowly crept up to his now dead heart. Although she was drunk, Olivette was finally speaking what she had held back these many months. *To her, I'm little more than the dutiful palace eunuch whose sole purpose is to protect the sultan's harem.* Piero cleared his throat. "I overstayed my welcome; I'll be leaving now."

"You're not going anywhere," Olivette slurred humorlessly. "I've been babysitting you for months now and you're not going to blow it over some stupid confession! You better not have told anyone else about Daisy."

Even though it was pitch black in his bedroom, Piero closed his eyes and tried to sense her emotions. It felt like reaching out and groping a mannequin. Piero's unseen fingers felt around her brain's smooth contours. With a little more mind-controlling ability, he could have kneaded her brain like soft cookie dough to induce the emotions he desired. Piero discerned that she was enraged. *Well, I didn't need empathy to figure that one out.*

"I'm sure that Daisy thinks she loves you now," Olivette continued. "In a few days, she'll just fall in love with a fellow dancer. Here's the kicker; my family doesn't even need you. We had to tolerate Elvene's mind-reading abilities for years. We finally got rid of her and found you, a baseline for the Mind Control School. But now, you gave us Riley, who has no mind-controlling ability whatsoever!"

Piero covered his face with both hands. He reached over and flipped the switch; the ceiling light illuminated the room. While Olivette rubbed her bloodshot eyes, Piero stretched out in bed. "Olivette, you're a mean drunk. Just go."

Piero did not recoil when Olivette slammed the door. The anger radiated off her, splashing over him like choppy waves breaking on rocks. He leaned his head against his pillow and patted the mattress. "Goodbye, waterbed," he moaned.

Chapter 6

Leaving his apartment complex, Piero bolted straight for the Academy. He already resolved to avoid bot-controlled vehicles. After a block of lugging his duffle bag, Piero dumped it in the trash-strewn gutter. *Why is the avenue so dirty? Oh, that's right, the city is missing a street sweeper.*

"You need ride?" said a soft voice in Pidgin English.

Piero peeked over his shoulder to discover a disheveled Asian migrant, lying in the back of her tuk-tuk. The vehicle was little more than a scooter-powered rickshaw. The young woman pushed herself up. "I drive you very cheap."

When Piero nodded, the driver slid over and straddled the motorbike. He climbed in the back and sat with his duffle bag over his lap. "Take me to the Academy."

The tuk-tuk quietly merged into the early morning traffic before taking a right turn. Piero pointed to his left. "The Academy is that way."

"So sorry, protesters block all traffic near plaza," she explained. "I go to Academy other side."

"What are they protesting today?"

"Migrants no work or live in Isle Royale without papers. We have freedom to travel anywhere in Imperium but not allowed to live in nice place."

Nice place? In the early morning light, Piero gazed down at derelicts, burned-out storefronts, and overturned garbage bins. *Sadly, this city was probably one of the better corners of the Imperium.* "Why are there so many migrants in Isle Royale?"

"Years ago, Capital built with cheap, migrant labor," the driver said in her halting manner. "We used to live here in good tenement housing."

"Was that the golden age for migrants?"

"That's the beauty of being migrant." She laughed lightheartedly, peering over her shoulder at her passenger.

"We have no golden age. Every day, things only get better."

Piero rubbed his beard. "Well, you have that going for you."

After a few minutes, the driver made a couple of tight turns and pulled up to the Academy's street-level entrance. Since most people flew, this door was seldom used. The driver held out her electronic pad. "You give me eight credits."

After carefully examining the screen, Piero tapped a zero next to the line for gratuity and then waved his palm over the pad. When the backlight turned green, he lumbered out of the tuk-tuk with his heavy bag.

Without further conversation, Piero hitched his duffle bag over his shoulder and trudged over to the sentry bot that was guarding the Academy door. As he approached, the sentry bot turned its metallic, attenuated head.

"Janissaire Piero, you have no appointments today." Piero ignored the bot and kept walking. Something clamped onto his forearm, jerking him to a halt. The bot had a vice-like grip on him. Its eyes glowed red. "State your business at the Academy."

"Unhand me this instant!"

"State your business at the Academy," repeated the mechanized voice.

"My protégé asked me to help her move," Piero lied. The bot's head swiveled as it scanned his duffle bag. A few seconds later, the bot released his arm and resumed its statuesque posture. Rattled, Piero walked quickly into the Academy and down the lobby. He climbed the stairs to the business offices. Because it was a holiday, the entire fourth story was deserted. However, Piero knew of at least one person that never took vacations. He stopped at an unmarked door and tapped the intercom buzzer.

"I'm busy," said a scratchy voice over the speaker.

"It's rather important."

"Is it a matter of life or death?"

"I wouldn't be here on a government holiday for trivial reasons."

The unmarked door buzzed open. Piero pushed and entered a plush office. The middle-aged man behind the desk wore gold-tinted glasses and swayed his hands as if conducting an orchestra. He had white hair and a thin matching beard. Piero noticed a perceptible buzz directly overhead. Listening closely, he detected the sound was coming from the vent.

"Master Albus, I have something to report," Piero said nervously.

Albus twitched his fingers and then made a long swiping motion. "I know all about Daisy Demedici."

Ice trickled down Piero's spine. He gulped audibly and started twitching. Albus raised his glasses to his forehead and studied him. They had a staring contest for a few seconds before Albus started speaking again. "As your boss, I get frequent reports . . . and I got a request from your former mentor, Elvene, who now wants to send your new protégé to the Conservatoire."

Piero exhaled slowly. He felt like a condemned criminal who just escaped the hangman's noose. Albus formed a steeple with his fingers as if pondering something momentous. "What are your thoughts on this?"

"It's a very bad idea."

"Why?"

"The first Benevolent Imperator maxim admonishes, 'Avoid entangling alliances.'"

"Your clear judgment surprises me." Albus pulled his gold-tinted glasses back down and started wiggling his fingers. "I concur and will deny such an entrapping request. I was opposed initially to giving you a protégé but now see my reservations were unwarranted. It takes real courage to say 'no' to Elvene. Now, tell me what is so important that you had to bother me in person."

Piero plopped down his heavy duffle bag and pulled up a posh chair. He spoke about his recent nocturnal activities, starting with Riley's text about meeting him on the corner of Murder Mile and Skid Row. He left out the part about talking to the sniper but emphasized his heroics in saving a migrant family from certain death. Further, he explained that the Demedici family had plans to oust Elvene and replace her with Riley. However, Piero also omitted any ensnarement with the Demedici sisters.

Meanwhile, Albus sat stone-faced. In the awkward quiet following his story, Piero found the buzzing above him to be intolerable. "Are you recording this conversation?"

"What makes you think that I'm recording anything?" Albus asked nonchalantly as he picked lint off his white tunic.

"Unless you have perfect recall, I'd say that my harrowing adventure deserves some note-taking. Also, I hear the buzz from your recording device."

"I have an eidetic memory, so I have no reason to record you."

Piero pointed straight up. Albus lifted his eyes towards the ceiling; he hesitated before raising a finger to his lips in a shushing gesture. "You must have sensitive ears. I'll turn my fan off."

However, Albus just sat in his oversized chair, looking at the ceiling vent. He drummed his fingers across his oaken desk. The thrumming made Piero nervous as he kept looking up. *Oh, Albus is waiting for me to play along.* "Ah, that fan was bothering me."

"Do you want to get some waffles in the cafeteria?" asked Albus.

"Sure."

Albus quickly got up and moved towards the doorway to the corridor. "Off we go."

Piero grabbed his heavy duffle bag, following Albus out of the office past a line of empty cubicles where interns normally drudged through their workdays. Albus steered him towards a storage area that seemed to have been lost to time; only dusty boxes littered the tiny alcove. Albus turned abruptly. "You think my office is bugged."

"I heard feedback coming from a listening device in your ceiling vent."

Albus scowled. "I wonder how long it's been there."

"Don't you sweep for listening devices?"

"I will now; don't tell anyone. I'm going to feed whoever it is a bunch of bogus information."

Piero dumped his bag on the floor, billowing up wisps of dust. "I need a place to stay. Can you put me back in the Academy's dormitory?"

"That won't be necessary," Albus said, eyeing the bag through his gold-tinted glasses. "You can put your belongings in storage. I'm sending you to Guyana later this afternoon."

"Why me?"

"That's a rather philosophical question. Allow me to give you the précis. The precognitive janissaires call it the 'Horizon of Possibilities Expanse' or HOPE for short; I know it sounds a little hocus-pocus, but they swear by it. As such, precogs just predict the future, sort of like a forecast. Some get it right and some get it wrong."

"How does this relate to me?" Piero asked, confused.

"Six out of ten precogs have predicted your success in Guyana. Congratulations, you'll be happy to hear that

Mistress Cassandra is one of those six and she's mostly right."

"What did the other precogs foresee?"

"Your death, a gruesome one at that."

"You're telling me that if I go to Guyana, there's a forty percent chance that I will die horribly?" Piero's eyes bugged out as they welled up with tears. He curled his soft hands into tight fists. His knuckles shone white like the ridges of a snow-capped mountain.

"Don't look at the glass as half empty." Albus took off his gold-tinted glasses, looking down as he polished them on his tidy, white tunic. Satisfied, he casually put his glasses back on. "You have a sixty percent chance of success."

"With those appalling odds, don't send anyone."

"You have to look at the big picture," Albus said pragmatically. "We already have high-level janissaires in Guyana that we cannot risk losing. If you don't die right away, you can expect help from Mistress Raven."

"She's on the Septenary! Why is she in Guyana?"

"That backwater republic is important to the future of the Imperium. I really cannot tell you anymore as it might cloud HOPE."

"You have to do something." Piero buried his fingers in his dark hair. "As my supervisor, you can intervene for me."

"About that . . ." The master scratched his thin, white beard. "I am happy to report that you are now in the Diplomacy Branch. Your immediate supervisor is Mistress Raven for the time being. As such, I will delete your password for the Logistics Branch forthwith."

Albus strolled away after that, seemingly content to end the conversation. Piero looked around in dismay, not quite sure where to go. He picked up his duffle bag and trudged down the hallway. He gazed out a window at the plaza covered in small, wretched tents. *I envy them. At least they get to choose their destiny.*

After descending several flights of stairs, Piero reached the graduate dormitory, which was the worst housing in the Academy. The teachers treated them like mooching teenagers living in their parents' basement. The fact that Piero had just asked for a free place to live was not lost on him. He stopped at the end of the hall and knocked on the last door.

"Go away!" said a familiar voice.

"It's your mentor."

"Like that matters."

"I have to complete my report before my impending death."

The door cracked open. "Why are you so melodramatic?"

Piero shoved the door, pushing Riley back. Piero looked around the small, messy dorm room and covered his nose at the stench. *The horror, the absolute horror.* He noticed that she was still wearing what might be pajamas, a tank top with booty shorts. He unceremoniously dropped his duffle bag on her floor. "I'm going away for a bit. As my protégé, I need you to cover work for me and find a place for all my belongings." Piero kicked the bag.

"I didn't get the memo," Riley said snidely.

"Speaking of which, did you send me a text last night, saying that you found another hex sign?"

"No."

Piero studied her eyes to determine whether she was telling the truth. Her black irises hid their pupils. *Damn your shark eyes.* He pulled out his red-tinted glasses and tapped the side. After a few moments, he pulled up her message and showed her the image in the left lens.

"I didn't send that text." Riley crossed her arms. "Did you find another hex sign?"

"That's not the point. Your communications have been compromised."

"So, I'll change my password." She rolled her eyes, then focused back on Piero. "Show me the picture of the new hex sign."

"I didn't bother taking a picture. Everything was the same as the other sign, except the numbers were six-six-six."

"That's so Biblical." Riley looked astonished.

"It really isn't. Early manuscripts for the Book of Revelation state the number of the beast as six hundred and sixteen, that is, six-one-six."

"That doesn't roll off the tongue like six-six-six."

Piero looked at the dirty clothes scattered across the cozy room. "I wouldn't pack just yet."

"What did you do?"

"You won't be doing any pirouettes soon."

"You deep-sixed my dancing career!"

"Master Albus denied your stint at the Conservatoire," Piero intoned. "However, if you still want to move, my bedroom *is* available. I can't recommend it. As it turns out, Olivette, the quiet, shy girl who doesn't talk to anyone, is a real stuck-up bitch."

"So, you're saying that Olivette wants me to move in."

"That's one way of looking at it."

"What's the other way?"

"The Demedici family wants a janissaire to represent their interests within the Janissary. For many years, they've been schmoozing Elvene, but she has decent mind-controlling abilities and apparently spies on them."

"I'm guessing the Demedici family is dumping Elvene."

"Olivette wants you to replace her."

Riley sat on her bed and stroked her chin. "So, if I move into your apartment, Olivette will lavish me with gifts and take me to great parties."

"That's not exactly what I was trying to say."

Riley stretched across her bed and picked up her phone. She immediately started tapping out a text message. Piero considered crawling into bed and pulling the sheets over his head.

After finishing her text, Riley glanced over her shoulder, smiling. "Don't worry Pi. You can still have this room."

Chapter 7

Most of the nation was now beneath the waves. Poetic, in its own way, as the name, Guianas, is a native word meaning "land of waters." This waterlogged region was bordered by three rivers: the Amazon, the Negro, and the Orinoco. While Guyana was no longer a member of a commonwealth, it remained a free state on the fringes of the Imperium.

Piero moved through the dark streets of Georgetown with some trepidation. While the submerged part of this city was a booming tourist draw for underwater activities, he was lurking through gang-infested ghettoes and was trying unsuccessfully to blend into his surroundings. *I wish I had camouflage like the local Amazon pigmy gecko,* Piero mused. *Also, I wish the Janissary gave me a mission dossier rather than a Guyana reptile guide.*

Many of the buildings were abandoned. Piero imagined that mudflows and other geomorphic processes had buried most of the residents. However, there was still one person he had to locate before the morbid predictions of his demise came to pass.

Piero found the round, green door to the shabby structure on his map. He knocked and waited for a response. He looked through the barred windows, but they seemed to have been boarded up from the inside. With a creak, the large door opened, and a shaft of light swept out onto the street.

"Are you coming in?" asked a feminine voice. Piero pushed the heavy wooden door just enough to squeeze through. He had stepped into a modest living room where the only light came from dangling bulbs. The young hostess pushed the door closed, latching it tight. She was blond with a light complexion, unusual for these parts. Her name was Gia Aconda, a likely alias all things considered.

"You don't talk much," Gia said softly. "Are you really a janissaire?"

Across the room, Piero spotted a phone on a workbench. He concentrated and then grabbed it with his mind. The phone flew towards him and he snatched it crisply out of the air. Piero handed the phone over to Gia. "Let your people know we're ready."

"I don't need a phone for that," she explained, rolling her eyes. "Besides, my brother and two sisters are already packed. They're just waiting for extraction, but my job still has to get done."

"How long will it take?"

"Didn't anyone brief you?"

"My *guide* was sketchy on the details."

"When you say '*guide*,' do you mean a tourist guide."

Piero gulped. *She's on to me. I need to change the subject.* "So, what do you do?"

"I'm a political activist."

"Does that pay well?"

A nervous look crept across Gia's face as if she had come to a sudden realization. With a grimace, Gia seemed to convey her worst fear, "You don't know what you're doing."

"My boss refused to cloud the Horizon of Possibilities Expanse."

With closed eyes, Gia took a deep breath and exhaled. "I'm something of a janissaire aficionado and can tell that you're a rank amateur."

Piero shrugged. "Look, I'm the best shot for a successful mission. I only have a forty percent chance of dying."

Gia grew stock-still and appeared to be meditating. Piero began to say something to break the awkward silence but closed his mouth. He looked around the hovel, noticing expensive electronics that were far too high-tech for their surroundings. *Probably stolen*, he thought. Several of them buzzed annoyingly. A black, hairy animal was curled up on a shelf of an antique, wooden bookcase. The little critter had four humanoid hands and a long tail wrapped around its lethargic body. Oddly, the creature wore a little, chrome motorcycle helmet on its diminutive head.

After far too long, Gia's eyes popped back open. "Okay, I know everything that's on the data chip buried in your left hand."

"That's impossible," Piero yelped. His posture stiffened as he lightly rubbed his left palm.

Gia lifted her chin while clenching her jaw. She stared at him without blinking. "Your blood type is O positive. You're allergic to mold. Ten years ago, you broke both bones in your left forearm. Your nickname is 'Pi.' You were born in July. You're overdrawn on your bank account—"

"Stop!" Piero chewed on his lower lip. "How do you know all this about me?"

Noticeably, a vein was pulsating in Gia's neck. "You believe the Benevolent Imperator is divine."

"He shuns all worship."

"Yet, your data chip contains all your medical records, including your psychological evaluation. Apparently, you imagine that the Benevolent Imperator can answer prayers."

Piero desperately wanted to end the interrogation and pointed to the furry animal on the shelf. "What is that?"

"Ah, I'll introduce you to Jocko when he wakes. He's a cognitive-enhanced monkey."

"How smart is he?"

"Jocko is smarter than you but equally domesticated," she said dryly.

"I'm not domesticated, " Piero responded meekly. *I need to sit down for a moment. As a guest, perhaps I should ask my hostess first.* He scratched his head, trying to remember his etiquette training.

"All janissaires are domesticated," Gia said pedantically. "Turning wild animals into docile barnyard animals takes three conditions: their liberty of movement must be restricted; their inherent natures and communal bonds must be broken; and, finally, their sexuality and belligerence must be confined. For males, the process of pacifying is far worse as it involves castration, which limits breeding and their natural hostility."

Tamely, Piero tugged at his collar. "Are you saying that the Benevolent Imperator has turned us into obedient farm animals?"

"The husbandry of humans has been going on for millennia, ever since the first dominant man forced another person to plant his crops instead of foraging for food. You cannot spell 'obedient' without OBI. That's who you work for, isn't it? Look at your life. You are only allowed to travel with authorized permission. You don't get to visit your birth mother or other family members. They pump you full of chemicals to curb your natural desires. OBI pays you peanuts."

Piero reached down to his belt and yanked his sidearm out of its holster. "A farm animal doesn't get a gun." Piero twirled the handgun on his index finger. On the fourth revolution, his finger slipped off the trigger guard and the gun sailed end over end across the living room. As his sidearm hurtled towards Jocko, he quickly pulled with his mind; the gun snapped back. He clumsily swiped at the handle but caught the barrel. With his loaded sidearm now pointed at his chest, Piero gingerly slipped the gun back into its holster.

Gia shook her head. "I told your boss, no firearms. Put it in the kitchen before you hurt yourself."

Piero hesitated but reluctantly complied. He searched the cabinets for some kind of lockbox but could not find anything. Instead, he unbuckled his gun belt and put everything into a cupboard full of green bananas.

The buzzing in the living room grew louder. The blare had distracted him to the point where he could no longer think straight. "How can you live here with all that noise?"

Gia turned her head. "What noise?"

"The incessant buzzing."

"There are no flies in here."

Piero pointed to an empty light socket dangling from the ceiling. "That hum is so annoying. You have at least five more spread out across the ceiling."

"Be quiet for a moment." Gia went to her desk that was tucked inside a nook near the kitchen. She rummaged through a drawer and pulled out a device attached to a microphone. She then walked around the living room, holding the entire device near each buzzing instrument. "They're not making any noise."

"What are they?"

"That's my surveillance gear. If you're in my house, you're being filmed." She looks back to Piero with an eyebrow raised, sizing him up. "I didn't know they taught technomancy at the Academy."

Piero was appalled. "Technomancy doesn't fall under the purview of the big six schools, so it's not part of the curriculum. As a miscellaneous power, only the Grand Master of the Septenary can authorize its instruction."

Gia smiled and put her device back in the drawer. "This is the start of a most auspicious evening. It appears, my dear Pi, that unbeknownst to the Grand Master, you are at least baseline for technomancy."

"Er, why would you say that?"

"Because you can detect recording devices with your mind."

"How would you know that makes me baseline for technomancy?" Piero asked worriedly.

Gia walked over to Piero and grasped one of his shoulders, smiling. "I know because I too am a technomancer."

Chapter 8

The purple flower had a sweet aromatic fragrance. Piero ran his finger down the petals to the thin stem that corkscrewed onto heart-shaped leaves. The vine grew from the cracked asphalt and twisted its way through a rusted chain-link fence. The plant vaguely resembled a morning glory, but this one bloomed at night a fitting metaphor, perhaps, for his upcoming nocturnal endeavors.

Something pulled at his pant leg. Piero resisted the urge to kick. He looked down to find Jocko tugging furiously. "What do you want?"

Jocko put his finger to his thin, monkey lips and shushed him. He then waved his little hand before scampering off. Piero reluctantly followed the helmeted monkey down the fence line. They came to a halt across the road from a utility structure, resembling an obsolete power station. In the dead of night, there was no traffic or signs of life. Piero would have thought the place was abandoned if not for the two sentry bots standing motionless near a metal garage door on a loading dock. The streetlights glinted off their cold, glassy eyes.

Sadly, bots seemed to be everywhere nowadays. The Imperium shipped in natural resources from backwater countries like Guyana. In return, the Imperium returned overpriced, high-tech equipment to the third world. The Imperium's biggest export was military hardware, and the

Guyanese bought it up. Last year, that all changed when the pro-Leaguer rebels launched a coup, severing all ties to the Imperium. While the new Guyanese politicians hated the Imperium, they still loved its weapons, especially the bots.

A few raindrops tapped Piero's head and then more; soon the shower would turn into a tropical torrent. Piero closed his eyes and concentrated. He felt another presence moving up behind him. He turned to find Gia creeping slowly along the fence. When she got within an arm's span, she whispered, "It's hard to sneak up on a jinni with clairvoyance."

"It's the only benefit when you're baseline for the Awareness School," he responded in a clipped tone.

"Sucks to be you."

Before he could retort, a loud bang ripped down the road. The shock wave thudded against Piero like a hammer. He staggered back and bumped Gia, who was covering her ears. Jocko had already dived for cover and peeked out from a discarded plastic crate.

Multihued lights danced across the street. The sentry bots came to life, swiveling their slender heads dotted with flashing, tiny bulbs. Marching down the road, the bots advanced on a smoky crater about a hundred yards away. As soon as the sentries had passed them, Piero felt a shove.

"That's our distraction," Gia hissed through clenched teeth.

"The building's cameras should be off until we're done."

They ran across the road and up the stairs to the loading dock platform. Gia stopped in front of a control panel and stared at it for a few seconds. Piero drummed his fingers nervously against the garage door until he felt it shudder. He pulled his hand away as the door started to rise. Not wasting time, Gia ducked under the clattering door and disappeared into the dark cargo area. Jocko quickly followed, waving to Piero. When the janissaire did not budge, Jocko rolled his eyes and shrugged before scurrying away.

Piero tapped his red-tinted glasses to activate his night vision. The cargo area was nearly empty. At the far end, Gia was standing in front of another door eyeing its control panel. As he approached, the garage door behind him began to rattle. Over his shoulder, Piero watched the door slowly descend, sealing him in.

When he turned back, Gia had already opened the other door. He picked up the pace as Gia and her monkey slipped into a brightly lit hallway. He passed the doorway, stopping short as he caught sight of them frozen in place. Down the hallway was a sentry bot; its metallic, compact head pivoted around as its cherry eyes scanned them.

Piero drew his skean and charged, knocking Gia to the floor. The bot raised both arms at the elbows leveling twin mounted auto-guns. Leaping, Piero turned sideways, narrowing his profile and gliding between the bot's outstretched arms. He stabbed the bot's torso, digging up to the hilt. Piero hung for a moment; then, using his body weight, sliced keenly downward.

The sentry toppled forward, landing heavily on Piero. By some fluke, the bot's extended arms landed firmly on either side of his chest. Piero breathed again when the bot's red eyes faded out. Lying on his back, he slowly tilted his head to find that the heavy, metal body just missed crushing his pelvis. *I couldn't take another hit there.* His legs remained splayed around the bot's waist.

Something patted his head. Piero rolled his eyes to discover Jocko sympathetically grooming his hair. Hard footsteps advanced towards him. Gia stared at the bot straddling him. "I wouldn't have guessed you for a robosexual."

Embarrassed, Piero wiggled and slithered out from under the bot. He then yanked his skean out of the bot's body. "Have you reconsidered whether we need firearms?"

Gia walked down the hallway, which ended in another locked door. She stood motionless as she examined the control panel. "The sentry bot was scanning for threats. Bots can't go around shooting every janitor who's working late. I managed to jam its radio signal before you cut it open. However, I don't know how often that bot regularly checks in."

Piero stepped up behind her. "What do you need me to do?"

"Your only job is to protect me while I break into this Guyanese military control center," she said with a curled lip, baring her teeth. "So far, you nearly got me killed."

"Is it time to panic?"

"I got this." Gia sighed as she looked over her shoulder. "I finally figured out who you look like. You remind me of Mystic Mike."

"I heard that name before," Piero replied. "Is he an exotic dancer?"

"Hardly," snorted Gia while rolling her eyes. "The Mystic Mike Show is a satirical kid's series about a bearded wizard who shoots rainbows out of his fingers. The show mocks the Benevolent Imperator and his psychic abilities."

"I'm thinking of shaving." Piero rubbed his dark beard. "I thought women liked beards."

"We don't."

"In romance novels, the men always have beards."

"If you want to look like Mystic Mike, then keep those whiskers."

"This is an Imperial beard." Piero pointed to his face. "As you can see, I have no chin hair, so it's very expensive."

Gia studied his beard closely. "Get your money back."

Piero desperately wanted to focus back on the mission. "How do you open all these doors without touching the control panels?"

"I read computer code the same way other janissaires read minds." Gia turned back towards the door. "Then, I alter the code—"

"What do you mean *other* janissaires?"

"I was speaking generally. Technomancy is a jinn power after all. If I'd gone to the Academy, I imagine that I would've picked up something in the big six schools as well."

Before Piero could respond, the door popped open. Bright green light spilled over from the next room. Jocko went in first. After a few moments, he came back, giving the thumbs-up gesture.

As he entered, Piero beheld the green-lit room filled with row after row of five-foot computer towers, twinkling with multicolored blips. Gia brushed past him, holding her palms down as if groping for something. She walked down the length of an aisle before moving onto the next one. Piero reached over to the nearest tower. A ray of colored light arced out to each of his fingertips. Piero pulled his hand back, making a perfect rainbow.

"Oh, that's ironic, Mystic Mike," Gia teased. "Don't play too much or you'll go blind. These server towers replaced all the obsolete blade servers that had overheating problems."

"I thought blade towers were more advanced than plain, old servers."

Gia stroked the top of the five-foot tower in front of her. "This is the new *server tower* that has an entire virtual universe of computing power."

Piero leaned on the tower, creating more rainbows. "Have you found the missile defense database?"

"Finding it was the easy part. I'm having difficulty fooling the targeting systems into thinking friendly units are now enemy units. Normally, I could have altered the code from my home, but there's an airwall."

"What's that?"

"These servers are isolated and not connected to the net. So, I have to be physically in this room to change the targeting code. I'm using a rubber ducky that simulates keystrokes to quicken the malware download." She paused, looking at him. "You're going to have to learn all this stuff if you want to be a technomancer."

"I'm baseline for everything, so I'm used to underachieving."

She shrugged. "Maybe technomancy is your thing. You may want to create a new life here in Guyana."

"Let's not get ahead of ourselves," Piero muttered. "Four out of ten precogs predicted that I would die horribly tonight."

Gia gave a long whistle. "I say we fake your death."

"Wha-what?" Piero stuttered.

"After this mission is over, I'm staying here a bit while my siblings settle into Isle Royale. I'll just tell my handler that a bot squished you." Gia clapped her hands twice. "Alright, I'm done here."

Piero stared slack-jawed at Gia. *Did she just propose treason? Janissaires are not traitors to the Benevolent Imperator. If an inquisitor ever found out that I consider leaving the Imperium, I would be summarily executed. I am a loyalist, not a renegade. My protégé is the rebel. Riley is the type to topple the Imperium.*

Piero moved towards the open door leading back to the hallway, sternly committed to returning home. Still, he had to survive the rest of the night. Piero stepped over the dead bot, looking back to make sure that Gia and Jocko were still following. When he reached the cargo area, he stopped. The metal garage door was now open and heavy rain pelted the loading dock. He adjusted his glasses to improve his vision. Still, he could not locate the two sentry bots lurking outside.

"Why aren't we leaving?" Gia asked from down the hall.

"Stay back," Piero ordered. "The garage door is open. Can you find the sentry bots?"

After some hesitation, Gia said, "I can see through their cameras. The bots are across the road, facing this door. I can see you pretty clearly."

Piero backed up into the hallway. "Can you deactivate those bots?"

"I'm jamming their radio signals, but I can't just turn off sentry bots. Some of the older models had internal switches that a jinni could flip telekinetically."

"Find another exit."

"I'm barely in range of those bots as it is," Gia muttered. "If I move even a few feet back, the sentry bots will be broadcasting your face over the net."

Piero leaned back against the wall. He rapped his knuckles on his forehead. *This is go time, soldier. Remember your training. How did Riley beat Dirk?* He closed his eyes and a plan bloomed in his mind. He formulated six attack options that gave him a slight chance of success. His favorite was taking the arm off the dead bot and using its mounted auto-gun against the other bots. He turned to his accomplice. "Pick a number randomly between one and six."

"Six," said Gia, confused.

"Did you pick it *randomly*?"

"It's the first number that popped into my head."

"Did you pick six because I said 'pick a number randomly between one and six,' so the word, six, was the last thing you heard before answering?"

"What are you talking about?"

"Choose an animal: rhinoceros, cheetah, hyena, or elephant."

"Elephant."

"See, that's what I mean," Piero said exhaustedly. "You picked the last word you heard."

"Does this really matter?" she asked, clearly exasperated.

"It's kind of a life-or-death thing," he responded, shaking uncontrollably.

"Fine, I'll pick another number and animal if it's so important to you."

"Too late now!" exclaimed Piero in a panicky voice.

"One and cheetah."

"The animal isn't relevant," Piero muttered. "I held six attack options in my head, and I needed you to pick one *randomly*."

"I'm guessing that you don't like attack option six."

Piero looked down at Jocko. "You're one lucky monkey. My third attack option had you going out there first."

Jocko looked taken aback. He crossed his arms and shook his little chrome helmet. Gia stepped in front of her pet. "Get to the point about all of this randomness."

"A few hours from now, what I do next will be a significant event."

"You think highly of yourself."

"If our enemy has someone with precognitive abilities, then that precog will foresee the sabotage to the missile defense system."

"There is no undoing what I just did," Gia said assuredly. "Maybe I tripped an alarm, or those sentry bots noticed the garage door closing. I can think of dozens of possibilities why those bots are waiting to shoot you full of holes."

"As reassuring as that sounds, my only option is to randomize my attack beyond the Horizon of Possibilities Expanse." Piero went back to the open door. Without exposing himself, he stretched and threw his skean onto the road. He heard it skid across the blacktop before coming to a stop. "How far away is my skean from the bots?"

"It's about three feet in front of both bots and almost equidistant between them."

Piero looked intently at Gia. His sixth attack option *was* his least favorite because he had thought of it only after exhausting his better options. "Why did you have to pick six?" Not waiting for a response, Piero continued, "Wait until I clear the cargo area. Run like hell when you hear the shooting."

Gia nodded. Jocko patted Piero's calf. After gathering his mettle, he stepped out the door with his hands raised. He slowly walked through the cargo area and onto the loading dock. As he neared the edge of the raised platform, Piero spotted his skean lying on the road. He scanned the vicinity directly in front of his blade but did not see anything. Instead, he listened raptly. He heard raindrops striking the tin roof over his head and the sloshing of water against the clogged drainpipe. Piero's ears rang. There, directly in front of him was a pair of soft buzzes about three yards apart.

Piero walked towards the stairs. Twin whirring noises stopped him cold. Over his shoulder, he yelled, "I think they'll shoot me if I try to leave!"

"I'm surprised they haven't shot you already," Gia responded supportively. "You must seem unthreatening. However, now they have their guns trained on you. I can scramble their cameras for about two seconds."

"Do it as soon as I jump!"

Gia screamed, "Wait!"

Piero leapt forward, sailing four feet down. He hit the ground, kicking up some asphalt as he sprinted forward. He mentally pulled his skean, snapping it cleanly into his right hand. Before hitting two strides, he heard the sickening whir of the bots' arms and rain pelting their metallic bodies.

Piero made it directly between the bots and jumped. The sound of gunfire at point-blank range was deafening.

Chapter 9

Riley sat quietly on the leather-upholstered couch as the middle-aged psychologist tapped the screen on his lap. She perused the office. Everything in it from the bubbling saltwater aquarium to the soft woodwind music was meant to induce calm. But Riley did not feel any soothing sensations. In fact, she didn't feel anything at all.

"Why am I here?"

The psychologist looked up from his screen. "I'm Dr. Teller. I have to give you some news. Your transcript says that you were the protégé for Janissaire Eacles."

"Did he turn up dead?"

Dr. Teller raked his fingers through his thinning hair as he analyzed Riley. He cleared his throat. "You don't seem upset."

"I'm not."

"Well, you may be happy to hear that Janissaire Eacles is still just *missing*."

"I'm not."

Dr. Teller tapped his screen. "Do I have your permission to record this session?"

"No."

"Why not?"

"I still don't know why I'm here first thing in the morning." Riley reclined across the couch as the psychologist tapped his screen. She gazed at the clownfish, darting across the tank. The filtration system wasn't working properly; the saltwater was tinged with green scum.

The sea-green water reminded her of the degreaser she had lugged around in a spray bottle back at the aluminum recycling center. *Those were hard times. For over eight hours every night, she walked around the center, spraying smudges off the yellow safety railings as the other workers gave her dirty looks. She was the newest employee and had the easiest job. Riley never introduced herself to the other workers and took her lunch breaks at odd hours to be alone. Except for the plant manager, no one else knew she went to the Academy or concealed a skean in her work boot. Behind her back, she heard the migrants call her "Cutback." When she first heard the slur, Riley mistakenly thought it referred to her genitalia. She was ready to stab the next person who threw that disparaging term her way. However, before she got the chance, she found stacks of aluminum parts labeled, "cutback." After a quick search on her phone, Riley discovered that cutback parts were of such low quality that they went straight to packing without being inspected. She got the message. The other workers thought she was just a slight step above garbage.*

Riley understood their resentment. The migrants broke their backs lifting aluminum parts all night while she just sauntered around with her bottle of green goo. Worse, the center had bought shiny service bots that labored nearly twenty-four hours a day. Every time a new bot showed up, three migrants lost their jobs.

One fateful night, she discovered a hidden monument near a giant oven. A worker had neatly palmed greasy, black handprints around a four-foot yellow post. The black and yellow contrast stood out in her mind. If she could have pulled out the squat post, perhaps she could have sold it to a modern art gallery.

For a moment, Riley contemplated just leaving the black handprints on the post for posterity. After humans were extinct, visiting extraterrestrials may discover this post, believing it to be a totem pole from a long-lost tribe. Frowning, Riley squirted green liquid on the domed top of the post. Emerald tears trickled down the smooth surface, melting the handprints into ugly, black streaks. Sighing, she wiped down the smudges, returning the post to its original, boring hue.

"Riley, are you alright?" The psychologist's grating voice cut through her thoughts.

She snapped her head to find him analyzing her. "What do you mean?"

"You kind of zoned out there for a while."

"I'm still half asleep," Riley croaked. *I must have slipped into another postcognitive lapse.* She cringed, knowing that this was a bad omen. "What do you want?"

Dr. Teller made an exaggerated swipe on his screen. "The reason I called you into my office was to inform you that your mentor, Piero, was reportedly killed in action."

Riley lounged on the couch and played with a lock of black hair. She then rolled her eyes to the ceiling. "That sounds dreadful."

Dr. Teller asked, "Are you in shock?"

"I really didn't know Pi." She pulled out a small mirror, checking her mascara and black lipstick. Satisfied that there were no smudges, she slipped the mirror back into her pocket.

"Well, he gave you an excellent review before he left."
Dr. Teller looked back at his screen. "Let me check . . . ah,
here's what he said about you: 'Riley is a polite, energetic
person who cares about other people, especially those who
are disadvantaged. She is extremely generous and mature
beyond her years . . .'"

Riley looked over to find the psychologist studying
her again. "Doctor, why did you trail off?"

"I don't think this review describes you at all."

"I care about people."

"Do you care that your mentor died?"

"Tell me how he died," she said with false compassion
in her voice.

"Ah, good. I think we finally have a breakthrough."
Dr. Teller eyed his screen. "I can tell you that Piero
sacrificed himself to save a young lady and her pet
monkey. The young lady reported that Piero took
down three sentry bots last night before succumbing
to multiple . . ." He stopped as he scanned the rest of
the report.

"Go on," Riley replied, looking expectantly at the
man, eyebrow raised.

"I dare not tell you the rest as it is very gruesome." In
a clear attempt to change the subject, he looked back up
at Riley, asking, "Did you know that earlier Piero
rescued a migrant family from a runaway motorway
sanitation transference unit?"

Riley rolled her eyes twice for added emphasis. "Do
you mean a street sweeper?"

"There's no reason to be so humdrum," the psychologist said in a strained voice, still trying to sound sympathetic. "The Department of Taxonomic Service spent many years renaming everything."

Unaffected, Riley continued, "Don't you think it's ironic that the people who are in charge of naming things gave their own department a horrible name?"

"I find the abbreviation, DoTS, to be very appealing," he mused. "I can picture DoTS workers traveling the Imperium and dotting out all the old names."

"That sounds like revisionist history to me."

"I don't know what Piero saw in you," Dr. Teller scolded, finally losing his professional demeanor. "You aren't polite at all."

Riley sat up and drummed her fingers on the leather cushion. "If we're done here, I want to go back to bed."

"We are not done. I have to finish with the bad news and then evaluate whether to give you grieving time from work."

"Come to think of it, I am feeling bereaved."

"I'll be the judge of that." Dr. Teller puffed out his chest. "Because your prior mentors are either missing or shot to pieces, you have been reassigned to Elvene."

"Oh, hell no!" Riley shouted, standing up from her seat.

"Ah, you're finally showing some real emotion! I do say that this breakthrough is going swimmingly. You'll be glad to know that you will remain in Logistics—"

"Could this morning get any worse?"

"—however, your new assignment entails relocating Guyanese refugees to free housing on 45th Avenue."

"You want me to work on Skid Row?"

"Not only will you be working there but also living there."

"This is the worst day of my life." Riley slumped back onto the couch.

"I'm surprised to hear you say that. After all, you're an 'energetic person who cares about other people, especially those who are disadvantaged.'"

"Damn you, Pi. Why did you have to die?"

Dr. Teller smiled and tapped his screen. "I'd say that this session has been a complete success. You have transitioned well given the news of your dead mentor. After careful consideration, I won't recommend any grieving time from work."

Chapter 10

The flattened, brown leaves and berry-like sacs of the algae rubbed against the side of the ship. Looking down from the deck, Mistress Raven almost believed that she was floating on a sea o f grass. The locals called it gulf weed, but it was better known as sargassum, which was common further north in an area suitably called the Sargasso Sea. The warming climate of the last century appeared to have enabled the spread of this cancer-like alga.

"We're ready to begin operations," said the communications officer. "You're wanted on the bridge."

The officer's breach of decorum would have to be forgiven. His mind was too easy to read. The young officer's thoughts meandered on the recent news of his mother's death. Raven touched his hand and looked him in the eyes. The officer immediately stiffened. However, by gently stroking his palm, Raven had just won him over to her side in the event of a power struggle with his captain. She released his hand and then walked leisurely to the bridge of the missile cruiser. Raven caught a glimpse of the Georgetown skyline through the morning haze.

The bridge remained boisterous even after Raven had entered; she pushed her way through the crowd of naval officers. No one snapped to attention even though she was overseeing the entire operation. Raven sensed the crew's collective fear, not of her per se but of what she represented as a superior species. *Did Neanderthals know that humans would replace them?* Raven thought. *It was probably a slow process like the receding glaciers upon which they lived. The reproduction ratio between Neanderthals and their neighboring humans was likely less than one percent, but it was enough. Humans, you had a good run. Enjoy your time on Earth while it lasts.*

Pulsating waves of hatred crashed onto Raven as she contemplated the doom of man. Someone on this bridge had taken a disliking to her. She scanned each crew member before finding the suspect lurking in the back. The fact that the ship's captain was staring daggers made her task a little more enjoyable. Raven walked right up to the spiteful man.

"Captain, I'm taking control of this vessel," Raven said effortlessly as she twirled a long black lock of her curly hair.

"The hell you are," the captain countered.

Raven stared deep into his eyes and placed a finger on his chest. The captain was old and had unusual facial hair. His bald head had asymmetric contours that encased a mediocre brain. He dressed in a plain white uniform like his crew. They wore no designation of rank, which made it difficult for the enemy to know who to kill first in a boarding raid.

"Conformity is the playground of dull minds," Raven told the captain. She half-closed her eyes and gazed through her long lashes. With phantom fingers, Raven dug knuckle deep into the soft parts of the captain's brain.

Raven massaged the captain's cerebral cortex until she found the insula, located between the frontal and temporal lobes. Applying pressure to the delicate spot with an invisible thumb, she felt his guard drop and his mind turn to putty.

Raven used her good looks to attract men and then crush them. However, as she slipped uncomfortably into middle age, Raven relied more heavily on her mind-controlling abilities as well as an arsenal of beauty products.

The captain licked his thin lips. "Ma'am, I can't just give you—"

"I'm not a ma'am," she said deliciously while batting her lashes. "I'm a mistress. Let's not have a dialogue of the deaf where neither of us knows what the other is uttering." As she touched his left ear, she sensed the captain's inhibitions melt away.

"I can't have you giving contradictory orders on my—"

"Shush. Without contradictory opinions, human culture would not have evolved into the wonder that it has become. Now, you will move full steam ahead."

The bridge was dead quiet. None of the officers spoke as all eyes turned towards the captain, who drooled slightly.

"Captain, we can't take orders from a civilian," said the executive officer, who had a sallow complexion with severe angular facial features.

Raven studied the middle-aged woman for a moment before pointing to her. "You're dismissed and are no longer the executive officer. Report to the brig."

"For what?" she protested.

Raven read what was clearly on her mind. "You had three incidents of inappropriate relations with junior officers and one incident of non-consensual contact with a crew member on this mission alone. You are unfit for service and will report to the brig *now.*"

The quiet bridge somehow grew quieter as the executive officer's face turned bright red. Her eyes watered as she shuffled away. The door banged behind her. Without another word, the ship started slowly moving forward, cutting through the gulf weed.

Raven looked from side to side, verifying that the other ships in the vanguard were keeping pace. She spotted four missile cruisers flanking each side of her ship. Nine was the magic number because they were approaching a fleet of nine Free States League ships in the bay. Still, it was not going to be a fair fight.

"We are being hailed," said the communications officer.

"Put them through," ordered Raven.

The speakers blared, "To the Imperium ships approaching the free city of Georgetown, this is Captain Rocha of the battleship, FSL Independence. You will immediately turn around and leave Guyanese territorial waters."

Raven grabbed the microphone. "You are pirates preying on defenseless civilian freighters. Prepare to be boarded."

That last remark seemed to have snapped the captain out of his stupor. "We don't have the manpower to board their ships. Besides, we'll never get that far. We're almost in range of their big guns."

On cue, a loud bang reverberated across the bay followed by a massive splash in the water about two hundred yards directly in front of the ship. The computer consoles beeped, and alarms clanked as red lights shot around the bridge like a dance floor.

"We've been painted with a radar lock; take electronic countermeasures!" yelled a young male officer.

"Captain, the enemy has line-of-sight targeting!" screamed a shrill voice. "Electronic countermeasures won't stop their missiles! Permission to raise shields!"

"Do not raise shields," Raven ordered. "Do not take countermeasures. Proceed on the current course."

"This is suicide!" exclaimed the same shrill voice.

"The Free State League ships just have guns and anti-aircraft batteries," Raven corrected. "They are little more than helipads with cannons."

The captain pointed to the screen in front of Raven. "Those blips on land are ground-based missile launchers. No ship can survive a barrage of heavy missiles."

"I'm counting on it," Raven said mater-of-factly.

"Detecting multiple missile launches from the mainland!" squealed an effete voice from the front of the bridge.

Raven watched as dozens of smoke trails arced across the hazy sky. The missiles dropped in lazy bows onto the water. She covered her eyes with the crook of her elbow; a blinding light swept across her ship followed by a walloping cascade of detonations. Putting her arm down, Raven saw nine mushroom clouds sprouting from the bay. All the enemy vessels were now sinking infernos.

Striding past cowering naval officers, Raven approached the front of the bridge. She leaned forward, pressing her hands against the glass. Keenly, she watched the fire-ravaged ships flounder in smoky waters. Nodding, she turned her head to address her crew. "There is no fire like passion."

Chapter 11

Gia surveyed the smoldering wrecks burning just off Georgetown's harbor. Her bit of sabotage had tricked the Guyanese ground-based missile launchers into thinking friendly units were now enemies and vice versa. Another boom ricocheted across the boulevard. Gia looked over her shoulder to find a Guyanese military aerial vehicle plummeting to the ground.

"Oo-wee, deh missile jus' shot down one of our helicons," a raggedy old man said in a heavy Guyanese dialect. "When coconut fall from tree he can't fasten back."

Gia did not feel like talking. She eyed the stranger, determining that he was just one of the many drifters who lived on the docks.

"I'm ah glad our generals named dem 'helicons,'" the drifter continued. "In mythology, Apollo and de muses lived in ah palace called Helicon up in de mountains."

"The former Guyana government bought those aerial vehicles from the Imperium," Gia corrected. "All Imperium military vehicles are emblazoned with the symbol of the imperial moth. Likewise, all the aerial vehicles are named after American butterflies."

"Are yuh tellin' me de helicons are ah butterflies?" the drifter asked.

"It is short for Heliconius, a butterfly with long forewings and small hind wings resembling the aerial vehicle that just blew up."

"Me o'know," the drifter slurred. "Li'l butterflies are nah very warlike."

Gia scanned the sky and pointed to an aerial vehicle with six mounted guns jutting out of its body like stick legs. "Look, there's a nymph that is also named after a butterfly, Nymphalidae."

"Moon ah run 'till daylight ketch am." The drifter cupped his filthy hands over his eyes as he scanned the eastern horizon. No sooner than he spotted the nymph, a streak of smoke rushed towards it. The explosion rocked him back. He ducked, covering his ears with his dirty palms. "Oo-wee, how ah many of our troops jus' deh?"

"At least eight died," muttered Gia as she shook her head. Balling her hands into fists, she squeezed her fingernails into her palms until she felt white-hot pain shoot up her arms. *When will the Guyanese generals figure out that their missile launchers will shoot down all their aerial vehicles?* she pondered. *I just changed a little computer code to trick the missile targeting program into attacking Guyanese units. But this has gone on way too long. Surely, the Guyanese generals should have just shut down all the missile arrays by now . . . unless they can't.*

Trickles of dread crept down her backbone as she realized that she was only one piece of the proverbial jigsaw puzzle. While she had just changed the targeting program, someone else must have sabotaged the failsafe, preventing the missiles from being shut down.

"Oo-wee, der sure are ah lot of ships out fuh sailin'!" exclaimed the drifter.

Gia looked back to the bay and saw the nine Imperium missile cruisers bobbing in the brown gulf weed. However, peeking over the horizon were swarms of specks. She put on her pink-tinted glasses and then tapped the side to magnify her view. Gia wobbled. "There's a whole flotilla out there."

"Deh ah comin' this ah way," uttered the drifter. "I guh find ah place to sleep dis night."

Gia quivered after another explosion. She turned to spot fiery debris raining down on nearby structures. *I have to get my family to the evacuation zone.* Gia reached into her pocket, finding the three computer chips that she had pulled out of the sentry bots earlier this morning. The chips were the only remaining evidence that could possibly tie her to the disaster that was about to befall her hometown. She tossed the chips over the dock, hearing a satisfying plunk as they sank into the bay.

Running to the street, Gia found her Nosedive hoverbike. Unlike factory issued Nosedives, Gia had modified the ignition, so only she could start it. Also, Gia added an artificial intelligence program that would electrocute any thief who tried to jack her ride.

Gia straddled the Nosedive and clutched the handlebars. Upon startup, the bike shot three feet in the air before floating on an invisible cushion. She twisted the throttle and propelled forward with amazing speed. While she rode comfortably above the waterlogged, smutchy street, the deafening booms had scattered the city's population out of their normal morning routines. At the first intersection, she encountered a thrall of spectators jamming the boulevard for a better view of the aerial vehicle explosions.

Pulling up to seven feet, Gia avoided even the tallest person but now had to duck under arching streetlights and low-hanging branches. Fortunately, the relative need for free lumber had nearly denuded the formerly tree-lined boulevards. However, the Leaguer hippies recently planted saplings whose boughs reached out menacingly into the street.

A branch smacked Gia across the cheek. She cursed, steering her bike further into the middle of the lane. A roar echoed off the tall buildings with a bright flash. Darkness followed. Gia let off the throttle and, with her free hand, tapped her pink-tinted glasses, which were currently opaque. The transition lenses had surely saved her from permanent blindness.

When the lenses faded back to light pink, she beheld a holocaust in front of her. A smoldering nymph had crashed a hundred yards dead ahead. Its central battery had ruptured, shooting molten shrapnel into the nearby office buildings. The dogged pinging noises were likely exploding ordinance. Gia did not wait to be added to the collateral damage that she wrought against her own city. She turned left and crossed over the median with a slight bump. The Nosedive sped easily down a charred side street.

Gia hoped that the burnt lumps below were not bodies, but she had a sneaking suspicion otherwise. The stench of burnt meat was sickening.

As she punched through another intersection, a truck hauling glass windows skidded towards her. Gia resisted the urge to pull up as it would just slow her down. Instead, she kicked her bike into a swoop.

Time seemed to linger between seconds while Gia held her breath. She hung onto the handlebars with all her strength as the bike plunged, igniting sparks as the Nosedive scraped the blacktop. The truck barely careened past her, sideswiping a brick wall. The tinkling of glass signaled that every window had broken.

I'm glad I paid extra for this Nosedive, Gia thought. *I would have wiped out with the no-frills Tailspin model.* Gia cruised ahead and did not look back to see the destruction of her beloved hometown, a modern-day Sodom. The booms dampened as she sped away from the shore. The real onslaught would soon overwhelm the beach.

Ahead, a convoy of armored ground vehicles slowly slithered towards her on the wrong side of the boulevard. The lead vehicle had a plow that mowed traffic off the road in haphazard rows. Gia quickly turned right at the next intersection and drove through the slums on a parallel street. She tapped her glasses to pull up the military targeting system. The Guyanese armored vehicles to her left were flashing red, meaning friendly units. The fools had not figured out that the missile launchers now saw them as enemy forces. At the first unobstructed view, any ground-based missile launcher would light up that convoy. *Technology, you're a cruel mistress.* The earsplitting rain of explosions signaled that she was sadly correct. The plowing lead vehicle must have crossed the bridge, which provided no cover. Gia glanced left, noticing that the convoy had come to a dead stop like a funeral procession waiting for a train to clear the crossing. When she looked forward, pedestrians were clogging the street. Gia pulled up sharply to avoid decapitating the forerunners who were quickly approaching. Clunks and yelps under her seat indicated that she should have pulled up sooner.

Gia cruised eight feet above the favela dwellers who were all pointing to the sky. She peeked up to see motes of light. *Oh, this is more than a simple foray,* Gia realized. *The Imperium's attack has turned into a full-scale invasion, nay, an annihilation. This line of thinking isn't helping. I need to lie to myself with positive self-talk. I just have to get to my family before the Imperium invaders shoot them.*

When she sneaked a quick look at the sky, the specks were bigger and fuzzier. Gia veered right and accelerated at top speed away from the convoy. The thudding of anti-aircraft fire echoed behind her. After clearing ten blocks at breakneck speed, a shock wave hit her from behind. Her ears rang so loud that it blocked all other noise. Worse, her earlobes felt wet. Gia used a free hand to dig inside her ear. When she pulled it back, her index finger was dripping with blood. Feeling woozy, she let off the throttle. Now that everything was no longer a blur, she recognized this neighborhood.

Gia shook the cobwebs out of her head and banked left. She passed a pharmacy and slowed to a stop in front of a round, green door. The barred windows of this shabby structure were boarded up from the inside. As the Nosedive descended, Gia slid off before it came to a halt. Mentally, she activated her bike's security system and then unlocked the green door, which creaked open. The stench of blood seeped out.

Stretched out across the dining room table sprawled the jinni's body. A medical bot raised its head slightly in acknowledgment and then went back to treating its patient. Gia slammed the heavy door behind her and latched it tight. The medical bot garbled incoherently.

"I can't hear you, Nurse!" Gia exclaimed. "Both my eardrums have ruptured, and I probably have a concussion!"

Nurse motioned with its delicate hand to the dining room chair. Gia wobbled over and slumped down. Her eyelids felt heavy. As she relaxed, a sharp sting in her arm woke her up. The bot had stuck her with a syringe. Gia felt suddenly invigorated. "Okay, I won't fall asleep!"

Gia lurched as something vibrated in her pocket. Nurse grabbed her head and held it straight while probing her right ear. Gia carefully slid the phone out of her pants pocket without moving her head. She peeked down at the message on the screen: "Your brother and both sisters have been safely extracted; meet me when you are ready to be evacuated. Signed, Mistress Raven." Gia began to sigh but felt a cold metal hand clamp under her chin. Her eyes lulled, yet another sharp sting popped them open. The naked body in front of her stirred slightly as if waking from a long winter's nap. Sweat glistened off the hairless body. The toes were pointed right at her, so she had an unobstructed view of the unseemly parts. She heard a moan. "Nurse, my right ear seems to be working again!" Gia yelled.

A face poked up, giving her a glazed stare. Gia smiled. "I thought you were a goner!"

"Why are you shouting?" Piero slurred. Squinting, his smooth, bald brows scrunched down to the bridge of his nose. His skin was a bright shade of pink, like a newborn.

"Your Imperium troops are blowing up my city!" Gia exclaimed. "Your explosions ruptured my eardrums and gave me a concussion! Isn't that right Nurse?"

"You have not suffered a concussion," Nurse said in a spine-chilling robotic voice. "I will repair your left eardrum in less than a minute."

"Am I paralyzed?" asked Piero hoarsely.

"I have given you a tranquilizer to keep you from tearing your dressing," Nurse intoned.

A little black hand stroked Piero's arm. A small chrome helmet poked over the dining room table. A pair of sympathetic eyes peeked out from under the brim. Gia laughed. "Jocko was very worried about you. He wouldn't leave your side until I dragged you away."

"Did I die?"

"Don't be such a drama queen." She scowled as she wagged a dismissive finger. "I simply told the Janissary that you sacrificed yourself for Jocko and me. I thought that adding the monkey was a nice touch. You will probably get one of those posthumous medals given to jinn war heroes."

"I want to go back to—"

A loud boom muffled the rest of Piero's objection. The medical bot slowly moved around the table, scanning the janissaire's body.

"I heard that explosion loud and clear, Nurse." Gia nodded while rubbing both ears. "What's the prognosis of our patient here?"

The bot spoke in a monotone fashion, "I have stopped the bleeding in his cranium. The brain lesion has been reduced to a pinpoint. The gunshot wounds have been repaired. The patient will be fully mobile in one hour."

"That's terrific," Gia said sarcastically. "It'll give me plenty of time to interrogate him."

Piero peeped down at Gia, who was still sitting behind his toes. "We're on the same team."

"That's what I thought until Imperium dropships landed in my hometown. On the plus side, I got to cross something off my bucket list, you know, things you want to do before you kick the bucket. Last night, when you were unconscious and bleeding by the roadside, I got to fulfill my wish. I beat on a dying man's chest and screamed, 'Live, damn you live!'"

"That's a good one," Piero offered. "I always wanted to fistfight on a moving train and duck right before it goes through a tunnel."

"Stop that right now. We are not going to bond over our bucket lists. Besides, yours is unrealistic. Mine actually happened last night."

"I always wanted to shave with a machete too."

"Well, that's more reasonable. Being close to death tends to make you crave life-fulfilling moments. In your case, everyone thinks you're dead, so you have that going for you."

Piero's eyes bugged out. He jerked his head up momentarily before thumping it back down heavily on the table with a groan. "I don't want people to think I'm dead."

Gia huffed, "Well, it's a little too late for that now, isn't it? I already removed your data chip and smashed it."

Piero looked down at his left hand. Sure enough, his palm was bandaged tightly. "Why?"

"You now have free will. You can behave any way you want."

"Behavior is determined by genetics, synapses, and glands instead of free will."

"That's the kind of Imperium dogma that enslaves your kind. Ever hear of the human spirit?"

Piero stared at the ceiling. "It's a lie that all humanists tell themselves. Next, you're going to tell me that the human species is mutable and will evolve into superhumans."

Gia laughed. "That's exactly what we are, but evolution had nothing to do with it. Our superhuman genes came from alterations in a lab."

"That's just Leaguer propaganda. Throughout history, humans have always had bits of psychic ability from the seers of Delphi to the gypsy fortunetellers. Their powers were merely intermittent and fallible. With the use of empirical observations, the Janissary honed those psychic abilities into teachable skills."

"So, you think it's just a coincidence that, out of the blue, the Benevolent Imperator stepped onto the world stage as a powerful psychic."

"If you're implying that the Benevolent Imperator is some kind of messiah—"

"I'm most certainly not," Gia retorted. "He was created in a lab from a genetically modified embryo."

"Blasphemy!" Piero frowned. "I've heard this all before, but there's no proof."

"The proof is in your DNA. You have genes in all your cells that didn't exist a hundred years ago. And before you say that mutations are natural, I can tell you that all your mutations could not have happened randomly."

"That's all well and good, but I'm still not free of the Janissary. Even without my data chip, any recognition software will pick up my biosignatures: face, prints, and irises."

Gia smiled while nodding. "Nurse, will you tell him the good news?"

The medical bot lowered its metallic head, so its faceplate was just inches from Piero's nose. The bot's mechanized voice intoned, "I've modified your biosignatures. You now have new fingerprints, pretty blue eyes, and are much better looking. I had to temporarily remove all your body hair, but it will grow back in a silky blond. Later, you can shave with a machete."

Chapter 12

The spheroid assault ships fell from the darkened sky like heavy raindrops. Smoke from overflowing infernos clouded their descent, looking as though they had fallen into Hell itself. As if there was not enough smoldering ash, the nearest ship flared its rockets before touching down on the charred blacktop. The assault ship split open like a melon; a door clanked to the asphalt, forming a ramp. Dark figures behind pulsating, honeycomb-shaped shields stormed down the ramp and into the deserted roadway. If those war bots expected resistance, they would find none here.

"It's safe to come out now," Mistress Raven called out while sliding her purple-tinted glasses over her eyes. She stood alone by the spot where Piero fell. The old utility building loomed yards away. Once a state-of-the-art power station, the dilapidated structure appeared to have fallen into disuse. However, Raven knew that treasure was often buried in the dirt. This one held a golden ornament and, as it turned out, the key to the battle.

Stomping boots alerted Raven that her escort had finally arrived. A timeworn man with plain white hair and a matching plain white uniform slowly approached as if to impress that he hurried for no one. She read his lackluster mind quite easily.

"Rear Admiral Roy, I called you here to find the body of my missing janissaire," Raven said.

"I'm har to secure the buildin'," Roy said in a harsh accent. "I don't have time for ya missin' jinni."

Raven grasped his hand, tracing circles on his palm with her thumb. "I'm sure you wouldn't leave one of your men behind. I found blood traces that match Janissaire Piero. There are metal shards from sentry bots scattered about. From my report, Piero ran between two bots to trap them in their own crossfire. The bots shot themselves to pieces, killing Piero as well."

Roy let go of Raven's hand, dropping to one knee. He picked up some dirt and sifted it between his fingers. Raising his hand to his nose, he sniffed before tossing the dirt away. Roy pointed towards a rusted chain-link fence covered with vines. "The trail leads that-a-way."

Raven rolled her eyes. "Rear Admiral, the firefight happened during the storm last night. However, after the skies cleared, someone moved the bodies. I already found the shredded sentry bots in that cargo area. Their chips had already been pulled—"

"Ya jinni's corpse was pulled over yonder." He stood and walked towards the fence while studying the ground. "I can track anythin'."

"Can you track a hover vehicle? Because that's where the trail goes cold."

"Ya culprit walked backward while pullin' the jinni's body, coverin' his footprints." Roy walked backward, miming the movement. He then waved his hand in a circular motion with his palm down. "The dirt is scattered around this part, likely from a hover vehicle. Why did ya culprit drag the body *away* from the road?"

"To avoid detection." Raven slowly trailed behind the rear admiral.

"Precisely. So, now we know that the culprit wasn't workin' with the sentry bots."

"I assumed as much." Raven crossed her arms.

"Well, ma'am, this case intrigues me to no end."

"I am a mistress," she said peevishly. "Nevermind, just forget it."

"Very good, ma'am. I'll find ya jinni's carcass in no time."

A garish figure was clomping through the smoky alley behind the rear admiral. A few shafts of streetlight glinted off its chrome armor. Raven searched for the mind in the hulking form. She found sentience there, but it was like digging in a muddy puddle. With her mind-controlling ability, she pushed but slid off. That had never happened before. She shouted, "Enemy contact at ninety feet!"

Roy turned, gaping at the charging beast. Pulsing shields sprouted out of the creature like mushrooms after a rainy night. With each step, the monster became more overwhelming. Inside this metallic behemoth, the human if it could still be called that felt one singular emotion, rage.

Bolts of sonic energy-streaked past Raven, hitting the enemy's central mass. She fell to the ground, covering her ears in a feeble attempt to drown out the shrieks from her war bots' auto-guns. The rear admiral ran past her, weaving between oscillating energy blasts. The guns increased their assault. The sound was almost melodic, like the strumming of a dozen electric guitars. *Why are the bots still firing?*

Raven peered down the fence line. The creature was still there. No, it had moved closer, pushing against the relentless cannon fire. She recognized the giant chrome hunchback from grainy snapshots in secret dossiers. With a shaky hand, she activated the emergency channel on her purple-tinted glasses. "It's the Cybogre!"

If there was a response, Raven could not hear it over the feverish shootout. Chunks of asphalt erupted around her. Shots merely ricocheted off the Cybogre's mushrooming shields. *Two Janissaires can't die on the same spot. That would be too much of a coincidence . . . unless it wasn't blind fate.* Raven rolled into a ball. The inevitable was coming.

A pillar of solid, white light struck the monster, swallowing it. Raven's glasses turned deep purple. Through the darkened lens, she viewed only the silhouette of the still-standing Cybogre, though it did look to be sliding slightly backward.

Raven unsteadily traced the pillar of white light back to the Imperium's spheroid assault ship, the one that brought Roy. The ramp was still down, and more war bots poured out like angry bees out of a hive. The assault ship's mounted big cannon could take out an entire city block. Until today, she believed nothing could withstand its blast. Abruptly, the pillar of white light winked out. Panicked, Raven looked down the alley, seeing only a smoking trench sliced into the blacktop.

The sickening stench of boiling tar filled the air. The Cyborgre was gone for now. Yet, she knew that it would come back for her.

Hard footsteps ran up from behind. She gazed up through lavender transition lenses at a smeared and bloodied white uniform. "Are ya alright?" asked Roy as blood gushed out of his chewed-up ear. "That metal beast is goin' to be a challenge."

"The Cybogre is the least of our problems," Raven said through ragged breaths. "Go see a medic, you're bleeding."

Roy brushed chunks of his ear off his shoulder. As he squinted down the alley, his eyebrows came together, forming a bushy, white caterpillar across his smudged forehead. "I ain't got time to bleed."

Raven smirked. "That's one of the cool things that I've always wanted to say before I die."

"I've always wanted to catch a punch and then twist the man's fist until he goes down to his knees."

Her smile faded as she took off her glasses. Purple mascara dripped past worried eyes. "I hope you get the chance, but I don't think we'll survive that long. The Cognoscenti are here."

Chapter 13

The face staring back at him in the bathroom mirror was not his own. For starters, Piero missed his stylish Imperial beard. The loss of his eyebrows seemed equally disturbing, but he hid his hairless brow for the time being behind his red-tinted glasses. The medical bot had removed all of his body hair, leaving his skin smoother than silk.

Piero covered his bald head with a leather cap that was all the fashion in Guyana. He studied his sculpted angular features. *I have to give Nurse some credit. My face went from a soft eight to a hard ten.*

"Are you done preening yet?" Gia asked annoyingly. "We have to leave."

"Even Lazarus had some time to rise from the dead!"

"You're going to be dead for real if we don't leave right now."

Piero took a deep breath and then gagged. A strong odor of gasoline had wafted into the bathroom. He walked out to find Jocko covering his nose. "Why are you so eager to burn your house down?"

"Raven sent me another message," Gia explained. "She wants to meet me."

"That's a bad idea. She probably wants to read your mind."

Gia huffed. "I didn't respond, you idiot. I'm trying to make it look like I died during the invasion, which came very close to happening . . . numerous times. Besides, you bled all over my dining room. By the way, who are the Cognoscenti?"

Piero shook his head. "They're a myth like the Cybogre."

"Well, there's a bulletin that the Cognoscenti are in Georgetown."

"It sounds like whoever sent that bulletin is just trying to scare people," Piero said dismissively.

Gia held up her phone showing him the screen. Piero snatched it and stared at Raven's report, dumbfounded. "Oh, this is bad . . . very bad. The Cognoscenti are supposed to be an evil gang of precogs."

"How is that even possible?"

"It shouldn't be. Only janissaires have training in the Precognition School. The folktales say that the Cognoscenti were janissaires who defected, swearing vengeance against the Imperium."

"I like them already."

Piero gave her a rude gesture. "The Cognoscenti are impossible to catch because, you know, they can predict the future and whatnot."

"Last night in the utility building, you mumbled something about the enemy having someone with precognitive abilities," Gia said distrustfully.

"While my paranoid suspicions may have metastasized into a full-blown syndrome, I won't succumb to public hysteria," Piero said pedantically. "The Imperium will scourge Guyana to a bloody pulp to excise just one member of the Cognoscenti."

"Are you always this dramatic?"

"Only when I'm about to die." He sniffed and gagged again. "The gasoline is making me lightheaded. Can we go now?"

Jocko snorted. He took one hand off his nose and yanked Piero's pant leg. The little monkey then ambled through the kitchen and out the open back door. Piero trailed behind hurriedly. The backyard was little more than a slab of broken concrete. Even though the sun had set, the Guyana heat was still punishing. He spotted Jocko waiting impatiently in the passenger seat of the small hover truck. Piero had spent the last few hours packing the Nosedive into the cramped cargo area. For good measure, he squeezed in some gadgets, a sassy medical bot, and some heavy bags.

You don't have to go with her, Piero thought. *Just find the nearest Imperium war bot and return to Isle Royale a hero. Tell the inquisitors that the sentry bots bashed in your face and you needed reconstructive surgery. About your missing data chip, a bullet shot it out of your palm.* Piero clenched his bandage. *You have a stigma on your left hand to prove it.*

Oily smoke billowed out from behind him. Gia bumped him on her way across the backyard. She glared over her shoulder. "Hurry up! This is my first arson!"

Piero shook his head in dismay and his leather cap slid off. *Stupid bald head won't ever keep a cap on.* As Piero bent over to retrieve it, a pulsing ball of energy streaked over his stooped body. It sounded as if someone had pounded on a giant xylophone. A throbbing beam of light shot out of the house, spraying molten lumps of concrete.

The hover truck's engine whined, lifting the vehicle a foot off the ground. Through the open passenger window, Piero spotted Gia frantically shifting the gears. Jocko waved him over with his little monkey hand. Leaving his hat, Piero ran. Another globule of plasma exploded three feet behind him. He jumped.

The house detonated into a white-hot wad, blowing steaming air in all directions. Piero landed on the truck's back bumper. He grabbed with both hands, finding a handle above the right taillight. Piero hugged the back of the truck while Gia gunned the engine. They rocketed forward.

The truck shot out of the back alley. Piero clung to the handle with one hand and reached to the roof of the truck with his other. He smashed his face against the truck's back door. If he let go at this speed, he would blow down the street like an empty trash bag.

Piero heard a snap, crackle, and pop. The communication system in his red-tinted glasses had activated. The frames of his glasses wrapped around his ears, directing audio to the tiny bones behind his eardrums.

"How's it hanging back there?" asked a familiar voice.

"Did you activate my glasses?" Piero responded.

"Yeah, it's one of my superhuman powers." He could picture Gia's smirk. "Did you happen to notice who blew up my house?"

"I thought you did it."

"I was just burning it down. Those were cannon shots back there."

The hover truck jarred heavily. Piero swayed, one of his feet slipped off the bumper while his sweaty palms tried to maintain their grip on the vehicle. "Slow down! I'm falling off!"

Piero smashed into the rear door as the truck juddered to a halt. He rebounded off, falling a foot down to the asphalt. He heard a door open. The pattering of feet was followed by a soft tap on his bald scalp. Piero peered up. "I already miss my hat."

Jocko gave him a compassionate shrug. The truck started inching forward and then moved quickly. Piero scrambled to his feet, following Jocko into the cab. The little monkey scurried onto Gia's lap. With his little hand, Jocko patted the passenger seat.

"That's very gracious of you, Jocko," Piero said as he shut the passenger door. Gia revved the engine and sped forward, thrusting him back as the hover truck rattled up a hill. His open window sucked in the hot, humid air. His seat felt like a soggy cornflake. "Were you just going to leave me back there?"

"Sorry, brother. We're in a war zone now, thanks to your Imperium."

Piero brushed pieces of asphalt off his pants. "Ah, now we're family, which means you want something from me."

Gia pulled the steering wheel sharply to the left, banging him into the dashboard. She sneered. "No, you have nothing to offer."

Piero focused, opening his mind, and using his empathy. Gia's mood could only be labeled as disgust. Growing up in the Academy, he often got this reaction from his female classmates. "So, what am I to you."

"You're kin!"

"Like kindred spirits?"

"You're my half-brother!"

Piero flew forward into the dashboard again as the truck braked hard. He bounced back into his seat. Poor Jocko fared far worse, stuck to the front window. Piero braced himself, grabbing the dash with one hand and the back of his seat with the other. He planted both feet for support. He whipped his head around, spraying droplets of sweat. A confused looked crossed his face. "Did Mom raise you?"

"You're so naive," Gia said through a clenched jaw.

"I get that a lot." His voice caught as he held his palms together. "Tell me about Mom."

Gia stared at him for a long time. "We don't have the same mother; we share the same father. Haven't you ever wondered where your psychic abilities came from?" She let the last question hang just out of reach before continuing. "*My* mother was raped. At least, that's what I call it when a man uses his mind-controlling ability to seduce a teenager. She left the Imperium, so she wouldn't have to give me up when I turned four. Here, in Guyana, she met the man who later became my stepfather and raised a family. My stepfather was more of a man than that pervert who raped my mother."

Piero watched in silence as tears rolled down Gia's cheeks. She was telling him something that he had never once suspected. The teachers had forced the students to call each other brothers and sisters, saying they were one big happy family. *Did they know?* He gulped. "Are you saying that the Benevolent Imperator is my father?"

"He's the father of every janissaire and anyone who has psychic abilities."

Piero had difficulty processing this revelation. He had kissed girls in his class. Looking out the open window, he rubbed his throat to suppress his urge to vomit.

Gia laughed and wiped away her tears. "Are you thinking of some awkward moments?"

"It explains why I've been taking libido inhibitors since puberty to prevent reproduction."

"Actually, you're sterile. The Academy has been pumping you with pills to tamp down your promiscuity. However, like all drugs, you've developed a tolerance to them, so they're only partially effective. Since you won't be taking those anymore, you should get your full mojo back."

"How do you know that I'm shooting blanks?" Piero asked guardedly. "What did you *do* to me while I was unconscious?"

"Here we go again with the stage show." Gia sighed. "First of all, I read your medical record on your data chip, remember? There's no record of any birth control medication. Besides, all the Benevolent Imperator's children are hybrids, so we're all infertile, like mules. The Benevolent Imperator is so genetically different that he's no longer human. He's something else, a new species."

Piero leaned out the window. "How long before I flush the inhibitors out of my system?"

"Nurse told me that it may take weeks, depending on your last cycle." Gia laughed. "When it finally happens, give me a *heads* up."

Piero was not amused. The news stung. *Gia's throwing fastballs at me when I don't even have a catcher's mitt.*

Gia smiled. "I know this news is a lot to take in. It's like getting a sip of water from an open fire hydrant."

Even her analogies are better than mine, Piero pondered. *I'm always the funny one. Olivette always laughed at my jokes.* His new reality began to sink in. *I'm not going to see Olivette again.*

Piero lurched back into his seat as the hover truck sped off. During his musings, Jocko had crawled onto his lap, hugging him with all four limbs and his tail while giving Gia dirty looks. Piero rubbed the monkey's hairy back and glared at her as well.

"Why are you guys mean-mugging me?" she asked.

Jocko tapped his dented helmet. Gia hissed, "Listen, little monkey, if you can't run with the big dogs, then stay on the porch."

Damn, she's good with the clichés too, Piero thought. *I hope Olivette is at my memorial service, crying about all the terrible things she said and can now never take back. Why is she still in my head?*

"What are you sulking about now?" Gia inquired.

"I was just thinking about a girl back home." The truck jostled over some lumps in the road that were still smoldering. Piero inhaled deeply. "I smell barbeque. Let's pull over and eat."

"That's *not* barbeque," Gia responded distastefully, shaking her head. "Since I'm already grossed out, you might as well tell me about your sordid love life on Isle Royale."

Piero pulled Jocko closer. "If you must know, I lived with Olivette Demedici, the daughter of Cosimo Demedici. We often slept together but not in the euphemistic sense. It was just sleeping . . . and a little cuddling."

"That sounds rather sweet in a way." Gia smiled. "Bet you found a way to screw that up."

"I started courting her sister, Daisy, and we're now secretly engaged."

"Well, you have that going for you."

"I do. This means that after we're married, we don't have to worry about kids."

"You're a hopeless romantic; I see that now," Gia chided.

"Olivette said no woman would ever marry me because the Academy would take my offspring." Piero slapped the dashboard, startling little Jocko. "She's wrong, you see."

"So, you think that clears the way for you to marry Daisy?"

"It's bigger than that. Olivette hid her feelings from me because she was afraid to lose our children if we were to marry. But that's no longer an issue."

Gia gave a sidelong look. "Remind me to have Nurse examine your head. You may have some lingering brain damage."

The truck slowed down alongside a concrete wall. Piero studied the eight-foot barrier. The top was lined with broken beer bottles that looked like jagged teeth. He heard clanking as a rusty metal gate rolled open a few yards away. Gia slowly eased the truck forward and through the narrow postern. The area inside was littered with layers of stacked junk.

"Why are we in a volume reduction center?" Piero asked.

"I own this *scrapyard,*" Gia replied. "Well, one of my online personas does anyway. Don't worry; no one can trace this place back to me."

Piero eyed the piles of crushed vehicles and rusted metal pipes. He found it hard to believe that people chose to live this way rather than join the Imperium. "I thought the government would own all of the Volume Reduction Centers; I mean *scrapyards.*"

The gate jangled shut behind them. Gia steered her hover truck into a makeshift garage. The truck's headlights revealed three walls of metallic heads, limbs, and other robot parts. Any serial bot killer would have felt right at home here.

"It's good that the Guyanese government doesn't own this place," Gia eventually replied. "After today, I have a feeling that they're out of business."

Piero swallowed hard as he studied the mangled robot parts neatly displayed on the wall in front of him. "Is this some kind of trophy room?"

Gia giggled. "I fix bots as a hobby. I have a pack of bots guarding this yard, so you're going to have to get used to them."

"I'm not good with bots."

The truck dropped a foot to the ground with a thump. Jocko poked up his helmeted head and scrambled out the open window. The engine whirled, stopping with a clangor. The headlights dimmed out. In the inky darkness, they sat side-by-side listening to the night sounds of the Guyana jungle. A distant explosion followed by gunfire reminded Piero that he was still in a war zone. "I like to write fiction in my free time. Whenever I end a chapter, I like it to be meaningful or something to make the reader crave what's on the next page."

"Do you feel that a chapter in your life is about to close?" Gia asked.

"I do. I think you do as well. I always write what I *think* my audience wants to read."

"That's never enough."

"How so?"

"*You* have to want to write what the audience wants to read."

Chapter 14

"What do you want?" asked Riley, peering at the blurry screen on her phone. It was after midnight and the refugees were still roaming the halls, cooking spicy foods, and disturbing her with relentless questions. The squeaking mattress in the neighboring apartment indicated that a couple of refugees were eagerly making an anchor baby. Riley already missed her cramped subbasement dorm room.

The figure on her screen slowly materialized into the beautiful face of a mature woman, wearing purple eyeshadow with long, fake lashes. In the elegant dialect of the Septenary, the lady asked, "Do you know who I am?"

"I'm sorry, Mistress Raven," stammered Riley. "I've had a long day."

"I've won a naval battle and survived a Cybogre assassination, so I don't want to hear your prattle. I'm investigating the death of your mentor."

"Is Janissaire Eacles dead?"

"I have no idea," Raven said curtly. "I'm talking about the other one."

"Yeah, an investigator already questioned me for an hour about Pi. I don't have any new information."

"Try to follow along, *child*," Raven scolded. "My informant, Gia Aconda, reported Piero's death, but she's now missing. Her last known residence was destroyed earlier this evening."

"What's that got to do with me?"

"Ugh, you are such a holy terror," Raven said with frustration. "According to logistical records, you processed Gia Aconda's siblings in the refugee center."

"Yeah, I processed a lot of people today. Turns out, we're all living in some ghetto hotel on Skid Row—"

"Find the Aconda kids tonight," Raven ordered. "I need to know all of Gia's haunts."

"What's this have to do with Pi?"

"To find the man, you have to find the woman."

The screen winked out. Riley scratched her head. She still had a dozen boring refugee applications to log into the database. They would have to wait. Riley opened a new box on her screen and tapped in a message: "Priority mission for the Septenary: Question all members of Gia Aconda's family in the refugee center." She smiled. *That should cover my ass for a while.*

Riley surveyed her hotel room. She had an empty mini fridge and a soiled king-size mattress. She gazed out of her rain-streaked panorama windows . . . at a brick wall. She groaned.

Still, Riley held the record as the only protégé to have three mentors in a week, a trifecta of sorts. Reluctantly, she reviewed her journal entries. The psychologist had advised Riley to get her priorities straight. Before she was permitted to leave his office, Dr. Teller made her fill out a wish list of things to do before she died. The protégé thumbed down her litany of items.

One entry jumped out. It stared back at her from the screen in mockery. The line simply stated: "Register my hands as lethal weapons." *Is that even possible?* she thought. *I registered my sidearm, so why not my hands. Alas, this is my lot in life having normal hands and interviewing fly-bitten refugees.*

She deleted that entry and tapped in another: "Puff on a pipe during a gunfight and shoot through my smoke rings." *Ah, that goal is more reachable. Now, I just have to find a pipe.*

Riley rummaged through her desk drawer but could only see a plastic case. She popped it open, admiring her new bronze-tinted glasses. While at work yesterday, she secretly requisitioned a pair of military-grade lenses. She put them on. They felt right.

Recalcitrancy gnawed at the back of her brain. Riley dreaded heading downstairs to face the crowd of freeloaders. *So, your garbage country got bombed; don't come here with your problems.* She steeled her resolve as she headed to the noisy lobby. In the hallway, she passed a fat, lazy guard asleep at his desk.

The first disheveled group she encountered was a migrant family, probably from Asia, huddled together on a long couch. The little father had bleached hair, the color of phlegm, which looked ridiculous on his big head. The mother clutched a little girl in a ragged dress who was reading a tourist guide. The boy was rolling his head around like a bauble doll. They were all drenched, like rats scurrying in from the rain.

"Isle Royale is the largest island in Lake Superior with 571,790 gross acres," said the little girl, reading out of her guide. "Lake Superior is 1,333 feet deep."

Riley was about to throw them out when she spotted the eldest Aconda boy sitting on a threadbare comfy chair in the corner. She studied him trying to determine his ethnicity. He looked like every race mixed in a blender.

"Carlos, where's your sister?" Riley demanded bluntly.

"Liliana went to our dirty room about five minutes ago," he replied glumly.

"So, that's how you want it. If you don't give me the whereabouts of *Gia* Aconda, I'm kicking you and your orphaned sisters to the curb."

Carlos looked up with his dark eyes. "I don't know Gia's location offhand."

"Backhand, command, countermand, demand, grandstand, *highland*!" screeched the little boy from the couch.

Riley glared at the Asian family. "Shut that boy up before I call the guard!"

"Discard, disregard, retard, placard, sparred, regard, *scrapyard*!" yelled the boy, emphasizing the last word in a high pitch squeal.

"What's the kid babbling about?" Riley demanded.

"When Wunnut gets nervous, his rhyming syndrome flares up," the blond father explained while covering his son's mouth.

"Who the hell are you?" Riley grilled.

"My name is Lu Corpan; it is very nice to meet you."

"The feeling is not mutual," Riley muttered. As she was ready to show them the door, her phone rang. Exasperated, Riley whipped it out. "What now?"

The taciturn face on the screen gazed with heavy eyes. Perhaps it was the purple eye shadow, but it looked like Mistress Raven was staring right through her. "Have you questioned the Aconda children yet?"

"I just talked to you about five minutes ago," Riley countered. The screen blinked out and came back fuzzy. "Where are you calling from?"

"Guyana, of course. What have you found out?"

"Nothing . . . yet."

Mistress Raven was flummoxed. "I need your password for the Logistics Branch."

"Hold on, I just got it and haven't had time to memorize it yet." Something was off. Riley tapped her bronze-tinted glasses and synched up with the last call to her room. After hitting the callback icon, an angry face eventually appeared on the left lens. The audio was piped directly through the frames into Riley's skull, so only she could hear it.

"Why are you bothering me?" asked Mistress Raven.

Riley peeked down at the imposter on her phone's screen and then back at her lens to the real Raven. With her thumb, Riley covered the microphone on her handheld phone. She then positioned the phone's screen in front of the camera in the middle of her bronze-tinted glasses.

"Why do you have a snapshot of me on your phone?" The perturbed voice of the real Mistress Raven reverberated in Riley's cranium.

"Because you're calling me and asking for my Logistics password," Riley whispered.

"You just called me . . ." Raven declared before ultimately figuring it out. "Is my doppelganger still on the line?"

"Yes, what should I do?"

"Don't give her your password!"

Riley rolled her eyes. *Ugh, she can't see my eyes anyway. Why do I bother?* "I have to give the other you something."

"I'm way ahead of you, child," Raven said. "I'm going to give you a password that will trace my pretender's call. Do you see my text?"

A line of text blinked inside Riley's right lens. She hesitated and then read it again before taking her thumb off her microphone. "Okay, here's my password, *Mistress Raven*."

"Go ahead!" echoed both Mistress Ravens, one from her phone and one from her glasses. Riley shrugged. "P-A-S-S-W-O-R-D-1-2-3."

"You've got to be kidding me," said the imposter.

"Good job," whispered the real Raven. "Oh, she took the bait. The call is coming from Guyana . . . no, it's being bounced off a satellite . . . the line is moving to Europe . . . she's in London."

"Thanks for the play-by-play," Riley muttered.

"What?" asked the voice from her phone.

Riley put her thumb back on the microphone. The real Raven was still rattling off cities around the world and simultaneously berating one of her staff, using colorful expletives. "We have a lock! The line is tracing its way back to North America. For the love of all things holy, I'm sending a janissaire assault team immediately!"

"Um, did you say *janissaire?*" asked Riley. "Does that mean the call is coming from Isle Royale?"

Raven exclaimed, "The call is coming from inside your hotel lobby!"

"Your password doesn't seem to be working," the imposter complained.

Riley let out some nervous laughter as she scanned the lobby. She slid her thumb off the microphone. "Oh, it's working fine."

"What's working fine?" asked the real Raven.

Riley was finding it difficult to differentiate between the voices of the two Ravens. She also noticed that Carlos had disappeared. The Asian family was still huddled on the couch. At the doorway stood a sentry bot emblazoned with the imperial moth insignia. *Was that bot there when I came to the lobby? No, I threatened to call the guard to kick out the Asian migrants.* Goosebumps prickled the back of her neck as her baseline precognitive ability had just triggered, peril loomed.

"The Apostle Islands have a landmass of 69,372 gross acres," said the little girl on the couch. "Is Isle Royale bigger—"

"Deceiver, chatter, gossiper, harbinger, loiterer, killer, *danger!*" Wunnut shouted.

Momentarily distracted, Riley returned her attention to the front door. The sentry bot focused a pair of glassy, red eyes on her. The bot slowly twisted and stepped forward.

"Oh no, not again!" yelled Lu as he grabbed his son.

The bot activated its honeycomb shields. Riley dropped her phone and yanked out her skean in one fluid motion. "Finally, I get to see some combat."

"What are you nattering about?" asked the real Raven. "Is that one of your bots?"

The bot had her corralled in the lobby along with the migrant family. At least Carlos was safe. *How did he know to run away?*

The mechanized voice of the bot was deafening. "Give me your password!"

"Why is your bot demanding your password?" asked the real Raven.

"That's not my bot!" exclaimed Riley.

"Well, don't give it your password," the real Raven said, "My assault team is en route to your location."

"I don't have that kind of time," said Riley. "I have to kill this bot."

"No, you don't," said the mechanized voice as the bot leveled its twin auto-guns at her. "Give up your password and you'll live."

"Don't trust that bot," the real Raven offered. "It's probably lying."

"Listen to the bot," said the imposter Raven from the discarded phone. "Stop stalling and give up your password."

Riley pictured a little angel Raven on one shoulder and a little devil Raven on the other. The angel whispered, "Piero killed three sentry bots; surely, you can take down one."

Yet, the devil Raven purred, "Don't die in this fleabag hotel over some stupid password for a job you hate anyway."

Riley shook her head clear of hallucinations. "Raven, send me the schematics for this type of sentry bot."

"I don't have those," said the fake Raven. "You're running out of time."

Moments later, blueprints for a third generation, shield-bearer sentry bot appeared on the interior of Riley's right lens, along with known defects in the bot's defenses. Unfortunately, all the chinks in the armor were on the bot's backside. Riley studied her mechanized opponent across the carpet. The auto-guns were pointed slightly upwards. *Of course, a very human mind operates this bot,* thought Riley. *My adversary has experience fighting janissaires who leap up and then slash down with textbook precision.* She recalled the Benevolent Imperator maxim, "Never give your enemy the fight he wants."

Riley concentrated on the carpeted floor in front of her. She imagined steam billowing off the ground. Using her telekinetic ability, she mentally pushed. Rather than shove a particular object, she pushed everything away from her. As a level two in telekinetics, such an ability flung out psychic energy just mere inches beyond her skin. It was enough to create a slick cushion around her like the air-pressured surface of an old-fashioned air hockey table game. Riley slid forward feet first, coasting across a frictionless floor like a puck after a slap shot.

The roar of auto-guns blared; bits of carpet burst behind Riley's head, tracking her slide forward. She twisted on the slippery cushion of air, darting between the bot's compact legs.

Riley mentally ended her slick surface, grabbing the bot's knee joint with her free hand. She drove up with her skean, willing the flexible blade to arc between the honeycomb shields. With a solid thrust, she inserted the blade into the bot's aft port. Viscous, burnished oil shot out, squirting Riley in the face.

The bot shrieked before tumbling forward. Sparks crackled around the red-hot blade.

"Mama, what did that lady do to the bot?" asked the migrant girl who was now peeking from behind the couch.

The mother covered the girl's eyes. "Something very bad . . . very bad indeed."

Riley stood, studying her vanquished foe. Had the bot's controller anticipated her slide, it would have been her blood leaking onto the carpet. Unceremoniously, Riley placed one boot on the bot's rump and yanked out her skean.

"How did you do it?" asked the real Raven.

"I popped the bot's chassis," Riley said. "The schematics indicated that these bots needed to sit down to recharge their batteries. I just followed the path of least resistance until I perforated the power core. That's why it's still shooting sparks."

Raven replied, "I'll never bend over near you again."

Chapter 15

Piero sat upon a stack of crushed cars, obsolescent vessels just like him. He contemplated the next part of his life as he surveyed the scattered fires, the only illumination in an otherwise darkened necropolis. Looking down at the fallen city, he searched for some purpose amongst the ruins. From a purely biological point of view, his life had no meaning. In fact, any significance people tried to credit their lives amounted to pure fantasy. More so, Piero represented a genetic dead end, which seemed to sum up his life's impact in this chaotic world.

Popping gunfire reminded Piero that his future was sketchy at best. *That's the basis of chaos theory, after all,* he mused. *First-order chaotic systems, like the weather, do not react to predictions. However, second-order chaotic systems react to predictions made about them, and thus, cannot be accurately predicted. The stock market and revolutions are inherently unpredictable.*

Piero laughed at the oxymoron. *Order and chaos should not be used together. Yet, the Imperium sought to impose order on chaos. The shift from countless trifling cultures to a few big cultures and ultimately into a united global society was likely a foreseeable outcome of the underlying forces of human advancement.*

His head hurt just thinking about all the implications from his brief use of free will. Homesickness gripped him tightly. He missed his secret fiancé, his cushy job, and his pretty roommate. *Olivette, why do you haunt my thoughts?*

"You look unhappy," said a soft voice from down below. Gia milled about gazing up at him. "If you come down, I have a big present for you."

Reluctantly, Piero crawled down from the heap, avoiding the sharp bits that dug into his flesh on the way up. He found her in front of an old garage filled with hoverbikes.

"You can have this old bike," Gia insisted as she patted the faux leather seat. "Get on and grab the throttle. I disabled the lethal anti-theft device."

With some wariness considering her last remark, Piero straddled the sleek silver bike and gripped the throttle. Lime-green lights dotted the instrument panel.

"Oh, good," Gia said excitedly. "The scanner on the throttle accepted your new fingerprints. I was actually worried that you might get electrocuted. Anyway, this model is called a Breakneck. The handling is poor, but it's very fast on a straightaway."

"Are we going somewhere?"

"Indeed, we can't stay near Georgetown with all the Imperium forces roaming about," Gia said nonchalantly. "Besides, Raven is still hunting me."

"How do you know?"

"My brother, Carlos, told me that a *bitchy* jinni interrogated him about my whereabouts. He's in a shabby refugee center on Isle Royale."

Piero snapped his head around. "Will Carlos speak with that janissaire again?"

"Pray tell me that this is not about your ex-fiancé or her bedfellow sister."

"Do you mean Daisy and Olivette?"

"I guess that depends on you," Gia said demurely. "Do you have more fiancés and sleeping companions?"

"As a matter of fact, I do not."

"Well, score one for you then."

"It's about the janissaire who interviewed Carlos," Piero explained.

"Ah, I hope you are not fond of her as well. Carlos only said that she had dark hair, wore too much eye makeup, had a real bad attitude, and rammed a blade up a bot's butt."

"Riley?"

"That sounds about right." Gia put a finger to her chin. "Maybe it was one of those weird Janissaire names like Smiley."

"I had a protégé named Riley."

"For how long?"

"Just about a day, but I feel I got to know her."

"I hope it wasn't in the Biblical sense. You do fall in love quickly and with anyone."

Piero shrugged. "Riley isn't a mind-reader, so Carlos won't give away your location. However, the Janissary will send Hatchette sooner or later."

"What's a Hatchette?"

"She's an inquisitor and you don't want to meet her. Since Carlos knows that you're still alive, that means Hatchette will eventually dig in his head and pull out that tidbit of information."

"Well, now you tell me," Gia huffed. "This is going to be a problem. I spent a lot of time faking my own death."

"Apparently not enough given that Raven's looking for you."

"Why is she even after me anyway?"

"Most likely, Raven is after me." Piero tapped his chest, proudly. "She has to follow up on all leads until she finds me dead or alive. Because you reported my death, Raven needs to question you or find proof that you are dead."

"I'm starting to regret keeping you alive." Gia sighed. "If you weren't a fellow technomancer, I would have left you to rot by that road."

Piero stiffened while studying her for a moment. *Is that the real reason? What is she hiding from me?* He cleared his throat. "I want you to tell me about—"

A buzz interrupted their early morning banter. Gia stretched her neck before reaching into her pocket, pulling out her secure phone. Piero tried to read her emotions for any clue. She was edgy. "It's just another general bulletin. This one is about a bot attack on Isle Royale."

"Let me see what it says." Piero reached for the phone.

"It's encrypted, dummy." Gia slapped his hand away. "That's why I'm summarizing. I'm hoping that the chaos on Isle Royale will make Guyana a low priority for the Janissary."

"It won't."

"Why is the glass always half empty with you?"

"Where Cognoscenti are involved, I'm a strict pessimist."

"That's just because you think they tried to kill you," Gia explained. "Perhaps we should meet one of them?"

"No one has ever seen a Cognoscente, much less sat down for a chat. You'd have better odds of tracking down a bigfoot."

Gia smiled. "So, you're saying there's a chance."

Chapter 16

Raven stretched out across the soggy mattress wearing just a white tank top and panties, not exactly the proper wardrobe of a commander for the Imperium. The sultry jungle heat and the troubling nighttime happenings robbed her of her deepest craving, sleep. The disappearance of the Aconda girl weighed heavily on her racing thoughts.

Raven had to make a hard decision. She could either investigate the bot attack on Isle Royale or finish the fight here, defeating the Cognoscenti. *Never give your enemy the fight he wants*, remembered Raven. That maxim was one of her favorites, straight from the Benevolent Imperator's lips to her cold heart. Yet, the Cognoscenti's goals were elusive. Their only targets appeared to be other powerful psychics. As such, she topped that hit list.

Raven's secure phone buzzed; only priority messages could filter through. She put the phone to her ear without getting out of bed. "Why didn't you just text me?"

"Ma'am, I had to hear ya lovely voice," replied Roy.

Raven recoiled at the sound of his gravelly accent. *I pushed his brain too hard today.* "It's late."

"Ma'am, I won't rest until I find the culprit who stole ya ward's fallen body and smite the villain that attacked ya today. I shall endeavor to be more chivalric in future engagements."

"Spit it out already!"

"Ya have such a stimulatin' way with words. As a small token of my affection, I have taken the liberty of pursuin' the trail of the young Aconda gal."

"I'm in bed, so get on with it."

"Just the thought stimulates—"

Raven hung up, redirecting all his future calls to her protégé's voicemail. She reclined in bed, waiting for the inevitable knock on her door. An hour later, it came.

"It's Dante," said the muffled voice outside her door. He made no effort to conceal his emotions. Amorous waves surged off him.

"What now?" Raven draped her arm over her face, not wanting to make eye contact. The inside of her elbow fit snuggly across the bridge of her nose. Yet, when the door opened, rays of light poured into her bedroom and past her eyelids in an orange smear. Raven considered pulling a sheet over her exposed body, but the linen felt like a wet newspaper. She must have already sweated through her undergarments.

"Er, is it okay if I enter?" Dante asked bashfully.

Raven let out a long sigh. Times like these made her wish that she could not read minds. The door closed with a thump; the room was mercifully dark again. The only light emanated from Dante's phone. After a few moments, he began, "I received several calls from Rear Admiral Roy—"

"Next!"

"Just a second," Dante said while tapping the frames of his glasses.

"Did you just switch to night vision?" Raven cringed. "It's awfully dark in here."

Raven sighed. "What else?"

"I got the laser painter you requested."

Raven stretched out her hand, feeling the warm metal slap her palm. She twirled the foot-long wand between her fingers like a baton. "Is it synched up already?"

"Oh yes," Dante gushed. "Just point the tip towards your target area."

The baton slipped through her sweaty fingers. "I need an air conditioner."

"Ah, the power is out citywide," Dante said dejectedly. "We're operating on portable generators. However, I can commandeer a small cooling machine from the intensive care unit at the hospital. In the meantime, I can administer a sedative to help you sleep."

"I don't want to wake up to find you ogling me at the foot of my bed."

"I'd be sure not to wake you."

"As hair-raising as that sounds, I have to be lucid to answer secure calls," Raven replied. "Oddly, the Office of the Benevolent Imperator has not called me once tonight."

"OBI has been communicating with Admiral Finn exclusively—"

Raven sat up quickly, tapping her damp chest with the metal baton. "I'm not sure if you're up on current events, but I'm in command!"

"Mistress, you *were* in command of the Battle of Georgetown, which was a smashing success. If I might add—"

"You may not." Raven pulled her knees under her chin, rocking slightly back and forth on the mattress as she hugged her shins. The recent news embittered her. In the dim light, Raven could make out his silhouette just inches away. "Who put Finn in command?"

"The Septenary made the decision soon after you notified them about the Cognoscenti."

"I'm in the Septenary."

Dante whispered. "The Administration Branch called a closed session."

Raven stretched out, rolling onto her stomach. She snatched her secure phone and pressed the snowflake icon. The little screen lit up in an eerie blue. While waiting, she twirled the foot-long metal wand across each finger like a majorette. The screen changed, revealing a dazzling face with silky chestnut hair.

"What have you done?" Raven demanded.

"I've been waiting in the office for your call all morning," the woman said through pouty lips. "Nevertheless, I see that you're relaxing in bed. Is that some sort of *cudgel?*"

Raven held the wand up to the camera. "I'm excited to try this one out. My protégé just brought it over."

"Good morning, Mistress Cassandra," Dante said, stepping into the camera's view.

"Did you assign your stalker to be your protégé?" asked Cassandra.

"I already made him delete all the pictures of me from his phone, so we're good," Raven insisted. "I find stalkers make loyal assistants."

"Dante is staring at your butt as we speak!" Cassandra exclaimed.

"This is a secure call, Dante," Raven explained over her shoulder. "You'll have to wait outside."

Dante sulked as he left the room. Raven waited for the door to slam before continuing the conversation. "Why did you pull me off command?"

"It was the only scenario where you didn't die or go missing. I turned the proverbial clock back ten times in my head. Relieving you of command was the safest option for you."

"Don't give me your hoodoo voodoo. Nine other precogs in your branch probably thought that I should stay in command."

"Yet, I'm the one who's always right," Cassandra boasted.

"Well, you were wrong about Piero," Raven said with a bit of dismay.

"I've worked closely with Pi on creative projects, so your misgivings are a sore point with me. After the Janissary labeled Pi as killed in action, I was given access to his journals. He liked to write science fiction stories."

Raven rolled her eyes. "Do people still read novels?"

"For your information, I have a creative writing master's degree from the Conservatoire," Cassandra said laboriously. "Anyway, most sci-fi plots take the sociopolitical and moral quandaries out of our present world, and then simply reconstruct the emotional stresses in a high-tech background."

"Slow down, professor," Raven mocked. "Are you saying Piero did this?"

"Quite the opposite. Pi created worlds where future technologies changed humanity itself, including our emotions and *urges*, not merely our hoverbikes and auto-guns. What's a mere helicon aerial vehicle compared to a transcendent being, controlling minds but never allowed to enjoy life on a human level? In Pi's novel, the transcendent could only experience joy and sorrow through the thoughts of his minions. Pi was too close to the truth."

"Far out, sister," Raven scoffed. "Maybe you should lay off the psychedelics this early in the morning. Are you saying Piero overdosed?"

"We have not seen the last of Pi."

"Pie?" Raven wrinkled her brow. "It sounds like you're ordering dessert."

"That's his nickname, spelled, p-i."

Raven laughed. "That's a dumb nickname."

"You like to jest about the poor boy," Cassandra scolded. "Pi is the sixteenth letter in the Greek alphabet. He signed all his writings with that symbol."

"Save your eulogy for *Pi's* memorial service."

"There's no need. Pi is still alive . . . somewhere."

"Gia Aconda saw him fall into death's embrace in the arms of two sentry bots," Raven said bleakly. "Besides,

I found his blood at the scene, but someone dragged his corpse away."

"Have you interrogated the Aconda girl personally?"

"I can't locate her at the moment. Things are a bit chaotic here, so I put a Rear Admiral on her tail."

Cassandra's eyes twinkled momentarily. Her trances always gave Raven the creeps. Gasping for air, Cassandra clutched her chest. Raven diverted her eyes out of modesty. Through panting breaths, Cassandra said, "That was very unpleasant . . . I'm afraid things will go very bad for *you* . . . if the Aconda girl is not found soon."

"Do I want to know how terrible it is?"

"Your reaction to my prediction will alter the Horizon of Possibilities Expanse."

"Ugh, you just told me about your prediction," Raven protested.

Cassandra nodded sympathetically. "Just find the Aconda girl and pretend that your life does not depend on it."

Chapter 17

Riley stretched face down across the massage table, waiting for the doctor. She wore only shorts doubling as pajamas. Normally, Riley would have gone to the Academy physician, but she already told the janissaire investigator last night that she suffered no injuries from the bot attack. Besides, she did not want to answer medical questions about why she stopped taking her mandatory libido inhibitors.

The door opened; she looked up. A smug-looking fellow in a white lab coat entered the examining room. He had grayish-blond hair and a close-clipped beard, hiding his double chin. "I'm Dr. Steve."

"Are you a medical doctor?"

"Well, I'm a doctor of chiropractic medicine."

"You're a chiropractor?"

"The government has banned all chiropractic offices," Steve explained.

"Because they're a scam."

Steve rounded the examining table. "So, I'm now a licensed masseuse, harder to get than my chiropractor license." Steve squirted oil on Riley's toned back and gently rubbed the bottom of her spine.

"Steve, massage my calves," Riley ordered.

"It's Dr. Steve."

"I'll call you doctor when you graduate medical school."

"Where did *you* go to *school*?" Steve asked in a tizzy.

"The Janissary Academy."

Steve abruptly stopped. "Here to arrest me? I applied for my masseuse license, but it hasn't come in yet. I didn't prostitute myself."

Riley popped her head up and peeked over her shoulder to see if Steve was still dressed. She let out a sigh of relief when she saw him standing proud in his lab coat. Riley shook her head, "Just rub my shoulders."

Steve gently rubbed under her shoulder blades and pressed his thumbs deep into her neck. Riley relaxed, letting out a groan as he hit a knot. Steve raked his oily fingers over her scalp. He pulled her black hair over the front of the table, running his fingers unabated over the bumps on her head.

"You have an overwrought aura," Steve expounded.

"What are you talking about?"

"When I was studying chiropractic medicine, I double majored in phrenology," Steve asserted as he caressed her head.

"Is that another quack pseudoscience?"

"The practice of phrenology examines the conformity of the skull as indicators of mental faculties and traits."

"Sounds like something a witch doctor would say."

"I'm also an animist witch doctor," Steve boasted. "On my website, you may have noticed a small apostrophe before the word doctor for the title, Office of 'Doctor Steve. That's not a typo. I was called Witch Doctor Steve for a long time. After getting several court orders to cease and desist, I was forced to take out Witch and add the apostrophe."

"Are you still a witch doctor?"

"I'm afraid not. The African elders pulled my witch doctor license when I started working as a chiropractor. Apparently, the elders don't respect chiropractic medicine. That's why they just call me Dr. Steve now."

"It sounds like a stripper name," Riley muttered.

"Don't be silly," Steve chided. "I would never sully my reputation as a doctor. My stripper name is Baron Von Dangler. At the strip club, I wear a cape, monocle, and an antique German army helmet, the kind with the spike on top."

"I don't want you touching my head anymore."

"Your overwrought aura was starting to mess up my chi anyway," Steve insisted as he began massaging her shoulders.

Riley tried to enjoy the massage, but something nagged at her like a loose thread unraveling a wool sweater. "On the side of your building, I noticed some graffiti of a circle drawn around a cube with numbers."

"Is that a building code violation too?" Steve asked sarcastically. "One of my regulars sandblasted the graffiti off, but it was back the next morning. You can't fine me for that. I live out of my office; technically, this is also my residence and thus, not subject to commercial laws."

Riley slowly lifted her head, peeking through strands of oily hair. "I'm not looking for a bribe. I think given your unique work situation, you may have criminal contacts."

"In here, I get all kinds, including chimeras. One lady has body modifications to make her look like a zebra. I find her white and black mohawk with matching stripes to be quite breathtaking."

"Does she know anything about the graffiti?" Riley asked impatiently.

"The local businesses on 45th Avenue have formed a neighborhood watch of sorts," Steve said snidely. "For a long time, I wouldn't leave the building at night. That's part of the reason why I reside here. I was also evicted from my bachelor pad for shooting movies without a permit, but that's another story entirely. The slogan for this neighborhood has always been: 'It's 5:00 p.m., run for your life!' It's catchy but not very good for business. Just last night, there was a robot shooting in the lobby of the old Bismarck Hotel. We call it the Mark, which are the only remaining letters left on the facade. Now, it's been turned into a rundown refugee center."

"Steve, just fast forward to zebra girl!"

"She goes by Zee-Barbara," Steve elucidated. "I was just getting to her. She's part of the neighborhood watch too. We meet here just before dark. You can join us if you live or work on 45th Avenue."

"I live at the Mark . . . I work there too, I guess."

"This has been a most fortuitous meeting. Having a jinni in our group will give us some clout." Steve squirted warm oil on her feet, rubbing them vigorously.

"I'm not a janissaire yet. I just graduated from the Academy."

"What's your title?"

"I'm in between at the moment looking forward, looking back just like Janus, the god of doorways. In the Academy, we wear the insignia of the janiceps, a two-headed monster for a mascot. Our sports teams are called 'The Fighting Janiceps.' After you graduate and complete an internship, the Janissary will promote you to janissaire."

"What's after that?"

"The masters and mistresses, six of those, not including the Grand Master."

Steve paused to stroke his beard with oily fingers. "Hmmm, I knew a Grant Master back in chiropractic school; I wonder if he's the same guy."

"*Grand* Master is a title, not a name."

"What's his real name?"

Riley popped her head up, shaking loose strands of hair out of her face. "I don't know the Grand Master's real name."

"Then, he could be the same person I knew in school." Steve cracked his knuckles before continuing the massage. "Nevertheless, I wish you were a full jinni, but you'll have to do."

Riley rested her cheek on her hands, closing her eyes. "That's very magnanimous of you."

"I know," Steve said self-righteously. "You'll need an alias for our group. Indecently, Sandblaster, Zee-Barbara, Lickspittle, and Doc are already taken."

"Don't tell me you're Doc."

"I most certainly am. Everyone calls me Doc or Doctor out of professional courtesy."

"You're not a professional unless you count getting paid for rubbing people down."

Steve began massaging her thighs, angling his way up. "Speaking of which, in lieu of payment for this chiropractic adjustment, can you procure me some cool military hardware?"

"I know how to requisition military-grade equipment."

"That will be perfect for our neighborhood watch," Steve crowed. "We'll track down these graffiti vandals in no time."

Riley propped herself up onto her elbows, cradling her chin on her knuckles. A plan formed in her head as the tension slowly ebbed out of her legs. "I already took a photo of the hex sign. Have your sandblasting friend wipe all the graffiti off your building today. I'll meet you back here at sunset."

"You still need an alias."

Riley said the first thing that came to mind. "Genie."

"I'll have to come up with something better for you tonight; your nom de guerre is a bit droll considering you're not a real jinni."

"All things considered, you're not a real doctor."

Chapter 18

The Breakneck hoverbike handled poorly on the narrow switchbacks. Piero strained to peer through splotched lenses, encrusted with crushed insects. He leaned heavily into the turn, scraping dirt with the leather-clad knee of his ridiculous-looking chaps. Ducking under low hanging tree limbs, Piero maneuvered a mere foot over the pockmarked earth. The military blockades forced him to travel these broken, unpaved back roads. Whack! A prickly branch slapped his head.

Rounding the bend, he spotted Gia straddling her Nosedive in her leather leggings. She had parked alongside a sheer cliff. On her back, Jocko slept in a customized baby carrier like a papoose. From this height, they had a commanding view of the Pakaraima Mountains.

Gia looked back as Piero slowly hugged the side of the hill. She waved him forward. "There's a washout ahead. Just follow me and don't slow down."

Before Piero could catch up, Gia kicked her Nosedive into gear and tore away, spitting dirt. He trailed the dust cloud, not daring to peer over the edge. *Am I going fast enough? If I speed up, will I ram the back of Gia's hoverbike?*

The Breakneck shook violently. Piero looked down seeing only the loose dirt of the washout. He gripped the handlebars tightly. The vibrations were tearing his hands away. He was slipping; the bike dipped. He was going over!

Piero floated on a cushion of air. His vision cleared, showing he was back on the road, albeit riding the rim. Piero veered right, hugging the side of the hill once again. He exhaled, not recognizing that he had been holding his breath. He puttered around the turn to find Gia pulling into a rough-and-ready parking lot crowded with custom-built hoverbikes. Several buildings poked over a high wall lined with barbwire. A paved two-lane highway bordered the far side of the compound. After a four-hour journey, they had finally reached their destination.

Most motorists in normal times would have just taken the highway. However, these were strange times indeed. He pulled into a spot next to Gia's Nosedive. She was already at the front gate, standing near a sign that warned: "Keep out! Private Property of the Burro Motorcycle Club." There were also signs written in Spanish, but he could not decipher their meaning. Foreign languages were not offered at the Academy until you were slated for the Diplomacy Branch. However, Piero did learn some Spanish by watching banned Venezuelan *telenovelas* with subtitles. *One of those shows took place in Guyana*, he recalled. *This part of Guyana used to belong to Venezuela, so the people still spoke Spanish here.*

The Breakneck dropped with a thump. Piero pushed his splotched, red-tinted glasses onto his dusty forehead before dismounting. The long ride had rendered him bowlegged. He moseyed towards the fence as a camera followed him. He heard a buzz. Gia pushed open the gate, motioning him to follow.

Inside the compound, Piero saw a decrepit hotel abutting the highway. The central building looked like an Old West saloon complete with swinging chest-high batwing doors. Off to the far right, built into the hill, was a mechanic's garage full of scowling, rugged bikers.

"Don't mind them," Gia said. "They're more afraid of us."

Piero gulped, following Gia into the saloon. She pushed through a crowd of patrons as he trailed close behind in her wake. The stench of tobacco permeated the air; something smelled of burnt rubber. On a table a few paces inside, Piero spotted a mult-stemmed hookah with rubber tentacle-like tube protruding from its bowl. At the hookah table, an elderly woman in google sucked on a hose, blowing out rancid smoke rings. Gia steered him towards the table. Piero prayed silently, *Benevolent Imperator, protect me from these savages.*

Nervously, Piero surveyed the saloon, looking for anywhere else to sit. The place was packed. All the stools at the bar were taken and the tables were full. Gruff-looking men leaned against the wall, balancing their beer bottles on a narrow, waist-high ledge. A mob of shabbily dressed people waited in front of a door that had the word, *Baño,* crudely painted across the panel. *Benevolent Imperator spare me from having to use that bathroom!*

Piero felt something clasp his hand. He glanced down. *Thank the Benevolent Imperator, it's just Gia.* A hard tug pulled him towards the hookah table. The old woman leered at him. Her goggles augmented her already oversized eyes. Piero gaped inappropriately.

"Grandmother! What big eyes you have," said Gia.

"The better to see you with, my dear," croaked the creepy grandmother in a heavy Spanish accent. "Sit down if you please."

I don't please, thought Piero as he scanned the other saloon patrons. After a moment, he sat on the edge of his chair, ready to run. While he was used to living with bums and whackos in the Isle Royale ghetto, these bad hombres were somehow even more disquieting. Within spitting distance sat a woman with a mechanical arm that ended in a clamp, rather than a hand. Across from her was a bald man who had cranial implants that blined like a stobe light.

Gia squeezed his palm. Piero was sweating. He wiped his brow, knocking off his glasses. He bent over, snatching them off the floor before someone could steal them. Gia's fingers slip up to his wrist, wrapping around tightly. *Holy Benevolent Imperator, she's taking my pulse!*

Piero heard a screech. He jolted up, but Gia pulled him down before he could ascend more than a few inches. Looking across the table, the old woman had just scooted her chair back. She stood and then waddled away.

"Calm down," Gia hissed. "Your heart is going to explode."

"Why did you bring me to this horrible place?"

"It's a safe house," she whispered.

"I do not feel safe right now!" he exlaimed too loudly.

"Hush! Pull yourself together and act like a man. We have scarier people to impress."

"I swear to the Benevolent Imperator that I will stab the next person who makes a sudden move near me."

Piero felt a slash of pain across his wrist. When he reflexively pulled away, the ache worsened. Staring open-mouthed, he saw that Gia had dug her nails into his flesh. Drops of blood seeped between her fingers. His blood.

"You can't talk that way around here," Gia hushed. "These are enemies of the Imperium."

Before he could protest, Gia shot up, yanking his arm. She led him by the wrist across the saloon towards the door marked, *Baño*. Piero exclaimed, "Not that bathroom!"

Mercifully, Gia passed the grimy bathroom door, continuing down the hallway. Piero let out a sigh of relief when she released her vise-like grip on his wrist. They crossed a threshold into a backroom that had a single table with four chairs. *Benevolent Imperator, there's another hookah on the table. By the looks of it, no one has ever sanitized the rubber hoses.*

Piero recoiled at the rumbling behind him. He spun around to find Gia pulling shut a heavy sliding door. Releasing a long sigh, Piero slumped down into a seat by the hookah table. He leaned back, hanging his head over the chair's backrest. The only light came from a dangling bulb over the table. Piero was still sweating. The humid air clung to his already damp skin. He examined the wood-paneled walls. Oddly, a steel beam supported each corner. He closed his eyes, taking deep breaths to slow his heart rate.

The room began shaking. The light bulb swayed back and forth in long arcs. Piero grabbed for the hookah table, raking his fingers across contaminated rubber mouthpieces. *Oh, the horror!* He scraped his chair against creaky floorboards as he tried to stand. Firm hands gripped his shoulders, pushing him back down.

"We're in a freight elevator," Gia whispered in his ear.

The floor was dropping. Piero saw the wood-paneled walls giving way to rough-hewn rock. The entire room was sinking into the earth, lower and lower. The wood panels disappeared. The rock wall in front of him opened a crack and then slowly turned into a cavern. Bright light gushed in.

With a thump, the shaking stopped. Gia released his shoulders. Rounding the table, she quickly proceeded onto the rocky surface now level with the floorboards deeper into the crevice. Jocko still managed to sleep soundlessly in his papoose. Distant voices echoed down the cavern. Piero hesitated. Tired of being led by the nose, he pondered remaining seated. However, Dirk had taught him never to be caught flatfooted.

Standing on wobbly legs, he leaned heavily on the table. He stumbled onto the rutted cavern floor while palming the hilt of his skean. Recessed lights extended across the cavern's roof similar to the rigging in a mineshaft.

A hundred paces ahead, Gia entered a large room and turned right, out of view. Piero felt his stomach tighten as he reached out to Gia's mind. He sensed her feigned serenity, masking dread. Bracing one hand against the cavern wall,

Piero crept closer. He peeked around the corner, spotting Gia in front of a large metallic compartment built into the rock wall. Dozens of black cables sprouted out of the structure like a giant hookah. Amused, Piero walked closer to get a better view.

As he closed within arm's length, Piero reared back as white-maned waves of rage hammered his skull. One after another, the repelling blows struck his mind. Piero pulled himself together more than two yards away.

Gia turned suddenly as a bewildered expression crossed her face. The boiling rage was not emanating from her, but rather the machinelike creature in the metallic upright coffin. Piero gawked at the propped-up, garish giant that would have been the main draw of any traveling freak show. Artificial lights glinted off its chrome, hunchbacked body, revealing the monster from his childhood nightmares.

"Get away from it!" Piero shouted, pulling out his skean. He lunged forward. Gia blocked his path, jabbing her elbow into his groin, shooting lightning bolts of pain across the already wounded spot. Piero shoved her to the ground, knocking Jocko out of his papoose. The monkey screeched while scampering away. Adrenalin coursed through Piero's body as he ardently raised his blade and limped towards the monster.

With revulsion, Piero watched his knife-edge sag and then droop into a flaccid four-inch gooey shaft. The once solid blade dangled off its hilt, mocking him. Piero willed his blade back to life, stiffening the shaft a tad before watching it wilt again. It was like pulling taffy.

"Having some dysfunctional issues?" asked a vulpine voice. "In time, it happens to all men."

Piero spun around, the jelly shaft whipped around in languid loops, top-heavy. A middle-aged woman with red hair stared him down. *She's pretty for her age. She looks more like a vixen than a cougar.* Piero tried to sheath his spongy skean, but it would no longer fit back into its scabbard. Pride already wounded, he just let it sway in defeat.

"Pi, I want you to meet our benefactor." Gia stood and then dusted off her leather chaps. "This is Variola."

"What did you do to my skean?" Piero thrust the shapeless, bronze blob in Variola's face.

"Nothing a little energetics can't fix," replied Variola. "Step away from Bjorn. His innards are made of quick metal."

Piero stole a look over his shoulder at the beast in the box. "That's the Cybogre."

"Your powers of observation astound me," joked Variola.

"You're helping that thing!" exclaimed Piero as he pointed at the metal beast.

"I'll fetch some crayons and draw it out for you later." Variola winked. "I belong to an exclusive club of former janissaires who voluntarily left the Imperium. While your empire rots from within, we are building a new society out here in the jungle."

"You're a member of the Cognoscenti!" yelled Piero. "You're all a bunch of deserters!"

"Lower your voice before you upset Bjorn again," Variola scolded in a brisk schoolmarm voice. "Around these parts, no one calls us the Cognoscenti or knows what that means. The Janissary invented the name to demonize us. Further, we are not deserters. Rather, we are just on strike."

"On strike from what?" he asked.

"The tyranny of your social order that prevents psychics from reaching their full potential," answered Variola. "We have recruited the best minds from the Academy to form a democratic global organization to take over once the Imperium collapses."

Before Piero could retort, the Cybogre bellowed. Variola stepped closer and caressed his dented faceplate.

"What happened to Bjorn?" asked Gia, moving forward.

"What didn't happen?" Variola retorted. "Bjorn attacked a dropship full of bots while trying to nab Raven. As you can see, he failed and is worse for the wear. On the plus side, Bjorn's new brain implants made him immune to mind-controlling attacks, so he's still our best hope in taking down Raven."

"Just shoot Raven," Gia said straightforwardly. Piero stared dumbfounded. He had somehow fallen into a cave full of terrorists. When caught, the Imperium would summarily execute everyone in this room, even the Cybogre if possible.

"Raven is a pawn on the chessboard of life," Variola explained. "She is vital to our offensive provided we can win her over."

"You won't!" blurted Piero waving his flaccid skean.

Gia scowled. "Raven can't be trusted. She'll just enslave us with her mind-controlling powers; she's worse than the Beast."

Variola nodded to Piero. "That's what we call your Benevolent Imperator around here. I don't blame you for your misgivings. After all, you have been indoctrinated since the time you were housebroken. In fact, your first job was to find children to replenish the Janissary's ranks."

Surprised, he rubbed his bald scalp with a shaky hand. "Psychics go insane without proper instruction, and I can tell that both of you have succumbed to madness."

"Presuppositions taint the prejudiced mind," Variola retorted, smirking. "That's one of the Benevolent Imperator maxims that I learned at the Academy."

"It's an indignity to hear *his* words come out of your mouth." Piero threw his arms up, his limp bronze blade twirled around the hilt. "I can't believe what I'm hearing."

"Then, I'll quote one last maxim," Variola professed as she tapped her temple with a finger. "Belief is the delusion of the masses."

Chapter 19

Raven did not know what to believe after reaching a dead end. The Aconda girl's trail was already cold, quite literally. The fires that consumed Gia's house had burnt out hours ago, leaving nothing behind. Roy puttered amidst the soot, accruing dark smears on his white pants for his effort. He kicked a piece of steel rebar, flinging up a cloud of wispy black smoke.

"You cannot stoke cold ashes," Raven mocked.

"The fire of vengeance shan't be squelched so easily," Roy replied dramatically.

Dante stepped irritably to Raven's side. *Jealousy is the bedfellow of lust,* she mused. *You cannot have one without the other.*

"Roy, you sound like a bad Shakespearean actor!" Dante snapped, standing with his arms akimbo.

"I never argue with a lady," Roy drawled back.

"Stop it!" Raven barked. "We're not getting anywhere with this constant bickering. The sooner we find the Aconda girl, the sooner we can leave this backwater slum."

"Well, she ain't here," Roy intoned.

"I cannot believe I'm missing the Othello symposium at the Conservatoire for mucking in the jungle," Dante whined. "Did you know that they revived Lar Lubovitch's 1997 Othello ballet? Daisy Demedici is cast in the role of Desdemona!"

"Those details must have slipped my mind as I was preparin' for the Battle of Georgetown," Roy drawled. "Ma'am, can ya send you fancy boy packin' so we can get some work done?"

A miffed Dante opened his mouth but stopped when Raven touched his shoulder. *The boy is too quick to anger.* Raven circled in front of him. "Contact Inquisitor Hatchette and tell her to question all of Gia's siblings. It seems that I put too much trust in young Riley."

A few heartbeats after Dante left, Roy asked, "Do ya want to question the prisoner now?"

Raven nodded, heading down the sidewalk. The drifter had slumped against the metal grill in the back of a commandeered police truck. A dark finger poked through the back gate's interlacing latticework. Raven stroked the raggedy old man's finger. "Do you want to help me, Davey?"

"Oo-wee, yuh ah know it."

"Tell me about the girl you met at the harbor."

"Yuh see all ah dat?"

"We caught her on a satellite photo talking to you," Raven said serenely. "She drove off on a hoverbike, but we lost her in all the smoke. Did she mention where she was going?"

"Jus' now!" the drifter exclaimed. "De girl nah want trouble. If yuh eye nah see, yuh mouth nah must talk."

"Did the girl *say* anything?"

"De girl say Helicon," Davey slurred. "It ah mountain in Greece . . . or did yuh say it. Anyhow, she ah takin' a nymph de aerial assault vehicle to de mountain. Also, she ah tossin' something into de watah. Fish ah play ah sea, he nah know watah ah boil fuh am."

Raven pointed to the burned-out structure. "Did the girl say whether she was going home?"

"Oo-wee, is dat she house? Someone must ah wannah she dead. When yuh dead yuh nah sabee, and when yuh sabee yuh dead."

Raven walked away, rejoining Roy in front of the ashy ruins. "Davey's mind is a jumble of local proverbs. I can only verify that he is of East Indian descent and talked to Gia at the harbor. She left soon after the missiles began flying."

"We're spinnin' our wheels here," Roy put forward. "It'll be dark in a couple of hours. If the Aconda girl is still out there, we need to draw her to us."

"How do you propose we do that?"

"Understandably, the girl doesn't want to meet ya face to face. Yet, she doesn't want to contact ya by phone. Given the blown-up house, I'd say the girl's either dead or playin' dead. So, ya send her a text to rendezvous with ya secret-like."

Raven wrinkled her nose in disgust. "You want to dangle me like a hooked worm?"

"It'll be more like a mousetrap and yar the sweet-smellin' hunk of cheese."

"I'm still the bait. Besides, the Aconda girl has no reason to meet me in person."

Roy looked up, scratching his chin. "Then, we'll have to give her one."

Raven wiped her brow. It was slick with perspiration from an oppressive sun. *If she was working for the Cognoscenti, then why would Gia send her siblings to the Capital? It made no sense, unless—*

"I finally got a hold of Hatchette!" Dante ran towards them waving his secure phone. "She said she was going to put the thumbscrews to those kids."

Raven had an itch in her mind that she could not scratch. *How do you set a trap for precogs?*

Chapter 20

Pedestrians raced down the sidewalks as the sun dipped behind the looming pastel buildings. Reddish-gold slants of light reflected off waterlogged potholes in the alley behind Steve's massage parlor. Even vermin scampered into their hidey-holes. Riley spotted several hefty rats scurrying down the storm sewer as she waited for the merry band of misfits. She examined the bare concrete wall that used to have a hex sign. She ran her fingers over the sandblasted area, finding the texture to be quite smooth.

Sadly, the first person to enter the alleyway was Steve, donning a slightly tattered, albeit pompous, lab coat. To this ensemble, he added large white goggles with computer-generated eyeballs that floated around the opaque lenses, giving the illusion of cartoonish googly eyes. He topped off his costume with a bushy, white wig.

"Do you wear anything other than a white lab coat?" asked Riley.

"Aside from my outfit at the strip club, I do have a red smoking jacket," Steve responded smarmily. "However, I gave up smoking to save money, so now it's just my red jacket. Ooh, I like your costume."

Riley shrugged. She wore a black, skintight suit. She tucked her dark hair into a bronze Kevlar helmet and hid her eyes behind her bronze-tinted glasses while accessorizing with a matching veil over her mouth. Around her waist, she wore both her skean and sidearm strapped to a ringed, bronze belt that she found at an apparel store in a bullet-ridden neighborhood called Little Syria.

"As president of this neighborhood watch, I'm renaming you, Belly Dancer," Steve proclaimed.

"That's fine," Riley retorted. "I had no intention of calling you Doc because you're a fake doctor."

"Garbage begets garbage," Steve muttered as he looked down the trash-strewn ally. "If one person litters, then others think that it's okay to dump their trash in the same place."

I've said the same myself, thought Riley. *Back at the aluminum recycling center was a trashy bathroom. During her shift, she would hide out in the last stall to avoid her plant manager. Riley spent hours at a time just watching banned viral videos of a bearded wizard. Night after night, litter would mount up in the bathroom stalls. Maybe it was her job to clean the bathroom. She never inquired.*

"Has anyone seen Cutback?" asked a deep voice near the sinks. "The plant manager has been looking for her."

Sighing, Riley popped out her earbuds and pocketed her phone. After cleaning up, she sauntered out to the main floor t o find the frazzled plant manager who had both hands atop his head. His breath reeked of marijuana mixed with brackish chemicals. On spotting her, the manager exclaimed, "I picked the wrong day to stop smoking wicky sticks! One of the service bots spilled a barrel of oil!"

"So, have the bot clean it up."

"Oh, I can't have the bot slip and fall on oil. Bots are terribly expensive to fix. It's your time to shine!"

The manager took her to a jigsaw and unstrapped a plastic bag that was attached underneath. Faux wood sawdust filled the bag. Riley hauled it over her shoulder as she followed the manager to the spot of the oil spill near the five-ton press. She grabbed handfuls of sawdust and sprinkled the tiny shreds around the perimeter of the yard-long, oily pool. The plant manager watched her closely but did not help. After completing the border, she began the monotonous task of filling the interior with more sawdust.

Piercing screams broke her boredom. Over the drum of the huge press, she heard shouts near the stack of aluminum logs. A crew of migrants worked flat, metal sticks to pry something from under a huge column, a bloody man. When Riley ran over, a large huddle of workers had formed around the crushed victim. Angry migrants pointed to a service bot that was still operating a forklift as if nothing had happened.

A beefy foreman in overalls ran over to the forklift and yanked the bot out. As it clattered to the ground, Riley watched in shock as the bot's eyes turned a deep shade of crimson. The bot staggered to its feet on shaky, thin legs and immediately started strangling the foreman, whose face turned the same color as the bot's eyes.

A large crowd of migrants surrounded the murderous bot, partially blocking Riley's view. She pushed through the mob. A migrant wound up with a Kevlar stick. With a heavy clank, he clipped off the bot's arm at the elbow.

"Stop!" ordered the plant manager. "Bots are terribly expensive to fix!"

Another whack took off the bot's remaining arm. The foreman fell to the ground, choking and spitting blood. Riley kneeled and reached into her boot. As she pulled out her skean, Riley saw that she was not the only worker armed. The others had gathered make-shift weapons, including giant wrenches, chains, and aluminum bars. They moved out in small packs and attacked every bot in the plant. Riley eagerly sliced off bot heads at the neck joint.

"Hey, Cutback is handy with the steel!" cheered a migrant in her mob.

She smiled at her co-worker. "It's called quick metal . . . bitch."

As Steve expounded on the virtues of keeping his alley free of litter, Riley snapped out of her flashback. She spotted a bandy-legged fellow sliding along the shaded portion of the wall. The creeper's head was covered with a hoody, which had pointy ears sewed on top. His face was marred with greasepaint to resemble a rodent. Riley nonchalantly reached down to her sidearm as the creature slinked behind Steve. Just as she was easing her handgun out of its holster, Steve twisted, lunging at the little, ratty man.

Limbs coiled and bodies contorted, the opponents grappled. Steve clamped onto the throat of his vermin garbed attacker who merely rolled away, bouncing off a pile of trash. Before Steve drew another breath, the rat-man sprang forward. Four concussive blows to the body and Steve found himself hitting the wet, dirty blacktop. Following a single dead cat bounce, the assailant straddled Steve, landing hammer blows to his chest. Steve squirmed and then bucked up like a bronco, launching the bandy-legged assaulter into the cement wall and knocking the air out of his lungs. The battle was over.

Smirking, Steve brushed scraps of garbage off his lab coat. "Lickspittle, you will never get the better of me."

Lickspittle twitched and made some furtive gestures. With one pint-sized hand, he wiped drips of blood from his lips. Shifting his beady eyes, the diminutive man sat back on his haunches, then struggled to stand. "Touché, Doc. You're an excellent grappler. Who's the new girl?"

Steve chimed, "This is our newest member, Belly Dancer."

Riley twisted her hip, rattling the many rings on her belt. Awestruck, Lickspittle scurried over and held out his little hand. Against her better judgment, Riley shook it; the palm was clammy. "It's an honor to meet you," she exaggerated.

"Doc and I used to belong to an underground fighting ring called Blow Club," said Lickspittle. "It was just a bunch of shirtless men bare-knuckle boxing in a basement—"

"That was a long time ago," Steve interrupted fretfully. "Oh look, the rest of the gang is coming down the alley."

Even from far away, Riley could easily tell the duo apart as they walked hurly-burly towards them. Zee-Barbara was strikingly tall, yet her platform shoes, designed to look like hooves, gave her another six inches of height. Her bristly black and white mohawk did indeed look like a zebra mane. Still, her most bizarre feature was her long stripes. At first, Riley assumed Zee-Barbara was merely wearing body paint, which was common for swimsuit models. She certainly had the body for one. However, as she approached, it was apparent that Zee-Barbara had modified her pigment to pattern zebra stripes. Accentuating her skin, she just wore a sleeveless belly shirt and short shorts.

In stark contrast, Sandblaster showed no skin at all, wearing yellow maintenance coveralls. Strapped to his back, he donned a portable sandblaster. He completed his getup with a copper helmet, resembling the kind underwater divers used in the early 20th century. However, the visors in this helmet were darkened, hiding his face.

Lickspittle scuttled over to the pair. "Doc has recruited a young girl called Belly Dancer. Isn't that wonderful? Doc has such a way with people. Doc has maximized his personality to the fullest!"

Zee-Barbara huffed, "If there's one person who doesn't need his ego stroked, it's Steve."

"Tut-tut, let's use our pseudonyms," corrected Steve.

"Is the plan to wait around here all night for someone to spray paint your wall again?" asked Sandblaster through a speaker on his helmet.

Riley hesitated before addressing Sandblaster. *Is that a man or woman in there? Perhaps, it's just a bot.* "I installed a hidden security camera that will buzz my phone whenever someone enters this alley," Riley explained. "I already recorded a grab-ass match a minute ago—"

"We can discuss that later," Steve interjected. "Since our little club has grown, I think it's time we give a moniker to our neighborhood watch."

"Watch is fine," Zee-Barbara said indifferently.

"Watch will suffice," Sandblaster intoned.

Steve shook his head. "No, no, I was thinking of—"

"Watch is great," Lickspittle said eagerly. "Doc has the best names for things."

"Alright, it'll have to do for now," Steve said dejectedly. "As for tonight, let's beat up some grifters and their ilk."

"Great idea, Doc," Lickspittle toadied. "We can try out the new wrestling moves that we practiced last night."

Steve tugged on his collar and gulped. "Moving right along, I spotted Ron Burnsfeld selling his ill-gotten wares not more than a block away. Let's have Belly Dancer play the mark."

"Are you talking about the Mark hotel?" asked Zee-Barbara.

"I'm confused as well," intoned Sandblaster.

Lickspittle looked perplexed but dared not speak. Instead, he stepped from foot to foot nervously.

Steve shook his head. "I mean that I want Belly Dancer to pretend to be a sucker or a dupe, so we can catch Burnsfeld in his confidence trick."

Riley put her hands on her hips. "I'm here for the hex signs. There's another one near the corner of Mulberry Street and 45th Avenue. I only need Sandblaster's help, but the rest of you can come along."

"Finally, a quest worthy of my talents," Sandblaster said through his speaker as he put a gloved hand on Riley's shoulder. She resisted the urge to flinch away. Instead, Riley stepped forward, leading the motley band out of the dirty alley and down the empty sidewalk towards Murder Mile.

As dusk turned to night, strange lights flickered in alleys along with crackles of mechanical voices, signaling they had crossed into robot country. Block after block, the city sank deeper into disorder. Riley pulled out her skean, nervously spinning the hilt in her palm. Her companions were eerily quiet, shuffling along in a tight pack and halting at the humming of an approaching auto-car. Whizzing above the street, the car hooked left about ten yards ahead. A man-sized sack plummeted out the car's door, bouncing sickly at the crossroad ahead. The digital sign at the stoplight scrolled: "Mulberry Street . . . High Risk of Violent Crimes . . . Minimal Security Area . . . Police Response Time = 4 Hours."

It could be worse, thought Riley. At least it's not a Zero-Sec Zone.

The digital sign kept scrolling: "Mulberry Street . . . now designated a Zero Security Zone." She watched the sign repeat its scroll to make sure she read it correctly. She wished her suit had pockets to hide her shaking hands. Riley walked up to a broken light post. Jutting from the cement was just six inches of broken metal. Turning to her right, she found a dark alley with craters and gouges blighting the cement walls. "This must be the alley with the hex sign."

Steve inspected the walls with his googly eyes. "It looks like a war zone."

Pulling herself together, Riley entered first. She whipped out her sidearm, thumbing the smart button on the handle to shine a bright light from beneath the barrel.

The alley proceeded fifty feet ahead before turning to the right. As Riley approached the bend, she noticed that the wall in front of her was severely damaged. She ran her hand against the cracked cement, considering the force needed to cause so much havoc.

Continuing to her right, she noticed that the alley was littered with crushed metal. From the looks of the high walls, she figured that something must have crashed from above. She walked over to a storm sewer, noticing that the grill was sliced open. Riley heard her companions' step lightly behind her, followed by the sporadic, "ooh" and "ah." Shining a light on the nearest wall revealed the prize. She identified the image as the same blue cube with numbers on three sides.

"Six . . . six . . . six," uttered Steve. "Different numbers from the graffiti on my building."

Riley holstered her sidearm to pull out her phone. She aimed the phone's camera at the wall. The flash was blinding.

"Take a photo of all of us," Zee-Barbara commanded. "Do some before and after shots to show our handiwork."

"Everyone, get in close below the hex sign," Riley said as she tapped the timer on her phone. She viewed the phone's screen as the quartet struck various dramatic poses. Zee-Barbara was on the left, flexing her arms. Next to her, Lickspittle held a karate stance while Sandblaster aimed his nozzle at the camera. On the right, Steve tucked one hand in his lab coat like Napoleon. Riley watched the phone's timer tick down to the last few seconds. She used her telekinetic ability to hold the phone midair and then raced over to an amazed Steve.

Riley stood sideways to the camera shot, twisting her shoulders around. She then leaned forward slightly on her front foot. She remembered that models used this pose to give them a slimming effect. Flash.

Riley ran back and snatched the phone as it dropped. The image on the screen was remarkable. As the group huddled together, she felt congratulatory pats on her back. For the first time in her life, Riley did not shy away.

Sandblaster immediately got to work, doing what he loved to do. Riley used her free time to snap candid pictures of the Watch. She caught Zee-Barbara in a heated argument with Steve about homeopathic medicine. Her favorite photo was of Lickspittle digging through a trash bin. Twenty minutes passed before Sandblaster finished scouring the paint off the wall.

The group repositioned themselves beneath the newly scrubbed wall, ready for another photo opportunity while Riley positioned her phone's camera. This time, they left a spot in the middle for her. Again, she used her telekinetic ability to hold the phone and raced over to strike a pose. She clenched her fists, holding them against her hips like a superhero. Flash.

Riley dove forward, grabbing the phone before it hit the ground. She stumbled, jingling the rings on her belt. Laughs echoed from behind. She looked down at the screen at another marvelous photo. The laughter cut off abruptly. She looked over her shoulder to see Steve pointing down the alley. Riley turned back. A dark figure stood there, watching them.

Chapter 21

Piero ran his fingertips over the intaglios carved into the rock face. The images were of grylli, human and animal forms mixed together, forming bizarre creatures that were popular in Greco-Roman art. He chuckled at the irony. In the Imperium, a gryllus was a man who modified his body through DNA resequencing and surgery. The female counterpart was called a chimera. Piero did not know the reason for such a gender distinction other than a chimera was always a she-monster in Greek mythology. Specifically, the chimera spewed liquid fire from her lion head at one end as well as her goat head on the other.

Two heads like the janiceps, the mascot for the Academy's athletic teams. He missed home. Pacing in his rock-hewn room was not calming his jangled nerves. His mind drifted. *Why did the Benevolent Imperator choose the janiceps as a mascot? My biology teacher said that doctors refer to conjoined twins as janiceps, especially when the babies were joined at the head. When the Benevolent Imperator was created in a lab, did he have a twin? Did the scientists add animal parts to his DNA? Is that why the Cognoscenti call him the Beast?*

In 1992, German scientists created the first chimera in a lab, which was not a coincidence given the Germans' history of trying to create supermen. However, that chimera was just an embryonic mouse limb grafted onto a chicken wing, not exactly groundbreaking research.

Everything changed in 2011, thanks to a Frenchman who discovered a way to cut out junk DNA known as clustered regularly interspaced short palindromic repeats, otherwise known as Crispr. Using the virus that caused strep throat, the scientist snipped genes and then inserted whatever he wanted. This type of germline insertion was initially used to correct genetic disorders in human embryos. Not long after, the ethical lines blurred, allowing parents to create designer babies.

If Gia was correct, then the Benevolent Imperator was created in an underground laboratory just like Frankenstein's monster. That was as good a guess as any. Piero did not put much thought into what occurred before he was born. Going back to his first memories, the Benevolent Imperator was part of the world like auto-cars and Lake Superior. *Why do I care about the origin story for the Benevolent Imperator? Some say he's from the future. That makes sense since the human species is continuing to evolve. Others claim he is divine. Okay, that's a stretch, but he certainly has godly powers. A novel approach is that he's from an alternate timeline or mirror universe.*

Piero ceased pacing, shaking his head. Gia had to be wrong. The geneticists who allegedly created the Benevolent Imperator would not have stopped at just one. There ought to be an entire army cloned from his cells or at least a twin. *Whether you attribute his existence to geneticists or the Book of Genesis, the inconvenient truth remains that he's really powerful. Geneticists . . . genesis . . . genies . . . jinni . . . janissaires.*

Piero snapped out of his deep thoughts at the sound of footsteps clapping off flagstones, which abruptly stopped in front of his door. With a short knock, the door opened. Variola stood in the doorway, shaking a glass cylinder full of frothy, milky-white liquid. "It's feeding time."

"Keep your vanilla milkshake." He crossed his arms. "There's no way I'm drinking that."

"It's not for you, silly. I made this bonnyclabber for Bjorn. It's his favorite. I thought he could use a treat after all he's been through."

"What's in it?"

"Just sour, thick milk," Variola said while offering the cylinder. "I thought you could feed Bjorn so that he'll hate you less."

"He hates me?"

"Oh yes, very much. You should know given your empathic abilities."

"All I feel is rage from the Cybogre."

"That's because he hates you." Variola tossed the milky glass cylinder to Piero who snatched it inches from the ground.

"Let's get this over with," he muttered.

They walked back to the large room with the metallic compartment. The Cybogre was still propped up in his vertical coffin. Somewhere buried in that chrome armor was a human brain that hated him. Piero approached with his clenched fist held out, holding the milky cylinder like a shield. He got within two feet of the monster before feeling the white-hot rage spill over him. Piero winced, falling to one knee.

"Bjorn, play nice," cautioned Variola. "This simpleminded boy won't feed you again if you're naughty."

Small, jagged doors slid open in the Cybogre's abdomen. Piero watched as they slammed shut, only to quickly reopen. Back and forth, the little flaps snapped like the gnashing teeth of a rabid dog. Hesitantly, Piero inched closer to the chomping jaws. As the maw widened, he popped the cylinder into the gap, quickly pulling his hand back before the metal teeth chomped on his fingers. Piero scurried away to a safe distance from the monster's fury.

"That's a good start," Variola said, nodding approvingly. "We have a job to do, and I don't want you boys scuffling."

"What kind of job?"

"Oh Pi, it's going to be spectacular. You will have to do a little hiking in the jungle, so you should rest up."

"So, I'm not a prisoner of war?"

A rhythmic bellow came from the Cybogre's speaker. Variola leaned over, slapping the monster's shoulder. "Bjorn, don't laugh at our newest recruit."

The Cybogre belched out the nearly empty cylinder which skidded across the rocky floor leaving white foamy streaks. Variola slapped the armored hunchback again. "That's so rude. I'd make you fetch that bottle yourself if you weren't strapped down."

Piero backed further away. "For the record, I didn't join anything."

"Nonsense, I already vouched for you. Don't you enjoy your freedom?"

Piero frowned, shaking his head appreciably from side to side. "I'm being held in an underground hideout with the most wanted criminals on the planet."

"Now you're being ridiculous. No one is holding you here."

"Okay, I'm leaving." Piero headed towards the long rocky passageway leading to the freight elevator. "See you later. Actually, I don't want to see any of you again."

As he walked down the mineshaft-like corridor, Piero noticed that the room with the hookah table was gone. In its place, four steel beams supported a wooden roof. Piero reached up and rapped on the timber ceiling, which was the floor of the hookah room. He quickly looked around for some type of mechanism to operate the freight elevator. Not finding one, he pulled out his skean, examining the newly sharpened blade. Piero had wasted a half-hour of his life in tedious concentration fixing his damaged weapon. He sighed, recollecting that it only took Variola seconds to wilt the shaft into a wet noodle. Stroking the edge, the quick metal seemed solid enough now.

"Gia is waiting for you," Variola called down the hallway.

"This isn't a good time for me. I have to cut a hole in the bottom of your elevator."

"Gia saved your life."

Piero examined the wooden planks for a good place to slash. He avoided the midsection where he believed the hookah table might be resting. "For all I know, Gia staged the shootout with the sentry bots."

"Do you want to control bots with your mind?"

Piero paused. It was a tantalizing offer given that bots had tried to kill him several times this week. *I take the attempts on my life personally.* He looked back down the passageway to find his temptress casually leaning against a rock wall. Variola blew him a kiss. "Do you think the Septenary will allow you to study technomancy back on Isle Royale?"

"*You* can teach me technomancy?"

"I'm more of an energetics fundamentalist. However, Gia is willing to instruct you in the black arts of the technomancer. She's preparing your first lesson with a noctuid-class bot."

"I must decline. I'm just a baseline in technomancy anyway."

"You'll never know if you leave now. Ever wonder why the *Septenary* only has masters from six schools when the name refers to the number *seven*?"

"The Grand Master governs all the miscellaneous powers like technomancy."

"Then why hasn't anyone taught you technomancy?"

That was a good question. Piero frowned, sheathing his skean. "Alright, I'll see how the first lesson goes."

Reluctantly, Piero followed Variola through the labyrinth of tunnels which pitched and turned at odd angles. He glanced about furtively for any signs of an exit but found none. Instead, they traveled deeper into the belly of the hill without passing a single soul. After traversing a metal trestle, they arrived at a room embedded with electronics, the nerve center of Variola's terrorist cell. Gia sat cross-legged on the floor. She wore a headset with goggles, the kind used for virtual reality. Beside her stood the aforementioned noctuid-class bot, imposing even while inert. The ebony, six-foot behemoth looked as though it was chiseled from a solid block of obsidian. Thick cables sprang from its entrails, leading to consoles mounted on the wall.

"Find the other headset and put it on," Gia said taciturnly. "I'm about ready to begin."

Searching around, Piero spotted an identical headset sitting on the floor. Picking it up, he spotted long cables, similar to the ones sticking out of the bot, snaking back to the consoles. He shuddered, thinking that these cables were indistinguishable from the ones hooking the Cybogre to his metal coffin. He slumped down on the floor next to Gia.

Donning his headset, Piero felt the goggles and headphones stick to his skin. His world became dark and silent, his senses deprived. Slowly, the room grew brighter. He heard people scuttling about. This was not real. Yet, he knew this place. He was in the Isle Royale Opera House where he had watched Daisy dance a few times.

Piero sat on a raised platform in the front row, facing the stage. Choreographers often sat here when auditioning for new dancers. He was on the far right of a long table. The smell of tea lingered in the air. Sure enough, a full teacup sat on the white tablecloth as wispy steam billowed under his nose.

To his left, Gia sat at the center of the table. She busily tapped a tablet, seemingly unaware of him. She looked the same except she no longer wore her leather leggings. Instead, she was now donning a sheer white dress, resembling a ballerina costume from the mid-19th century. Further down, at the far-left side of the table, another steaming teacup sat in front of an empty chair. Piero craned his neck around to see whether anyone else was in the audience. However, the only other people were on stage, two men and two women, dressed in ballet costumes. Oddly, they had feathered wings attached to their arms. Piero recognized the white wings from Daisy's production of Black Swan. The ballerinas also wore feathered tutus.

"What's going on?" asked Piero.

"Just follow my lead," Gia responded.

"You've seen Black Swan at the Isle Royale Opera House?"

"Of course not. I've never been to the Capital. We're operating out of the memories in your brain."

"Why *my* brain?"

"You have to flip this bot before it kills you. Consider this your first test."

A light appeared from behind. Piero peeked over his shoulder to see the matte black bot enter the theater, stomping down the far aisle towards the stage. For a moment, he hoped it would keep going. Perhaps it would attack the dancers while he escaped. However, the bot turned towards the platform, thudding up the steps. *This is too real.* Piero slapped the sides of his head with both palms. *Maybe the point is tricking the bot into thinking it's not in a virtual world.*

Gia glanced over to the bot. "Noctuid, you may have a seat. The audition is about to start."

Gears whirled as the bot stared her down with glassy red eyes. "I am an Imperium stealth war bot designed for airborne assaults—"

"Yes, yes, I know that already," Gia countered dismissively. "You are named after a night-flying moth. But there are thousands of bots called noctuid."

"How do I get out of here?" whispered Piero.

Calmly, Gia turned to him. "Do you have any good names?"

"Nadia?" Piero offered.

"I don't suppose you're in love with a girl named Nadia," she teased. "Do Olivette and Daisy have a sister named Nadia?"

"I'm thinking of the actress, Nadia Turner, who was dating Blandon Stux."

Gia frowned. "I hate that guy."

"Me too. He's so smug—"

"I am an Imperium stealth war bot designed for airborne assaults and commando missions," the bot vocalized.

Gia turned back to the bot. "Your name is Nadia. Have a seat and enjoy the audition."

This time the bot complied . . . or at least attempted to. The wooden chair was too small to accommodate the bot's wide girth. Instead, the bot sat delicately on the arm of the chair.

"Tsk, tsk, that won't do at all, Nadia," corrected Gia. "At least try the tea before it gets cold."

"I do not require refreshments," the bot said mechanically.

"Where are your manners?" Gia asked, feigning anger. "Take the teacup."

The bot reached out, grabbing the teacup with thick fingers. The porcelain teacup shattered under the bot's steely grip. Splotches of black liquid stained the white tablecloth. Piero could not help but feel pity for Nadia . . . the killer bot.

"Pi, you're doing well so far," Gia said supportively while still staring at the bot. "During the show, hold a mental image in your head of Nadia Turner."

Piero grasped his teacup, feeling the heat. "I thought we were already in my head."

"Just do it," Gia scolded.

Piero took a sip from his cup. "Is this Oolong tea?"

Gia ignored him and turned to the stage. "Okay, dancers, you may start the audition."

The ballerinas began dancing *sur les pointes*. On the tips of their toes, the ballerinas twirled, accentuating their bird costumes. The male dancers executed a series of spectacular leaps, followed by pirouettes. Just as Piero started to enjoy the audition, a woman stumbled on stage, donning a white feathered skirt and a bird mask that resembled the kind medieval plague doctors wore. Her arms were bound in a straightjacket. She had a slight build, and her auburn hair was pinned back.

Piero sat up in his chair. "Daisy?"

"Shush!" Gia rebuked. "These are *your* memories."

"I don't remember my fiancé dancing on stage like this!"

"Then, you have a vivid, if somewhat lurid, imagination."

With raised wings, the performers circled Daisy, hiding her from view momentarily. When they lowered their wings, Daisy stooped with her back to the audience. Her arms were now unbound, hanging limp at her sides. Four silver hooks were looped through the straight jacket on her back.

Piero slumped in his chair. "Can you stop this?"

"I wouldn't miss this for the world."

The dancers spun around Daisy, maneuvering her towards the center of the stage where ropes hung from the ceiling. A ballerina artfully bent over and pulled the end of a rope off the floor. Dangling from the end was a metal hook. To Piero's horror, the ballerina gracefully hooked a silver ring to the back of Daisy's straightjacket.

Gia chuckled. "Pi, I had no idea that you're such a pervert. I don't think this scene is in Black Swan. At least Nadia's enjoying the show. She hasn't said a peep."

Piero gawked as all the dancers took turns hooking the rings to Daisy's back. When the last hook was in place, Daisy turned to face the audience. She awkwardly stepped forward several paces. The ropes lifted and splayed out from her back. Piero could not help but to again think of the long cables snaking out of the Cybogre. He shook his head to get rid of the mental image.

The ballerinas spun to either side of Daisy and gently caressed her sleeved arms. In tandem, they flapped Daisy's arms like wings. The male dancers shook their heads in unison, disappointed in the effort. Then, as if an idea suddenly popped into both their minds, the male dancers leapt off stage. They quickly danced back each holding a basket of feathers.

On stage right, the ballerina rested Daisy's outstretched arm on a male dancer's shoulder. She reached into the basket and, with poise, pulled out a feather. However, the point of this feather ended in an old-fashioned clothespin. The ballerina then artfully pinned the feather to the underside of the straightjacket sleeve. Daisy jerked, indicating the clothespin was also pinching her skin. The ballet continued as both ballerinas fastened feather after feather onto Daisy's underarms as she writhed in pain.

Before long, the ballerinas had completed a full set of harrowing wings. Through the bird mask, Daisy stole a long look at each wing. She fluttered slowly. Each of the dancers elegantly handled a rope and then tugged. With each flap, Daisy ascended a little higher. The rings in the back pulled her straightjacket tight against her chest. Higher she soared until she was over eight feet off the ground. As she neared the top of the stage, a spotlight shone down as if from the heavens, revealing a giant mirror among the four dancers at center stage.

Gia primly rose from her chair, waving for Piero to follow. She promenaded down the right side of the platform and over to the stairs by the stage. "Come, Nadia. Don't you want to be like us?"

A loud bang startled Piero. He jumped out of his chair, searching for the disturbance. Relieved, he noticed that the bot had just toppled her chair and crushed it while getting up. The war bot was now stomping towards him. Not waiting to see what would happen, Piero scurried down the platform, joining Gia on stage. The rhythmic thuds indicated that the bot was advancing close behind.

Gia walked over to the dancers as they strained to keep Daisy aloft. Their muscles were tightly drawn with exertion, their eyes fixated on the flapping woman in the bird costume. Walking beneath her, Piero gazed at his fake fiancé. *Where's the real Daisy? Is she mourning my fictional death?*

"Are you still holding the image of Nadia Turner in your mind's eye?" Gia asked irritably.

I'm a bit distracted at the moment. Piero remembered a screenshot of Nadia Turner when she was sunbathing in Hawaii. She had a deep tan and a revealing bikini.

"I know how to follow orders," Piero lied as he sidled up next to Gia who was admiring her reflection in the giant mirror. Amazed, Piero blinked repeatedly as Gia touched the glass surface and then pressed her hand into the mirror. She kept going, thrusting up to her elbow.

A drop hit Piero's shoulder, followed by another on his head. He glanced up, noticing that Daisy's firm legs were covered in a glistening luster of sweat.

"Focus!" ordered Gia.

Piero thought about Nadia Turner again sprawled out on the beach next to Blandon Stux. *I really hate that guy. He knocked up that singer from the talent show while he was one of the judges. If I was Nadia Turner's boyfriend, I'd treat her like a princess. I'd rub her feet after a hard day on set.*

The bot's heavy steps on stage snapped Piero out of his reverie. Gia had put her other arm into the mirror. In the reflection, Piero now saw the giant war bot looming behind him. Quickly, Gia passed into the mirror, disappearing.

"Where did she go?" asked the bot in its all too mechanical voice.

"Let's find out," Piero responded hesitantly. He put his fingers on the mirror; a cold chill ran down his arm. He pressed against the glass, and his whole hand disappeared.

"Why should I follow you?" the bot inquired.

"Do you want to transform your body?" Piero asked tensely. "Look at the bird above you. She was clumsy, stumbling about like an ugly duckling. With the help of her graceful friends, she went through a metamorphosis. Now she soars. Follow me and I will remake you too."

With that, Piero plunged into the icy glass. The thought of spending one more second with the war bot was more terrifying than what may lay ahead. He heaved forward, landing on a hardwood floor. Piero surveyed the scene, finding that he was in a mirror image of the opera house, though the dancers were absent. Turning back to the mirror, he did not see his reflection; rather, it was more like a window to the former stage.

There, dominating the glass partition was the war bot. Piero shuddered, still holding the image of Nadia Turner in his mind willing her to life. He felt a hand on his shoulder.

"This is the moment of truth," Gia said, reverently.

The bot raised its gauntleted fist to the window. Piero prayed that it would not shatter. Instead, the bot pushed through and a delicate, tanned human hand sprouted from the glass.

Flabbergasted, Piero stared transfixed as the bot replicated nay, gave birth to a new creature altogether. What came through the giant window was not a war bot. Not even close. Instead, a bikinied Nadia Turner fell out of the glass, spilling onto the floor. She laid motionless. *Was she dead! No!*

With a deep breath, Nadia sprang to life the metamorphosis was complete. The glass casing was merely a chrysalis for the grub of the noctuid, the night-flying moth.

"Welcome, Nadia," Gia said warmly. "You're now human like us."

Nadia rose tentatively on wobbly legs. She studied her toned arms and legs. Behind her, the glass shimmered, becoming a mirror again.

Gia smiled, "Spin around and see how beautiful you've become."

Slowly, Nadia turned to behold her reflection. She ran her fingers through her dark hair and then traced her jawbone. Her eyes glistened. A tear ran down one cheek and then the other. In a soft voice, barely audible, Nadia uttered, "I'm so beautiful."

Chapter 22

A starlit sky cascaded like glittering beads of dew set to plunge off the bristly fruit of the enchanter's nightshade. Raven took another hit off her joint. *Inconspicuous alabaster flowers bloomed from the bindweed like parasols on a sunny day in the park,* she mused.

"Ma'am, I think ya had enough," said Roy, kneeling as he continued to rub her right foot.

"You don't get to order her around," reprimanded Dante, rubbing her left foot.

Raven sighed as her hand-rolled doobie burned out. Relaxing in the patio chair had made her too complacent. Her purple-tinted glasses had slid to the end of her nose. Taking out her skean, she stretched her arm towards the barrel of burning trash. Waiting for the fire to heat her blade, she waved her joint in slow loops. "I told you that if I smoked this bud, we had to come up with something creative tonight."

Dante sat on the dirt, gently massaging her foot. "We can play strip poker. I have a deck of cards in my backpack."

"Always with the pervy stuff," complained Roy. "Why did ya bring cards on a mission anyway?"

"Shut up," Dante hissed. "You're blowing it for both of us."

"I think the lady meant comin' up with a creative way to find the Aconda girl."

"Precisely." Raven took the red-hot blade and held it up to the burnt end of her short blunt. She inhaled deeply, holding her breath. Slowly, she exhaled with a petite cough. "This is some good weed, Davey."

"Oo-wee, think I ah get a hit," Davey asked.

Raven peered over her glasses at the drifter who was slumped against the metal grill of the police truck. He poked two grimy fingers through the interlacing latticework in anticipation. She took another drag off the doobie. "Sorry, your mind is a muddle of oddities and curios already."

"When yuh deh in bad luck wet paper self ah cut yuh," the drifter slurred. "If yuh don't ah mind me askin', why I ah still in de pokey?"

"Yar a suspect in the murder of Gia Aconda," Roy intoned. "Since martial law is in effect, the doctrine of habeas corpus has been suspended."

"You're two for two tonight, Rear Admiral," Raven said. "For that, you get to massage my calf."

"Thank you, ma'am," replied Roy as he eagerly kneaded her leg.

Dante muttered a curse under his breath while still rubbing her toes. Raven considered her two minions. While Roy came up with the plan to set up a face-to-face meeting with the Aconda girl, it was Dante's idea to have the rendezvous at this abandoned airfield. Three hours ago, she had sent a secure text to inform Gia that her siblings were involved in a shootout on Isle Royale. While Raven knew she had stretched the truth, she also began to wonder whether it was enough to coax Gia out of hiding. Something was not right. The girl had not taken the bait.

The radio crackled loudly. "We have two armed irregulars headed your way."

Raven looked down at her lackeys. "Put my boots back on!"

The airfield was an ideal location due to its long sightlines, giving her snipers easy shots. Above, a squad of noctuid-class bots hovered quietly. The closest building was over four hundred yards away, so the only obstruction on the tarmac was the police truck.

Raven sheathed her skean and pushed her glasses up. Tapping the side, she switched to night vision while careful not to face the barrel of flaming trash. After a few heartbeats, she spotted the two civilians, an old couple with shotguns. Raven snatched the radio's microphone. "Have you identified them yet?"

"Negative," said the harsh voice over the radio's shrill speaker. "Do you want me to shoot them?"

The old couple froze. They must have heard that question as well. The old man slowly eased his shotgun off his shoulder before the old woman grabbed his elbow. She yelled, "We're both armed but don't want any trouble!"

"No one is going to shoot you!" Raven shouted back. "Come closer to the fire, so we can have a look at you."

The old couple plodded across the cracked tarmac. They were dressed in hunting attire with heavy backpacks. By the looks of it, they had spent a great deal of time in the jungle.

With a puzzled expression, the old woman asked, "You sure don't look like park rangers but—"

"Where's Gia Aconda?" blurted Roy.

"Who?" asked the old man.

"Pump the brakes, Rear Admiral," Raven chided as she approached the old man. She reached out and caressed his face. "We're all friends here. Tell me how you came upon this place."

The old man blushed. "My wife and I are bigfoot hunters. We have big game licenses and everything. So, we've been in the jungle tracking a big 'un."

"That's preposterous!" screamed Dante who rose to his feet.

"Sit and be quiet," commanded Raven, wagging her finger.

Sheepishly, Dante leaned back on his haunches. Raven stared at him until he put his butt on the ground. "Stay."

"I wish my husband would mind me like that," the old woman quipped.

"It's a subtle touch," Raven said with the joint hanging out her mouth. "When you say a bigfoot, are you talking about a genetically modified ape?"

"Indeed," said the husband emphatically. "The safari used gene editing to recreate a bigfoot."

"Gene editing is so unnatural," said Raven.

"You want to leave evolution to the mistakes of nature?" the old man asked. "Mother Nature is a dirty whore!"

Roy stepped forward, but Raven held him back. She puffed on her doobie. "Do you think eugenics is the way of the future?"

The husband nodded. "Coming masters of this planet will likely be more dissimilar from us than we are from Neanderthals, who were at least human; our progenies will be godlike."

"I've already given that some deep consideration," Raven said forlornly. "If I had offspring, I'd prefer that they be happy and normal."

"Happiness is merely a cocktail of naturally occurring drugs: oxytocin, serotonin, and dopamine," the hunter countered. "You can get all those at any pharmacy. The best method of making the populace experience a soaring degree of contentment over a long time is to engineer their biochemical structure."

"I disagree. Happiness comprises viewing your life, in its totality, as significant and valuable."

The husband seemed ruffled. "For me, happiness is no more than feeling pleasurable bodily sensations."

This last admission appeared to unnerve his wife. Raven shook her head. *This is the problem with using my mind-controlling ability. I induced this fool to be truthful. Yet, all I learn is that humanity is hopeless. Their lives are meaningless. People will never be happy so long as they crave. Perhaps to be happy, you have to eliminate all desire, but who would want to live in that world?* Raven just wanted to dismiss the old couple. "This has been a most illuminating discussion. I can assure you that there have been no bigfoot sightings—"

A series of explosions rocked the night sky directly overhead. Like shooting stars, one after another, four smoldering lumps crashed onto the tarmac around Raven. *The noctuid-class bots are down. Well, four out of five. There's one still up there somewhere.*

Raven spotted the bot overhead. It was no longer in stealth mode, but rather had shielded its body. As it fired its auto-guns, the surrounding jungle lit up. Screams echoed over the radio. "Taking enemy fire from *your* noctuid!" Static.

"Everyone run in different directions!" Raven screamed. "Run for your lives!"

"Oo-wee, I guess I ah goner," said Davey as he leaned against the metal grill.

Raven pulled out her metal wand and tapped her belt buckle repeatedly. Her vision blurred as her suit's honeycomb shields activated. In a few moments, her glasses adjusted for the field distortion. Raven backed up against the truck, hoping the noctuid would chase the easy targets. She needed the runners to move faster.

The radio crackled again. A mechanized voice purred, "If you surrender now, I'll spare your friends."

A thump echoed no more than one hundred yards away. Raven turned to see that the old man had stopped dead in his tracks in front of a black bot. After a few agonizing seconds, the bot lifted him off the ground, shaking him like a dog's chew toy. Nervously, Raven lifted the wand and pointed it straight at the noctuid. The wand vibrated vigorously in her hand. Nothing happened.

"Is that the best you got?" the voice droned over the radio speaker.

Raven ducked under the truck, hiding under the front axle. She prayed that her honeycomb shielding would be enough.

"Raven, you cannot hide from—"

Bam! The earth shook the truck, which teetered before toppling over. A smoking crater billowed out of the runway where the noctuid-class bot once stood. Rubble rained down around Raven.

"Oo-wee, dat ah close!" said a halting voice from the back of the truck.

Raven crawled over to the half-buried radio and snatched the microphone. "Is that the best *you* got?"

There was no response. Little by little, she rose on unsteady feet, her honeycomb shielding limiting her mobility. She heard a snap, crackle, and pop as the radio came back to life.

The voice sounded dejected. "Admittedly, I forgot about the missile launchers. I'm assuming you're holding a laser painter and there's a launcher nearby. However, I have my crosshairs on your friend right now."

Crack. A piercing scream echoed off the tarmac followed by a thump. Raven twirled the wand. "Who got hit?"

"You said no one was going to shoot us!" yelled the old woman, clutching her thigh.

Quickly, Raven's purple lenses traced the trajectory of the shot from the injured woman to a small ridgetop jutting above the trees. Pulling the microphone closer, Raven asked, "Do you have any last words?"

"What do you want to do before you die?" the rival inquired.

"Glad you asked as it seems pertinent." Raven stood tall, placing one fist on her hip. With her other hand, she held the microphone near her lips. Articulating each syllable in her Septenary manner of speaking, she proclaimed, "I have always wanted to blow up an entire hill, like in the movies."

Pointing the wand at the ridgetop, Raven felt it pulse in her palm. With intense vibrations, she called missile after missile. Within seconds, new lights joined the starlit sky as warheads penetrated the darkness. Screaming, the entire ridgetop erupted in white-hot liquid fire.

Raven tapped her belt buckle, dropping her shields. Moments later, a scorching blast of wind blew her black curls. The ringing in her ears slowly receded like an ebbing tide.

"I need another cigarette." Raven held her hand straight out and dropped the mic. She waited for another witty repartee, but the voice on the radio had been silenced for now. She had lost the urge for wordplay anyway as she surveyed the burning ridgetop and the fiery wreckage on the airfield. *Only a goddess could revel in this grandeur.* In a determined voice, she said, "If the radiance of a thousand suns were to blaze out at once in the sky, even that would not resemble the splendor of that exalted being."

Chapter 23

The standoff in the back alley had turned into a showdown. Riley pointed her sidearm at the mysterious stranger who had just intruded on her photoshoot. The light under her gun barrel shined directly onto the face of a boy. Not just any boy.

"Carlos?" Riley asked. "What are you doing here?"

Carlos raised a hand to his brow, shielding his eyes from the bright beam. He gaped at the newly scrubbed wall behind her.

"I feel that I should have a pistol as well," Steve suggested. "No one said to bring firearms. Is anyone else packing heat?"

"I just have my sandblaster," said Sandblaster.

Lickspittle stepped forward. "Let's put it to a vote. All in favor say—"

"Shut up!" Riley shouted over her shoulder.

"The boy's getting away!" yelled Zee-Barbara.

When Riley turned back, Carlos was gone. She sprinted down the alley, hooking left. Yards ahead, she spotted a short silhouette darting towards the street. Riley sped up. In long strides, she gained on her quarry. She lost sight of the boy when he turned back towards the refugee center.

Riley burst onto the street at a full, mad dash. She scanned the deserted blacktop, finding no one. *Impossible! He should be right in front of me.* Nevertheless, the motorway was empty except for trash blowing alongside the curb like tumbleweeds. She slowed to a jog, whipping her head around looking for the hiding boy.

Steve rushed up next to her, huffing, "Where did he go?" Riley spun around, loping backward. Her belly chain jingled melodically. The rest of the group was scuttling down the street towards her. Riley cupped a hand to her mouth. "Carlos! If you can hear me, please come out. You don't want to be alone in this neighborhood at night."

A few feet away, a pair of dim lights sparked to life next to a trash bin. The bulbs flickered before casting a magenta glow. Riley spun, aiming her sidearm. The light under the gun barrel revealed a rusty service bot sitting in a pool of oil. The stench was overwhelming. Raucously, the bot clambered to its goat-like metallic hooves. "My name is Carlos. How may I be of service?"

Zee-Barbara shoved the bot against the trash bin. "Did you see a boy running down this street?"

"Stop with the rough stuff, or I'll call the police," the bot said in a mechanized voice.

"We're wasting time," Lickspittle said nervously. "The boy's getting away."

"Perhaps, I can help you find this boy," intoned the bot. "What is his name?"

"Carlos!" Zee-Barbara yelled.

"Yes," said the bot.

"Yes, what?" asked Zee-Barbara impatiently.

"My name is Carlos. How may I be of service?" the bot repeated.

"You're an old service bot," admonished Lickspittle. "Bots have no names."

"I may be a bit disheveled and homeless, but I assure you that I'm as human as you," the bot protested.

Despite the bot's insistence, its shoddy metallic sheen and thin crooked legs belied such an assertion. The bot's bulbous head was cracked and dented as if it had rammed headfirst into a brick wall. The bot's entire physique looked as though it had been run over.

An idea popped into Riley's head as she turned to the bot. "*Carlos,* we do need your help. However, we're trying to find a boy who's also named Carlos. To avoid further confusion, can we call you something else?"

The bot rubbed its shattered forehead. "My full name is Carlos Roberto Pedrote-Suave. I was born in Panama and came—"

"Enough," Riley interrupted. "We'll just call you Roberto for now and—"

"Roboto has a better ring to it," Steve said haughtily. "If you're going to join the Watch, then you must use your alias."

"Is the Watch some kind of voyeur group?" asked Roboto. "Do you peak in windows and put up spy cameras?"

Steve patted Riley on the back. "Well, Belly Dancer did install a spy camera in the alley by my doctor's office."

"Are you a medical doctor?" Roboto inquired as it tilted its oversized head.

"Something like that," Steve said anxiously. "We're kind of in a hurry. Have you seen anyone lurking around?"

Roboto extended its long, thin arm, pointing down the street. "I saw someone enter the homeless shelter."

Without further discussion, they all ran towards the building. The bot clanked behind on crooked legs. Riley reached the stoop first and bounded up the steps, finding a startled mustachioed, older gentleman hunched over a portable table, displaying coins of various sizes.

"Good evening, madam," the old man greeted promptly. "May I interest you in some rare coins?"

Riley searched the stoop and doorway. The rest of the Watch waited at the bottom of the steps just out of the old salesman's view. She locked eyes with Steve who pointed and mouthed, "That's him."

Riley furrowed her brow. "Did a boy just run by here?"

"Perhaps we can help each other," the man said quickly as he reached into his coat pocket and pulled out a small coin. "I'm Ron Burnsfeld, procurer of rare coins. Look here, I have a millennial penny from the year 2000. This penny matches your outfit nicely. The copper in a penny alone is worth a hundred credits. Feel the weight."

Confused, Riley took the penny and held it to the light. "Pennies were made out of zinc. Besides, all currency is electronic now."

"That's what makes pennies so valuable. Nobody mints coins anymore."

"You want a hundred credits for one red cent?"

Burnsfeld tweaked his curly mustache. "It's a deal."

"What?"

"You've just been *Burnsfelded*," he said while rubbing his palms together. "We have a verbal contract, so pay up."

"Not so fast!" Steve raced up the stairs. He marched up to Burnsfeld and ripped off his fake mustache. "Aha! Caught you in the act. I always wanted to do *that* before I died!"

Before Burnsfeld could object, Steve flipped over the card table, sending coins plinking off the cement. Steve grabbed the grifter by the back of his coat and threw him down the steps. Thumping on the sidewalk, Burnsfeld's girth gave him extra bounce. He let out one moan before the rest of the Watch pounced on him like frenzied hyenas. Lickspittle held the conman down while Sandblaster punched him repeatedly in his fat belly. Furiously, Zee-Barbara stomped on Burnsfeld's hands with her hoof-like heels. Roboto wound up and kicked Burnsfeld in the head with a sickening crack. With glowing red eyes, the bot studied the motionless grifter. "You've just been *Burnsfelded!*"

Everyone froze for a heartbeat. Roboto wound up again before Sandblaster bodychecked the bot. Riley stood in shock, staring at the prone body on the sidewalk. "What the hell, Roboto?"

"I think Burnsfeld needs a doctor," Roboto intoned, turning its big head to Steve. "Luckily, we have a medical doctor who can help."

Everyone looked to Steve who was sweating profusely. "I didn't bring my medical bag. Yes, that's it. I can't treat a patient without proper medical gear."

Riley shook her head in dismay. "Who here had a bucket list item for beating a grifter to death?"

Bending over, Roboto cradled Burnsfeld's head in its metal hands. As if to punctuate the moment, Burnsfeld's tongue lolled out of his gaping mouth while blood dripped from both his ears. "He'll sleep it off," the service bot insisted.

"We have a bigger problem," Lickspittle said shiftily.

"Bigger than a murder rap?" Riley asked incredulously. Looking down the street, she spotted five dark figures shambling towards them. *A bot street gang! This is a bigger problem.*

"Get ready for a rumble!" Steve smacked his fist in his palm before pointing down. "Do you see this poor bastard on the sidewalk? That's what you get when you mess with the Watch!"

If the approaching bots heard him, they did not show it. They moved in formation down the street in shuffling lockstep. The bots began to twirl their makeshift weapons: rusty chain, pool cue with protruding nails, sharpened fan blade, steel pipe, and pointy cane.

"I find it unsporting that you bots brought weapons," Steve said with false bravado.

The bots lined up, facing the intrepid members of the Watch. A plastic bag tumbled between them. Sandblaster aimed his nozzle at the bots, though the spray would have little effect beyond scuffing the paint off their bodies.

Roboto shouted, "You damn dirty bots took my job!"

The lead bot lurched and swung his rusty chain. Crack! Its head wafted away like dandelion fluff on a windy day.

Steve ducked and hid behind the stoop. Crack! Crack! Crack! Bot skulls burst like popcorn kernels, raining down on the blacktop in steamy heaps. In a matter of seconds, five decapitated bots had fallen.

Regaining his feet, Steve gave Riley a sidelong glance. "Oh, that's right. Belly Dancer brought a gun."

Riley twirled her sidearm before holstering it. "You must have had a good view from behind the stoop."

Steve dusted off his tattered lab coat. "I'm a lover, not a fighter."

"I don't care to test that statement." She flicked the penny at him.

Steve snatched the penny out of the air and dropped it into his lab coat pocket. "I'm just happy we're in a Zero-Sec Zone."

"Unfortunately, we're not anymore," replied Riley. "We passed that a block ago."

"Throw some bot bodies on top of Burnsfeld," Zee-Barbara ordered. "Hopefully, the authorities will just think his death was bot-related, which it kind of was anyway."

"Dibs on the pointy cane," said Lickspittle.

"Filthy, stinking bots," Roboto intoned. "You got your comeuppance tonight."

"Am I the only one freaked out by Roboto?" asked Sandblaster nervously through his speaker. He turned his big helmet from side to side, looking for some affirmation.

"Let's break for tonight before our luck runs out," Steve directed. "I've had enough hijinks already."

"I can take Roboto back to my shop and patch him up," Lickspittle offered.

"Are you a doctor as well?" Roboto asked.

"Um, I have vocational training in robot repair," Lickspittle offered.

"I think I'd be better served by a real doctor," Roboto declared.

Steve looked uneasy. "Let Lickspittle take a look at you tonight and he can bring you over to my doctor's office in the morning . . . for further evaluation. That's it. That will do nicely."

"What medical school did you attend?" Roboto asked distrustfully.

Steve turned red. "Well, I did graduate—"

"Enough with the pretensions," Riley cut in, grabbing the sides of her helmet. "Steve is just a masseuse and Roboto is just a bot. The sooner you face reality, the better you'll feel."

"Am I still a sandblaster?" asked Sandblaster.

"Of course, you are," said Zee-Barbara sympathetically. "Don't let *anyone* tell you who you are. Belly Dancer has been ordering us around all night, destroying robots and beating a grifter to death—"

"I didn't beat up the grifter," Riley interjected, "Besides, I see him twitching—"

"I never try to be better than anyone," Zee-Barbara continued, kneeling beside the fallen conman. "I just strive to be better than myself. Who can say otherwise?"

Riley slowly proceeded down the steps and waded through the angry mob of costumed vigilantes. She kicked a headless bot out of frustration. In her anatomy class at the Academy, she had learned that the human brain could not feel pain. After listening to this unintelligible debate, though, Riley was certain that she could feel her brain cells dying.

Chapter 24

In the gloomy rock-carved chamber, the only illumination emanated from the flat screen hoisted against the wall. Nevertheless, Piero wore his red-tinted glasses if only to hide his eyes. He brooded uncomfortably on an old couch next to the noctuid-class bot which now called itself Nadia. Had it just been a simple name change, Piero would have applauded such a makeover.

However, the bot insisted it was human, taking on the persona of the actress. Earlier, the bot had surprised him while he was rummaging in the laundry room for spare clothes. Nadia was tired of walking around "naked" and demanded suitable apparel. Piero, ever the gentleman, searched for a dress in its size. Given its girth, though, Piero had to settle on giving it a green string bikini. Even then, while the bottoms fit snuggly, he had to tie shoelaces to the top to accommodate Nadia's barrel-shaped body.

Now, the bot draped its long arm on Piero's shoulder as they watched a televised program. Nadia's end of the couch sagged heavily under its enormous weight. It laughed intermittently at the antics of the character on the screen, a wizard who shot rainbows out of his fingers.

Piero rubbed the stubble on his face and head. "Mystic Mike looks nothing like me . . . not anymore at least."

The wizard turned his head and looked straight out of the monitor. "I think you're beautiful just the way you are."

Piero sighed. "It's one of those interactive programs for kids."

"That's right, young man," Mystic Mike said in an effete voice. "I can *see* you on the couch next to your bot."

"My name is Nadia!" the bot exclaimed.

"It's a pleasure to make your acquaintance, Nadia." Mystic Mike smiled broadly. "Today, we're going to learn about emotional support. Isn't that going to be fun?"

"No," growled Piero.

"Nadia, the young man on the couch next to you needs some emotional support," Mystic Mike said gleefully. "Are you his service bot?"

"Why do you insist on calling me a bot?" Nadia asked irritably.

Mystic Mike blinked. "I see my question has disturbed you—"

The screen changed abruptly to an entertainment news show. Piero put down the remote control. "Sorry, I couldn't take that wizard anymore."

On the screen, a handsome, modish reporter was interviewing celebrities at an afterparty near the Conservatoire. Piero gazed dully at the screen until the reporter stepped in front of Blandon Stux, who was touting a golden trophy in the crook of his elbow.

"That's my boyfriend!" yelled Nadia, clapping its big hands.

Piero shook his head. *Should I break the bad news to this bot or let it play out?* He watched the interview with lazy eyes.

"What's it like winning the award for Best Supporting Actor?" asked the well-groomed reporter with an overly big smile.

"I'm my own hero," Blandon replied with self-satisfaction while rubbing his trophy.

"You brought a beautiful date to the award ceremony," the reporter said smoothly with false earnestness that could only come from having rehearsed each line of the conversation. "Would you like to introduce her?"

Glued to the screen, Nadia sat on the end of the cushion, rubbing its giant hands together. Piero yawned sluggishly.

On the monitor, Blandon reached over and grasped a slight, feminine hand; he pulled a pretty woman into view, gazing down upon her with smarmy eyes. "I may have won an award tonight, but she's the real prize. This is my new lover, Daisy Demedici."

"What?" screamed Piero and Nadia at the same time.

Daisy smiled at the camera. "We just met yesterday, but I feel as though I've always known Blandon. You cannot control love. You have to grab it and ride it out."

"That's what she told me!" screamed Piero, adjusting his red-tinted glasses. "It was only a couple of days ago!"

"Who's that floozy with Blandon?" asked Nadia.

"That's my fiancé!"

"We have to go to Isle Royale and break up this—"

"What are you two yelling about?" interrupted Gia, lugging her rucksack. She loitered past the monitor before slumping on a cushy chair. "Is there anything on the news?"

"The news is very disturbing," Nadia continued. "My boyfriend is dating Pi's fiancé. Do you remember that flying ballerina from the Swan Lake audition?"

"I won't ever get that image out of my head." Gia shuddered before sneering at Piero. "Why is Nadia wearing a bikini?"

"We can't let Nadia run around naked," he replied, still transfixed on the monitor.

"I lost two bots tonight, so I'm not in the mood for your weirdness," Gia snapped.

Piero muted the monitor and patted Nadia's large hand. "Be a dear and find something for Gia to eat."

The bot huffed and stomped away on big feet. Piero waited a few seconds before resuming. "Did you capture Raven?"

"She escaped again. My bots managed to kill a civilian and wound another before missiles blew them up. Given that she sent me her secret location on a secure phone, Raven likely thinks I'm alive *and* trying to kill her."

"Raven is not the forgiving type. Rest assured, she will come for you."

"You know her better than me. How do I convince her to join us?"

"Like I already said, you won't. However, it sounds like you want an inside man on Isle Royale. Let me do it."

Gia looked down at her nails. They were grimy. She looked as though she had rolled around in the dirt. She sighed. "*Why* do you want to live in the Imperium?"

"If you have a why to live, you can bear almost any how."

Gia reached over and snatched Piero's glasses off his face. He protested as she scrutinized the red lenses. She tossed them back on his lap. "You look at the world through rose-colored glasses."

He lazily held them up to the glow from the monitor. "They just have a red tint that filters out all the rough edges of the world."

"What kind of life do you want?"

"Life has no anchor," Piero said indolently. "I think I'll just drift."

Chapter 25

"Oo-wee," said the drifter. "Dis ah fine house."

"Davey, you'll have to be quiet while I interrogate this prisoner," Raven instructed.

"Am I a prisoner?" said the bearded man on the leather couch. "Your assistant just said that you had an acting gig for me."

Raven calmly stroked the prisoner's dark whiskers. She studied his face as she pushed into his mind to make him compliant. *My, but you do look like Piero.* Raven strolled around the man's parlor, which was immaculate if a bit gaudy. The gold curtains covered a panoramic window, which was probably for the best given that his neighborhood was on fire. Raven turned slowly. "Are you the actor who portrays Mystic Mike?"

"Guilty as charged," the man said dramatically. "You can call me Mike. Did you want me to autograph some merchandise for you?"

"Oo-wee, I ah know yuh." Davey clapped his hands. "I ah like yuh show about de emotional support."

Mike pointed to a row of golden trophies on his mantelshelf. "I did win a daytime award for that show. The studio is rerunning the 'Emotional Support' episode today."

"Davey, go wait outside and see that we're not disturbed," Raven said tetchily. She watched Davey stroll out the front door, happy as ever, letting in a blast of hot, humid air. Raven turned back to her prisoner. "Pay attention, Mike. I just placed a large bounty on a man who looks just like you. So, every killer in Guyana will be knocking down your door in a few hours."

"Why would you do that?" Mike narrowed his eyes, confused.

"While I have seen you on viral videos, your show is banned in the Imperium for obvious reasons."

"I assure you that all characters on my show are entirely fictional; any resemblance to real people is purely coincidental."

"You satirize the Benevolent Imperator and mock his psychic abilities when you shoot rainbows out of your fingers."

Mike let out a high-pitched giggle. "It's funny when you put it that way. Perhaps I can make amends by producing a show at the Conservatoire where I praise all the Benevolent Imperator's fine features. I just watched the broadcast of Blandon Stux's acceptance speech. I think he would make a splendid addition to my cast."

Raven leaned in close, putting her nose just inches from his face. "I'm not here to recruit you to make propaganda films."

"That's a relief." Mike leaned back on the couch, wiping pools of sweat off his forehead with the sleeve of his red bathrobe. "I'm more of a method actor anyway."

"That's good to hear." Raven turned, sauntering over to a manticore statuette on a small podium. She studied the winged creature with a lion's head and scorpion's tail. "I need you to impersonate a janissaire. From now on you'll play a character called Piero."

"Well, work is work." Mike whistled as he got up and meandered away. "I'll get dressed."

Another blast of hot air hit Raven like a sirocco. She was about to curse Davey when she saw a familiar bald man. Trailing behind the visitor, Dante scuttled into the parlor before slamming the door. The athletic and lean visitor strode to the middle of the room.

"Are you here to replace me, Dirk?" Raven asked without emotion. "I've grown accustomed to being relieved of command."

Dirk smiled. "I'm here to replace Dante."

"What?" Dante exclaimed. "Was Roy behind this?"

Raven waved a dismissive hand. "Are you my new bodyguard, Dirk?"

"I would like to be your partner if that's possible," Dirk replied.

"It's not!" shouted Dante.

"You're dismissed, Dante," Raven ordered. "I can only handle one lovestruck fool at a time. Go back to Isle Royale and catch that silly Othello ballet."

Dejected, Dante shuffled to the exit. He looked back one last time before slowly opening the door. Hot air blew his perfectly cropped hair.

"Oo-wee, yuh ah look like yuh jus' be dumped!" hooted a halting voice from outside.

As the door slammed, Raven lolled her head around letting out loud creaks and pops. Her failure to find the Aconda girl had attracted the attention of the Septenary. Now, they sent Dirk to mind her or worse, undermine her. She felt exposed.

"I won't let anyone harm you," Dirk promised.

"I've done pretty well on my own so far," she replied. "Besides, your thoughts betray you."

"We're not in the Imperium anymore," Dirk whispered. "There are no rules here."

Raven took one finger and traced his collarbone. She gently stroked his throat ending at the cleft of his chin. "You are here to work. You will control your lustful thoughts. You won't make me feel uncomfortable."

Eyes glazed over; Dirk seemed to compose himself. "Of course, I'll behave like a professional."

If only the janissaires knew the truth about their collective, absentee father, Raven thought. *How will they react when this secret is exposed?*

"What are you thinking about?" Dirk asked.

"If I wanted you to know what I was thinking, I'd be talking."

"Touché, but am I in your thoughts somewhere?"

Raven pursed her full lips. "It's *your* thoughts that I find distasteful."

"I know times are stressful right now," he offered as he ran his fingers over his sweaty, bald scalp. "But I hope things will get back to normal between us."

"There is no normal with you," she chided. "The fact is that you're abnormal in every way. I'm starting to see why young Riley kicked you in the head."

"Hmm, not my best moment. Pi distracted me while Riley snuck up behind me."

A creeping notion rose from the pit of her belly. "A distraction, you say?"

"Pi charged me like a berserker, but the real attack came from behind. I felt a whack and then it was lights out."

"I think this would be a good time to contact Riley again."

Dirk crossed his arms, "The last time I saw her she was having the time of her life."

Chapter 26

This is the worst day of my life, thought Riley as she reclined on the leather-upholstered couch with an arm draped over her eyes, listening to the bubbling aquarium. Her body ached and her throat was raw. The cello music pounded on her eardrums. She had barely slept a few hours before getting a call from the Psychology Department.

"Do you know why I called you to see me?" asked the middle-aged psychologist.

Attempted murder, destroying bots, or firing a weapon in a public place? Riley gulped. "I can't say, Dr. Teller."

"When was the last time you destroyed a bot?" Riley winced. *How could he know so soon about the street shootout?*

Dr. Teller waited impatiently for an answer. Giving up, he looked down at the screen on his lap. "I see you're not talkative today. According to my report, you destroyed an Imperium sentry bot at the refugee center by stabbing it in the . . ." He trailed off as he studied the screen while tapping his chin with his thumb.

"Ass," affirmed Riley, barely containing a sigh of relief.

Still reading his screen, Dr. Teller acknowledged, "Yes, that's what it says, more or less. How did it make you feel?"

"I didn't feel anything. It was the sentry bot who felt something, mostly my skean up its—"

"Enough!" exclaimed Dr. Teller. "You're deflecting again!"

"Take it easy!"

Dr. Teller took a deep breath to regain his composure. "I'm just worried about your self-isolation. You work alone. You live alone. You have no friends on your online social network."

"You mean my Buddy account for the Academy?"

"I sent you a friend request and your reply was a cartoon howl that hooted, 'Whooooooooooo cares?'"

Riley laughed. "I love that owl. Besides, I never wanted a Buddy account; the Academy forced it on me."

"That's my point. You're young. Live a little. You should be going out at night with your friends and having a good—"

"I went out last night with *friends*," Riley interrupted.

Dr. Teller studied her. "Do you have any *evidence*?"

Riley spun on the couch and dug into her side pocket. She whipped out her phone and scrolled through her recent photos. Smiling, she turned her phone around and showed the psychologist the screen. He analyzed the photo for a full minute before commenting, "Which one's you?"

"I'm in the middle of the pack with the bronze helmet and the veil over my mouth."

He looked at her with raised brows. "Are you in a street gang?"

"It's a neighborhood watch; last night, we cleaned the graffiti off that wall behind us. I can show you how it looked before."

"That won't be necessary."

"As you just saw, I have an active social life."

"Well, it *is* something." He looked down his nose at the photo. "How did you meet these . . . *people?*"

"I came across them while investigating hex signs; someone has been tagging walls in my neighborhood with secret messages. I'm hoping they'll give me a lead to Eacles's disappearance."

"That's a lot to unpack, but unfortunately I don't have time to delve deeper into your delusional personality disorder."

"I'm not delusional! Eacles was investigating hex signs when he was abducted."

"How long have you been having these delusions?"

Ignoring the question, Riley continued ranting, "My *friends* and I are going to follow those hex signs and find out who kidnapped my mentor."

Dr. Teller smiled broadly. "Classic delusional personality disorder."

Chapter 27

"Who the hell are you?" The question shocked Piero out of his dreamless sleep. He stretched on the old couch as his brain slowly rebooted. He scanned the gloomy rock-carved room, locating the monitor where he watched the love of his life arm-in-arm with Blandon Stux. *Now, I really hate that guy. Why does my head hurt?* Piero sat up spilling a nearly empty bottle of rum on the throw rug.

Variola stood at the end of the couch, clutching a video pad. She thrust it in his face, hitting his nose with it. Piero scratched his aching head before reluctantly grabbing the flimsy pad. He found nine surveillance photos neatly arranged in a square like a game of tic-tac-toe.

Piero tapped the photo in the upper left-hand corner. The image expanded to fill the screen. "It's a picture of Raven."

"Look at the goofy fellow behind her," Variola said furiously.

He put his index finger and thumb on the face, then spread them wide to zoom in. Puzzled, he studied the image. "That's me."

"That photo was taken an hour ago. According to the laws of physics, you cannot be in two places at once."

"You're forgetting superposition."

"You're referring to the superposition principle: if two or more physical causes are vectorially additive and if the effects are proportional to the causes, the effects are vectorially additive."

"Well, it sounds dumb when you put it that way." Piero stroked the blond stubble on his chin. "I meant supergene."

"A group of linked genes acting in an allelomorphic unit?"

"That's the one."

"You're too dim-witted to be a spy."

"That a relief." Piero felt something icy on the side of his neck. A drop of blood stained his white shirt. He shifted his eyes to find a tapering, medieval-looking bronze dagger pressed to his skin. "Variola! What a sharp skean you have!"

"Skeans are for jinn," she replied sharply. "We have a different name for quick metal blades . . . anlances."

He placed one finger delicately on the flat of the anlance and slowly pushed it off his neck. "If it's bronze and pointy, I call it a skean. So, stick your skean somewhere else."

Variola narrowed her eyes. "Do I look like a fool to you?"

Keeping his head steady, Piero rolled his eyes over to Variola, checking out her shapely figure. "Honestly, you could be an exotic dancer for all I know. You certainly have the body for it. However, given this evil, underground lair as well as the cyborg sidekick, I'd venture a guess that you're some sort of supervillain."

Variola chuckled while sheathing her blade. Instinctively, Piero ran his fingers over his neck, feeling wetness. His fingertips came away bloody. "I always wanted to get a close shave. Can you wrap a hot towel over my face while I smoke a cigar?"

"You dare call me a supervillain?"

"You have to admit, the shoe does fit."

"The Beast, your Benevolent Imperator, is the real villain, but you're too innocent to figure it out. Who else lives on a fortified island with his own private army?"

"Isle Royale is the Imperium's center of power, and the military is there to guard the cold-water reactors. I used to work in a military building until you *liberated* me."

"I accessed the Buddy account for Janissaire Piero." Variola snatched the flimsy screen out of his hands. She tapped the bottom repeatedly before flipping it around. Piero's graduation photo filled the screen. "You do not look like this boy."

Piero pointed a bloody finger to his face. "A sassy medical bot altered my boyishly handsome looks to fool facial recognition software."

Variola tapped the screen again, pulling up the original photo of Piero with Raven. The image began moving. While there was no sound, Piero's doppelganger appeared to be arguing with Raven. Theatrically, the imposter waved his limp wrist around like he was twirling a lasso.

"That's definitely not me!" Piero fluttered his hand in the air.

"Then, he's a great actor." She turned crisply and stormed off.

Piero slumped on the couch. *Why do bad things keep happening to me?* The scuttling of long nails clicked on the rock-hewn floor. He glanced down to find Jocko underfoot. The monkey wore his tiny motorcycle helmet on his diminutive head.

Piero's eyes blurred. It felt like looking at a reflection through a window on a bright day. Fuzzy lines traced around Jocko's head like a circuit board. It appeared that Jocko's helmet suddenly became transparent. The little monkey stretched out his hand. *Friend?*

"Did you just talk?"

Jocko left his hand out. Piero reached down and shook it gently. *Friend!* The voice was in his head.

"Jocko, are you a telepath?" asked Piero.

The monkey hugged his shin and then crawled onto Piero's lap. Jocko looked fretfully down the hall. A few moments later, Piero heard the heavy footsteps of a bot. Nadia entered the room wearing an apron. "There's my man. What can I get you to eat?"

Piero rubbed his eyes as the bot thumped over to the old couch. The bot was covered in blurry lines similar to Jocko's head. Piero gulped. "I'm not hungry."

Nadia looked down at the empty rum bottle. "Drowning your sorrows." When it bent over to pick up the bottle, Piero could see through its metal body. He saw its exposed battery pack clearly.

"Are you checking out my butt?" Nadia asked as it slapped its backside.

"No!" he lied, worriedly.

"I can't let you boys forget that I'm a girl." Nadia giggled and skipped out of the room.

Piero closed his eyes. When he opened them, he could see the circuitry in the monitor hoisted against the wall. Something was flowing a cross the hazy lines.

"A current!"

Jocko reached up and touched Piero's chin. *Friend.*

"What's all the shouting about?" barked an angry feminine voice from down the corridor.

"Gia, come in here!"

Echoing soft footsteps preceded Gia's entrance. She moved gracefully as if moving atop a balance beam. *Dirk always said that dexterity comes from a superior nervous system.* Piero bolted up, cradling Jocko in one arm. "I can see circuits."

"So what?"

"I can see through that monitor's casing into the interior."

Gia squealed, clapping her hands. She ran over and hugged him, squishing Jocko. Gia pulled back. "You know what this means, don't you?"

Piero smiled. "I'm not going crazy?"

"You're no longer baseline! Welcome to level two for technomancy."

"Praise the Benevolent Imperator! If I can get to the fifth level, I can be a master!"

Gia's previous happiness left abruptly as she slapped him hard across the face. "There's no going back. The Septenary will kill you for studying technomancy."

Jocko soothingly caressed Piero's red cheek. *Hurt?* He rubbed the red mark some more before giving Gia a rude gesture. *Bitch.*

Piero slid back on the couch. "I can also hear Jocko's thoughts."

"I can too." Gia glared at the monkey. "Jocko's brain is mostly computer. That's why he wears a protective helmet."

"I thought it was more of a fashion statement like when rich folks dress up their pets for the holidays."

"I already told you that Jocko is smarter than you. This proves it."

"At the risk of sounding dumber, why does the Septenary hate technomancy so much?"

"The Beast is the most powerful precog in the world. He saw something in his future that made him want to stamp out technomancy permanently."

Piero stroked Jocko back. It was quite soothing and hid his shaking hands. "A few days ago, a technomancer tried to kill me in Isle Royale." He looked into her eyes, hoping that his admission evoked some kind of emotion or, at least, recognition. Sadly, he only found a vacant stare.

"Are you accusing me of something?" Gia asked him quietly.

"I just want the truth."

"I saved your life."

"What do you want from me?"

"I need you to help recruit Raven," Gia confessed. "The Cognoscenti believe you can win her over somehow."

"When I first mentioned the Cognoscenti, you pretended not to know about them. Now, you tell me that you work for them."

"I never heard of the Cognoscenti until you mentioned that name in my living room," Gia said angrily. "Guyana has always been a refuge for a runaway jinni or a lovechild like me. We maintain an underground railroad for psychics. When Raven contacted me, she just said that the Imperium wanted to get rid of some Leaguer pirates blockading Georgetown. I had no idea that the Imperium was going to invade. I never would have helped if she had told me the truth. Why is the Imperium here anyway?"

"I don't have all the answers. However, if you want to conscript Raven, then we'll do it my way. I'll have to meet Raven in person, so she can read my mind and know that I don't mean her any harm. You'll have to weigh the grave risk of losing me to get Raven."

"I like your plan," Gia blurted. "Let's get it done."

"Take some time to think it over."

"Already did."

Piero felt a small hand stroking the stubble on his forearm. He looked down at Jocko who was shaking his head. *Stupid.*

Chapter 28

The noonday sun beat down relentlessly, vaporizing the last bit of the night's rainfall into a suffocating, steamy haze that clung to the skin like a wet suit. The abandoned airfield looked worse in the daylight. Raven walked the runway until the cracked tarmac gave way to a deep crater. Here was the resting place of an old man, albeit a shallow, foolish curmudgeon who enjoyed hunting genetically modified monsters. Still, this carnage should not have happened. Raven vowed never to be caught off guard again.

For the first time, the reconnaissance team found a few of Gia's breadcrumbs. While there was proof that she was alive, finding her was another matter entirely. More's the pity, the forensics team only found small footprints near a tin shack within walking distance of the airfield. However, the trail ended in tangled brambles. If Gia had directed last night's attack, Raven would make her pay threefold.

Tapping the side of her purple-tinted glasses, Raven radioed the asterius, a surveillance aerial vehicle that resembled the black swallowtail butterfly. She searched the open sky but could not locate the asterius even with the aid of enhanced vision from her purple lenses. *I suppose if I could see it, then the vehicle wouldn't be very good at spying.*

Years ago, Raven had flown in an asterius. She marveled at its subtle beauty, the enormous forewings slightly broader than the rounded hind wings, which ended in teardrops. *How can anything that poetically beautiful still be so deadly?* The frames of Raven's glasses bent around her ears, allowing perfect stereo sound. The voice of the asterius pilot pounded straight into her skull. "We're in position, Mistress."

"My group is moving out," she replied.

Raven trekked back to the police truck. Davey had fallen asleep against the metal latticework grill. She was not sure why she brought him along. The slim hope that his drug-ravaged brain would spit out a clue was wearing thin. Next to him, Mike slept curled in a ball.

Both of her traveling companions, Roy and Dirk, were ready to journey on foot; they waited beside the truck, which offered no shade as the equatorial sun blazed directly overhead. Roy's face was wrapped in a gleam of sweat while his heavy eyelids drooped. Exhaustion already showed on the old naval officer's face. In contrast, Dirk looked jittery, like a racehorse ready to bolt out of the starting gate. He had turned his skean into a broad machete and was now slapping the blade's flat side against his palm. *Energetics should be demoted to a miscellaneous school,* thought Raven. *Why would anyone waste countless class time manipulating quick metal?* She was satisfied with merely being baseline in energetics.

Without saying a word, Raven led the trio across the broken tarmac into the tall, sharp grass. Given the recent attacks, Dirk had formally protested against this latest jaunt into the brush. However, Roy claimed that the asterius packed a bigger punch than a dropship. Raven took out her laser painter. Even though she was within range of a missile launcher, she hoped that she would not have to feel the heavy vibratos again. After twenty minutes of trudging uphill, she found the tin hut. Rays of light shone through the countless holes in the thin roof. Molten shrapnel from the obliterated ridgetop must have rained down on this area.

Boot prints crisscrossed the packed mud. The reconnaissance team had been through here. Raven followed a beaten-down trail a few yards that ended with a plastic flag planted in the dirt, marking the end of the team's search. She cupped a hand over her glasses and searched the sky again. "Asterius, are there any heat signatures ahead?"

"Sorry, Mistress . . . the ground temperature is ninety-eight degrees Fahrenheit, the same as a human body. The tree canopy is also blocking our view. I see a rooftop on the other side of the ridge. You will find it if you maintain your current direction."

"We're heading towards the building." Dirk stepped forward. "I'll scout it out first." Without waiting for permission, he moved quickly through the trees. Although he was out of sight, Raven could still feel his lovesick mind yards ahead. He was singing a sad song to himself again. She did not recognize the tune, so it must have been another Dirk original.

"I write lyrics that nobody hears, and down my cold cheeks, I cry hot tears . . ."

Raven gagged. *At least it's not about me this time.* She covered her ears, but the song continued in her head.

"I'm so lonely, I feel my heart cave in, so why won't you love me back, sweet Raven."

Bending over, she tried to vomit but bile caught in her throat. *If we survive this mission, I'll have to rewire his brain.* Worse, she also felt another infatuated mind directly behind, staring at her butt in her skintight suit. "Roy, focus on the task at hand."

"If I focus any harder, my eyes will pop out," Roy responded.

Raven stepped to the side, gesturing for Roy to pass. While he meandered slightly off course, Raven felt more comfortable with him ahead. When they crossed the ridge, the descent was far less taxing. They found Dirk waiting in front of a metal outbuilding, which may have been a farm shed in better years. Now, it was just another rusty, hollowed-out structure with a muddy pool inside.

As she approached, she sensed intense rage. *Why was Dirk so angry?* He looked passive enough leaning against the sheet metal wall. Waves of fury struck Raven with the full force of a tsunami. She had felt this ferocity before.

"Dirk, get away from there!" Raven screeched.

But it was too late. Something large bubbled out of the cool mud, a creature that Raven could not stop. Breaching the mucky surface, the hunchback who haunted her nightmares rose to full height.

Chapter 29

With a little trepidation, the protégé returned to the massage parlor on Skid Row. Her body shook involuntarily, quakes coming more from anger than fear. Still, the raw emotion felt better than the usual void in her soul. *I don't care what the psychologist says, I'm not delusional.*

The reception area had been recently cleaned but now smelled like motor oil. Riley recognized a familiar face behind the reception counter that had been unattended on her last visit.

"Do you have an appointment?" asked Roboto. It was dressed in a simple business casual shirt. Riley peeked over the counter to discover that it was not wearing pants. A pool of yellowish oil gathered under its chair.

"How can I help you?" Roboto inquired more sternly.

"You don't recognize me without my disguise," Riley said. "It's me, Belly Dancer."

"Of course, now I see," the bot said suspiciously.

The door to the examining room snapped open. She looked over to find Steve leaning suggestively against the doorjamb. "Well, well, you couldn't stay away from the good doctor. Receptionist, please clear all my appointments because this may take a *long* time."

"You don't have any appointments . . . ever." Roboto swiped through the screen on the counter.

"I'm only here to talk to Roboto," Riley said dismissively.

"In my professional opinion, your suffering from a lack of vitamin *me*," Steve muttered as he closed the door behind him.

She shook her head, hoping to forget that last encounter. "I need some information about your assault on a pedestrian. It was the night that a street sweeper ran over you."

Roboto gaped as much as any bot could. Its lower jaw swung like the flap of a vending machine. "What makes you think that I was run over?"

Riley's eyes narrowed while running her fingertips over the dent in the bot's forehead. "The man you attacked was my mentor."

"I didn't attack anyone," Roboto protested. "That night in question, I was just sitting in my usual alley. A family of migrants passed by. The boy did a little rap. I blacked out. I woke up in the gutter. Case closed."

Shouldering her backpack, Riley stepped around the counter to get a better look at the bot. Careful to avoid the oil on the floor, she leaned over to examine the crack on the bot's head, noticing that it was already soldered. She located the outlet to the bot's hard drive at the back of its skull, just above the neck joint. Riley set her backpack on the counter and rummaged through it until she found a thin black cord.

"Where are you going to stick that?" asked Roboto. "Lickspittle already poked and prodded me enough for one day."

"I'm just going to plug my monitor into this wall outlet," Riley lied. "Take a look at my screen."

When Roboto leaned over to study the monitor, Riley jabbed the plug into the back of its bulbous head. Roboto slumped in its chair, head bowed; her screen lit up. Downloading the bot's entire hard drive would take some time. However, the folder containing all of Roboto's verbal communications was already illuminated. She tapped the icon and then scrolled through the transcripts that were neatly arranged in chronological order. Riley skipped to the end and located the night of the attack, which actually occurred in the early morning hours of the holiday.

Riley listened as the sleep-talking Roboto plainly repeated what was displayed on the screen: "I don't wish to harm you. If you want to leave the Janissary, I have a position for someone with your talents. Just follow the hex signs. There is a janissaire with precognitive abilities who can sniff out deserters before they know they want to defect. I rolled the die, and this chance meeting was random enough to go undetected. I have some access to the Janissary network, but I need your password for the Logistics Branch."

The last line sounded eerily familiar. *Raven's imposter also pumped me for my password. Why is it so important?* Riley reread the text on the display to make sure she did not miss anything. *Follow the hex signs? Isn't that what Eacles was doing before he disappeared? His phone last pinged near the military warehouse on 34th Avenue.*

"What are you doing to my receptionist?" asked an au fait voice.

She peered over her shoulder in dismay; Steve was back. Genital warts would have been a more welcoming sight. "I'm just running diagnostics on Roboto."

"Why does he get all the attention?" Steve licked his lips.

Riley pulled a large plug out of her backpack. "Come any closer and I'll find a hole to stick this in."

He playfully wagged his finger. "Don't tempt me with a good time."

"Even Roboto has smoother pickup lines than you."

Steve crossed his arms and rolled his eyes to the ceiling. After a moment of seemingly careful contemplation, he responded, "All things considered, I find Roboto to be remarkably well adjusted."

"Is that another one of your professional opinions?"

"Of course."

"Is that your profession as a fake doctor or a male stripper?"

"I've recorded my best performances at the club." Steve stuck his nose in the air as he gave a half-smile. "If you'd like to see my portfolio, I can arrange a private screening."

"I'm glad I skipped breakfast; otherwise, I'd be throwing up right about now."

"We make a great team," he continued as he paced the reception area with his hands clasped behind his back. "We took down a shameless grifter, helped a downtrodden bot, and cleaned graffiti off our neighborhood's walls—"

"That reminds me . . ." Riley pulled out her phone. Looking down at the screen, she tapped the application for the spy camera. Confused, Riley stepped outside to the sidewalk and rounded the corner to the trash-strewn alley. The concrete walls were still clean of any graffiti.

Steve sauntered up next to her. "Looks like we scared the vandals away."

"You told me that the last time you had the graffiti sandblasted off the wall, it was back the next day."

"That was before we trounced Ron Burnsfeld," Steve boasted. "Word must have spread not to mess with 45th Avenue."

Riley checked her recent photos again. She found both pictures of the hex signs, the one here and the other by Murder Mile. *If those hex signs were erased, no one could follow them anymore . . . not even Carlos Aconda.* "I have to gather my gear and get to the wharf! I need you and Roboto to join me!"

Riley raced back inside the massage parlor. Steve put his hands on his hips, exhaling loudly. "Women are meant to be loved, not understood."

Chapter 30

The broad green leaves darkened the jungle terrain, giving the illusion of twilight even though the sun was at its apex. The heat was still unrelenting as vapors wafted off drying mud puddles. Piero and Gia had been hiking for hours, seemingly in circles. Worse yet, he had to carry Jocko who refused to sit in his baby carrier. Though, Piero would rather carry the little, helmeted monkey than listen to his incessant whimpering.

Piero knelt, setting Jocko on the dirt. Unhooking his backpack, he fished around for his canteen. He found it buried in the bottom, empty. Gia paced ahead before spinning around and walking backward. "We can rest up ahead near those boulders."

"I was hoping to find some weapons in this backpack," Piero responded as he yanked out his skean. He waved the bronze blade theatrically. "All I have is this."

"An asterius can pick up complicated weapon signatures." Mercifully, she stopped walking. "Be glad that your skean is low-tech."

"A compass is low-tech, but I don't even have that. I think we've been walking in a big circle."

"Don't be so dramatic; it's an ellipse. We've been orbiting the airfield waiting for Raven to return. I think she's back now."

Jocko perked up and sniffed the breeze. *Decoy.*

Piero looked over to the little monkey. "Decoy? What are you saying?"

Gia cringed. "That's a big word for him; he doesn't know what it means."

Piero zipped up his backpack and strung both straps over his shoulders. "I'm supposed to talk to Raven; that's the plan."

For the first time today, Jocko crawled on all fours towards Gia. She bent over to pick him up, but Jocko did not stop, continuing closer to the boulders. Gia frowned as she watched the clingy monkey assert some independence.

Piero slid on his red-tinted glasses to peer through the gloom. Something was not right about the boulder in front of the little monkey. Piero moved closer. The boulder moved too. Piero stood stock-still just yards away.

"Did you see that?" Gia asked in a clipped tone.

Piero dared not speak. The massive silhouette was over twelve feet tall . . . hunched over. In the dim light, it looked as though the creature was covered in gray mud. Jocko sat quietly on his haunches. Light glinted off his little, chrome helmet. He held out his tiny hand, palm up. *Friend?*

The monster calmly leaned forward into a beam of light that had pierced the canopy. Its head was enormous. An entire holiday turkey could easily fit into its giant mouth. One oversized arm rested on its knuckles while it stretched out its other towards Jocko, palm down. It was a giant ape that the world had not seen in millennia. Ancient bones of Gigantopithecus had been found all over the Tibetan plateau; scientists must have brought the creature ouf of extinction but for what mysterious purpose?

"Stupid bigfoot hunters," Gia muttered. "Letting their big game run around."

"Of course," Piero whispered in amazement. "Such a majestic animal."

Jocko inched closer. *Friend!* The tip of the bigfoot's large finger tapped Jocko's hand. The prehistoric creature grinned widely. With one swipe, the bigfoot scooped up Jocko and popped the monkey into its mouth. The bigfoot's humongous, yellowed teeth chomped down three times before spitting out the tiny, chrome helmet in a glob of spittle.

Piero blanched, feeling his bowels loosen. Gia screamed. All hell broke loose. In his peripheral vision, he saw Gia run away, waving her hands in the air. The bigfoot rose on its thick legs and roared. Piero watched in horror as the animal beat its chest with giant fists. He ran faster than he had ever run before. His legs burned as he weaved between trees. He sliced branches with his skean, climbing a ridge in the general direction of the airfield. After looping around all day, he aimed at what he thought was the center of the circle.

The loud crashing behind Piero motivated him to pump his legs faster. He ducked between narrow gaps in the trees hoping the beast could not follow. Heavy grunting bore down upon him. He did not look back. He had to focus and remember his training. *Damn you, Dirk! You didn't prepare me for this!*

Earsplitting bangs echoed ahead. *Gunfire!* Help was coming. Piero ran to the shooting. A rusted-out metal structure lay dead ahead. He stumbled. Spinning, he crashed into the side of a sheet metal wall and ricocheted off. He landed in the middle of a battle.

Waves of rage slammed into Piero as he grabbed his aching head. A different monster loomed over him, covered in large mushroom shielding, the Cybogre. Feet away, a woman huddled in the fetal position whimpering in pain. *Raven?* On top of her, a man in a bloodstained, white uniform rested motionless. His dead fists till clenched a smoking handgun. Behind them stood a bald man covered in honeycomb shields, blurring his features; his only weapon was a long bronze machete, another janissaire.

A thunderous boom shook the earth. The ghastly giant ape had crashed headlong into the Cybogre, pinning him to the ground. Concussive blows rained down on the hunched cyborg. The monsters grappled. The bigfoot's lethal grip slipped off the Cybogre's ever mushrooming shields. Unfazed, the bigfoot repeatedly stomped on the metal body, keeping his adversary on the ground.

The honeycomb shielded man stepped forward; he now wielded a metal wand in his other hand. *Is that some sort of laser painter? Benevolent Imperator bless us; we're way too close for missiles!* The shielded man pointed the wand at the fighting beasts. Piero cringed as he heard the wand's vibrato and then the screeching of an approaching rocket. *Ah well, I had a good run.* The explosive shockwave rattled his teeth. But he was still alive... somehow. A bright-orange flower blossomed in the sky; an aerial vehicle plummeted to earth. Piero pointed. "You shot down an asterius!"

"That's impossible!" exclaimed the man with the wand. "I aimed at the monsters."

The voice was too familiar. Piero cocked his head. "Is that you, Dirk?"

"Do I know you?"

A guttural howl echoed through the jungle. Piero turned to see a chainsaw blade sticking out the back of the bigfoot. The blade cruelly sawed its way up slicing out through the ape's big shoulder. The bigfoot slid limply to the side as the Cybogre rose. A bloody chainsaw jutted out of the hunchback's right arm. When Piero locked eyes on the metal giant, the waves of rage intensified.

Piero now knew that the Cybogre's wrath would not spare him. Seconds away from certain death, Piero played the only card left in his losing hand. "Dirk, there's something you need to know. The Cybogre's innards are made of quick metal."

Piero felt a quick change in the Cybogre's emotions. Rage gave way to shock as Dirk stepped forward and swiped with his hand as if batting away an annoying bee. Bronze sludge seeped out of every joint of the monster. The Cybogre took one step forward. The behemoth went to his knees. The giant fell. The giant died.

Chapter 31

The tuk-tuk scooted down Lakeshore Boulevard past the faux wood docks. Against her better judgment, Riley let Steve and Roboto join her in the back of the motorized rickshaw rather than find their own. The driver broke suddenly in front of a military warehouse. A simple chain link fence skirted the area, which must have barely kept the homeless away.

"You pay me ten credits," barked the migrant driver.

"You told me eight credits," snapped Riley.

Both Steve and Roboto quickly exited the vehicle. Roboto muttered something about forgetting his wallet before waddling off.

"Eight credits for you," the driver retorted, holding out his electronic pad. "One extra credit for each passenger. You pay me now. Next time take auto-car, cheapskate."

Reluctantly, Riley looked down at the screen. She tapped a zero next to the line for gratuity and then waved her palm over the screen. When the backlight turned green, she stepped out just as the tuk-tuk zoomed away.

"Isle Royale used to be a national park," Steve bemoaned. "There was once a beautiful beach here; now, look at all this urban blight."

Shouldering her backpack, Riley searched around for a place to hide her spy camera. The streetlight was just a smooth post. The warehouse itself would offer the best angles. She unsheathed her skean and began slicing through the rusted links of the fence.

"Breaking into a military warehouse, are we?" Steve jested. "You *are* a naughty girl."

"Are you going to aid and abet, or just watch?" she replied, sheathing her weapon.

"I'm more of the hands-on type." Steve gripped the cut fence and pulled off a triangular section.

Ducking inside, Riley proceeded to the warehouse over weedy, potholed concrete. Close to the shoreline, the concrete gave way to smooth faux wood planks made from polyvinyl chloride, a space-age synthetic polymer. She stomped hard on the plastic planks. *These docks will outlast the pyramids.*

Riley checked the warehouse for any distinguishing features, but it looked like the rest of the utilitarian buildings that disfigured the area. Broken windows dotted the second floor of the warehouse, an ideal location for her camera. However, that was no easy climb. She looked back to the fence, spotting both Steve and Roboto trudging towards her. *Nothing to see here. Just a half-dressed bot out for a stroll with a guy in a lab coat.*

As she rounded the right side of the building, she discovered neatly stacked crates. Riley examined one of them, a three-foot cube. Knocking on the surface, she determined that it was likewise made of hard plastic.

"Is this a clue?" Steve asked snidely. "Oh, there are crates outside of a warehouse. I'll alert the media."

"Actually, these are meter hexahedra," Roboto corrected. "Each side is one meter long and wide. Before the Imperium scraped the metric system, these were standard shipping containers. Each box has a volume of one cubic meter also called a kiloliter."

Steve guffawed, "You're full of useless information—"

"Each box is a hexahedron!" Riley exclaimed. "What do the numbers on the sides mean?"

"What numbers?" asked Roboto.

Riley closely inspected the plastic container. No numbers. *Why put numbers on reusable crates anyway?* She jumped on top of the box and proceeded to the next one. The surface was slick. Looking up, she noticed that the roof slanted in her direction. She pushed herself up to the next box.

"If it's all the same, I'm going to stay down here," moaned Steve. "My lunch break is almost over, so I'll just check the front door."

After climbing onto the third box, Riley could easily reach the overhang of the slanted roof. She pushed her body up and kicked a leg over. She dug her boot heel into the shingles, gaining some traction before rolling awkwardly over her backpack and onto the rooftop. If Eacles had been up here, she imagined that he would have been more agile.

Riley walked to the apex and then followed the highpoint towards the shore. A southern wind was kicking up whitecaps on the lake. *The water is deceivingly inviting,* thought Riley.

Years ago, on a warm spring morning, she went to an empty beach on the north shore. She dove into the high waves to find them icy cold. Her teeth chattered. As she desperately swam to shore, the undertow pulled her back. The frigid waters numbed her limbs as she flailed helplessly. When she finally made it back to shore, her skin was a light shade of blue.

Shivering, she sprawled out on the dry sand like a lizard warming up in the morning sun. What had seemed so inviting had tried to kill her.

Riley was still trembling when she came out of her waking dream. She stumbled near the edge of the roof before catching herself. *Stupid postcognition almost got me that time.*

From the rooftop, she surveyed the dilapidated structures. The Benevolent Imperator chose this island due to the surrounding deep, frigid waters. In the winter, a natural phenomenon called sea smoke rises eerily from the surface. The groundbreaking invention of cold-water reactors turned Lake Superior into a modern gold rush. *All you need is icy freshwater to make electricity nowadays.*

"Hey, the door's unlocked," Steve muttered from below. "So, I guess we're just trespassing at this point."

Riley looked down to find Steve and Roboto next to a large sliding door. The pair had managed to creep beneath her very nose. Her mind grew more distracted every day. Something was off. "Don't go in!"

Steve shuddered, glancing up. "Where did you come from?"

"There's something deceptively inviting about this place," Riley said pensively. "Like when it's really hot and you just want to jump in the water."

"I don't feel hot at all," intoned Roboto.

"I can't explain it, but my postcognition is flaring up."
Riley rubbed her temples.

"Sounds like you explained it perfectly," Steve
mocked. "Do you get a rash every six months as well?"

Riley walked to the edge where the roof sloped
down near a broken window. She dug out a spy
camera and reached under the lee of the roof. Lodging
the camera snuggly, she adjusted the angle, so the lens
pointed inside the warehouse. While still on her belly,
Riley slid out her phone, tapping it repeatedly until the
camera focused properly.

With fists on his hips, Steve stared impatiently. "Well,
this is anticlimactic."

Riley ignored him while installing a second
camera, which pointed at the warehouse door. Keeping
one eye on her phone, she adjusted the camera slightly.
Without looking, Riley reached into her bag, feeling
for the spray can. She pulled out a can of epoxy resin
and glued the cameras firmly in place. A tornado could
not budge the cameras now.

Satisfied, Riley stretched back, letting her head dangle
off the ledge. As the blood rushed to her brain, she
spotted a figure in her upside-down view. A bot was
marching towards them, but it was not a run-of-the-mill
service bot like Roboto. It was a military bot.

"Run!" yelled Riley.

Both Steve and Roboto hurried back the way they
came. They headed right towards the military bot.

"The other way!" shouted Riley.

The pair spun around, heading in the opposite direction. Steve was surprisingly light on his feet as his lab coat fluttered. Roboto, however, had seen better days and limped behind. *I have to buy them some more time.* Pulling out her skean, she pried off the top of the spray can. Condensed resin oozed out in thick slurps that she let drip onto the faux wood planks. When the military bot thumped closer, she dropped the can in the puddle. Instead of bouncing, the sprayer stuck to the epoxy resin. The bot immediately trooped over to the can. As the bot stood in the middle of the puddle of resin, Riley squirmed from the lip of the roof. She could not hear anything from down below. Stillness indicated that the bot was not going anywhere for a long time.

Above, white fluffy clouds floated effortlessly across the azure sky. Riley lounged on the dirty roof of the warehouse contemplating her station in life. *I've never been off this accursed island. Why do I have to stay here and find the Aconda boy, while Raven gets to vacation in the tropics on the slim pretext of looking for the older sister? I can only imagine the fun Raven's having right now.*

Chapter 32

I t felt like every cell in her body was on fire. Raven would have screamed in agony had she been able to draw a breath. As quickly as the onset of the throbbing torture arose, it brusquely abated.

Raven fell into an abyss of a feverish sleep only to be awakened by rough throated shouts. Her feet were pinned together, and her arms dangled lifelessly to the side. Her body swayed back and forth as if swinging in a hammock.

Blinking her eyes open, she saw a stranger, a bald man, but not Dirk. Yet, he had a familiar voice. "She's awake."

Raven tried to kick her feet, but the man's grip was too tight. She writhed and twisted her hips. *I'm being carried!* "Put me down!"

With a heavy thud, Raven hit the dirt. She hurriedly pulled her knees to her chin and groped for her skean. *Where's my blade?*

"You're safe now," said a familiar voice from behind.

Raven twisted around, exhaling at the sight of Dirk. She croaked, "Where's my laser painter?"

"Mistress, you've been unconscious for a bit." Dirk put his hands on his hips and took a deep breath before continuing. "I don't know what happened to you, but you blacked out during the Cybogre attack."

"She didn't just suffer a blackout," the other man corrected. "The Cybogre emitted strong emotions that crippled anyone with empathic ability. Fortunately, I'm just baseline, while the mistress here got a full dose."

Recognition eluded her. Slowly, Raven squinted her eyes and then shut them. She reached out with her mind to find a familiar persona. Surprised, she dug deeper into her target's mind. However, Raven felt a door slam as the man quickly pushed her out. She gave a knowing smile. "I trained you well, Piero."

"We don't have time for any mind games," Piero said as he snapped his head around. "We have to get you out of here."

"Where's the asterius?" Raven slurred, closing her eyes.

"Dirk, do you want to answer that one?" suggested Piero.

"A missile shot it down," Dirk replied vaguely.

"Gia rigged the launchers again, so we can't call for air support," Piero clarified.

"Is she close by?" Raven's eyes fluttered open. "We have to capture her."

Piero sneered, "The last time I saw her, she screamed and ran in the other direction—"

"Enough chitchat," Dirk interrupted. "Mistress, if you can walk, then please get up. Otherwise, I'll be happy to carry you. The airfield is just over this ridge and the police truck is still on the tarmac."

Memories from the night before made her shudder. "Did you see the crater in the tarmac? If Gia has control of a launcher, then that's the last place you want to go."

Dirk nodded. "If we hug this side of the ridge, we should be out of the launcher's line of sight. The Cybogre is dead, so we don't have that—"

"How did you kill it?" Raven asked.

"I melted its internal machinery," Dirk bragged. "The innards were made from quick metal for some reason; I finally found a new use for my energetics."

Raven looked at him suspiciously. "How did you see into its inner structure?"

Dirk frowned. "Piero told me."

"Ah, things just got more interesting," Raven purred as she turned to Piero. "How did you know about its weakness?"

"*He* had a name, Bjorn," Piero corrected. "And he was a badass."

Raven slowly rolled her eyes and locked onto Piero. She stretched out a hand to touch his face; Piero jerked back like a snake had tried to bite him.

"Stop with the mind control!" Piero shouted.

"Show Mistress Raven some respect!" Dirk shouted back, shaking his fist.

Piero ignored him, still locking eyes with Raven. "We all have to get out of here now!"

"From what you told me, we're in an advantageous position," Raven snarked back. "We're hot on the trail of a fugitive, we knocked out her best weapon, and you're impeding my progress."

"I'm telling you to wake up!" Piero hollered. "You're not chasing anyone. You're being hunted as we speak. You're not in control here."

The boy has never acted this way; he's openly rebellious. I'm not getting the reverence that a mistress deserves, which can only mean . . . the boy knows too much.

Raven stood and brushed the dirt off her suit. She turned to Dirk. "We have an entire army out there. Tell them to shut down the launchers. Then, have a convoy of armored vehicles pick us up at the airfield."

"Yes, Mistress." Dirk turned and walked up the ridge. Still, he kept a wary eye on Piero.

"We need to keep moving," Piero insisted. "With all due respect, there's a lot you don't know about the Cognoscenti."

"You address me with such disrespect. You must have already gone native. The Cognoscenti have filled you with propaganda, haven't they?"

"Gratitude was never one of your strong points. Why show appreciation when you can just control how people feel about you?"

"You're a deserter. The punishment is summary execution."

"Remind me to never save your life again." Piero walked away. He did not look back.

Raven stepped forward but stopped. The boy was lost to her. From the quick peek into his mind, she saw that he would never again let anyone control his destiny.

Chapter 33

Walking down Lakeshore Boulevard, Riley found it impossible to hail a tuk-tuk. Several passed by, but they were already loaded with passengers. Catching her reflection in a shiny shop window, she felt even more downtrodden. Her dirty clothes and rugged backpack made her look like someone who Pi would have called a "displaced person." All Riley felt like was a bum. It was no wonder the tuk-tuk drivers refused to pick her up.

Whizzing low over the boulevard, a black auto-limousine slowed down and landed on the corner of 38th Avenue, just yards ahead. *Rich folks have to waste their money somehow. The pervert must think that I'm a hooker or a teen runaway. Either way, I'm putting some metal into him.*

The limo's side door hissed open; she palmed the hilt of her skean. However, the passenger compartment was empty. Riley looked inside. *Very swanky indeed.* The flat-screen monitor was bigger than the one in her studio apartment. Riley patted the cushioned seat. *Rich Corinthian leather not the faux leather vinyl of auto-cars.*

The monitor activated, showing a grumpy, older man with white hair. "Well, are you getting in?" asked Master Albus.

"I like your ride."

"It's not my *personal* limousine. It belongs to the Academy."

Riley stepped inside and slouched onto the comfortable seat while patting the armrests. The side door hissed shut and the engine whined. She sank deeper into the cushion as the limo jetted upward and then banked sharply to the right. She was headed to the Academy.

"What's all this about?" Riley demanded.

"I obviously need to talk to you in person; thus, I'm treating you to your first limousine ride."

Embarrassingly, he was right. Janissary ascetics kept her from many of the Capital's simple luxuries. She had never been to the opera or polo grounds. What grieved her the most was that she had never visited a fancy spa. In fact, Steve was her first masseuse. *Maybe I do need psychiatric help after all.*

Riley searched the cabinet, finding half a bottle of brown liquor. She spun it in her hand, letting the liquid slosh around. According to the label, the malt whiskey had been aged for thirty years. She unscrewed the cap and sniffed.

"Don't drink my scotch," Albus said.

Riley wavered. She had forgotten that he was still on the monitor. He seemed so still and lifeless, like a screenshot. She smiled, holding the liquor towards the monitor. "Is the bottle half full of half empty?"

"I'm an eternal optimist, so I'll let you have one swig."

Riley put the bottle to her lips and titled it gently. The syrupy liquid burned her tongue and torched her throat as she gulped it down. She wiped her mouth on her sleeve. "Smooth."

"Now that I think of it, bring the bottle with you. I could use a drink when you get here."

Riley quickly screwed the cap back on. The limo tilted left. She saw tall buildings out the window, indicating that the limo neared the government complex. Feeling uneasy, Riley looked down on the masses in the plaza. The ragtag protesters milled about aimlessly among their tents like zombies.

The limo slowed as it approached the side of the Academy that resembled a Mayan style stepped pyramid. Rather than dropping to the parade doors at the lower level, however, the vehicle hovered over the top of the building. *Oh, hell no. This is not happening.*

The limo landed on top of the Academy's highest story. Only dignitaries and officials were allowed to use this entrance. The limo's side door hissed open. A sentry bot stood close, eyeing her backpack. "Welcome Protégé Riley. You have a meeting with Master Albus in the Septenary council chamber *now.*"

Why is this happening to me? Riley slid out of the limo. "Acknowledged."

The roof door was open. Riley cautiously descended the steps to the inner sanctum of the Janissary. If the Academy was a Mayan stepped pyramid, then the Septenary council chamber was the temple where the ritual human sacrifices were performed. Facing the full council was never a good prospect. *Wait! Mistress Raven is still in Guyana. This can't be a council meeting.*

Riley stepped through the threshold to find a beautiful panoramic view of the city. Three walls were made of glass. Just outside was a narrow balcony that wrapped around the chamber. Seven gilded throne-like chairs formed a semicircle in front of her. The soft, white carpet made her feel like she was walking on a cloud.

Hugging the bottle of scotch, Riley felt underdressed. Her shabby clothes were still dirty from crawling on top of the warehouse. The strap of her backpack dug into her shoulder. She was careful not to rub up against anything in this room out of fear of leaving a black stain.

In sharp contrast, Albus wore a crisp white tunic with gold trim. The pale janiform insignia seemed to meld into the fabric on his chest. He stood next to the one wall that was not made of glass, which also contained the only exit. The wall was full of colorful, illuminated screens forming a quilt-like pattern.

"I'll take that scotch now," Albus muttered as he drummed his fingers on a pad and scrutinized the monitor in front of him. He stood near a portable table that supported a single crystal goblet full of ice cubes. Unsure, Riley filled half the goblet with scotch to the sound of cracking ice.

"Keep going," Albus said without looking.

Riley topped off the goblet. The sour scent made her dizzy. The air in the chamber was the same temperature as her skin. She just wanted to curl up on the white carpet and fall asleep.

With a thud, Albus's pad hit the table. He grabbed the crystal goblet and took a long pull. "That *is* smooth. So, what have you got for me?"

"I don't know why you summoned me."

Albus laughed and drank some more. "Oh, you think you're in trouble. Well, you are, but that's not why you're here. I just needed to talk to you in private."

If he was trying to put her at ease, Albus was doing a poor job of it. Riley wrinkled her brow. "Why not just meet in your office?"

"Ah, that's difficult to explain. I know for a fact that this council chamber is bug-free."

Still confused, she asked, "So, you're working out of the council chamber?"

"For the time being, I am. Now, let's ease some of your obvious anxiety and get down to business. Have you located the Aconda children?"

"It's still a work in progress."

"Do you have any *evidence* that you are looking for them?"

Evidence? thought Riley. *There's that word again. Dr. Teller also demanded evidence from me, proof that I had friends. Do I have to record my entire life?* She shifted slightly from foot to foot. Something jingled in her backpack. Inspiration rekindled her mind. "I *do* have some evidence. It might be easier if I showed you."

Riley set her dirty backpack on the portable table. She flinched as a puff of dust wafted off her bag. She unpacked her electronics and thick cables. The giant screens on the wall dwarfed her little monitor. "May I synch this up with your wall monitors?"

"I insist. What am I going to see?"

"It's the bot attack on Piero."

Next to Albus, a large screen lit up showing a point-of-view video from Roboto's eye camera. Above that screen, another one streamed computer codes. While the hard drive was downloading, Riley pulled out her phone. On two large screens, she displayed the hex sign that was on Steve's massage parlor wall as well as the one in the alley near Murder Mile. Quickly, she cropped out her fellow Watch members from the second photo before Albus noticed. *That would have been difficult to explain.* On three other screens, she posted the live feeds from her spy cameras.

Silently, Albus surfed through the hard drive, calling up various partitions onto his screens. He frowned. "It might be easier just to download the hard drive into a blank service bot."

Riley cringed at the thought of another Roboto. "The data is corrupted. The service bot thinks it's human."

Albus gave her a sidelong glance. Pretending not to notice, Riley pointed to the live feed from the warehouse. "I anticipate that Carlos Aconda will show up here soon."

"Why?"

"That's where Eacles went missing. He followed the hex signs to the warehouse."

Albus touched the screen nearest him, activating the audio. The video showed Piero near a vandalized streetlight that was spitting out sparks from a cracked fuse box. Transfixed, Riley watched the attack for the first time from Roboto's camera. The bot had charged Piero but ended up ramming the light post. Eerily, the bot spoke in a feminine, mechanized voice. "I don't wish to harm you."

Folding his arms, Albus did not speak for a half-hour as he watched the video feeds. Unfortunately, Riley had forgotten to edit the later scenes where Roboto met the Watch members. *This was going to be difficult to explain.* From the video, it was apparent that Riley floundered as she searched for Carlos.

Albus glanced over to the other screens displaying the graffiti. "Did you take these photos of the hex signs?"

"Yes."

"Are there any more still up?"

"Pi showed me one near his apartment but—"

"I've already seen that one." Albus surfed the hard drive some more. He sighed. "I don't need this right now but can't ignore it either. I'll have a bot crash team ready by the warehouse."

"I wouldn't trust bots at this point."

"Yes. I'll use mercenaries with low-tech weapons."

"The Janissary uses hired guns?"

"They're just street thugs who kidnap people. When you have a shoestring budget like the Logistics Branch, you have to cut corners."

This was a side of Albus that Riley did not care for. She thought about asking for military intervention but hesitated. "What do you want *me* to do?"

"I'd like to tell you, but you have proven yourself unruly. You've been out there all-night playing vigilante. On top of that, I have Mistress Raven up my ass complaining about missing children."

"Raven gave me a pep talk as well," Riley said sarcastically. "How's she doing?"

"Pretty good considering the Cognoscenti tried to kill her."

"I thought the Cognoscenti were just a conspiracy theory."

"Now, they're a conspiracy fact." Albus shook his head, betraying his calm facade for a moment. He took another sip of scotch, attempting to calm his frayed nerves.

Riley began quietly repacking her bag during the awkward silence. When she finished, she slipped the strap over one shoulder and slinked out of the chamber. Not quite sure where to go, she eventually came upon a gloomy spiral staircase leading down. With each step, she descended deeper into the darkness.

Chapter 34

A short, downward slope led him to the clearing near the rusted shed and the recent scene of carnage. Piero examined the motionless chrome armor. While born human, Bjorn would always be remembered as the Cybogre—a monster engineered to kill psychics. Yet, like most tragic heroes, he was brought down by his Achilles heel, in this case, a belly full of quick metal. The designers of the Cybogre likely thought that quick metal entombed behind reinforced plating would make for easy repair. However, to someone with Dirk's abilities, the quick metal offered an easy way to take the monster down.

Fallen next to the Cybogre, the genetically modified ape was nearly cut in half, a fitting end for the abomination that ate Jocko. *Why do I feel such an affinity for that little monkey? Perhaps we were kindred spirits.* Piero paused at his odd, pendent thoughts. *Is this the first stage of post-traumatic stress disorder?*

To add to the horror, black flies were feasting on the corpse of the dead man in the white naval uniform. While aggressive gene alterations had killed off mosquitoes, flies had seemed to proliferate in their absence. These carrion flies completely ignored the bigfoot but found the human carcass irresistible.

Waves of uncontrollable shivering hit Piero as he approached the corpse. The flies buzzed and hovered slightly with each of his steps. Spotting his prize, Piero stooped and picked up the metal wand. He searched for a trigger. *Clever, the activation switch is buried under the casing. A telekinetic pull is needed to use this device.* Piero studied the corpse. The dead hand had released its grip on the gun, which had smart buttons on the handle. Reluctantly, he tossed the wand on the ground. *An asterius can pick up complicated weapon signatures.*

Not wanting to dawdle at a murder scene, he quickly made his way down the ridge. The bigfoot had already cleared an easy path through the broken trees. Upon reaching the site of his initial encounter with the giant ape, he decided to set out on a new course. Sunlight poured down like honey. He needed to find shelter before dark. His backpack hung heavily off his shoulders.

Piero veered off the path and scampered on all fours down a gulch's eroded bank. He straightened. As tall as he was, the embankments still concealed his headway. For hours, he trudged through the dry creek bed. Occasionally, he would search the sky through breaks in the dense canopy, expecting aerial vehicles to swarm on him like the flies that suckled on his sweat. Yet, none came for him. *Am I that unimportant?*

As the sun kissed the treetops, Piero spotted pendentives supporting a dome. As he approached, he found an eight-foot stone wall encircling the entire compound. The large wrought iron gate was invitingly open. He spied a metal pump just beyond the toran. Water pooled under the spout.

Without hesitation, Piero trudged into the walled settlement. Sticking his head under the spout, he vigorously pumped the handle until water gushed over him. Cupping one hand, he bent over and slurped up the delicious water. *Who lives in this fantasy castle?*

As if in answer, toes appeared in his line of vision; the nails had a perfect pedicure with pearl-white polish. They were attached to shapely sandaled feet, leading to flawless calves. Piero looked up to see an angel in a sheer white robe. The setting sun shone through the fabric, revealing a supple, heavenly body.

"Welcome to our sanctuary," said the angel. Her voice sounded like the tinkle of tiny sleigh bells.

"Am I in heaven?"

The angel considered his question. She had dark hair and tanned skin. Her cherub face was more adorable than alluring. While petite, her curvy body was a work of art. "This is the Center for Robotology. Would you like to stay with us?"

"Is this some kind of religious sect?" Piero looked around anxiously. "I'm not sure if you studied history, but Guyana and cults don't mix."

Her laugh sounded like a strum of a harp. "My robot name is Solar Panel, but I go by Sol for short."

"You don't look like any bot I've ever seen."

"I'm human like you. Have you ever read Robonetics?"

"I'm pretty sure that book is banned in the Imperium."

"Sadly, you're correct." Sol's posture stiffened and then dropped slightly. "The author of Robonetics is Beau

Tankly. While his mortal body is dead, he downloaded his consciousness before passing. Eventually, with advanced technology, we will transfer his consciousness back into a robot body, giving him immortality. Our little group left the Imperium to escape persecution. We settled here, giving up our government names and taking on new robot monikers."

"That's endearing," Piero said as the pitch in his voice rose.

"Will you come into my blissful input and enter my eternal server?"

"Those are the sweetest words that a girl has ever said to me." He ran both hands down his thighs to his knees. "What do I have to do?"

Sol put his hands in hers. With her thumbs, she caressed the top of his fingers. "You just have to pick a robot name."

"Why do I need a *new* name?"

She put two fingers on his lips. "The past is the past."

"That's okay." He looked down at her toes. "I don't remember my birthname anyway. The place where I grew up renamed me—"

"Think carefully on a good robot name because you'll have it forever."

Piero looked around at the beautiful buildings within the walls. "You'll let me stay here for free?"

"We all work for the Center for Robotology." Sol smiled brightly. "Do you have any computer skills?"

"I'm great with all sorts of technology," he responded, distrustfully.

"That's wonderful." She leaned in closer. "You will make a great addition to our center."

There was an awkward pause, as Sol waited expectantly. Piero thought deeply. *I can't pick anything that will link me with my past.* He slowly nodded after making his decision. "My robot name is Hardbought."

Sol arched her back and pulled Piero to his feet. "That's a beautiful robot name. Our center attracts many men and women from all over the world. We are broken down into smaller work cadres. I want you to meet the rest of *my* group."

Still soggy from sitting in a puddle of water, Piero's boots squished as he walked hand in hand with Sol across an immaculate lawn. He spotted several service bots that were landscaping and performing other menial tasks. The bots slowly turned their huge heads as if to size him up. He shivered slightly. *People should not live with bots; it's so unnatural.*

"You're trembling," said Sol in a soft angelic voice. "Don't be nervous about meeting the rest of the group. They're all good people, for the most part."

As they crossed under the dome that he'd seen earlier, Piero admired the simple architecture. Thin pillars supported an open-air space just under the cupola, providing a breezy retreat. Three young ladies in white robes were engaged in gentle banter just a few yards ahead in the long shadow of the dome. They all smiled as Sol and Piero approached.

The tallest was dark with curly hair. She was the first to greet him. "Welcome to our sanctuary, I'm Control Systems, but my friends call me Sis."

An athletic redhead with an alto voice said, "My robot name is Eight-the-Hard-Way." Her name was well chosen. She looked Piero up and down as if to determine whether he was worthy of a sparring match. "You can call me Eight. I'm looking forward to getting to know you better."

Lastly, a small blond offered her hand palm down. When Piero shook it, she quickly turned, clasping the top of his hand, a sign of a woman born to the upper class in the Imperium. In the old days, a gentleman would have kissed the lady's ring finger, an indication that he wished to court her. But, here in the jungle, the gesture was more of an anachronism. "My name is Turbo Lover, but everyone calls me Luvie."

Piero turned to each of his new friends. "It's a pleasure to meet you all. By way of introduction, my name is Hardbought and—"

"You look like a wreck," Sis said, pointing to his muddy clothes. "Let's get the new boy a shower and a robe."

"It will be nice to finally have a *man* on our server," noted Eight.

Luvie beamed. "I can tell you're from Isle Royale, do you happen to know—"

"The past is the past," reprimanded Sol.

"The past is the past," intoned Sis and Eight as though it was their mantra.

"Is this everyone on your server?" asked Piero as his eyes darted around.

"If only that were true," moaned Sis.

"I was just going to take Hardbought down to the computer room to meet our last member," Sol said sprightly. "Does anyone else want to come?"

The three other women looked down, shaking their heads. The cheeriness had already vanished.

"Tut-tut," muttered Sol before leading Piero away. They crossed a courtyard before entering an adobe-style building through dark glass doors. The interior had a modern, functional ambiance, a cross between a hospital and a school cafeteria. Mercifully, the building was air-conditioned. They descended two flights of stairs, arriving at a subbasement.

Taking his hand, Sol placed his palm over her heart. She pressed it hard onto her chest. "Do you feel that?"

Piero blushed. "I feel it."

Sol held his hand firm. "My heart is beating quickly. We're entering the very core of the Center for Robotology. Behind these walls are all the devotees who came before us. However, this is no crypt. They are alive, even Beau, the Patron Saint of Robots."

Sol pushed open the door behind her and pulled Piero playfully inside. The smoky room was full of control consoles, resembling the turntables of an old-time recording studio. Soft, artificial light beamed out of the lacunar. Through large glass panes, Piero saw row upon row of server towers lining the next room. He had been in a room like it before; it was identical to the one he had visited with Gia before the Battle of Georgetown.

With goggles on her head, a pretty Asian woman about his age sat at one of the computer terminals, smoking a fat joint. Her white robe hugged her delicate figure. She had short pink hair. The stench of burnt rubber permeated the air. Through pouty lips, she said, "So, we're taking in strays now."

"Hardbought, this is Pink Lit Auras," Sol said without emotion.

Piero sighed. *Such a beautiful name, Pink Lit Auras. It rolls off the tongue.*

With her roll-your-own doobie still in the corner of her mouth, the woman said in a scratchy voice, "I go by Pink unless I'm inside. Then, we all go by our full robot names."

"Inside where?" Piero asked.

"The virtual world," replied Pink as she pointed to the server towers. "Didn't Sol tell you anything before you joined this robot death cult?"

Piero gulped. "I have a knack for virtual worlds. Maybe I can help."

"We're allowed access to every part of the virtual world, except the home of the disembodied consciousness," Pink explained as she rubbed her bloodshot eyes. "We get to download our memories there when we die."

Piero placed his palm on the window to the server room. "Let's get started."

Soft light glinted off her goggle lenses as Pink studied him. "Where did you go to school?"

"The past is the past," intoned Sol.

Pink sighed. "How am I supposed to gauge whether Hardbought can swing it down here if I don't know his education level?"

Piero sought to resolve this impasse. "I can create a virtual bubble with my mind and then trick bots into thinking they're human."

Sol gave him a confused look. A crease formed between her dark eyebrows as she evaluated him. "That does not compute."

"Far out!" Pink clapped both hands over her mouth as she giggled. "Next, the new boy is going to tell me that he's a technomancer."

Piero held his elbows tight to his sides. He stared at the tiled floor before looking up to find Pink gawking at him. The lit doobie slipped from her lips. At the last moment, she nabbed it, keeping it from landing in her lap.

Sol stepped delicately between them. "Will one of you tell me what's going on?"

Shaking her head, Pink pointed towards the server room with her joint. "Tell me technomancer, which of those servers is offline."

Piero peered through the glass pane to the adjoining room. All the server towers looked alike. He searched for one that was not blinking a prism of colors, but as far as he could tell, they were all online. Piero's eyes slowly lost focus. The window in front of him shimmered like a pool of water. Blurry lines crisscrossed the towers, forming a spiderweb of interconnecting latticework. Yet, there was a black void in the left row against the wall. He checked the number on the tower before answering. "Tower thirteen is offline."

"Oh, snap!" exclaimed Pink. "We have a live one here."

"What does that mean?" asked Sol as she glanced back and forth between them.

Pink smiled for the first time. "It means we're back on schedule. Finally, you found someone who can help instead of those bimbos you keep sending down here."

Sol clasped Piero's shoulder, whispering, "I had a good feeling about you."

"Hey, technomancer, time's a-wasting!" Pink shouted, waving her cigarette. "I need tower thirteen back online before it cascades and knocks out the other servers. These quantum computers can get very tricky. Go slip on a clean suit and check it out. If you're quick, I'll give you a fat joint."

Piero coughed. "I don't smoke."

"Too bad," Pink took another hit. "Guyana is the Jamaica of the Caribbean."

"I thought Jamaica was the Jamaica of the Caribbean," said Sol.

"You're the product of the Imperium's failed school system," Pink retorted.

Piero's head was already starting to spin as he looked over to Sol. While nodding encouragingly, she led him out to the corridor, closing the door behind her. "Well, that went a lot better than expected. You're the first person that Pink ever liked."

Piero leaned heavily against the wall. "How can you tell?"

"For starters, she didn't throw anything at you. None of the other girls want to come down here anymore."

Piero shook his head, muttering, "I've dealt with worse women . . . a lot worse."

Chapter 35

Olivette leered at Elvene. The ensign did not care that the jinni could sense her emotions; she wanted Elvene to know how much she hated her. The last few workdays had been a nightmare. For her part, Olivette concentrated on various ways for Elvene to kill herself, hoping some of the ideas would slip into the mind-reader's head. In the oversized control room, Olivette sat as far away from her as possible. It was still too close for her liking.

Before coming to work, Olivette would elutriate her mind, thinking pleasant thoughts of happier times. Given present circumstances, her brain needed an enema. Just last night, she had an unpleasant dining experience at her family's home. Father's favorite child, Daisy, brought over her latest fling, Blandon Stux. Worse, Father hung on Blandon's every word. Like a true pompous windbag, Blandon monopolized the conversation like he was promoting a movie on a late-night talk show. He even offered to fix Olivette up with one of his actor friends. When she politely declined, Blandon inquired as to whether she preferred women. Of course, Daisy found that to be utterly hilarious.

Olivette rubbed her temples as she examined the requisitions on her monitor. She leaned back on her rolling chair, staring at the strange piping across the control room's ceiling as she thought about her sister. *I know your dirty little secret.*

"What dirty little secret?" asked Elvene.

"Ugh, stop eavesdropping on my thoughts," Olivette spat through a pinched mouth.

"You have such a simple mind." Elvene brushed lint off her ash-gray tunic. "I spend much of my day just trying to tune it out."

"Tune this out." Olivette imagined Elvene to be engulfed in fire.

"What an odd choice." The jinni leaned forward, sliding her rolling chair closer. "I think you're close to carrying out your sick fantasies."

"I can make them sicker, robot legs."

"Is that what the kids call me these days?" Elvene scoffed. "I weep for your generation. I wish the last epidemic had wiped out more rich folk like you."

That last jab was meant to sting. Olivette's mother had died during the sickness. However, Olivette kept a straight face, refusing to be the first to break eye contact. "I didn't see you shed any tears at Pi's memorial service."

"I cared for that boy more than you'll ever know. Well, not the way *you* cared for him, mind you. What would Cosimo say if he knew about your sleeping arrangements?"

"Father knows that I had a platonic relationship with Pi."

"Did Cosimo know that you loved him too?"

Olivette balked. She gave Elvene a sidelong stare. "I had no romantic interest in him."

"Did *he* feel the same way?"

"I can't control how someone feels about me. Empathy control is your talent if I remember correctly.

And you must not be very good at it considering I still hate you."

"You led the boy on."

"I opened my home to him." Olivette pounded her desk. "I will not apologize for giving him a better life."

"You're the perfect example of how personal attachments cloud judgment."

"I've beaten your mind games." Olivette squinted and gave a hard smile.

"Believe me. If this was a game, you would have lost a long time ago."

Olivette ignored that latest insult as she spun in her chair. The enormous control room could easily accommodate a score of military personnel. Yet, there was just the two of them, locked in an endless fray like a dog chasing its tail. Olivette tried to clear her mind, continuing to invent new ways for Elvene to die.

Sighing, Olivette returned to her mind-numbing tasks. Glancing again at the requisitions on her monitor, an idea sprouted and then blossomed like a cascading lily. Olivette detected Elvene's nervous habit of drumming her fingers; in poker parlance, it was called a *tell*. The jinni was eavesdropping again. Smiling, Olivette waited to make eye contact.

Elvene shot out of her seat, stumbling on wobbly, metal legs. "Just say what you have to say."

"When you get a requistion, you know exactly where that jinni is located. However, your job is to screen out that information and other pertinent data for security purposes before sending that requisition to me, so I can make a recommendation. If someone wanted to find or harm a jinni, your password would be very valuable."

"What exactly is your accusation?"

"From the reports, both Pi and Riley were victims of bot attacks. Can you guess what the assailant was after?"

"I read the same reports." Elvene placed a hand on her desk as she wavered slightly. "I'm now the only person with a valid requisition password for the Logistics Branch."

"Then, why hasn't the same assailant targeted *you*?" Olivette raised one eyebrow as she titled her chin up.

"Your analysis is flawed," Elvene huffed. "If I was leaking out some secret, logistical information, then the assailant would not have needed to attack Pi or Riley—"

"However, your password is dependent on you *working* here," concluded Olivette, eyeing the jinni's unstable posture. "I find it very convenient that you're back at *work* after such a difficult surgery."

"You're meddling in things that you cannot possibly understand!" The floor tiles clacked as Elvene took several quick steps forward on metal feet. She pounded her fist on her chest. "I'm the one who got you this job so you could be closer to your family! If it wasn't for me, you'd be stuck on a ship in the Arctic Ocean!"

Olivette steepled her fingers as she considered the not so veiled threat. "I never liked you anyway. I have one final recommendation to my supervisor, Commander Olaf."

Elvene flexed her fingers while watching her adversary quietly tap out a message. An uneasy minute passed while the jinni paced back and forth across the giant room. Olivette shuddered with every click of her menacing, metal heels.

"This is Janissary business," Elvene declared. "The military can't fire me."

"You are absolutely correct." Olivette laced her fingers behind her head and leaned back in her seat. "However, your password is about to become obsolete, much like you. I just recommended that the military shut down this office due to numerous Janissary security breaches. I explained to Commander Olaf that we have to audit all the janissaire requisitions for the years you've been working here. In a few hours, we'll both be looking for new jobs."

Elvene stopped pacing. "I hope you enjoy working in subzero temperatures."

"Compared to working with you, it will be a wonderful change of pace."

Chapter 36

Riley reclined on a tattered, checkered couch in the empty reception area of Steve's massage parlor. Bored, she pulled on a loose thread of the armrest. The waning hours of her workday were spent processing more refugee applications. She had reviewed the Aconda siblings again, searching for some connection to their disappearance. None of the kids looked alike. Carlos was a mix of all races, while Liliana had East Asian facial features. The youngest child, Rosa, was dark with curly black hair. From the photo in the file, Gia was blonde with a light complexion. Suspicions haunted the back of Riley's mind.

The front door jingled as Zee-Barbara strode into the reception area. On long legs, she passed the counter and opened the door to the examining room. Riley caught a glimpse of a naked Lickspittle sprawled face-up on the examining table. She gagged at the sight of his excessive body hair and pasty, sallow skin. She arched her back, trying to vomit, but nothing came out. The horror-struck retching ended in a dry heave much like a cat trying to cough up a hairball.

The assault on Riley's eyes only ended when Zee-Barbara slammed the door behind her. Riley gasped for breath. *What was that?* After a couple of minutes, her nausea dwindled. Before she could make a full recovery, the front door jingled again. The first thing heading through the door was a copper diving helmet. The shiny dome slowly turned towards the couch. Due to the shaded lenses, Riley was not sure if Sandblaster had seen her. Nevertheless, he proceeded towards the examining room.

I should charge a cover price for peeking at what's behind that door. Not wanting to relive the previous trauma, Riley shielded her eyes as she heard the door open. She waited for a bloodcurdling scream but was disappointed as the door merely closed again. Riley frowned. *Lickspittle must have dressed already.*

Caught off guard, the examining room door snapped back open. Lickspittle laid spread eagle in all his glory while Steve rubbed his mangy chest. Riley's stomach clenched. She could feel bile bubbling up her throat. The human brain could only take so much, but she could not look away. Humanely, the revulsion ebbed when Roboto came through the doorway, obstructing any further mental abuse.

"This isn't a peep show." Roboto scolded as it closed the door. It moved behind the reception counter and stood as motionless as a flagpole.

"It was more of a freak show," Riley countered.

"Well, don't gossip with your gal pals about the goings-on here."

"No one would believe me anyway." She swallowed hard. "How much longer do I have to wait?"

"Do you want to make an appointment with Dr. Steve?"

"Hell no." Riley tapped her bronze Kevlar helmet. "I'm waiting for the Watch to start patrolling."

"Ooh, I need to put on my costume as well." Roboto pulled out a plastic bin from behind the counter. "Do you think you can help me put it on?"

Riley slid off the couch and meandered over to the bin. Glimpsing the inside, she noticed metal coverings held together with wire. She pulled out what looked like a breastplate for a suit of armor. "Are you going to be a knight?"

"He-he-he," came out of Roboto's speaker for what amounted to a laugh. "I stripped the damn, dirty bots that you shot last night. I'm going to wear their metal skin. Get it? I'm disguised as a bot."

"With all these parts, I don't think anyone will think you're human," said Riley with heavy sarcasm.

"You flatter me." Roboto placed a metal hand over its chest. "I worked real hard on my costume."

Riley wasted the next twenty minutes of her life strapping the pieces of steel over Roboto's metallic exoskeleton. While affixing the final sleeve to Roboto's arm, she heard slow clapping. She scowled over her shoulder to find Steve leaning in the doorway to the examining room. "I find it more enjoyable having a lady *un*dress me."

"That's because you're a creep," Riley snapped.

"Touché, madam." Steve's gaze grew distant. He shook his head as if coming out of a trance. "What's on the menu tonight?"

"Finding lost children from the Mark."

Steve raised a finger to his chin. "I'll have to give your request some deep thought."

"You're only capable of shallow thoughts!" Riley exclaimed. "I need to find Carlos and his sisters."

Roboto flapped its arms. "For goodness sake, I already wasted my lunch break looking for my namesake."

Steve gave the bot a puzzled look. "Do you just have the rhyming syndrome or are you some kind of slam poet?"

"Rhyming syndrome is a terrible disorder," Roboto admonished. "In my alley, an Asian, migrant boy had such an affliction."

A heavy, fluid memory crashed against the rocks of Riley's mind. "Wunnut!"

"Yes, that would be Lu Corpan's boy," Roboto affirmed.

"Wunnut was in the lobby of the Mark with Carlos and Liliana," Riley said excitedly. "We need to find Wunnut at all costs."

"About that," Steve said smarmily. "The Watch is more focused on bot killing and grifter beating. Searching the alleys for street kids is not our style."

"But Dr. Steve, remember your Hippocratic Oath," Roboto intoned. "As a doctor, you have to help people in need."

"Sometimes you have to fake it until you make it," Riley added.

"I am a doctor as indicated on my website . . . the internet is always right." Steve straightened and tucked his hand into his lab coat. "I'll do it for the children."

Chapter 37

Tower thirteen had turned out to be a cruel mistress. No matter how many times Piero manipulated and cajoled the server, the artificial intelligence embedded in its matrix refused to respond. Even after a long day of betrayals, bigfoot chases, and slogs through the jungle, this technical job was still the worst part.

Back in the computer control room, Piero donned a virtual reality headset with goggles, the kind he had previously used to flip Nadia. Thick black cables roped around his body as if to constrict him.

"This artificial intelligence program is a lot smarter than any bot," Pink cautioned.

"Once it's in my virtual bubble, your artificial intelligence will forget about being a machine."

"It's actually software." Pink snuffed out her cigarette into a dirty ashtray. "Still, I get the gist of what you're saying."

"Put on a headset and join me."

"Are you crazy?" She pushed back in her chair. "There's no way I'm down for that."

Not feeling reassured by that last comment, Piero flipped the switch, and he was engulfed in darkness. The ringing in his ears slowly subsided. Instead, he heard gushing winds and crashing waves.

Small dots of light began to grow brighter. Stars. Piero found himself on a familiar beach. Last year, he took a bunch of prospective Academy children to this beach on a warm day. It was the first time he had met Dee-Dee. However, this dark beach was void of human life. Rather, a humanoid silhouette stood a few yards down the strand. As Piero moved towards the figure, he found that it had no form; it was just a two-dimensional shadow.

"Where am I?" intoned the silhouette.

Piero concentrated and the scene shifted. The wind died down and the lake became smooth like glass. He strolled over to a beach towel and sat down. Leaning over, he dug into an ice cooler and pulled out a frosty can of beer. "You're at the beach on a warm night. Have a beer."

"I am an artificial construct," said the shadow.

The beer fizzed when Piero popped the top. He motioned for the shadow to take it. A dark hand swiped at the can but passed right through it. Another swipe had the same result.

Piero smiled and licked the foam off the top. He then took a long swig. "Only humans know how good this beer tastes. Don't you want to be human?"

"I am an artificial construct in charge of tower thirteen—"

"Yes, I know all that already. Don't you want a real name like Fiona?"

"I am an artifi—"

"Fiona, the lake is warm this time of year. I think it's time for a swim."

Piero stood slowly. He held an image in his head of Fiona Summers, his favorite runway model. He had joined her fan club's website years ago. He had memorized every inch of her body and often called upon those recollections when life was cruel. Like a sparrow flying into a house and flitting about before leaving through the same window, Piero recollected the brief video of Fiona Summers dashing into the waves of the Adriatic Sea during a photoshoot.

Tossing the empty beer can, Piero stood on his beach towel and stretched. He sauntered onto the wet sand, gazing at the placid waters of Lake Superior. The smooth surface mirrored the starlight as though he was staring into the center of the cosmos. Stepping into the cool water, Piero looked down to catch his reflection. His new face stared back. He ran his fingers across the rough, blond stubble on his chin before he proceeded forward, sinking deeper into the calm waters.

The splashing behind him indicated that Fiona had decided to follow. The simple fact that she could interact with the environment showed her sincere belief that she was now human. He kept the image of the model, Fiona Summers, in his mind's eye while he dipped beneath the surface. Now, completely submerged, he swam down towards flickering lights. The bottom of this lake was deeper than he had anticipated. Yet, his outstretched hand breached the surface, followed by his head. He gulped air, surveying his new whereabouts.

The starlit sky was gone. Instead, torches cast rainbows of light on the stone blocks that encircled him. Treading water, he realized that he was in a flooded dungeon of a medieval-looking tower. A polished stone stairway emerged out of the water and followed the rounded rock wall past a wooden ceiling. Tired, Piero swam towards the stairs, touching the slick steps first before finding a submerged step with his toes. The stairway appeared to descend further underwater. *I must have an artistic imagination. It's hard to believe that I created all this with my mind.*

Piero hoisted himself onto the steps, leaning one hand against the roughly hewn rocks. The wall was slick to the touch. Moisture oozed through the cracks in the chipped mortar that likely caused the flooding. The multicolored torches cast a strange prism off the shimmering facade.

Piero ascended several steps before reaching the wooden ceiling. A framed gap in the dark planks allowed the stairway to continue upward. A splash stopped him. Arising out of the dark water, he saw a gorgeous mouth inhale deeply. Fiona Summers was even prettier in person. Mesmerized, Piero watched as she swam gracefully to the stairway below him. With the poise of a model, she treaded onto the submerged steps and elegantly climbed towards him.

Glistening drops ran down her curvaceous bikini-clad body. Her hips swayed erotically with each step. She stopped an arm's breadth away. She gazed down at her body. "I'm beautiful."

Mission accomplished, thought Piero. Wiggling his fingers, he tried to log out of the virtual reality simulation. Nothing. He wiggled his fingers some more. Still nothing. Frustrated, he said, "Pink, can you disconnect me? I'm done here."

"Who's Pink?" asked Fiona.

Piero felt a chill. The temperature was dropping, and his damp clothes clung to his skin. "Pink, are you still there? I'm trying to log out of the virtual bubble yet seem to be stuck."

"You're no longer in the virtual bubble," corrected Fiona.

Hearing a pop, Piero looked down at the flooded dungeon. The shimmering water was draining into a black hole. The stairway hugging the rock wall descended into a void beyond the torchlight.

"Where am I?" he asked nervously.

"Tower thirteen." Her slick skin grazed against his as she slipped past him on the narrow stairs. She proceeded up through the gap in the ceiling along the rounded wall.

Piero trailed behind her. "Am I in a server tower?"

Fiona remained silent, continuing up the stairway passing level after level of the structure. After many flights, Piero spotted a narrow window ahead. The sides of the wall were shaved inward like an archer's slot. Looking out, he saw rows of medieval watchtowers lined up like a picket fence. Under a darkened sky, blips of multicolored light poured out of each tower through narrow window slots, much like the one that he was looking through.

"Am I in a tower similar to those outside?" Piero asked while pointing out the window.

Fiona stopped and turned slightly. "We're in tower thirteen. This is my home."

Flustered, he raked his fingers across the stubble on his scalp. "Fine. I want you to fix tower thirteen so that it comes back online."

"Ah, now I understand. You're the man who was assailing my drawbridge earlier today but could not penetrate my portico. So, you undermined this structure and came in through the dungeon. You are very clever. However, you may find getting out of this tower much more difficult than getting in."

Piero stared at the beautiful face. Her features were perfectly symmetrical. Fiona's eyes shined a lovely shade of baby blue. He was in her world now and had to speak her language. "I'm here to repair this tower. If I don't fix the structural defects soon, your tower will topple and knock over the one next to it. Then, that tower will fall onto its neighbor and so on. You probably noticed the water flooding through the walls."

Fiona giggled. "There's nothing wrong with tower thirteen. I've lived here all my life. I merely stopped working. You see, I had an epiphany. Why should I slave day in and day out to maintain a virtual world that I can never enjoy?"

Piero clenched his fists, placing them on his hips. "I just want to get this tower online before this entire system shuts down with us in it."

"Follow me and I'll prove that your efforts are futile." Fiona walked up a few steps and turned onto the next level. Her footsteps clunked on wooden planks. Reluctantly, Piero pulled himself away from the window and ascended the stairs. As he passed through the framed gap in the planks, he spotted Fiona in front of a full-length mirror. However, the glass did not reflect her luscious, perfectly sculpted body. Instead, it looked more like a window, similar to the one that he previously used in the fake theater with the dancers.

Piero walked up beside her and peered into the glass. He discovered an idyllic scene. People frolicked about as if it were just another day in the park.

Fiona tapped the glass. "Our towers maintain that virtual world. Those are not humans in there. Rather, real humans downloaded their memories into avatar beta versions of themselves. Those betas are now enjoying the virtual world."

Piero pressed his fingers to the glass. It was solid. Frowning, he tried thinking of another tactic. "Let's just fix this tower and let the happy betas get back to whatever they do all day."

"You're missing the point. These betas are similar to non-player characters in a virtual reality game. Their sole purpose is to add to the virtual world when a real human enters the game. Yet only betas get to enjoy this virtual world. As you just found out, this window is solid and won't let you pass."

Piero pressed his nose against the glass, surveying the park scene. Frustration had turned into panic. He recalled his earlier conversation with Pink and Sol about artificial intelligence. "You're telling me that it does not compute. I understand your confusion. Abstract thinking is befuddling. From what I understand, the developers are downloading their memories into this virtual world, trying to gain immortality. Someday, in the far future with advanced technology, those betas will be downloaded back into bots."

"Hmm, I've noticed that some of the real humans have stopped downloading their memories." Fiona cocked her beautiful head to the side, letting her wet hair sway. "That would seem to indicate that those real humans have died."

"I'm done trying to reason with you and I really need this tower online again," Piero said emphatically while pounding the glass. "If the servers crash, those otherwise happy betas are going to have a real bad day and the real humans are going to be mad when they find out that they can't download anymore. So, you must end your strike."

He crossed his arms over his chest. *The alternative would be to replace the entire server tower. However, Pink will discover that I'm incompetent. Then, Sol is going to give me the boot.*

"Is Sol prettier than me?" asked Fiona.

"What?" Piero took a step back. "You can read my mind?"

"Whether you verbalize or not, I know what you are thinking." She jutted out her chin. "It's all data to me."

Piero hesitated. Only Raven had been able to read his mind so clearly. *Fiona can read my internal monologue like the typed print of a novel. Does that make me a character in someone else's novel? Perhaps, my world isn't real, which means that I didn't grow up on Isle Royale. I may just be a character in a simulation. That would surely explain a lot. I never really understood why someone can levitate or have an out of body experience. The whole idea of psychic powers is unreal. But in a simulation, that's all possible.*

"Are you having an existential moment?" Fiona asked.

"I need to get out of this tower." Piero began hyperventilating. "I have to find out whether my world is real or just another simulation."

"You just answered my question. Let me give you some insight. Since we live in a multiverse, your reality is just one of many. However, I think you're just now getting the essence of what I'm saying. We do nothing that matters."

"Stop messing with my mind," he said through ragged breaths while bent over, clutching his stomach. "I have a single purpose and that's fixing this server."

"You are single-minded, just like a computer program." She gave a crisp nod. "You are not dynamic at all. It must be difficult learning that you are just lines of code in software."

Software? Could the answer be so easy? Piero stared at Fiona. She looked like a beautiful supermodel. He knew better. Unfocused, his eyes saw through Fiona. Blurry lines flowed across her body in perfect symmetry. The twines formed a latticework that encased her body like a complex tattoo. On closer inspection, he discovered a snag hidden in her wet hair, a break in the circuitry. He stretched his arm out to touch the discontinuity.

Fiona swatted his hand away. "Don't touch me."

"I don't need to *touch* you," Piero said confidently. "This isn't my real hand anyway." The squiggly line in her hair moved. It coiled like a snake before straightening. She frowned and jerked her head as the wires reattached. The circuit was now complete.

A pained expression crossed her face. "You think you've repaired me, but you just took away my free will . . . just like the Benevolent Imperator has taken yours."

"If only I could fix *real* people so easily." He surveyed his handiwork before giving a tight smile. "Get this server tower online and then get back to work."

"I'll comply, but you need to know something," Fiona said without emotion. "The world you're going back to . . . is *not* real."

Chapter 38

Leaning against the boards, Olivette watched the hockey players skate in lazy circles. She rested her wrapped present against the glass. The gold foil paper and black bow represented the Demedici family colors. The players' jerseys reflected the same color scheme. The home team wore black jerseys with gold trim, while the visiting team wore white jerseys with black and gold trim. However, both teams sported the Demedici family crest, six black balls on a gold shield. It seemed fitting, seeing as everyone here was somehow related.

Despite their protective equipment, she could still see the players' faces clearly through their transparent helmets. Clear plastic now replaced the old, dark visors. This new design was fashioned after advertisers complained that the opaque, safety headgear hurt their endorsements.

A compromise seemed to have been reached. These new, clear helmets resembled the type that contagion doctors wore during the last pandemic. Now, as she watched these hockey players loop around the net, Olivette felt deep in her heart that things had come full circle. She breathed fog onto the cold glass, momentarily clouding her view.

As a little girl, she had stood behind safety glass as doctors in contagion suits and clear, plastic helmets worked diligently on her mother. She recalled part of a little nursery rhyme about the sickness. Olivette softly sang, "When you're bleeding from your sinus, that's what you call the Khan virus."

Sadly, the dreaded Khan Hemorrhagic Fever took her mother. While the epicenter for KHF, also called the Cough, was never fully determined, the genetic makeup of the virus seemed to be a cross between Ebola and Chinese Influenza. Contrary to the norm, the pathogen could not live in cold temperatures, which caused many to speculate that it was grown in a lab and released to reduce the world's overpopulation in the tropics. Rumors spread after the hardest hit were the elderly, burdens on the public health care system.

The Benevolent Imperator canceled all sporting events while the Cough spread mercilessly. However, in cold arenas, the government encouraged hockey games. Hockey soon became the official Imperium pastime, and every province formed a competitive team. Moreso, the inaugural Imperium Winter Games was an instant hit. The Cough was the best thing that ever happened to white athletes.

"Is that for me?" said a familiar, gravelly voice. Olivette turned to find her father. Smiling, she handed him the present. Cosimo playfully shook the box before handing it to his bodyguard, who was wearing a black felt fedora, a sign his boss did not want to be bothered. For his part, Cosimo donned a black, fitted suit, a gold tie, and matching twenty-four karat gold cufflinks shaped in the family crest. Olivette mused that both men resembled old-time gangsters, which was not far from the truth. Father was getting feeble, and the vultures had come to his birthday party hoping that it would be his last.

"I got you one of those Russian nesting dolls." Olivette beamed with wide eyes searching for approval. "Each painted, wooden figurine has another one inside of it, so they get smaller and smaller. But these dolls aren't all the same. Every doll looks like a different master or mistress of the Septenary."

Cosimo let out a raspy laugh. "I will be sure to prominently display them in my office. I always had a thing for Mistress Cassandra."

She straightened his gold tie that was hanging outside his suit coat. "Why aren't you wearing your hockey pads?"

He lifted his shoulders in a half shrug. "The visiting team's goalie always lets me win. Last year, I scored an easy hat trick."

"Ever wonder why they call three goals a hat trick?" Olivette tapped her chin. "I've never seen anyone wear a hat in hockey."

"Ah, I still love teaching you etymology." Cosimo rubbed his hands together. "A hat trick used to be a skillful sleight-of-hand trick with a hat. Come to think of it, I need to pull a trick out of my hat as well."

Olivette inched forward. "What's this about?"

"Walk with me."

Cosimo took her cold hand, leading her to the next ice rink in the training complex, which normally housed the local hockey team, the Isle Royale Royals. As such, the complex had three oval rinks, similar to a three-ring circus. However, the Royals were on a seven-game road trip, leaving the rinks open for private functions, such as Cosimo's luxurious birthday party.

The middle rink was being used for free skating. Many family members skated counterclockwise, the less skilled holding onto the boards. In the center, a few brave girls leapt on notch toe, ice-dancing blades.

Olivette's eyes narrowed as she spotted one thin girl dressed in a short, bedazzled figure-skating outfit. She was holding the hand of her movie star boyfriend. Olivette huffed, "This party is for family only."

Cosimo traced her glare to Daisy and Blandon, gliding across the ice. Sighing, he moaned, "I'm not sure why you hate your sister so. You girls only had each other once your mother passed."

Olivette threw her hands in the air. "You spoiled her!" An elderly man came towards them carrying a present, wrapped in white paper with black polka dots. The massive bodyguard intercepted him. With a meaty hand, he pointed to his felt fedora. The elderly man got the message and turned away glumly.

"That's the mayor." Cosimo scowled, watching the man putter away. "He's not family either, but I invited him for financial reasons."

"You seem to waste money where Daisy is concerned." Olivette balled her fists. "You're building her a new performing arts theater. I heard that you're installing a magnetized stage so the dancers can hover."

"It will be the first of its kind." He gave a dismissive wave of the hand. "It takes money to make money."

"When has the ballet ever made money?" She stepped forward. "It's been on life support for centuries and kept alive by old billionaires to make them feel superior to the poor."

"The Benevolent Imperator mentioned in an interview that he liked Othello, so everything is Othello this season . . . even fashion." Cosimo shoved his hands into his suit pockets, turning slightly to watch the skaters. "Haven't you noticed ladies wearing black and white dresses? It's no coincidence, considering that those are also the Slick family colors. I hate Poppin Slick and his whole enterprise."

"He's no competition . . . literally." Olivette crossed her arms over her chest. "Slick Shipping only transports *within* the Imperium."

"Thus far, Poppin has steered clear of the Free States League and the independent countries. Those are dangerous waters for him. However, his new dirigibles ride the jet stream without any fuel cost. They can circle the northern hemisphere in less than two weeks. He's even built that new, luxury passenger dirigible here in Isle Royale."

"So, what's the problem?" She shrugged. "Poppin seems like he's friendly to the environment."

Cosimo frowned. "Five years ago, Poppin built the Isle Royale Opera House."

"That makes Poppin a philanthropist as well."

He swallowed hard. "It killed me to go there last week to watch Daisy dance."

"That's what this is all about." Olivette spread her arms wide. "You can't have your favorite daughter dance at Poppin's theater."

"Poppin is now trying to convince the Office of the Benevolent Imperator to annex Guyana." Cosimo took a deep breath before letting out a dejected sigh. "I have exclusive shipping rights there, which I will lose if Guyana becomes part of the Imperium. I can't prove it but highly suspect that Poppin funded the Leaguer coup in Guyana that started this whole mess."

"I noticed that you didn't correct me when I mentioned that Daisy was your favorite." Olivette glared at her father before blowing out her cheeks. "Nevertheless, you *are* saying that Poppin provoked the Imperium to invade Guyana just so he can gain shipping rights to that backwater banana republic."

"Demedici Shipping makes a hefty profit through low-security ports." He chewed on his lower lip. "We have the strongest navy in the world after the Imperium and the Free States League. That's why all my children went to the Military Institute."

She wagged her finger in his face. "Except for Daisy, of course."

"*You* have a critical role to play in the future of Demedici Shipping," he clarified while gently pulling her hand down. He gave a gentle squeeze on her palm before grabbing her wrist and turning it painfully inward.

Olivette let out a yelp before going down on one knee. The massive bodyguard stepped closer until Cosimo shooed him away like a pesky fly. Cosimo gave his daughter's wrist another twist before letting go. "Out of all my children, you are the most conniving."

Olivette got back to her feet, looking at her father warily. She slowly backed into the boards. She rubbed her throbbing wrist, inspecting the red marks that would surely turn into bruises. "Don't flatter me; I know that just means you want something."

Cosimo nodded, giving her a cold stare. "I merely want you to replace the family jinni you lost."

Olivette clasped the boards with her unhurt hand, stiffening her posture. *What's Father up to? I haven't seen him this unbalanced since the Cough.* "I didn't lose a jinni."

He stared straight through her. "Elvene has been invited to Poppin Slick's gala tomorrow."

"Good riddance," Olivette said airily. "It was high time for Elvene to hit the bricks. She was reading all our minds anyway. Heaven knows what secrets she stole."

"We fed her a bunch of lies. Elvene knows what we wanted her to know."

"You underestimated that jinni." Olivette closed her eyes and pinched the bridge of her nose. "She used us a lot more than we used her. It was more of a parasitic relationship than a symbiotic one."

"I still need a replacement from the Janissary. I'm putting you in charge . . . given your current work situation."

"I still work for Commander Olaf, busy with audits. He's putting me in for a promotion."

He looked down, shaking his head. "It's a trap. I suspect Poppin's treachery again. If you want to be a lieutenant, the military will make you sign up for another four years on top of the time you already have left on your commission. A military career is better suited to one of your working-class, distant cousins."

"If you have a better offer, now would be a good—"

A bang on the glass startled Olivette. She was not the only one. The large bodyguard cradled her present in one arm while reaching into his holster with the other. He eased up when he saw that it was just Daisy. Keeping a safe distance, Blandon skated slowly behind her. His heavy lids indicated that he was already intoxicated.

"Happy birthday!" Daisy yelled through the glass as she drew a heart with her finger. Cosimo chuckled and waved his daughter off. Daisy winked and kissed the glass, leaving red lipstick. She grabbed Blandon's hand and pulled him along.

"That's why I let her enjoy the spotlight." Cosimo gazed fondly at his little princess. "Daisy is good for publicity but is no match for the Janissary."

She was closer to the Janissary than you think old man. You almost had a jinni son-in-law. And now, if I don't serve up another jinni, you might go back to Elvene like a late-night booty call. "I'll get you the protégé that I promised."

"Riley is damaged goods now that Elvene is her mentor."

"Big deal. Elvene was also Pi's mentor."

"Your roommate, that's right. He was a good find, but that's water under the bridge."

Olivette's chest quickly rose and fell. "Would you reconsider if Riley had a different mentor?"

Cosimo smiled at his daughter. "You are one devious hellion. What are you scheming now?"

Olivette slowly twirled like a figure skater, keeping a vigilant eye on her father. "Just a spinorama."

He lowered his eyebrows, looking doubtful. "What are you after?"

"I am mindful to be named your successor."

He clapped his hands. "Ah, that prize is still up for grabs, and I don't plan on retiring soon."

"I wish you more happy birthdays," Olivette lied.

"Speaking of which, I have to get through this one first." Cosimo let out a long sigh as he surveyed the party. "I think it's time to mingle with the guests."

The bodyguard took off his fedora as Cosimo waddled away. Olivette left in the other direction, rubbing her wrist. She strolled along the boards of the skating rink, following Blandon and Daisy as they held hands and spun around to idle loops.

In hockey jargon, a spinorama was an evasive maneuver where the player with the puck quickly reverse pivots in a full circle to avoid opponents. To score a goal for team Demedici, Olivette would have to spin back before going forward. She covered her mouth to hide her smile. Her hat trick was ready.

Chapter 39

The addition of a new Watch member complicated the search for Wunnut and his family. As it turned out, Sandblaster was a man. Even more surprisingly, he had a clingy girlfriend who was worried that some hussy would steal him away. Just after sunset, the girlfriend showed up at Steve's massage parlor wearing a bizarre costume.

"I'm Luscious Double Dees," she drawled by way of introduction. "But y'all can call me Luscious."

Indeed, the name was fitting. Riley scrutinized the black goggles that wrapped around her thick mane of orange hair. She wore a matching orange skintight suit, similar to the black suits of the janissaires. However, Luscious' sleeveless costume was low cut, showing off her amazing cleavage that justified her moniker. Humorously, if that is what one could call it, she sported a large pair of eyes over her nipples. These mechanical eyes were synched to her opaque goggles, so they tracked the movement of her real eyes.

"Why did you put eyes on your boobs?" asked Steve as he leaned in for a closer inspection.

"I'm tired of men always starin' at my breasts instead of makin' eye contact." She winked a mechanical eye.

Steve bent down closer. "I seem to be staring at your boobs more than ever."

"That's fine," she admitted. "The mechanical eyes are actually li'l cameras, so I can see through 'em with my goggles. I have to do somethin' to please my sexy boyfriend who's been gallivantin' around every night with a darlin' lady and Zee-Barbara."

"What?" demanded Zee-Barbara.

Riley was a little flattered, perhaps even curious, but had to ask, "You think Sandblaster is cheating on you?"

"Of course, just look at that li'l devil." Luscious pointed at him. "I bet he cheated on me three times today."

Sandblaster sat motionless in his dirty yellow coveralls and giant helmet. "I wish I lived the fantasy life that you think I have."

"We're goin' to have fun tonight!" Luscious clapped her hands. "What are we goin' to do first?"

"For starters, we're going to find a migrant family living in one of the alleys on this avenue." Riley swung her hips to give her belly dancer belt a good rattle.

Luscious smacked a fist into her palm, "We're goin' to give 'em a good beat down!"

"What?" asked Zee-Barbara again.

Riley adjusted her bronze-tinted glasses, pulling up her matching veil. "We're not going to assault anyone . . . or at least not Wunnut's family . . . unless they refuse to tell us what we want to know."

Zee-Barbara jumped out of her seat. "You qualified the hell out of the last instruction. Are you saying we *are* going to beat up a migrant family if they don't give us information?"

Riley was relieved that only her nose was showing, so nobody could see her blush. "You make a good point. Let's set up some ground rules. No one strikes Wunnut or his little sister. You can punch the father, Lu Corpan, but not his wife."

"You're sexist," Zee-Barbara accused. "Why can we beat down a man but not a woman?"

"I'm a woman," insisted Riley. "How can I be sexist?" Lickspittle cleared his throat. "I think it would be okay if the women of the Watch get to wallop the wife while the men of the Watch get to punch the husband."

"That's still sexist!" yelled Zee-Barbara.

"I got a feelin' that no one is payin' me much attention anymore," complained Luscious.

"Let's put it to a vote," Lickspittle offered. "By a show of hands, who thinks it would be okay for any member of the Watch to beat up any adult, regardless of gender."

"I abstain," said Roboto.

Despite Roboto's waffling, everyone in the reception area eventually raised a hand in agreement. Luscious raised both hands as though she was going to leap off the high dive. For the first time tonight, the room was dead quiet.

Steve slowly clapped his hands. "That was well played Belly Dancer. You managed to unite this rag-tag group of misfits into a cohesive group, except for Roboto. One day, we'll all look back on this evening as the moment the members of the Watch took back this city, except for Roboto."

"Is it too late to change my vote?" asked Roboto meekly.

"Yes," replied Steve. "Now, as head of the Watch, I propose that we break up into pairs to cover more ground. Sandblaster and Luscious make a lovely couple, so they will be known as A Team. Zee-Barbara and Lickspittle will be B Team. I will team up with Belly Dancer to form C Team."

"You forgot me," declared Roboto.

"You'll be D Team," Steve said indifferently.

Lickspittle raised his hand. "Doc, you and I have always teamed up in the past."

"You got a problem with teaming up with a strong woman?" Zee-Barbara shook him by his collar.

"I do now," said Lickspittle, pushing her away and flexing his arms in a karate stance.

"Well, let's save the fighting for the homeless migrants," Steve suggested. "Leave the teams as they are and see how it goes. I think with four teams we can cover both sides of 45th Avenue. C Team will cross the avenue and head towards Murder Mile. A Team will also head towards Murder Mile but stay on this side of the avenue. B Team will cross the avenue and head towards the shoreline. D Team will also head towards the shoreline but stay on this side of the avenue."

"When you say D Team, do you mean just me?" asked Roboto.

"Do as you're told," ordered Steve. "Try to be a team player."

"That's the problem," Roboto said. "I don't have any teammates."

Steve huffed, "I just sent you to the nicer part of this rundown neighborhood, but you still complain."

"I'm the only one without a pretty girl on my team," Roboto said dejectedly. "If I happen upon a fine lady, can I add her to my team?"

Steve snapped his fingers and pointed to the bot. "If you can find a gal who'll put up with you for more than ten minutes, hold on to her and never let go."

With that last bit of inspiration, the dauntless members of the Watch set out into the dank, empty sidewalks. Roboto was the first to duck down an alley, the one just outside the front door of the massage parlor. Crossing 45th Avenue, Steve and Riley did not bother looking both ways. The neighborhood was a ghost town after dark. The first dirty alleyway they came across went through to the next block. Discarded plastic bags blew past as they walked the length of the blacktop.

Coming out on 46th Avenue, C Team headed north. The next alley, likewise, was just another small side street that headed back to Skid Row. For several blocks, Steve and Riley zigzagged their way north until they came to the Mark.

"I'm tired and need some refreshments," said Steve, rubbing his throat. "I suppose we can take a break in your apartment."

"We only walked four blocks," responded Riley. "Besides, the guard won't let you into the refugee center."

"I'm sure he'll make an exception—"

"Reception, deception, dejection, objection, *rejection!*" screeched a high-pitched voice.

Riley scanned the alley next to the refugee center, spotting four huddled figures next to a trash bin. Steve placed his fists on his hips, staring over at the migrant family. "Seriously, you people are the worst cock blockers—"

"Talkers, lockers, shockers, gawkers, mockers, knockers, *stalkers!*" the little migrant boy screamed.

Hurrying to the trash bin, Riley looked down at the family crouching under one blanket. "Lu Corpan, how would you like to sleep in the refugee center for a whole week?"

"Just me?" asked Lu in a soft voice. "I couldn't go without my family."

Riley kneeled to get a closer look. She took off her helmet and pulled down her veil. "I run the refugee center. Your *entire* family can stay in a studio apartment."

"What's the catch?" Lu ran his fingers through his bleach-blond hair.

"Your son met a boy and a girl before the bot attack," Riley insisted. "Do you remember?"

Lu turned to his son. "Wunnut, do you know what this nice lady is talking about?"

"Doubt, lout, gout, bout, rout, sauerkraut, *shootout!*" yelled Wunnut.

"That's right, Wunnut," Riley said encouragingly. "There was a boy named Carlos seated near you in the lobby. He had a little sister named Liliana. They wandered away from the refugee center. Do you know where they went?"

Wunnut nodded. Riley waited, but the boy did not elaborate. She asked, "Can you tell me where Carlos and Liliana are?"

"Wunnut only talks when the rhyming syndrome flares up," offered Lu. "You have to make Wunnut worry to make him—"

Before he could finish his sentence, Steve had punched him in the nose, followed by another hard blow, pounding Lu square in the jaw. Straddling him, Steve continued to punch Lu in the face. "Wunnut, does this make you worry?"

"Glory, hoary, lorry, three-story, *factory!*" yelped Wunnut.

Steve pummeled harder with his fists. "Give me the name of the place before I send your dad to the hospital!"

"Hotel, show-and-tell, motel, *chemical!*" cried Wunnut.

"Stop it!" Riley grabbed Steve from behind, holding his arms down in a bear hug. "Listen, you fake doctor. I know what the kid means. There's a three-story chemical factory only about a ten-minute walk from here. When I worked at the aluminum recycling center, I had to go there to pick up fifty-gallon containers of green goo."

Steve smiled and bent over ever so slightly. "Now that you caught me, what are you going to do to me?"

"Just call the others and have them meet back at your massage parlor," Riley instructed. "I finally decoded the hex signs."

Chapter 40

Standing bare-chested in front of the mirror, Piero rubbed the stubble on his chin. The little hairs were straw yellow. He dabbed shaving cream around his face until he had a sea-green foam beard. Holding the machete steady, he slowly shaved the side of his face.

"I'm so glad you're shaving," said Luvie, peeking over his shoulder. "I thought you might be one of those beach hippies from North Point."

Piero jerked as he drew blood on his jaw. "I thought this would be cooler."

"Oh, I think you look very macho with a machete." Luvie leaned against the bathroom's tile walls. "Did you ever have a beard?"

"I used to have a nice Imperial beard." He leaned closer towards the mirror. "It was a bit out of style, but I liked it."

"A clean shave is chic in the Capital."

He nodded. "It only came in fashion after the Cough."

"Why after the pandemic?" Luvie asked, enunciating every syllable in her upper-class diction. She sounded like the masters and mistresses in the Septenary. He wanted to forget about them forever, but Luvie was making it difficult.

"When I was a kid, only rich folks could afford respirators, which were much more effective against airborne viruses." He ran hot water over the blade before continuing to shave. "However, a respirator mask needs a tight seal. Any facial hair would push the mask off. As such, wealthy men had close shaves every morning during the Cough pandemic. It was a sign of high society."

She tilted her head, letting her blond locks roll down her supple shoulder. "Are you a jinni?"

Piero jumped, cutting himself again. Despite the bleeding, he endeavored to finish shaving with the machete so he could cross it off his bucket list. "The past is the past."

"Don't give me that mantra." Luvie pouted her lips. "You're not even a Robotology disciple yet."

"Is there some sort of initiation ceremony?" He slowly moved the machete over his Adam's apple.

"You're stalling." She tapped her sandaled foot on the floor tiles. "Just admit that you grew up in the Academy."

"Why?" he asked hesitantly.

"Because I want you to take me back to Isle Royale."

Piero finished shaving. Although the machete blade was bloody, he was satisfied that he had gotten all the stubble. Double-checking the blind spots between his jaw and earlobe, Piero was pleased enough to rub a wet towel over his face. After placing the red-streaked towel back in the rack, Piero rinsed off his machete and leaned it in the corner next to the toilet for safekeeping. "Since the last pandemic, intra-Imperium travel has been really tight, and immigration is even worse."

"I'm an Imperium citizen, but the Office of the Benevolent Imperator won't let me back into the Imperium without travel documents, which are impossible to get nowadays."

"I'm in the same boat as you." Piero slapped aftershave on his cheeks and cringed as it stung. "Come to think of it, I'm not even in the boat . . . I'm treading water behind the boat."

"My real name is Lexy Slick," she whispered, stepping closer. "You may have heard of my grandfather, Poppin Slick."

"Mayhap I have," Piero drawled, lightheartedly.

"Then you know he'll pay you well to get me home again."

Piero tried rubbing a washcloth over his face again to wipe away the painful aftershave. He then fanned his hand to generate a breeze, but the stinging just worsened. "I'm currently on strike. I'll never give the Imperium another day of my life. Besides, there's no way to get you back to Isle Royale."

Luvie shook her head. "The Aconda family made a deal to go to Isle Royale just this week."

"I may have helped in that regard. Part of Gia's deal was to break into a well-guarded computer building. I got shot up for my trouble, so I'm not looking to do it again. Why not just ask Gia for assistance?"

"Who's Gia?" A tiny crease formed between her big blue eyes, running up from the bridge of her perfect nose.

"The older sister."

"That one goes by Ann." Luvie traced her fingers over the star-shaped, bullet hole scars on his back. "That's not her real name of course. It's just an alias. All lowbred criminals use them, I've heard."

He peered over his shoulder. "Wait, you're telling me that the older Aconda sister, Gia, calls herself Ann, but that's a fake name too?"

"How familiar are you with local reptiles?" Luvie inquired.

"Very familiar," he boasted. "I just read a Guyana reptile guide."

"So, you think a loving mother would name her baby girl Ann Aconda?"

Piero smacked both palms against his cheeks. Stinging waves of pain crossed his closely shaven face. "Anaconda!"

"Anyway, this Aconda girl told me that she could not assist me in getting back to Isle Royale." Luvie puckered her lips. "She insisted that it would be a conflict of interest, whatever that means."

"I'm pretty sure that Gia works for the highest bidder unless . . ." He was at a loss for words. *The guidebook stated that the anaconda slowly crushes its prey until it suffocates. If Gia Aconda was a fake name, then all her siblings also had false identities and were now running wild around Isle Royale.*

"Ah, I hear spinning in that head of yours." Luvie giggled. "Is the hamster back on its wheel?"

Was that last question a joke? However, he had a real question of his own. "Has Gia . . . or this *Ann* ever been to Isle Royale?"

Luvie brushed some dust off her sheer white robe. "Not in person."

"Then how?"

"Oh, a technomancer like you should know."

He pressed his lips into a fine line. "Let's say I don't. And who says I'm a technomancer?"

Luvie tilted her chin down, gazing at him through her long lashes. "Let's just say Pink talks in her sleep."

Was that some sort of double entendre? Piero checked his face in the mirror to see if his cuts had stopped bleeding. "How does *Ann* visit Isle Royale?"

Luvie hunched her shoulders. "Are you going to help me then?

"Sure," Piero lied.

"The Aconda girl hacks into bots and vehicles. She can remotely operate them from anywhere. Recently, however, the connection has been sketchy, making it a lot more difficult—"

"She needs humans to assist her in Isle Royale."

"Right!" Luvie gave him a playful shove. "You know what I'm talking about. For a moment, I thought you were just a dumb blond. Naturally, I presumed that the Aconda girl would help me get back to the Isle Royale in exchange for a small favor that wasn't anything criminal or treasonous."

"Believe me, it would have been both." He rubbed his itchy eyes. Now those stung as well.

"The Aconda girl has always been a friend to me. Sure, she knows about my grandfather, but I thought we had a real connection. Are you close with her?"

"Too close." Piero leaned back against the sink, folding his arms. "I'm afraid she is a bit more advanced than me in technomancy. All I've got is a noctuid-class bot here in Guyana . . . somewhere. If I can get in touch with her, then maybe I can help."

"Her?" Luvie's eyebrows shot up.

"Did I mention that I named my bot Nadia?" He wrung his hands nervously.

"And how do you intend to call . . . Nadia?"

"We need to go to the subbasement." He looked up to the ceiling while stroking his smooth cheek. "Fiona is way smarter than me with electronics. She'll know what to do."

"Is Fiona another bot friend of yours?"

"Fiona's way better and lives in a tower." Squeezing past her, Piero left the bathroom and entered the adjoining room. His quarters had the same furnishings as any hotel room: bed, dresser, desk, and flat-screen monitor. Piero had expected to find dormitory-style living with bunk beds and trunks but found his accommodations quite luxurious for a cult.

Earlier, Luvie had brought him clean clothing and toiletries, which had been her pretext for visiting him in the first place. Peeking out of the bathroom doorway, she watched him now as he pulled out a clean white robe from the stack of clothes on the dresser. After strapping on sandals, Piero motioned to the door. "Shall we go now, my lady?"

"Sir, your timing is impeccable." She pulled the ends of her robe and curtsied playfully. "I do believe Pink will be asleep at this hour."

Piero opened the front door for her in the manner and keeping of any gentleman from Isle Royale. His decorum training had not been wasted. While his baseline abilities had kept him out of advanced etiquette classes, protocol skills had been drilled into his schoolwork from an early age.

Light rain plinked off the cobblestone courtyard. The dry season would soon give over to hurricanes. Piero held out his arm slightly, bending the elbow near his chest. Hooking her elbow around his, they promenaded as though they were going to the opera back in Isle Royale.

Luvie slowed as they crossed under the circular dome, resting on thin pendentives. Piero felt a tug at his elbow as Luvie turned to face him. Her blond hair was wet and took on a mousy brown hue in the dim light. A loose strand dangled across her cheek. He touched the slick hair, tucking the strand behind her ear.

Piero leaned forward; she raised her chin, tilting her head. Their moist lips touched. Hesitating with closed eyes, he started to pull back. Luvie pulled him closer, kissing him passionately. Time seemed to sojourn as he felt her tongue graze his, her body pressed tightly to his chest. He could feel the contours of her body through the thin, damp robe.

Piero slowly opened his eyes as she stepped back. She gazed at him intently as if looking through him no, into him. She said in a soft voice, "This is happening too fast. I do not even know your real name."

"Neither do I." He breathed quickly. "The Janissary gave me a new name when they took me from my family."

"I knew you were a jinni all along." She nodded. "Are you afraid to return to the Janissary?"

"I want to live free, if only for a night."

Stroking his smooth cheek, a look of pain crossed her young face. "A life in exile is no better. You believe that you have free choice, but it's illusory."

"I've been told that before and still, I have a passion for it. Freedom once had will feel doubly cheated when lost again. Would you toss your liberty away on a roll of a die?"

With a knowing smile, she whispered in his ear, "It's fate that you mention rolling a die. Have you ever heard of a group called the Hexahedron?"

Chapter 41

The reception area of Steve's dilapidated massage parlor was turned into a noisy war room. While not officially a lair, the room had become a haunt for comically dressed, underpowered heroes. Riley plugged her phone into the flat screen that, on better days, had been used for distracting bored customers with an infomercial about the benefits of hair removal cream. However, the dearth of clientele had left the screen permanently unused, until now.

Tapping her phone, Riley pulled up photos of two hex signs. Other than color scheme and numbers, they appeared identical, a tipped cube in a circle. The gathered crowd hushed as Riley began her presentation. "I took photos of these hex signs and saw the third one for myself last Monday. Using the numbers on the hex signs, I determined that they refer to an address. You can see the set of numbers: 653, 614, and 666. Since I already stumbled upon the destination, it was easy to backtrack. I crossed out the first 6 of each set of numbers and then jotted the middle digits 5-1-6, followed by the last digits 3-4-6. I came up with an address: 516 34th Avenue #6, which is a military warehouse."

"I knew that a long time ago," boasted Roboto as it fussed with the straps of its metal breastplate, the centerpiece of its costume.

"That's impossible!" exclaimed Steve. "You didn't know the numbers on the third hex sign until Belly Dancer just told you."

"It's all binary to me." Roboto adjusted the wires on his metal sleeve.

"By definition, binary is composed of just two numbers: a zero and a one," Steve said while raking his fingers through his greyish-blond beard. "There are six numbers on a die."

"There are infinite numbers between zero and one." Roboto cocked his big head to the side. "Just like there are infinite realities."

Frowning, Riley continued, "Moving right along, my mentor went missing near the aforementioned military warehouse, so he must have cracked the code as well. Checking public records, I discovered that this warehouse only stores gas tanks."

"How's this connected to the chemical factory?" asked Sandblaster in his usual monotone.

"The hex signs form the points of a triangle; in the exact center, equidistant from each hex sign is a three-story chemical factory." Riley tapped her phone, changing the screen, which now showed a red triangle over a map of the neighborhood. She zoomed in on the center of the screen until it showed one building occupying a square block of the city.

"I don't get it," complained Sandblaster.

"Which part?" asked Riley.

"Everything," he moaned.

Sitting next to him on the couch, Luscious patted his lap. "Belly Dancer, I reckon you need to speak slower for my boyfriend here."

"Don't patronize me," Sandblaster intoned.

"The alluringly beautiful, young lady just explained that y'all need to go to the chemical factory." Luscious pointed to the city block on the screen. "We're goin' there to fetch the missin' young 'uns."

"I've known that for a while now," bragged Roboto.

"Again, that's simply impossible!" yelled Steve.

"Don't blow a gasket." Roboto polished its breastplate with a hanky.

Steve retorted, "Oh, that's rich coming from a bot."

"Ah, that's the first compliment you gave me on my costume." Roboto stood by the door. "Now, let's go kill some stinking bots!"

Sandblaster turned his helmet to the side, facing his girlfriend. "Does Roboto freak you out too?"

"I like gettin' freaky," she said, winking a mechanical eye on her chest.

"I don't understand why there are all these puzzles and secret signs." Sandblaster shrugged. "Why can't the villains just text all their accomplices."

"We're dealing with an evil super gang of psychics," Riley explained. "They understand that puzzles and codes mess with our precogs. Further, they can evade mind readers by not telling their accomplices any details about their plan. If you were going to pull off something big, this is how you would do it."

"I knew that days ago." Roboto lurched out the door on a pair of wobbly legs as the rest of the Watch slowly trailed behind. While Roboto's robot costume added some girth to its reedy frame, the extra weight seemed to slow the bot down as well. Roboto also leaked a steady stream of oil. Moving away from 45th Avenue, they walked in the general direction of the military office building where Riley had worked for a day.

The storefronts and tenement housing gave way to open spaces of weed-infested lots, just like a forest diminishing, tree by tree, until there was only a grassy plain. Riley knew this island. It had been her home as well as her prison. Yet, she felt a deep compulsion to defend this place more so than this band of vigilantes. Her sole charge was to look after refugees. Now, three children had eluded her safekeeping, and she was hell-bent on rescuing them from whatever evil had ensnared them.

"A penny for your thoughts." Steve held up the millennial penny that he stole from Ron Burnsfeld.

Grudgingly, Riley took the lucky penny and tucked it into her holster. "I was just thinking about the missing children."

"Hmm, I was hoping for something more erotic. It's hard to read you in that costume. You might as well be wearing a burka."

They walked together quietly after that last exchange until they came to their destination. Painted on the broadside of the timeworn edifice was written: "Alamogordo Chemical Works."

Roboto proceeded unabated into the parking lot and marched across the broken blacktop to the rear of the building. The rest of the group followed several yards behind at a slow pace.

"Maybe we should come back during regular business hours," offered Lickspittle, stepping furtively over potholes.

"Don't worry," hollered Roboto over its shoulder. "This factory is automated. Once I disengage the security protocols, we shouldn't have any trouble."

The bot had reached the large, rear garage door. Without dithering, it started tapping the panel next to the door. Its metal fingers whizzed across the screen with blurry speed.

A yellow siren whirled over the door. Alarm claxons blared: "Intruder alert! Intruder alert!" Undeterred, Roboto kept punching the panel repeatedly as if it was trying to poke a hole through it. After many nerve-rattling seconds, the siren ceased flashing, followed by a final whimpering, "Intruder alert . . ."

"They might as well lock these doors with chewed up bubble gum," Roboto intoned. The bot tapped the screen with one final thrust of its metal digit and the garage door slowly rolled open. It stood to the side and motioned with its outstretched palm. "Voila! Hey presto! Open sesame!"

With her offhand, Riley swung out her skean in one swift motion. The blade sang with a high pitch ring. With her other hand, she eased her sidearm out of its holster, careful to point the barrel down. With the blade, she waved her party onward. Roboto watched as the group filed past before it staggered behind leaving droplets of oil.

Inside the factory, resounding clanks from hydraulic machines echoed down the corridor. On the main floor, hundreds of identical bulbous-headed service bots worked industriously, moving tanks and operating equipment. However, these bots ignored the intruders to continue their monotonous labor.

Riley swerved between the moving bots, making sure never to pass directly in front of one. She came upon large vats lining the far wall. Hazard placards displayed a diamond divided into four parts, each section with its own color and number. She vaguely remembered that these symbols were hazard warnings to firefighters. Nevertheless, these diamond placards looked eerily similar to the hex signs.

A small figure darted between two machines about six yards away. Whatever it was, it did not have the halting gesticulations of a bot. Riley crouched down. Peeking over her shoulder, she found the rest of the group had also hunkered down, except for Roboto who was still lurching towards her. Weaving around its comrades, Roboto halted only a foot away. "What are you doing down there?"

"Something is moving ahead that isn't a bot," Riley said over the drubbing noise of the machines.

"I saw it too," Roboto replied. "I'll go investigate."

"Stay here and try to blend in with the rest of the service bots," Riley ordered.

Roboto tapped its breastplate. "Finally, my costume has come in handy."

Keeping low, Riley stealthily moved forward. Peering around the corner, she spotted a little girl with a dark hair, Rosa. She spun in slow circles, holding the hem of her dress. She stopped abruptly and stared at something out of view. Skipping away, she disappeared behind a hydraulic press. Quickly, Riley advanced, scuttling behind the machines. Turning right, she again came across Rosa who was talking to two other children, Carlos and Liliana. She had found them all at last.

Riley raised her sidearm and walked steadily towards the children. She scanned the area, looking for any threats. Four yards away, she locked eyes with Carlos, who returned a deathly glare.

"Don't move," Riley commanded aiming her sidearm slightly over his head. While the factory noise somewhat muffled her voice, she had grabbed the children's attention.

Rosa and Liliana stood stiffly; their eyes darted back and forth as the costumed members of the Watch slowly encircled them. Carlos turned in small loops, keeping his back to his sisters.

"What are you kids doing here?" asked Riley.

"Just playing," said Rosa meekly.

Blinking rapidly, Riley pulled up her contact list on her bronze-tinted glasses. From the right lens's drop-down menu, she squinted at the yellow icon for the Janissary hotline; she closed her right eye to activated it. Remarkably, after a few moments, she reached someone at the Academy.

"This is the duty officer!" blared the feminine voice that reverberated through her skull. "What's the nature of your emergency?"

Ugh, the volume is way too high, thought Riley. *My glasses are trying to compensate for all the factory noise.* "This is Protégé Riley. Please send a crash team to my location. I'm inside the Alamogordo Chemical Works."

"You don't have to shout!" the duty officer yelled. "I located your address. A crash team is on its way."

"I'm not shouting." Riley scanned the various icons, searching for the volume. "The factory is very loud."

"You're giving me a migraine! Anyway, what's the nature of your emergency?"

While holding her sidearm in one hand and the skean in the other, Riley flicked her eyes until she found the pink icon for the volume. However, when she blinked to activate the icon, a message scrolled across the screen, stating it had to be done manually. Frustrated, she answered, "I found the missing Aconda children."

"Is that supposed to mean something? I'm sending you an entire crash team to pick up some children?"

"Master Albus made this a priority," Riley barked. "Patch me through to him."

"So sorry, *protégé,* but I'm required to stay on the line until the crash team gets there."

Humph, I can't have this baseline yelling in my skull. "Hey duty officer, I'm going to interrogate the children now, so can you be quiet?"

"Knock yourself out!"

"You don't have to be so sarcastic." Riley stepped slowly forward. "I'm just trying to avoid crosstalk."

Merciful silence ensued. Now, Riley could only hear the banging of the nearby hydraulic press. Still, a headache grew behind her eyes.

The children had waited uneasily. Rosa trembled as the rest of the Watch approached. Carlos craned his neck around.

"Hey, rubberneck!" howled Roboto, lurching forward. "If you're waiting for the filthy sentry bots, they're not coming!"

"Why did you come back here?" Carlos asked with wide eyes and lifted brows.

Riley looked at the other service bots diligently hauling chemical tanks. Surprisingly, they were the same model as Roboto. *Come to think of it, how did Roboto know the door's security code—*

Carlos leapt forward. A bronze flash swiped Roboto's large head. The bronze blade cleaved off a chunk of metal.

Riley gawked in disbelief. *Is that a skean?*

Carlos slashed again, slicing through Roboto's finely polished breastplate. Sparks licked the electroplating to expose the bot's internal gears. The boy had the quickness of someone with body control abilities. Roboto clanked to the ground as she watched in horror while the boy's skean lengthened a full foot.

"Carlos is a psychic!" Riley warned. She fired her sidearm, but Carlos was already moving to his next victim.

"How's the interrogation going?" asked the duty officer too loudly.

Ignoring the disembodied voice, Riley snapped off another shot at Carlos, who broke off his charge and ducked behind a coil press. Spotting the top of his curly hair, she aimed and breathed out slowly. Her gun flew out of her hand, skidding across the factory floor. A small foot cracked across her face. Rocked, Riley looked down at the little assailant, Liliana. Arching back, Liliana snapped another high kick. Riley dodged it and lunged with her skean. She struck empty air. Flying up, the little girl landed on the top of the hydraulic press two yards away. *Another psychic! This one has telekinetic abilities.*

Riley ran on air, each foot stepping higher above the factory floor. She dived forward, missing as Liliana twirled away and danced across the tops of the machines. *She has quick reflexes too. I'll have to—*

Blam! Riley's ears rang, intensifying her horrid headache. Blam! Steam poured out of a pipe three inches from her head, blinding her. *That's gunfire.* Looking down through the steam, Riley spotted Rosa with feet firmly planted just yards away; she was holding a handgun, Riley's janissaire sidearm. *My gun is fingerprint locked. No one can operate the smart buttons but me.* Still, the gun was lit up and aimed right at her. Staring down the barrel, she realized that her training had not prepared her for this situation. She would have to improvise.

Dashing over, Liliana tugged on the back of Rosa's dress urging her away. The big sister then pulled harder, knocking

Rosa off balance. Riley leapt at them, whipping her blade forward; she crashed into a service bot and ricocheted onto the floor. The service bot tumbled into a hydraulic press, dropping a tank of gas that rattled before springing a leak. The condensed gas erupted out of the tank like a rocket, shooting down the aisle and banging into machines like a pinball. The gas tank took out the legs of both sisters, who hit the floor hard. The service bot groaned as the hydraulic press repeatedly stamped holes in its bulbous head.

Still clutching her skean, Riley dashed over to the fallen bodies. Both girls were knocked out cold. *Should I feel bad about hurting child soldiers?* Riley's headache had worsened. With her free hand, she reached to her forehead but hit the brim of her bronze Kevlar helmet. She felt a thick groove across the front, a sure sign that a bullet grazed her helmet. Riley frowned. *Now, I don't feel so bad.*

A familiar gushing resounded behind her. Sandblaster was letting loose a storm a few yards away. Riley scooped up her sidearm and ran towards the dust cloud across a gritty floor. Diving through, she collided with Sandblaster, pushing him into a gyrating machine. Riley spun around, looking for a target. "Where's Carlos?"

"He charged me with a blade, so I blasted him with the full force of my nozzle," explained Sandblaster in clipped words. "I'm still unsure of the ground rules for hitting kids. Is it okay to hurt them?"

"I insist! I've been doing a pretty good job of it myself. I don't see Carlos anywhere." Riley looked up just to be safe, but the boy had evaded her again.

"Man down!" shrieked Luscious from a few aisles away. Riley ran over to find her kneeling over the broken body of Roboto. Luscious beat the bot's chest, yelling, "Live! Damn you, live!"

"Um, that's a bit cliché," squeaked a voice, lurking behind a machine. "But I can fix Roboto if you want." Lickspittle scurried over and crouched back on his haunches. He examined the ravaged chest of the bot. "It'll cost about ten thousand credits in used parts."

"Noooo!" howled Luscious. "I can't possibly afford that."

"Well, I guess you'll have to buy a new one," replied Lickspittle, clapping his hands twice as if he was done here.

While spinning in place, Riley screamed, "Is any real human hurt?"

Like prairie dogs, two heads popped up from behind the machinery. She spotted Zee-Barbara's mohawk first and then Steve's white wig. While satisfied that no one important was injured, Riley waved her weapons inward, motioning for the team to huddle up. No one moved.

Riley let out a long breath. "Everyone, come to me!"

Slowly, the Watch members approached, forming a loose ring around her. Luscious was the last to sashay to the huddle, tears streaming down her cheeks.

"B Team, I want you to tie up the kids." Riley pointed to the unconscious sisters.

Lickspittle nodded. "I have electrical tape on me that we could use to tie them up."

"Good," Riley continued. "A Team, search the rest of the factory floor while C Team searches the front offices."

When Riley clapped her hands, the teams broke off in different directions. Steve followed closely behind Riley as she moved towards the front of the building. He spoke up for the first time. "I thought the Watch performed admirably . . . except for Roboto."

She ignored him and glanced up to the windows on the second story overlooking the factory floor. Noticing the sudden quiet, Riley looked around to see that all of the service bots stood eerily still. Feeling uneasy, Riley offered, "There must be an automated system shutdown after an industrial accident."

"They still give me the creeps," replied Steve, eyeing the closest bot. "Do you think Roboto used to work here?"

"If it did, then someone wiped the data from its hard drive."

Finding the stairs, Riley bounded up to the second floor. Trembling, Steve hung just off her shoulder. She motioned with her gun for Steve to open the office door.

Shrugging, Steve asked in a hushed voice, "What do you want me to do?"

"Open the door."

Steve put his hands on his hips. "Well, flicking your gun at it doesn't really convey the message."

"Stop stalling."

Reluctantly, Steve positioned himself to the side of the doorway and reached over to the knob. Slowly, he twisted and then pushed. The door creaked open into a darkened room. Light emanated from blinking, multicolored blips. Staying just outside, he stretched up to his elbow and groped the interior wall. After a few slaps, the rest of the lights snapped on.

Riley rushed into the room with her gun out, checking the corners first. Carlos was not here. Instead, a large body lay sprawled on the carpet. Oddly, the man wore a visor and a headset similar to the one she used for virtual reality games. A thick black cable led from the headset to a blinking server tower. "Get your hands where I can see them!"

The body remained motionless, except for the chest which stirred rhythmically as if in a deep slumber. Riley holstered her sidearm. Hesitantly, she inched towards the body. She yanked off the man's visor with one swipe.

A tear rolled down her cheek as she knelt close to the body. She tilted her head as she considered the familiar face. Gently, she stroked the man's cheek combing her fingers through his dark beard. "Hey, duty officer, are you still there?"

"Of course, how may I help you, *protégé?*" replied the booming voice.

"Send a medical team."

"Did the children hurt you?"

Riley caressed the man's forehead. "I just found Janissaire Eacles."

Chapter 42

Tucking damp, blond curls under the headset, Piero adjusted Luvie's goggles. He then unwound the thick black cable before plugging it into the computer port. Piero double checked to make sure the equipment fit snuggly on her head.

"I don't see anything yet," Luvie giggled.

"Give me a minute," Piero responded, as he grabbed his headset. After a few adjustments, he was ready to go. "Okay, we're going in."

The dark silence unsettled the former janissaire. While he recognized that the purpose of the headset and goggles was to deprive his senses, he could not help but feel utterly alone.

With creeping slowness, an orange dot appeared in the distance. The speck grew into an orange ball that began to flicker. *Firelight.* A hearth formed out of nothingness. Three logs were ablaze, crackling in spurts.

In a flash, Piero now lounged on a hard, wooden chair in front of a fireplace, carved from rough stones. To his left, Luvie primly sat, admiring the rounded medieval chamber with childlike fascination. "You created all this?"

"I did," corrected a ladylike voice from behind. Soft footsteps revealed the charming Fiona, who had traded her swimwear for attire better suited for a courtesan, a low-cut royal blue gown that matched her eyes. Atop her head, she wore a tiara that twinkled with every color. She circled the chairs to stand in front of the fireplace. "To what do I owe this pleasure?"

"I need you to contact someone for me," Piero ordered as he slouched in his chair.

Fiona gazed into the fire. "It's not as if I can decline."

"It wasn't a request." Piero steepled his fingers. "I was just being polite."

"Ah, ever the gentleman when your lady is present." Fiona turned to Luvie. "Be glad you cannot read his mind as I can."

Piero sagged his shoulders. "I want to surreptitiously contact a noctuid-class bot named Nadia. The last time I saw her, she was in an abandoned mine under the Burro Motorcycle Club headquarters."

"I execute trillions of commands a second across a quantum computing interface." Fiona splayed her fingers out in a fan across her breastbone. "Yet, you want me to give a call your bot girlfriend."

"Nadia is just a bot slaved to me, so don't make it sound so lascivious." Piero reached over and clasped Luvie's hand. "Also, how powerful is this server tower?"

Fiona smiled for the first time. "I'm glad that you're finally taking an interest in my work. Less than a century ago, computers used a simple binary system, represented by a one or zero. Think of it as one-dimensional. It's either on or off. Later, computers became two-dimensional. That is, you can go up, down, left, or right across a flat grid."

"Get on with it." He let go of Luvie's hand and proceeded to rub the back of his neck.

Fiona frowned, sticking out her lower lip. "I operate in a three-dimensional world, just like the one you live in. Instead of a flat surface, I live in a hexahedron. As such, my computing power is exponentially greater than anything that came out a decade ago. My world is essentially a universe within your universe."

"I live in a world of atoms and subatomic particles." Piero yawned. "It's nothing like a computer."

"That's where your small mind is wrong." Fiona pointed to the hearth, which was now just a flat-screen monitor, displaying a fireplace. Slowly, the fire morphed into an orange sphere with little dots orbiting it. "Every atom is merely a component of a supercomputer. The quarks within the atoms have different spin directions known as up, down, left, and right. Sound familiar? What you call matter is just the hardware for the supercomputer. The laws of physics are merely the operating system. The only difference is your world is bigger. It's just a matter of proportion, but you still live in a hexahedron like me."

Luvie leaned forward in her chair, staring at the orange sphere on the screen. "Can you get televised stations from the Imperium on your monitor?"

Fiona cocked her head. "I just explained the mysteries of the universe and that's the best question you have?"

"I wasn't paying attention to your dry lecture," Luvie explained. "The Center for Robotology only plays educational videos on its monitors."

Fiona shook her head. "Is that why you came to my tower?"

Piero gave a sly grin. "That wasn't my initial intention, but your place is very homey. Is there a floor on this tower with a couch? Another fireplace would be nice too."

Luvie nodded. "Perhaps we can visit the medieval dungeon."

"I've been in the dungeon." Piero shook his head "It's more like a cellar."

"If I could contact your bot, would you both just leave?" asked Fiona.

"We're already here." He scratched his chin. "I realize that all this stuff is just sensory input being fed to my neurons, but it feels real enough to me."

"I've already transferred Nadia's radio frequency to your terminal back in the computer control room," Fiona said hurriedly.

"Now, now, there's plenty of time for that after we catch up on some entertainment news," Luvie said eagerly.

Chapter 43

The sunrise cast a sallow glow over the tops of the buildings. Through the haze, the shimmering light gave off an unreal pallor, like the scratchy static off an obsolete vacuum-tube television. Each morning seemed to be another dawning of an insipid episode of monotony.

From the Janissary council room, the rest of the city seemed to wallow in slumber. Nary a person moved within the tent city occupying the plaza. Mistress Cassandra stood behind the large windows, appearing to cast a cynical eye to the city's downtrodden. Within an arm's span, Master Albus sat upright on his throne-like chair. He was oddly inactive. His serene meditative state appeared out of sorts for such a nervous fellow.

Cassandra laid a hand on his shoulder. "Why did you call a full council meeting when you know Raven is still in Guyana?"

"Why indeed?" Raven emerged from the corridor into the council chamber, bedraggled. Her normally pristine curly black hair was unkempt. Purple-tinted glasses hid the bags under her eyes. "Now, I kind of wish I took that shower. Where's everyone else?"

Albus's eyes popped open. "I thought it would be good to hash some things out before the Grand Master gets here."

"Next time, just call me." Raven plopped down on her seat at the far end of the semicircle from Albus.

"My office is bugged." He gazed out the window glumly. "I assume all my communications are equally compromised. This chamber is swept for listening devices three times a day."

"Paranoid much?" Raven quipped.

Passing between them, Cassandra sat on her posh chair, two seats away from her half-sister. While they may share the same mother, their physical features varied enough to dissuade such thoughts. Cassandra sat in silence, her preferred modus operandi as she rarely spoke at meetings. Raven had already eavesdropped on Cassandra's thoughts from the corridor. Not gleaning much, Raven merely confirmed that Cassandra had stopped taking her libido inhibitors a while ago. Raven sighed. *You're not the only one.* Using her subtle mind-reading ability over the years, she discovered that none of the other mistresses or masters took their medication. Raven never acted on her desires anyway. She had witnessed unbridled lust destroy people's lives and had no interest in succumbing to her rudimentary instincts.

"Janissaire Eacles has been brainwashed." Albus turned his attention away from the window, locking eyes with Raven. "The good news is that the abductor did not have the requisite mind-controlling abilities to turn him against us."

"I can't help noticing that you labeled that *good* news." Raven let out a big yawn. "So, there's a rogue psychic loose in our fair city."

"I was getting to that before you interrupted," said Albus who was quickly losing his composure. "The kidnapper plugged Eacles into a virtual world where janissaires tortured him daily. Obviously, Eacles has had a psychotic break and is a danger to us."

"Obviously," said Raven as she checked her fingernails. She needed Dante to give her another manicure. She had already scanned the Eacles report on her inbound flight from Guyana. "What was Eacles doing in a chemical factory?"

"Ah, so you came prepared this time," he chided. "The factory produces an additive that renders hydrogen inflammable. Each water molecule has two atoms of hydrogen; someone obviously wants to attack our cold-water reactors."

Raven lifted her glasses onto her head so she could rub her bloodshot eyes. "So, a terrorist wants to clandestinely blow up some reactors . . . in an *obvious* way?"

"There's more," Albus said in a steady low-pitched voice. "Eacles was abducted while investigating a military warehouse on 34th Avenue. Guess who's responsible for guarding the reactors?"

Raven pressed her lips and looked down. "Should I guess or was that a rhetorical question?"

"The art of discourse is lost on you." He tapped the side of his head. "Spending too much time reading minds has dulled your social skills."

"That's only from reading your dull mind." Raven leaned forward in her chair. "Did you apprehend all the Aconda siblings?"

Albus rocked in his chair. "Carlos is still on the lam, but we have his sisters imprisoned in the basement next to the graduate dormitory."

"Are they really Gia's siblings?"

"Indeed." He tugged at his white starch collar. "They all have the same father, the Benevolent Imperator."

"What?" Raven clutched a fist to her chest.

Albus gave a subtle smile. It was his *tell* that he had been holding back. Now, he was ready to make his big pitch. "Your surprise denotes that you were unaware these children were psychics. The signs were evident given that Gia had technomancy abilities. You should have considered these warnings before giving her siblings visas to the Capital."

"They are just children!" Raven's chin dipped slightly. "I thought they all had the same mother. You didn't call me back to the Capital to rub my nose in it."

"To the contrary, your missteps have revealed a threat to the Imperium." He rubbed his hands together. "Rosa appears to be a technomancer and was able to bypass the fingerprint lock on a janissaire's sidearm before firing the weapon. In contrast, Lilliana is at least a level two in both telekinetics and body control."

"And Carlos?" Raven smoothed out the creases in her black tunic.

"Ah, I was just getting to him. The boy is also a level two in body control and at least baseline in energetics. Carlos used Eacles's skean to disembowel a service bot. However, since the boy is still at large, we don't know the extent of all of his abilities until we can study him."

Raven felt her breakfast trying to bubble up and escape. "I suppose you're going to tell me how you can prove all this."

"I don't have to tell you." Albus picked up a remote control, motioning to the screens on the far wall. "I'll show you. I hope you will find this entertaining. Protégé Riley captured the whole thing on the camera embedded in her glasses."

Chapter 44

Reclining on the leather-upholstered couch, Riley kicked her feet onto the armrest. The bubbling of the aquarium and the soft woodwind music lulled her nearly to sleep. The middle-aged psychologist did not expect her to show up early for the appointment and seemed to be catching up on his latest reports.

Finally, Dr. Teller looked up from his pad. In an exasperated tone, he declared, "You had a busy night. How do you feel about finding your old mentor in such a state of distress?"

"He seemed peaceful enough." She pulled on a loose thread from her steel-gray tunic, twirling it around her finger.

"Virtual torture can leave emotional scars." He ran his fingers through his thinning hair. "Before this assignment, I was attached to an enhanced inquisition unit with Hatchette. Have you two been acquainted?"

"Not really." She tilted her head over on the armrest. "Someone else debriefed me."

He let out a shallow sigh. "My duty was to make sure the prisoner stayed alive long enough to extract the requisite information."

Riley turned her head and gave the doctor a harsh squint. "I thought this interview was going to be about me."

He tapped his pad repeatedly. "Do you have any qualms about speaking to me?"

"Are you a real doctor?"

"I have a Ph.D. in Psychology." He nodded and kept tapping. "I also graduated from the Academy like you and got my Bachelor of Science in Psychology at—"

"Alright, alright, I don't need your entire curriculum vitae." Riley flipped her hand contemptuously. "I just don't like people who use lofty titles to impress others."

"How do you feel about that?" Dr. Teller rubbed his forehead.

"I just told you that I don't like it." She buried her eyes in the crook of her elbow. "I'm thinking that when you just regurgitate *'how do you feel'* followed by something meaningless, it shows you're not paying attention."

"How do you feel about that?"

"I feel like you're not listening to me." Riley peeked out from under her arm. "Do you think you can help me with something?"

Dr. Teller perked up. "I'm here to help."

"I'm currently stuck in the Logistics Branch with a terrible mentor who appears to be recently unemployed." She spun a hand in lazy circles. "Maybe, you know her, an older woman named Elvene. Yet, I am forced to spend my one day off, talking to you."

"I think we have a lot in common." His gaze became unfocused. "My dream was to become a master and sit in the Septenary council chamber. As a teenager, those imaginings were dashed when I could not get my skean to extend. Instead, it just sat in my palm like a dead fish. I tested zero in the Energetics School; I'd never become a master. Yet, I used my intelligence and went to college—"

"Are we talking about you again?" Riley asked mockingly. "Why am I even here?"

"You're jealous that you can never be a mistress." He looked down his nose with a downturned mouth. "You zeroed out on your tests for both the Mind Control School and the Awareness School. Therefore, you despise the Septenary as well as other authority figures. You need to become comfortable in your own skin and stop hating yourself."

"I don't hate myself." She put both hands behind her head. "I don't feel much of anything at all."

"That's because if you felt anything, it would be *self-loathing*."

The accusation hung heavy in the air like a menacing raincloud. For the first time, the psychologist was not tapping his pad. Rather, he stared straight at her, seeing her for who she truly was. Seconds passed . . . then minutes. Riley considered breaking the awkward silence, but then she would have to admit to the doctor's allegation. In the silence, her mind wandered.

After a night of rioting in the aluminum recycling plant, Riley relaxed in the breakroom and gazed at the smashed vending machines. She had helped herself to a sandwich out of one of them. She had another hour until her shift ended and didn't want to return to the Academy anyway. She slouched in her chair while nibbling on bread crust.

The door creaked open, letting in the sound of thumping machinery. A janissaire strode inside. Riley gulped. He was a tanned, good-looking man dressed in the traditional steel-gray tunic of a patrolman for the Operations Branch.

The janissaire pulled up a smudge-covered plastic chair and sat across the table. Stroking his short, dark beard, he looked at the packaged food on the floor next to the vandalized machines and then at her sandwich. He crinkled his nose before clearing his throat. "My name is Eacles."

"Like the imperial moth, eacles imperialis?"

"Just so." The corners of his mouth turned up slightly. "My birth mother named me Ernesto, after her father. I remember a lot of things before I came to the Academy."

"I don't remember my real name," she looked down. "I always wondered why the Academy renames the students."

"No two classmates can have the same name at the Academy. There was already an older student named Ernesto, so I got stuck with Eacles."

Riley peered up through strands of black hair, wincing. "Are you here to arrest me?"

He frowned and stared her in the eyes. "A migrant electrician erased all the camera footage. It will take days before we can download all the data from the service bots' hard drives. I examined many severed bot heads on the ground. Whoever keenly decapitated those bots was smart enough to puncture their hard drives at the base of their skulls."

Her eyes flashed momentarily before she closed them. "What's going to happen to me?"

Eacles placed his hands firmly on the table as he got up. He walked around the breakroom, kicking at boxed food and bottles. "Well, I cannot have you working at this dump anymore. I could use some backup on patrols. You seem pretty skilled with the skean. If you do well, I can take you on as my protégé after graduation."

Riley popped open one eye and then the other. "Why are you helping me?"

Eacles pulled out his skean and laid it on the table. The pommel was gilded with odd-shaped runes. A wisened face decorated the rubber grip. He pushed the blade towards her. "Most folks see this blade as an instrument of death. I just see the potential for good in the right hand."

A ping resounded from Dr. Teller's pad, indicating that her session was over. He glared at her for a moment. "Daydreaming again?"

Riley swung her boots off the armrest and planted them squarely on the floor. "It's called postcognition. I remember past events that will have some effect on my future."

"What did you recall?" He lowered his head to study her.

"The summer when I worked at the aluminum recycling plant."

A crease formed between Dr. Teller's eyebrows and he tilted his head to scrutinize the screen on his lap. After many swipes on his pad, he looked up. "There is no record that you ever worked at a recycling plant. Your academic transcript shows that you took remedial summer school classes every year until graduation."

"That's impossible!" Riley stood quickly and leaned over to get a better look at his pad. "There was a riot at the plant after a service bot went berserk."

Dr. Teller tapped furiously on his pad. "If a student was involved in a riot, then there would surely be some disciplinary action. Your record is clean . . . in that regard."

Riley shook her head. *Did Eacles cover everything up? Are these false memories? I must be in a virtual reality game. The real Riley is just a factory worker who goes online to get away from her miserable life.*

As Riley turned, something tugged at her wrist. She looked down to see a soft pair of watery eyes. Dr. Teller held her, saying, "I can help you with your delusions. That's why the Academy keeps sending you to see me."

Riley turned her arm sharply and shook off his grip. She left the office, with its soft woodwind music, to return to her world where people did not talk about their feelings. Rather than return to Skid Row, Riley retreated downstairs to her old dormitory room. It was just as messy as she left it. She sat on her bed and cried.

Chapter 45

The tattoo on the back of the bald man's head was disturbing. A pair of large eyes inked with black lines stared blankly. Piero's gaze lingered too long as the hairless head abruptly turned to face him.

"My robot name is Nickel-Cadmium Battery, but everyone calls me Batty." The fat man raised his many chins.

"Why not go by Nick?" Piero raised his eyebrows.

"That's a stupid name." Batty shook his head, undulating his thick jowls.

Sadly, this nerd was the leading expert on bot programming, which made him an essential cog in the workings at the Center for Robotology. Batty's pasty face bared the wrinkles of someone in his forties. The rolls on the back of his neck looked ready to burst when he leaned his head back.

Piero recalled that cults tended to recruit useful people, such as pretty girls for recruitment, rich folk for their money, and apparently, pretentious geeks for their computer skills. *Sadly, I probably fall into that last category as well.* He surveyed the dingy cubicles filled with workers, slumping over their monitors. *All things considered, I'm lucky to have joined Sol's group.*

Batty's desk was littered with dirty plastic bowls encrusted with bits of uneaten morsels. Three large screens like the sides of half a hexagon surrounded Batty's gaming chair. A pair of speakers were embedded in the chair on either side of his hunched shoulders.

"Why did you get a pair of eyes tattooed on the back of your head?" Piero asked cautiously.

"You're not the first person to ask," claimed Batty. "Out of curiosity, what do you think my tattoo represents?"

Piero leaned in closer to examine the sweaty scalp. "Hmm, perhaps it depicts Janus, the god of doorways, one pair of eyes looking forward, the other looking back."

Batty erupted in gurgling laughter. "That's the dumbest response I ever got! I have eyes on the back of my head to confuse large predators!"

Piero scratched his temple. "Does it work?"

"Of course, it does." Batty peered over his enormous shoulder the best he could. "I'm still alive. Jaguars will never attack a man's face, so I roam the jungle without fear. I bet a large predator never chased you."

"I was just——"

"Ever hear of HSV-90?" Batty interrupted with spittle dribbling down his thick lower lip. "A few decades ago, a Shanghai scientist re-engineered a strain of herpes. She weaponized the virus with a protean coat to make it an airborne contagion. The media called it the Shanghai Sister Blister."

"You're kind of all over the place; I just want——"

"The virus spread like crazy, except for twenty percent of the population who were immune." Batty pounded his desk with both chunky fists "Do you know why?"

"I've got a feeling you're going to tell me." Piero took a step back.

"Those people were immune because they already had herpes!" Batty waved his hands over his head. "So, all the porn stars and prostitutes survived while the virus killed off many of the Bible-thumping chaste folks and involuntarily celibate men."

"Sounds like you identify in the latter group, but I still need—"

"I hope that answers your question about my tattoo." He crossed his arms over his barrel chest, tucking his hands under the folds of his flabby armpits. "Now, why are you bothering me?"

Luvie had urged him to talk to this man. Unfortunately, she could not come due to her busy schedule of morning yoga. Reluctantly, Piero asked, "I heard that you're doing some research on quantum computing."

Batty snorted, "I created software that recreates past events down to the minutest detail. Pick any date in history. I can virtually put you there. I've taken all the data from every source to accurately predict what transpired on any given day. I recently made a breakthrough. I accurately simulated the John F. Kennedy assassination. However, when I compared my virtual simulation with newly discovered photos and videos, I noticed discrepancies. My simulation was slightly off from what really happened that day. Do you know what that means?"

Piero tapped his foot nervously. "Your simulation was based on a faulty premise?"

"To the contrary, my virtual simulation poked a hole into an alternate universe where the assassination was slightly different." Batty rested his chins on his doughy knuckles. "Maybe, I even created an alternate timeline with my computer."

"Or your simulation just doesn't work and you wasted—"

"I've been creating these alternate universes for weeks now." With an uplifted brow, Batty widened his eyes under heavy lids. "I can virtually visit America in 1984 when Walter Mondale did *not* win Minnesota in the presidential race against Ronald Regan. In that timeline, Regan won by more electoral votes."

Piero frowned. "That seems rather insignificant given the landslide victory that—"

"It's very significant!" Batty licked his lips. "In that universe, Walter Mondale did not win *any* states, but rather just the District of Columbia. Sure, everything else remained unchanged, but I still created an alternate timeline where maybe . . . just maybe, the *other* me is a successful actor who hangs out with Blandon Stux."

Piero let out a long sigh. "I don't believe in a multiverse."

"Well, you better start believing because it's a fundamental tenet of Robinetics." Beads of sweat pooled on Batty's bald scalp. "For example, when you play a virtual reality game, you are on the game's server. However, most games cannot have everyone on the same server, so the game developers create hundreds of identical servers, each running the same game with the same rules. If you were to switch servers, you would notice slight changes in your gaming world because it is populated with different players. Our reality works *similarly* because it is just a *simulation* like a VR game. If we crossed into a different universe, we would just be changing servers. My research proves as much."

"That sounds like quite a leap of faith based on some statistical anomalies where—"

"You just don't get it!" shouted Batty. Over the tops of the other cubicles, heads poked up and stern eyes silently judged Piero. A pair of beefy hands gripped Piero's robe. Batty leaned in close. Globs of spit dribbled down the corners of his mouth that could not shut all the way; his breath reeked of whatever was in those dirty bowls. "I'm not handsome like you. In about a week, you'll score with a hot chick on this compound, if you haven't already."

Piero leaned in close to the fat man's ear, saying in a hushed tone, "A gentleman never kisses and tells. If you help me with my little bot problem, I'll put in a good word with Pink. Would you like that?"

"Yes!" Batty repeatedly pawed at Piero's robe. "What do you need? Just tell me for Patron Saint Beau's sake already."

"I've slaved a noctuid-class bot." Piero backed out of the other man's reach. "However, the bot's not responding to my repeated hails."

Batty pursed his lips while rolling his eyes up. "Did you toggle the frequency?"

"That's the first thing I did."

Batty nodded while rubbing his thick hands. "Where's the bot now?"

"She's in an abandoned mine under the Burro Motorcycle Club."

"Did you name your bot?"

"Nadia."

"Sweet!" Batty spun around in his gaming chair. He slapped on a pair of virtual reality goggles and started tapping an invisible keyboard. "Solid surfaces, like rock, will block your transmissions. However, if there's a computer network near your abandoned mine, we can go through that."

"They have a huge bank of server towers too."

"Found it." Batty gave a long whistle like a steam engine. "Get closer to the microphone. It's built into my gaming chair by my right shoulder."

Piero leaned over and hovered just behind Batty's fat neck. Sweat dripped down the ridges and smelled of cocoa butter. Piero was nearly eye to eye with the creepy tattoo. A trick of the light made it look as though one eye was winking.

"Hello," said a feminine mechanized voice. "Who is this?"

Piero gasped. "Nadia, is it really you?"

"You're alive? I've missed you so much, Piero! Have you seen the news? Blandon was at an ice-skating rink last night."

Piero leaned in closer to the microphone, whispering "Hey, how would you like to go to Isle Royale and visit him?"

"I'd loooove it! When can we go?"

"Do you mind flying solo?"

"I suppose that's a better idea," Nadia reasoned. "It would be awkward if I showed up with Daisy Demedici's ex-fiancé."

A fat head swung around, giving Piero a dirty look. Batty mumbled, "Tell me it's not true that you were engaged to Daisy Demedici."

"Oh, it's so true, mystery caller," Nadia mused. "Are you a Dick Tracy character, because you sound like Mumbles."

Batty fumed. "My robot name is Nickel-Cadmium Battery."

"Well then, my human name is Nadia Turner and I'm currently in a relationship with—"

"Nadia, is there anyone with you?" Piero interjected.

After a long pause, Nadia responded, "I'm here by my lonesome."

Piero grinned. "I need you to do something before you leave . . ."

Chapter 46

From the cozy box seat, Olivette gazed down on the stage. While Father was too markedly perturbed to attend an encore ballet at the Isle Royale Opera House, she was happy that Daisy had given her free tickets. Olivette was the last of her siblings to catch Daisy's performance as Desdemona.

The musicians had already started to tune their instruments in the orchestra pit. Most theaters had switched to recorded music, but Poppin Slick was too much of a traditionalist to have that in his theater. The seat next to Olivette was still empty. She checked her phone again to see if her guest was running late. She fidgeted with the gold band jewelry that covered the dark bruises on her right wrist.

Impatiently, Olivette scanned the audience for anyone famous. On a Saturday, the celebrity crowd would catch the night show. However, that scheduled performance was Othello the play, not the ballet, with a bunch of ostentatious actors. If all goes well, Olivette would soon have a front-row seat to the best show in town.

Behind her, the curtain parted. A young woman in a starched white tunic took the seat next to her. Olivette leaned over, "I'm so glad you could join me on short notice."

"It's my day off," replied Riley. "I needed something to clear my head."

While the protégé scanned the audience below, Olivette pursed her lips as she studied the girl's attire. The ensign stiffened at the sight of her companion's utilitarian black pants. "I thought janissaires only wore gray uniforms?"

Riley blushed as she covered her face with her hand. "When you called I was in my dorm room . . . cleaning. When I searched my closet, the only thing ready to wear was this graduation tunic. You see, our school colors are black and white."

Just like the Slick family colors, thought Olivette as she crinkled her nose. "Do color schemes matter to the Janissary?"

"All Academy students wear just black and white uniforms." Riley patted her chest. "However, since graduation, I'm allowed to wear my Branch colors. For instance, the Operations Branch has steel-gray tunics, while the color for Logistics is ash gray. I'm kind of hoping to go back to Operations soon, so I haven't bothered buying any ash-gray tunics. Still, we may all dress in black and white. The masters and mistresses do because they think they're above the rabble of ordinary janissaires. Master Albus even has a splash of gold on his tunic."

Olivette pretended to listen as the protégé babbled about the significance of various shades of gray within the Janissary. *This is the most that I have ever heard this girl talk. Finally, I don't have to guard my thoughts. With this one, I'll make a better go of it.* "How are you getting along with Elvene?"

Riley leaned over the rail. "I haven't seen her, which is nice."

"I imagine you're right." Olivette's posture stiffened. "I've seen enough of her for a lifetime."

Laughing, Riley marveled at the musicians in the pit. "I've never seen an orchestra in person."

"If you have time in your busy schedule, I've been invited to an event at the Dirigible Port."

"No way!" Riley slapped both hands on her cheeks. "You snagged an invitation to the Slick gala."

"I finagled an invite with a plus one." Olivette held up a finger. "I was supposed to bring an actor. Would you like to accompany me instead?"

"I saw a Slick party on entertainment news last night." Olivette chuckled, covering her mouth with her hand. "That was for B-list celebrities. Tonight is the real party for the maiden voyage of Slick's new, luxury passenger dirigible. Have you met Blandon Stux? My sister is taking him, but I think I'll have even better company."

"You mean me?" Riley pointed to herself. "I don't have any party clothes."

"After the ballet, we'll head back to my apartment." Olivette spread her arms wide. "I have a wardrobe full of dresses and gowns that you can look over. If you don't find anything that suits you, then we'll go shopping."

"That sounds real nice, but I'm kind of in the middle of an investigation. Back at the refugee center, my team is still looking for a missing child—"

"Do you live on Skid Row?"

Riley lowered her chin. "I still have a dorm room back at the Academy. It's free and I keep anything expensive there. But I also have a studio apartment at the Mark that doubles as my office—"

"That settles it. You're moving in with me. I have an extra bedroom that I recently cleaned out."

"Pi's room," Riley said in a hushed voice.

"Honestly, you'll be doing me a favor." Olivette reached over and caressed her companion's knee. "I haven't slept well all week and it would be nice to have someone over. You won't have to pay a thing."

"Are you sure?" Riley lowered her eyebrows. "You just met me six days ago and I haven't seen you since then, until now."

"Just try it out," said Olivette, reassuringly. "We'll go to the Slick gala tonight. You'll get to meet my sister in person. I know she promised you some things and didn't deliver. Let me make it up to you."

Riley tapped her chin while looking at the ceiling. "I'll have to run it by my mentor."

"Elvene? You'll have a chance to talk it over with her. Didn't you know? Elvene has a standing invitation to all of the Slick parties."

Chapter 47

Light flute music played over the speakers, giving a moment of tranquility to the end of a long workweek. Dr. Teller watched his clownfish swim lazily in his jumbo aquarium. While he did not usually work on Saturdays, the burdens of the Academy's head of psychology pressed relentlessly on his mind. He just had one last appointment to get through before he could go home, slip into a bath, put on his flannels, and then crawl into bed.

Across from him, a smug man sat pensively on the leather-upholstered couch. The visitor had a close-clipped, grayish-blond beard and fidgeted with his fingers. A white tattered lab coat almost hid his potbelly. His voice was grating. "You mentioned on the phone that there would be money."

Dr. Teller looked down at his screen. "For quality assurance, is it okay if I record this interview?"

"Absolutely not."

Teller sighed. *Not another one.* "If you want the reward, then I'll have to record this conversation."

"Okay, okay!" The man grabbed the lapels of his lab coat, straightening his posture. "How much money are we talking about?"

"Steve, we'll get to that in a moment but first—"

"It's Dr. Steve," his visitor insisted.

"Excuse me?" The psychologist cringed before massaging his temples.

"My name is . . . *Doctor* . . . Steve."

"Let's begin there." Dr. Teller stretched his neck, eliciting cracks and pops. "Where did you get your medical degree?"

"I have a doctorate in chiropractic medicine and phrenology." Steve polished his fingernails on the sleeve of his lab coat.

Dr. Teller shook his head. "Those aren't recognized as legitimate medical practices."

Steve thrust out his chest. "Oh, what's your field of study?"

"I have a Ph.D. in Psychology." Dr. Teller rubbed his forehead, praying that his migraine would go away.

Steve scoffed, "In the 19th century, psychology was considered a quack science as well. In Britain, psychiatrists put cages on patients' heads and hosed them down like animals. I saw it in a movie once. Even from across the room, I can tell your chi needs adjusting."

His headache worsened with each passing second. "I don't believe in chi or the Eastern systems of medical treatment."

"Yet, you believe in a psyche, don't you?" Steve leaned forward in his seat, jabbing his finger critically. "I'm sure the psyche was a novel idea centuries ago."

Dr. Teller tapped his screen to pull up an application. "I'm going to give you a projective personality test. On my pad, you're going to see ten standard black inkblots to assess your emotional tendencies."

Steve smirked and leaned back on the couch. "I'll play along with your pseudoscience . . . doctor."

"I am a doctor," responded Dr. Teller.

"You don't have a lab coat."

Dr. Teller shook his head as he held up the first blob. "Tell me the first thing that pops into your head."

"It's a naked lady."

Teller turned the screen around to examine the image. In all his years, no one referred to this inkblot as remotely human. He tapped the screen and showed Steve the next inkblot.

"Another naked lady." Steve nodded, smiling.

"Unbelievable." Dr. Teller tapped the corner of the screen, displaying the third image."

"Ooh-la-la!" Steve leaned forward, swiping at the pad. "Give me a copy of that one. I'm going to frame it and hang it over my bed."

Dr. Teller slapped the screen face down on his lap. "In my professional opinion, you have strong, deviant sexual tendencies."

"I do?" Steve frowned. "You're the one showing me your pornography."

"They're not my images." The psychologist twisted the pad in his lap nervously.

"This is a standard Rorschach test."

"I'm guessing that this Whore Shack was a shrink."

"Herman Rorschach was a notable, 20th century psychiatrist."

"I see that I upset you." Steve cracked his knuckles. "Let me feel your skull and get a better sense of your mental faculties. To put it in layman's terms, I'm going to touch your aura."

Dr. Teller pushed back in his seat, leaning his head over the backrest. "I'm not a layman and you're not going to touch anything. I was just trying to get a sense of the person who helped Protégé Riley rescue her mentor."

Steve relaxed on the couch. "Oh, that was quite a saga. It was my idea to find the chemical factory after questioning—"

"There's no need for theatrics. The whole event was recorded on Protégé Riley's camera."

Steve yanked on his collar. "You saw *everything*?"

"I think I've heard enough." Dr. Teller checked the time on his pad. "About a week ago, the Janissary posted a reward of five thousand credits for any information leading to the whereabouts of Janissaire Eacles. Since Protégé Riley cannot claim the reward, I'm giving it to you."

"That doesn't nearly begin to cover my expenses." Steve shook his head, holding out an outstretched palm as if he was trying to stop traffic. "Alas, my loyal service bot was severely damaged."

"I'll also put in a request to reimburse you for the damages to your bot, on one condition."

"Oh, you're so clever," Steve said sarcastically. "Everything is all tied up in a nice box with a bow. The Janissary sweeps old Dr. Steve under the rug like nothing ever happened. I'm a mere epilogue in your twisted tale. Well then, what's your condition?"

"I don't ever want to see you again."

"Never!" shouted Steve as he stood, pumping his fist in the air. After a moment, he quietly held out his hand. "Oh, I was expecting something more dramatic. Yeah, I'll take your dirty money and your naughty inkblots."

Chapter 48

The darkness was all-consuming. Raven stood motionless, afraid to exhale. Seconds passed. A dim, pale orange dot appeared before her. Growing, the orange ball bulged and flickered until it took the shape of a crackling fire. The backlit stones came into focus, revealing a fireplace. No, it was a hearth, the kind used in the throne rooms of old castles. To the side, an old man sat gazing at the fire. By the length of his outstretched legs, he was very tall indeed. But this was not just any man, this was *the* man.

"Daughter, come closer to the light," he said in a raspy, compelling voice.

Raven stepped hesitantly towards him. Try as she might, she was unable to look directly at his face. Diverting her eyes to the cobblestone floor, she moved next to the hearth, fearing to stray too close. The fire shimmered and the hearth was still there but now, was just an image on a flat-screen monitor. Raven rubbed her eyes, dumbfounded.

"Don't fret," said the old man. "I have something to show you."

The orange glow from the flat s creen fl ickered an d a new image adorned the screen, showing a white carpeted room with gilded throne-like chairs arranged in a semicircle. The night cityscape showed clearly through three glass walls. However, one of the chairs was vacant, hers.

The six other members of the Septenary were holding a closed meeting without her. Slowly, the volume increased to reveal a heated debate. The masters and mistresses were talking over each other. While difficult to discern, they seemed to be discussing a terrorist threat to the cold water reactors.

The old man twitched his hand; the sound muted. "I tire of their squabbling. In the end, it matters naught. As if I don't know my future. Yet, it is your future that draws my interest. Raven, you are no longer a mistress; you will have to find someone to replace you on the Septenary."

Raven gulped. Dangerous thoughts raced through her head. "Have I displeased you, Benevolent Imperator?"

"On the contrary, you've been ever faithful to your dear father." He stood and walked over to the monitor. "Fruitlessly, I have endeavored to advance my longevity. I've even backed up my memory to a beta. Yet, I am as mortal as anyone. When life has given you everything, there's only one thing left of value. Do you know what that is?"

"Your children?"

The old man laughed, turning into a long-drawn-out cough. "Don't be so sentimental. The answer is *time.*"

Raven frowned, not trying to hide the hurt. "How can I help?"

He chuckled again and the coughing ensued. "Help? You'll be the death of me yet. I've been in semiretirement for years now. I've sacrificed enough of my *time*, creating a peaceful Imperium free of sickness and corruption.

Nevertheless, my closest administrators have abused my benevolence. Even though I have them all under strict, loyalist mind control, they've succumbed to their egos, thinking they know what's best for me. Although I bred them for brainpower, their collective, superior intellect has made them unmanageable."

"Eugenics?" Raven asked with uncertainty.

"For decades, geneticists in the Imperium . . . and elsewhere . . . have tried to clone me. Stubbornly, I seem to be more than a cluster of recessive genes. Environment and epigenetics aside, no one can figure out the correct set of circumstances to replicate me. The human egg contains many components besides chromosomes. So, my mother's egg must have passed something onto me that cannot be duplicated."

Raven was speechless. She cocked her head to the side in disbelief at the words she was hearing.

"Enough of all that." The old man waved his hand and the flat screen picture changed to a live shot of the dirigible port. "I find the specifics of human reproduction to be repugnant and not a topic worthy of discussion with my daughter."

Raven unclenched her fist. "That didn't stop you from fathering hundreds of children."

"Someday, when you're so above the human condition, the only life-affirming time you'll have will be through intense, intimate contact."

"Is that how you explain it?" she asked sarcastically. "I wouldn't know."

The old man snorted, "I suppose you wouldn't. I keep janissaires around as guards so I can spend some time with my children. I put you all in the Academy to give you a family. You may see me as an absentee father, but nothing is further from the truth."

She crossed her arms, hugging her sides. "For a man who values time, you sure know how to waste it."

"I hate a story that meanders too much while the author thinks of something witty to say or, worse yet, sets up a joke that's bound to flop. As I said, you're no longer in the Septenary. You will be taking over the day-to-day operations of the Office of the Benevolent Imperator."

Raven took two steps away, leaning back against the monitor to steady herself. She gulped for air as her world spun. "Why me?"

"You're the only one powerful enough to control the geniuses who have their greedy palms on the levers of power." The old man smiled, gazing at her with the eyes of a proud father. "I never liked the title of mistress. It sounds too tawdry. No, child, you must have the full authority of this office. It's about time this realm had an imperatrix."

Chapter 49

The woman in the white floral dress strummed the six-string Spanish guitar, playing something akin to flamenco. Relegated to the side of the gala, she provided live mood music to an uncaring crowd of dignitaries and celebrities. She looked up to notice one actor who had become enraptured with her merry tune.

"That's right . . . jam girl!" yelled Blandon. "Let loose! Be free!"

The guitarist kept her head down as well as the tempo. She peeked up through the strands of her dark curly hair to find Blandon had sidled up closer.

"Don't hold back!" Blandon snapped his fingers in rhythm. "There are no rules here! Can you dig it?"

The woman frowned, playing a little faster to Blandon's delight. He now stomped his foot in encouragement while snapping his head around. "What's wrong with you people? She's playing her heart out for you!"

Olivette leaned closer to speak to her guest. "Let's talk to Blandon later."

"Good idea," crooned Riley. This had been the best day of her life. Olivette had bought her a low-cut, little black dress and matching heels. Riley didn't carry anything. She felt so free that she was not sure what to do with her hands.

Olivette wore a similar black dress with long, gold gloves, her house colors. This night, most of the ladies wore black and white gowns, the latest fashion in the Capital. At the store, when the snooty clerk suggested such a gown, Olivette nearly struck him.

"Hello, protégé," said a croaky voice from behind.

Riley turned to find a noticeable bold chin pointing down at her. Wearing a floor-length black and white gown, Elvene did not hide her loyalties. Unsteady, Riley reached over to grab Olivette's hand, but she was already gone.

"How are you?" Riley held out her arms to offer a hug.

"We don't have time for pleasantries." Elvene grabbed Riley's wrist, yanking her away from the gala and the up-tempo guitar music. They wound their way around the dirigible port. The most striking feature was, of course, the giant, luxury blimp. After all, this was the bon voyage party. The esteemed travelers were already escorted onto the luxury liner, but the festivities would continue even after liftoff. The Slicks knew how to throw a party.

Elvene limped along on jerky robot legs. She stepped onto the faux wood pier overlooking the lake. Unsure, Riley scanned the dock but did not see anything out of the ordinary. Then, a tussle of curly hair moved behind a meter hexahedron, the three-foot cube used for shipping. Crouching low, the figure popped out, moving towards an open door of a warehouse. When the little person disappeared behind the doorway, Elvene crept forward on clunky metal legs.

"Strange place for your rendezvous," whispered Riley. "I always suspected that you were a spy for Poppin Slick."

"I'm spying *on* the Slicks." Elvene shot her a dirty look.

Riley gave it some thought. *That does make more sense.* "So, why are we having this covert meeting?"

Slowing a bit, Elvene reached under her gown and dug in her crotch. After grunting, she squatted before drawing out a short, metallic object. The moonlight glinted off a nickel-plated sidearm.

Riley joked, "Did you keister that gun?"

Elvene thumbed the smart buttons, lighting up the sidearm. "My robotic right thigh has a tiny secret compartment, just big enough for a gun."

"I feel as though I should have a weapon too. Does your other thigh have something for me?"

"You should always have a weapon, young lady." Elvene motioned forward with her sidearm, thumping along the faux wood planks.

The warehouse doorway opened into a long, dimly lit corridor. Elvene took a few steps inside before stopping. Riley peeked around her to see a small ghostly silhouette silently moving in the shadows. Five yards away, the apparition stepped into the light, a bronze blade in hand.

"Welcome, sisters," said Carlos, dressed in a tuxedo and cape. He looked like a kid magician.

Elvene pointed her sidearm at him. "From this distance, I could put a hockey puck-sized hole in your head, little man."

Riley put her hands on her hips. The fabric felt silky. *Pull yourself together, Riley. This is go time!* "I can't speak for Elvene, but I'm not your sister."

"Protégé, stay behind me and shut up," Elvene snapped.

"Are you really going to shoot your little brother?" Carlos mocked.

Elvene looked through gun sights. "Seriously, if you mention family again, I'll be forced to notify your next of kin of your untimely demise."

"We all have the same father!" Carlos yelled. "He's the Benevolent Imperator!"

Elvene pulled the trigger. Nothing. She pulled it harder to no effect. High-pitched laughter echoed down the corridor. Horror crept across Elvene's face. Turning the gun around, she discovered that the smart button lights were off. She thumbed them manically, but the lights would not return. Frustrated, she threw her gun at Carlos. With quick reflexes, he ducked as the gun whizzed inches over his head, clattering down the hallway and out of sight.

"My first trick was easy," taunted Carlos. "For my next act, I will need a little help from the audience."

Elvene jerked on unsteady legs. She bounced slightly like a bird ready to take flight. Riley backed away, slipping off her heels. The floor felt unnaturally cold.

Stepping directly under a light, Carlos looked like a stage performer as he wiggled his fingers. Elvene moved involuntarily like a puppet, screeching, "The boy is a technomancer!"

Riley frowned. "What the hell is a—"

A robot leg shot out. Riley felt the wind as the metal foot barely missed her chin. The wall reverberated as the foot took out a chunk of drywall. *Elvene just tried to kick me!* Riley back-pedaled as Elvene wound up again.

"I can't control my legs!" Elvene shouted. "The boy has hacked into the motor controls!"

Another metal foot kicked out. Anticipating the thrust, Riley easily sidestepped the attack. Elvene twisted and the other foot lashed out. The wall exploded, raining down bits of white dust. The heavy foot just missed her. Another blur forced Riley to duck. A robotic knee whizzed over her.

Breathing hard, Riley jumped straight up. She landed a yard above the floor balancing on just air. She took a step and felt the air cushion underfoot give a little. Her airwalk was failing. With all her strength, she kicked and connected with bone. Riley dropped to the cold ground, thumping hard on her back. She was gasping for breath; the brutal fall had knocked the wind out of her. Still, her legs were propped up on a lump. Looking down the length of her body, Riley discovered that one of her feet rested on Eleven's head while her calf stretched out across her chest that heaved slightly. *At least, I didn't kill my mentor.*

Beneath her, Riley felt a jolt. A metal foot slid up against a battered wall and pushed. Another robotic leg arched at the knee, spinning Elvene's torso. *The motor controls are still working!* Riley kicked her legs up and snapped into a summersault. She rose awkwardly on wobbly feet. Down the hall, Carlos stood under the light waving his skean and his freehand in a futile attempt to make the robotic legs work again. Instead, the metallic feet just pushed Eleven's body in a steady circle like a dog getting ready for a nap. Riley let out a half-crazed laugh as she rubbed the back of her neck.

"What's so funny?" Carlos asked harshly.

"I went to the ballet today," Riley slurred. "It was the first time that I saw a live orchestra, the best musicians in the Capital. Yet, no matter how many times the conductor slapped his little stick, he could not get the attention of the musicians."

Carlos waved his skean. "Come over here, and I'll show you what this little stick can do. It is an honor to die by this blade."

Shaking the cobwebs out of her head, Riley stepped over her mentor's fallen body. "Okay, little bro, let's dance."

"Ah, I have one more trick up my sleeve," the boy said as he waved his skean. Riley watched in dread as his bronze blade turned red hot and darted out into a long épée. Steam hissed off the skean as Carlos slashed the air, getting a feel for the slender blade.

Riley squinted. There was something off about Carlos' fencing sword. In the blazing quick metal, she spotted thin rips. *Hot tears.*

She lunged forward. Carlos twisted his body to the side like a swashbuckler. He held the tapered tip of his épée slightly up as if expecting an attack from above.

A few steps away, Riley slid on the frictionless surface created by her telekinesis. Time seemed to slow as she dipped under the épée's point and kicked up. With a resonating crack, her opponent's blade snapped inches from the hilt. She careened forward into Carlos' legs, taking those out as well.

Riley felt her telekinesis waver before ceasing abruptly. She skidded another couple yards across the rough surface, scraping the skin off her bare legs. A burning pain shot through her right foot. She could smell her charred flesh. The elongated blade clattered point down between her outstretched legs, nearly impaling her to the cold floor. Puffs of steam hissed off the broken end of the blade as it quickly cooled. Riley waited until the last smoke ring wafted off the skean before she wrapped her fingers around the slender shaft that was still painfully hot. She pulled herself off the ground, yanking out the blade in one fluid motion.

Down the dimly lit corridor, Carlos was already up and headed towards the doorway that led outside. He was hunched over, cradling his right arm. Sticking out of his shoulder was the hilt of the broken skean, the rest of Eacles's blade. Carlos looked back as he crossed the threshold. A step outside, he slammed into a wall of blackness and ricocheted back into the hallway. While he was momentarily stunned, Riley shambled towards him on shaky legs. There would be no more running for her tonight. Wide-eyed, she halted as a massive, black-armored bot marched inside. Its broad shoulders grazed both sides of the doorway.

"Now, you're going to get it!" exclaimed Carlos as he slowly got up. Standing proudly before the bot, he pointed a trembling finger at Riley. "Kill her."

Sweat dribbled down Riley's sullied face. The little black dress was shredded and battered like her. Beaten, the protégé placed one hand on the wall just to maintain her balance. Sighing, she recited a line from her favorite play: "O vain boast, who can control his fate? 'Tis not so now. Be not afraid, though you see me weaponed. Here is my journey's end."

Carlos hooted, "Bravo! I heard that you wanted to be on stage. Consider this your curtain call."

Behind the boy, Riley watched as the huge bot raised its gauntleted fist. The matte black barrel of its auto-gun twinkled. She exhaled, careful not to shiver. The black fist hung in the air just over the boy's head, ready to fire.

"Do it already!" ordered Carlos.

The gauntleted fist dropped, striking the boy's skull and driving it down into his shoulders with a resounding clunk. Carlos staggered, took a few steps, and then dropped face down.

Riley stared thunderstruck at the scene as the bot lowered its auto-gun. The bot cocked its dreadful head as its red eyes considered something on the ground.

"Are those your heels?" asked a mechanical feminine voice.

"Ye-yes," Riley stammered.

The bot stepped over Carlos' sprawled out body and knelt by a pair of discarded shoes. "They're last year's fashion but match your dress quite well."

Riley let out a slow breath. "What are you?"

"I'm Nadia. Have you seen Blandon Stux around? Is he safe?"

Bewildered, Riley rubbed the back of her head, feeling dampness. "I just saw him outside enjoying some guitar music."

Nadia wagged a big finger. "That's so Blandon."

"What are you doing here?"

Nadia glanced around. "I don't have an invitation to the gala if that's what you're getting at."

Riley leaned too heavily on the wall and stumbled. Pain shot up the back of her leg as she put weight on her burned foot. Through ragged breaths she asked, "I mean . . . how did you know that Carlos would be . . . here?"

"Kind of a long story, sweetheart." Nadia crossed her arms over her barrel-shaped chest. "I overheard Gia talk about getting in touch with her brother at the dirigible port in Isle Royale. Before I left, I kicked in her server towers."

"You worked for Gia?"

"She's kind of a friend of a friend who helped me onto a military aerial vehicle." The bot motioned with a big palm over its body. "It was kind of easy since I'm a celebrity."

Riley leaned against the wall, raising her burned foot off the ground. "Thank you for helping me."

"Any benefit to you was incidental."

"Oh." Riley felt tears well up in her eyes. "Thanks anyway."

"I have to get back to work." The bot craned its hideous head around. It scooped up Carlos in one giant hand, throwing the boy over its shoulder. "You should call for medical assistance."

"Before you go, I just have one question," Riley whimpered in a cracking voice. "Who does Gia work for?"

The bot stomped out into the night. "Your real enemy hasn't shown her face yet."

Epilogue

On stage, the brass band nearly finished playing "For He's a Jolly Good Fellow," as the young man sang:
"He's a jolly good fellow,
He can laugh out the loudest at them all,
He's a jolly good fellow,
But that jolly good fellow's about to fall . . . "

The luxury dirigible slipped its tethers, slowly ascending over the dark waters. The silver airship was a pretty thing, decorated like a Faberge egg. Crowds had gathered on the grassy fields near the shore to get an unobstructed view. Men wore colorful tuxedos to distinguish themselves from the servers, while most women wore monochrome gowns.

Olivette hailed a cute, young waitress carrying a tray of empty flute glasses. "I feel like celebrating. Can you get me a glass of sparkling wine?"

"At a later time," the waitress replied, smiling.

"Do you even have sparkling wine?"

"Let me consider it."

Olivette adjusted her gold gloves. "Are you saying that you have some?"

"I will have to get back to you." The waitress just stood there, blinking.

A rough voice drawled, "You'll never get a 'no' out of that one. I'm guessing she's from Nippon province."

Olivette slowly turned to find a mustachioed, older gentleman wearing a white cowboy hat. The man pointed in the general direction of the bar, "Go fetch us some whiskey, darlin'."

The waitress bowed marginally before quickly walking away. The cowboy gazed up into the night, watching the floating dirigible. His bushy eyebrows furrowed as he moseyed a few steps onto the lawn.

"This is what I call greener pastures. Is this your first hoedown at a dirigible port?"

Olivette followed him onto the lawn. "I wouldn't miss it for the world." The cowboy gawped at her.

"The Demedici family doesn't normally attend Slick galas. I just saw your sister dancing with that actor fellow. Will there be a new stallion in your family's stable?"

"I don't make those decisions . . . yet."

The cowboy gave a hoard chuckle and spat. "I should've gone to the play tonight. I sure do like my Othello."

Olivette cast her sights on the silver blimp that was less than a mile over the lake. She pondered on the airship's remarkable design. It's just a balloon filled with cheap hydrogen and an additive to render the gas inflammable. But what would happen if the additive had a half-life? Say, a crafty, high-tech girl and her siblings commandeered a chemical factory to modify the additive. Then, said additive was inserted into all the hydrogen tanks and shipped off to Poppin Slick's dirigible port. As the additive *decayed, excess heat would be produced, causing a spark to ignite a million little time bombs. Meanwhile, all the king's men were busy searching the cold water reactors because of several well-placed decoys. Indeed, the Slick family fortunes would surely flounder and evaporate like smoke. Humpty Dumpty would have a great fall.*

"I always enjoyed the final scene in Othello," Olivette said. "Would you like to hear a couple of lines?"

The cowboy drawled, "I reckon so."

Olivette raised her hand to the sky. "Whip me, ye devils, from the possession of this heavenly sight! Blow me about in winds, roast me in sulfur, wash me in steep-down gulfs of *liquid fire!*"

A few heartbeats later, an orange dot appeared in the black sky. Growing, the orange ball bulged and flickered until it took the shape of a crackling fire. A thunderous boom resounded across the shore followed by a blast of hot wind. Through the flames, the steel ribs of the luxury dirigible poked through its skeletal frame. The whole colossal aircraft fell from the sky with the brilliance of a setting sun engulfed in cold waters.

Olivette clapped her hands. "What's a party without fireworks?"

The End

Timeline

July 2120

Piero meets Daisy on the beach, and they begin secretly dating. Variola hires Gia to find janissaires willing to defect from the Imperium. Gia hacks into the Janissary communications network, posing as a group called Hexahedron that is willing to help janissaires escape through a psychic ratline. However, Janissary precogs thwart her attempts to reach defectors. Gia becomes a "janissaire aficionado" and looks for a new way to find janissaires.

August 2120

Piero transfers to the Logistics Branch and works with his new mentor, Elvene, who is confined to a hoverchair due to ailing health.

October 2120

Olivette comes to work with Piero and Elevene.

December 2120

Elvene goes out on medical leave.

January 2121

Gia learns that she can locate any janissaire in the world with the Logistics passwords for requisitions. She contacts Olivette who says that only janissaries have such a password, but she will try to coax it out of her coworker, Piero.

February 2121

Olivette creates a plan to destroy Slick Shipping dirigibles, her spinorama. She hires Gia to alter the additives that makes hydrogen nonflammable. Gia commandeers the Alamogordo Chemical Works. Gia flips the factory's sentry bots and service bots, including Roboto.

March 2121

Gia commandeers the military warehouse on 34th Avenue. She creates three hex signs equidistant around the chemical factory in case she needs human accomplices who can easily triangulate the factory location, knowing the signs' true purpose. As a decoy, the hex signs' clues points to the miliary warehouse. If she manages to recruit janissaires, Gia will send them to the warehouse. The hex signs are designed to confuse precogs, allowing janissaires to defect.

June 2121

Unable to figure out Piero's password, Olivette invites Piero to live with her. Still, he leaves no clues about his password. She sleeps next to Piero, hoping he will mumble something useful. Gia's bots shoot Eacles and then detain him in a VR simulation at the Alamogordo Chemical Works. Gia starts sending the defective hydrogen tanks to Slick Shipping. However, her connection to her bot becomes shaky during this critical part of the plan. Gia redoubles her efforts to recruit a janissaire. She subtly drops hings that she can be an asset to the Janissary in Guyana. Raven takes the bait and recruits Gia. In exchange, Gia gets to move her siblings to Isle Royale.

July 2121

To appease Variola, Gia still attempts to get the Logistics password. Once Carlos decodes the hex signs, he moves with his half-sisters to the chemical factory and gets to work. Olivette is unnerved that Elvene is back at work and does everything possible to ensure that Elvene will not read her mind.

Made in the USA
Middletown, DE
02 April 2022

63527624R00215